UNGIFTED

UNGIFTED
GORDON KORMAN

BALZER + BRAY

An Imprint of HarperCollins*Publishers*

Balzer + Bray is an imprint of HarperCollins Publishers.

Ungifted
Library of Congress Cataloging-in-Publication Data
Korman, Gordon.
    Ungifted / Gordon Korman. — 1st ed.
        p.   cm.
    Summary: Due to an administrative mix-up, troublemaker Donovan
Curtis is sent to the Academy of Scholastic Distinction, a special school for
gifted and talented students, after pulling a major prank at middle school.
    ISBN 978-0-06-174266-8 (trade bdg.)
    ISBN 978-0-06-174268-2 (lib. bdg.)
    ISBN 978-0-06-224007-1 (Scholastic ed.)
    [1. Behavior—Fiction.   2. Middle schools—Fiction.   3. Schools—
Fiction.   4. Gifted children—Fiction.   5. Robots—Fiction.   6. Robotics—
Fiction.   7. Humorous stories.]   I. Title.
PZ7.K8369Un   2012   2012008408
[Fic]—dc23   CIP
                                                                        AC

Typography by Erin Fitzsimmons
12 13 14 15 16   CG/RRDH   10 9 8 7 6 5 4 3
❖
First Edition

For the highly gifted Lev Jensen Iserson

*And special thanks to Coach John "Motch"
Motchkavitz and the award-winning
Great Neck South High School
Robotics Team #2638*

UNEARTHED

DONOVAN CURTIS
IQ: 112

I want a refund from ancestry.com.

They traced my family all the way back to the revolution. And in all those forefathers and fore-mothers, aunts, uncles, and cousins, there was nobody like me. No bigmouth hung for treason; no "classe clowne" who they stuck in the stocks and threw rotten vegetables at. The closest match was this guy in the Civil War who jumped off a battlement, whatever that is. And he only did it because the Union army was firing on Fort Sumter. That's what they put on his tombstone anyway. It sounds like a pretty good excuse to me.

I did things like that. If there were any battlements in my neighborhood, I'd probably jump off them all. And not because of any army. I'd do it just to see what would happen. "Reckless," my mother called me. "Poor impulse control." That's the school psychologist. "You're going to break your idiot neck one day, or someone's going to break it for you." My dad.

He was probably right. They were all right. But when the *thing* is right there in front of me, and I can kick it, grab it, shout it out, jump into it, paint it, launch it, or light it on fire, it's like I'm a puppet on a string, powerless to resist. I don't think; I *do*.

It can be little things, like throwing darts at a pool float to test my sister's swimming skills, or spitting back at the llamas at the zoo. It can be more creative—a helium balloon, a fishhook, and Uncle Mark's toupee. It can even be the smart-alecky comments that got me voted Most Likely to Wind Up in Jail in my middle school the last two years running.

"Our fans are great; our team is nifty! We're going to get blown out by fifty!"

See, that was probably not the wisest thing to say

on the day of the big game against our basketball archrivals, Salem Junior High. But I didn't just say it; I broadcast it over the PA system to the entire school. I don't know why I did it. The cheer was already fully formed in my mind—the poster advertising the big game had planted it there. It was definitely going to come out. Why share it with only the two Daniels, who were with me in the office awaiting sentence for our spitball war, when there was a perfectly good microphone a few feet away, unattended and live. Okay, it wasn't live. I had to flick the switch. I even had pom-poms—well, a crumpled piece of paper for sound effects.

The howl of protest that went up all around the building surprised even me. It was like I'd gone from house to house, poisoning everybody's dog. It was probably for my own good that I wound up in detention. If I'd been free in the halls at three-thirty, I would have been lynched. The sense of humor at Hardcastle Middle School didn't extend to their precious basketball team.

"Why'd you say we're going to lose, man?" asked Whelan Kaiser, starting center, peering down at the top of my head from his six-foot-four vantage.

Why? There was no logical explanation for what

3

I did. It had to come from my DNA. That's why I needed ancestry.com.

I was the only kid in detention that afternoon. All crimes had been forgiven in order to pad the audience for the big game against Salem, which had to have already started. All crimes except mine—dissing the basketball team. Even the Daniels—two-thirds of the spitball war—had been cut loose while I was doing time.

The Daniels weren't at the game. I knew this because they were skulking in the bushes outside the detention room, making grotesque faces at me through the window. If they could make me laugh—and it wasn't easy to hold back—I'd be in even more trouble. As it was, Mr. Fender was checking his watch every thirty seconds. He wanted to be at the game, not babysitting me.

Finally, he could bear it no longer. "I'll be right back," he told me sternly.

The instant he was gone, the window was flung open from the outside.

"Come on!" hissed Daniel Sanderson. "Let's get out of here!"

"He's coming back," I protested.

"No, he's not," scoffed the other Daniel—Daniel

Nussbaum. "He's going to the office to watch the feed from the security camera in the gym. You've only got ten more minutes. If he's any kind of basketball fan, you're golden."

I was out the window like a shot, breathing sweet, free air. See what I'm saying? The open road called, and I took it. This time I'd needed a little help. That's where the Daniels came in. They helped me a lot. They'd helped me to the office with our spitball fight, and helped me to the PA mic by daring me to do it. With friends like them, sometimes I wondered why I would ever need enemies.

I turned on them. "Thanks for letting me take the fall alone. Your support was really touching."

Nussbaum shrugged innocently. "I couldn't take credit for your poem."

"It wasn't a poem. It just happened to rhyme."

"I've been meaning to talk to you about that," Sanderson put in. "Don't you think that's kind of dorky? I mean, who rhymes anymore?"

"Nobody," I conceded, "except the entire hip-hop community." I bounced a pinecone off his head, which only made him grin wider.

We were at the top of the hill, looking down on the gym we shared with Hardcastle High. The parking lot was jam-packed. A roaring cheer spilled out of the building.

"Man, you couldn't fit a Hot Wheels car in there!" Nussbaum exclaimed, taking in the crowded lot. "Salem-*vs*.-Hardcastle is the place to be."

"Let's go check out the score," said Sanderson. "We can see if our 'nifty' team will lose by 'fifty.'"

"Yeah, Donovan, nice school spirit," Nussbaum added. Like *he* had any.

We started down, the Daniels jostling each other absently. A kind of friendly belligerence came naturally to those two. Maybe they were descended from the Hatfields and the McCoys. I'll bet the Daniels had never checked it out on ancestry.com.

And then The Moment was upon me.

I must have passed the statue of Atlas a thousand times going back and forth on the campus of the Hardcastle Public Schools. Yet somehow it was like I'd never seen it before.

It was not the titan's broad powerful shoulders supporting the bronze globe of the world and heavens that seemed so different. But since when did Atlas have such a big butt? Seriously, I knew he was a titan; but I didn't know that the most titanic thing about him was his caboose. He looked like a reject from *The Biggest Loser.*

Suddenly, I was striding toward the statue, in an almost trancelike state. I picked up a fallen tree branch and made my approach.

Nussbaum noticed my zombielike concentration. "Dude, what are you doing?"

I didn't answer, and he didn't really expect me to. He knew me. They both did.

I cocked back the branch, and unloaded a home run swing. The impact vibrated up through my arms to my brain stem, and into every cell of my body. The branch shattered in my hands.

I have to say that this was always the best part of it for a guy like me—the split second the tomato hits the car; the very brief flight as I drop from the edge of the roof to the pool; the instant that the balloon lifts the toupee and the sun's rays glint off that shiny bald head.

Or, in this case, the *go-o-o-ong!* sound from the statue's bronze behind. The payoff. It was usually downhill from there. Sometimes literally.

Atlas shivered as the vibration traveled through his metal body. The celestial sphere shivered too, rocking

7

dizzily on his muscular shoulders. At that point, I noticed for the first time that the sculpture wasn't a single piece of metal, but two, bolted together at the nape of the titan's neck.

Corrosion is a terrible thing. It was all in slow motion, but there was nothing you could do to stop it. With a crack, the bolt snapped, pieces whizzing out of sight. The ball of the world and heavens toppled and hit the ground with a *whump!*

I was still wrapped up in The Deed, lost in The Moment. It took the twin gasps from the Daniels to break the trance. And by that time, the heavy ball was already rolling.

Oh, no . . .

The big bronze globe careened down the hill toward the gym, picking up speed as it went. I ran after it, although what I thought I could do to stop it, I have no idea.

"Help me!" I called to the Daniels. But they were heading in the opposite direction. They liked to watch me do stuff; they had a lot less interest in hanging around for the consequences.

Heart sinking, I projected the course of the runaway globe. The prognosis was not good. It was hurtling straight for the parking lot, where a lot of innocent cars were waiting to get bashed in. Desperately, I threw myself headfirst at the juggernaut. When my shoulder struck the heavy metal, it felt like running into a brick wall. If it changed the direction at all, it was about a millionth of an inch. Flat on my face now, all I could do was watch.

The globe screamed down toward all that expensive machinery, bounced off an upturned curbstone, and caromed toward the building. The cars were safe, but the world and heavens were now on a collision course with the basketball game.

It pulverized the glass doors, sending up a blizzard of shards that obscured the entrance. I heard a very sharp whistle blast, like the referee was calling a foul on Atlas, or possibly me.

There was another relative on ancestry.com. He wasn't very much like me. I doubt I would have remembered him at all, except for his name—James Donovan. I'd wondered if I was named after him, although my mother claimed she'd never heard of the guy. He emigrated from Ireland in 1912, which would have been fine except that the ship he picked was—think Atlas here—the *Titanic*.

As decision makers, he and I were pretty much on the same level.

But get this: He didn't die. He was plucked from the freezing water alive.

James Donovan was a *survivor*.

If I'd inherited any of those skills, I had a sinking feeling they were about to come in handy.

UNIDENTIFIED

DR. SCHULTZ
IQ: 127

To be the superintendent of a school district like Hardcastle, with its forty-seven buildings and more than thirty thousand students, was a huge responsibility. A lot of administrators would have hundreds of complicated rules to follow. I only had one: No screwups.

So when I took time out of my busy schedule and burdensome duties to attend a middle school basketball game, I expected to see orderly students, good sportsmanship, and happy alumni. What I did *not* expect to see was a giant metal ball blasting into the gymnasium, scattering players like tenpins. Not only did it create a dangerous situation, but it also reflected very badly on the Hardcastle schools.

Miraculously, no one was injured. Still, there was a lot of chaos as the parents of the players rushed to their sons on the floor in an effort to protect them from whatever this onslaught was.

I knew instantly. That globe was part of the statue of Atlas that stood on the knoll overlooking the school. And it certainly hadn't rolled itself down to the gym. I raced through the shattered door and onto the lawn. I could see the ribbon of crushed grass all the way back to the figure of Atlas, who looked peculiar, bent under the weight of absolutely nothing.

The culprit lay in the flattened path, raised up on his elbows, staring at the damage, guilty. "You, there!" I called.

The boy tried to scramble up and run, but he couldn't get any traction on the squashed turf. By the time he found his feet, I was upon him, and he was caught.

"Come with me to my office."

His shoulders slumped. "Yeah, okay." He looked as worried as he ought to be. I drew some small satisfaction from that.

The administration building was on the very same campus, but the boy didn't speak on the way over, not even to protest his innocence. A fat lot of good that would have done him. I had him dead to rights. And the evidence—a four-hundred-pound bronze sphere, and the damage it had caused—spoke plainly about what he had done.

At last, we reached my office, and I glared at him across my desk. "Do you know who I am?"

He shook his head, and had the grace to look a little scared.

"I am Dr. Schultz, Superintendent of the Hardcastle Independent School District. And I'll have your name and your school's name right now."

"Donovan Curtis. I go here—I mean Hardcastle Middle, where, uh, *it* happened."

I wrote the information on a piece of paper on the cluttered desk in front of me. "Well, Donovan Curtis, I don't have to tell you that you're in big trouble right now. You're lucky that no one was hurt or even killed by that stunt of yours. Why would you do such a thing?"

"It was an accident."

If he thought he could get away with an excuse like that, he had picked the wrong administrator. "A giant metal ball doesn't plow through a building by accident."

He spoke up again. "I hit the statue with a branch, but I didn't think the world would fall off."

"You didn't think—"

My secretary, Mrs. De Bourbon, came bustling in, looking worried. "I'm so sorry to disturb you, Dr. Schultz, but you're needed urgently back at the gym. Someone called the fire department from a cell phone, and you're the only one with the authority to send them away." She frowned. "Nothing's on fire, is it?"

"No, of course not." I was halfway to the door when I hesitated. What to do with the boy? He was looking hopeful, as if he were home free. But believe me, he wasn't. It would serve him right if I left him sitting here, cooling his heels, while I went out to deal with the mess he'd made! But who knew how long that would take? By now those firefighters could be finding code violations in the gym! And I had a dinner meeting across town. . . .

I skewered him with my most severe expression. "You can go. I'll send for you tomorrow morning, and we can continue this discussion."

14

He was out of there like a shot. I wasn't far behind him when Mrs. De Bourbon called me back.

"I'm sorry to bother you again, but Student Services needs the list of the new candidates for the gifted program."

I sighed. Did everything have to pass through me? I was only one person! "It's on my desk, Cynthia. You can't miss it."

What a nightmare! There was damage to the gym floor in addition to the doors, which were a total loss. The foundry that had made the statue had gone out of business five years ago, so good luck getting a replacement globe for Atlas. The district's insurance agent was on vacation for the next two weeks.

I missed my dinner meeting and my dinner. By the time I got back to my office, I was almost insane with aggravation. This was exactly why I couldn't tolerate screwups. There was no such thing as just one. The first led to the second, and pretty soon they were coming at you in battalions. I needed to accomplish one real thing on this miserable day, and I knew exactly what it was going to be: I was going to call that boy's parents and let them know the damage and chaos their son's vandalism had caused.

I scanned my desk for the paper where I'd written

15

his name. It was gone.

I scoured every item on that desk, and not just once. Nothing.

"Cynthia!"

But she had already left for the day.

How could this be? That boy must have snuck back in and stolen the paper, hoping I'd forget his name among the thirty thousand students I'm responsible for! Well, he was wrong about that! His name was—his name was—

Sudden overpowering chagrin.

I had broken my only rule.

UNEXPLAINED

DONOVAN CURTIS
IQ: 112

If I didn't die of stress that night, I probably never will. Each time the phone rang, I was convinced it was Schultz, calling to rat me out to Mom and Dad. Every knock at the door meant the police were here to arrest the guy who'd bombed a basketball game with the weight of the world. Whenever my dad's BlackBerry pinged, I was positive that was the news-flash. It didn't make for good sleeping. It didn't make for *any* sleeping.

Mom was shocked at the sight of me over the breakfast table. "I was studying," I told her with a yawn wide enough to drive a truck through.

"You look like Wile E. Coyote after the Roadrunner dropped him off a cliff," said my sister, Katie. She was twenty-six, and had moved back in with us while her husband was deployed to Afghanistan with the Marines.

"Thanks, Miss Goodyear," I retorted absently. Katie was seven months pregnant, possibly with a baby hippo.

"One more wisecrack about my sumo stomach and I'll sit on you," she threatened. "You think this is a vacation for me?"

"Not for you; for *Brad*," I returned. "He's got an eleven-thousand-mile buffer zone from all this sweetness and light."

I regretted it the instant the words passed my lips. Normally, the two of us could go back and forth insulting each other for hours. But Katie lapsed into a melancholy silence, a far-off expression in her eyes. It wasn't hard to figure out the cause of her reverie. The father of her unborn child was on the opposite side of the world in a war zone. And even though First Lieutenant H. Bradley Patterson spent most of his time inside the armored shell of a tank, it had to be on her mind that her husband was in a risky line of work.

Mom came over and placed her hands reassuringly on Katie's shoulders. "Brad's surrounded by the best-trained people with the best equipment money can buy."

But her daughter's mind turned out to be elsewhere. "Beatrice is coming."

"Beatrice?" Mom echoed. "You mean Brad's dog? I thought she was staying with your mother-in-law."

"She *was*," Katie explained miserably. "But Fanny called me this morning. She said she can't cope, and she's coming this afternoon to drop off Beatrice."

"We're getting a dog?" I asked, mildly interested.

"That mutt hates me," Katie moaned. "That's the reason she was supposed to go to Fanny in the first place. Beatrice will never forgive me for taking her place in Brad's life. For all I know, she blames me for getting him shipped out. Like I make deployment decisions for the Marine Corps."

"She's your dog too, Katie," Mom lectured. "And we'd be delighted to take care of her while Brad's serving his country. Right, Donnie?"

"I'm not touching the poop scoop," I said firmly.

My mind was on Schultz, not dogs, that morning. At school, I waited to be called to the office. Between classes, I searched for the summons taped to my locker. Nothing. The anxiety was eating me up from the inside. When the PA announcement finally came, it was almost a relief.

"Would Donovan Curtis please come to the office? Donovan Curtis to the office."

It was the longest walk I'd ever taken. At each open door, hostile faces glowered out at me. Remember, I was still the guy who disrespected our beloved basketball team. When the news got around that I was also responsible for unleashing the runaway globe that bowled out the gym, I was really going to be Public Enemy Number One.

At last, I rounded the corner, and the glassed-in reception area came into view. To my surprise, the avenging angel waiting for me was not Dr. Schultz, but Mr. Fender.

"When you serve a detention with *me*, Mr. Curtis, you serve it to the end. And you don't leave until *I* tell you it's time. . . ."

He went on for a while, trying to scare me, I guess. The poor guy had no way of knowing that, considering the payback I was expecting from Schultz, a rampaging grizzly couldn't scare me. He cut me loose, though, explaining that, thanks to the damage to the gym, we students had "suffered enough."

I had a sneaking suspicion Schultz wasn't going to see it that way.

I couldn't say how much anybody had actually suffered, but the disaster at the basketball game was definitely the hot topic at school.

"When the glass blew out, I thought it was an explosion!"

"Like a terrorist attack!"

"Did you see the statue with the top part missing? It looks like my grandfather when his back goes out!"

"I heard the gym floor is permanently messed up!"

"When they catch the guy who did it, they're going to hang him on a meat hook!"

"Yeah!" Nussbaum chimed in. "I pity that poor loser! His life isn't worth a used Kleenex!" He turned to me. "So, Donovan, when do you think you're going to get busted?"

"Shhh!" I pulled the Daniels into the boys' room, and checked the stalls for possible eavesdroppers. "This is no joke! The walls have ears!"

"Dude." Nussbaum was offended. "We'd never rat out a friend."

"Listen, that call was a false alarm—just Fender for skipping out of detention. I don't understand why

Schultz hasn't come after me yet."

"Maybe he doesn't know who you are," Sanderson suggested.

I shook my head. "He wrote down my name. I told him where I go to school. He's the superintendent. He's got access to every file and record there is."

"Yeah, did you pick the wrong guy to get caught by or what?" Nussbaum agreed. "The head honcho of the whole district."

"I'm wondering if it's not as bad as it looked," I mused in a low voice. "A little cleanup, a little wood polish—"

"I heard they're going to have to redo the whole gym floor," Sanderson put in. "It costs, like, zillions of dollars."

"And don't forget the glass doors," Nussbaum added. "You're a dead man walking."

I totally agreed. So why wasn't it happening? All day long, and the following days too, I squirmed while rumors spread like head lice and the Daniels predicted my downfall. There was no escape from the tension at home, where reports of firefights in Afghanistan dominated CNN. Then, on Wednesday, Katie's mother-in-law dropped off the dog.

The times I'd seen Beatrice, she was a rocket-powered

hairball. But the cinnamon chow chow that slunk into our house was listless and mewling.

"What's wrong with her?" Mom asked.

"She's dying!" Fanny declared dramatically, and tried to walk out the door.

Katie held on to her arm. "How do you know? Did she get hit by a car? Is she sick?"

Her mother-in-law wasn't interested in the details. "I can't cope with this at my age!" And with that, she was gone.

Mom reached down to pat the dog. Beatrice snapped at her hand. She tossed a warning growl over her shoulder at Katie, just in case she might be contemplating a similar move.

"She's too mean to die," I observed.

"She can't die," Katie said tragically. "Brad loves her."

"Brad loves *you*, too," I returned. "What does that say about Brad?"

"He'll never forgive me if something happens to her!"

"Well, that's not exactly fair, is it?" Mom put in. "If anything went wrong, it was on Fanny's watch, not yours."

"That's her whole modus operandi," Katie argued.

"The minute she saw the writing on the wall, she dumped the dog on me! And how can we take care of Beatrice if she won't even let us go near her?"

As if in answer, Beatrice picked herself off the floor, walked over to me, and lay down on my feet.

"Donovan!" my mother exclaimed.

"What did I do? I didn't do anything!"

"Beatrice likes you!" Katie said in an awed whisper.

"So?"

"So you can look after her," Mom reasoned, like this was a huge honor.

I declined. "Forget it. Besides, if Brad is such a baby about Beatrice, you have to wonder if he's the right person to be in charge of a twenty-million-dollar tank."

But when Beatrice refused to eat, I had to hand-feed her a few lumps of liver-flavored kibble. When it was time to take her out, I was the only one she would allow to put the leash on. When Katie made her a bed in the basement, she wouldn't even go down the stairs. I knew I was going to have a roommate. Just call me Dog-Whisperer Donovan. As if I didn't have enough hassles.

Dad came home at six, bringing the mail. "There's a letter from the school, Donnie. Is there anything you want to tell us before we open it?"

By that time, my tongue was stuck to the roof of my mouth, so I just shook my head and waited for the ax to fall.

Who knew how much trouble I was in? Suspended? Probably. Expelled? Not out of the question—especially since Schultz thought I'd done it on purpose. I *had* done it on purpose—the hitting-the-statue part, anyway.

While Dad read, I monitored the telltale vein in the top left corner of his forehead. It bulged a little, but not nearly as much as it had during the aftermath of the toupee liftoff. That had to be considered an encouraging sign.

At last, he handed me the letter. "You have an explanation for this?"

"I—I—" Where would I even start?

My eyes fell on the page.

To the parents of DONOVAN CURTIS:
The time has come to recognize your child's hard work
and commitment to excellence as a student in the
Hardcastle Independent School District. This letter is
to inform you that DONOVAN has been selected to
attend the Academy for Scholastic Distinction (ASD),

a special program geared toward gifted and talented
students, tailored to their exceptional abilities and
extraordinary potential for academic achievement. . . .

It said more—a lot more, about school transfer paper-
work, and registration forms, and which bus route
would take me to my new placement at the Academy.
I barely saw any of it. My eyes couldn't get past words
like *excellence, distinction, gifted,* and especially *Donovan
Curtis.*

Gifted? *Me?* I was the guy who skateboarded down
waterslides and shot a Super Soaker at an electric fence.
When people heard my name, they thought, *Don't try
this at home!* not *gifted.*

I wasn't being expelled; I was being *promoted.*

Dad was grinning from ear to ear. "I always knew
that the real problem was they just weren't *challenging*
you."

Mom looked worried. "Is everything okay?"

"Donnie's gifted!" Dad crowed.

"It's a mistake," Katie scoffed. "The kid's about as
gifted as a caterpillar. He brings home a B and it sets
off six days of skywriting and fireworks."

Much as I hated to agree with Katie, she had a point.
My grades weren't terrible, but they were nothing to

write home about. Come to think of it, I *remembered* the day all the nerds and brainiacs took the special aptitude test to see who got into the gifted program. I remembered it because nobody even asked me to give it a try. And I wasn't insulted because I *wasn't gifted.*

My eyes skipped down to the bottom of the page.

My heartiest congratulations once again. Your child is a credit to the Hardcastle Independent School District.
Sincerely,
Dr. Alonzo Schultz
Superintendent, HISD

Schultz.

The only program Schultz would recommend *me* for was Alcatraz. Didn't he realize who I was? I mean, the guy made a point of getting my name so he'd know exactly who to burn at the stake!

It came to me in a giddy flashback to the day of The Incident. Right after Schultz let me go, his secretary asked for the roster of new kids for the Academy. The superintendent's response was the last thing I remember before bouncing out of there.

His exact words: "It's on my desk, Cynthia. You can't miss it."

Had that big doofus scribbled my name on the gifted list by accident? And everybody else thought it was there because it was supposed to be? It seemed crazy, but it did explain the two inexplicable things going on in my life right now: 1) why Schultz hadn't come to kill me yet, and 2) why I'd just been invited to go to genius school.

I laughed out loud. People thought *I* acted without thinking? This was a thousand times worse than hitting a statue with a twig. It was a shoo-in for the Bonehead Moves Hall of Fame!

"What's so funny?" Dad asked.

I almost spilled the beans. How many chances do you get to show that the guy who runs the entire city school system is an even bigger dipstick than you are? Besides, it's not like my parents weren't going to find out *eventually*. Sooner or later, Schultz would realize his mistake and . . .

Or would he? The only district officials who saw me that day were Schultz and his secretary, and neither of them had ever met me before. They worked in the administration building, not Hardcastle Middle School. The paper my name was written on was surely gone now, crumpled up in a wastebasket or fed through a paper shredder. The one thing the superintendent knew about me was the school I went to. That was the only way he could get to me.

The gifted letter tingled in my hands. If I was at the Academy, he wouldn't be able to find me. It was the realm of brainiacs and goody-goodies, the last place you'd look for a kid who put a bronze globe through a glass door.

A tiny voice spoke up from the depths of my spleen: *Forget it. Not in a million years. You won't last ten minutes in the gifted program. There's never been anybody more ungifted than you.*

Mom was flushed with happiness. "I always knew this day would come. It was only a matter of time before people realized how special you are." She sniffed back a tear of emotion. "Beatrice was our good-luck charm. Things are finally starting to turn around for this family. I can feel it."

"I feel it too," added Dad, putting his arms around her. "Wait a minute—*Beatrice?*" His eyes strayed to the hall, where the languid chow chow was chewing on his newspaper, reducing it to an inky pulp.

Up until that instant, I honestly don't think I was going to go through with it. But since Brad had shipped out and Katie had moved back in, the tension in our house had been simmering just below the boiling point. And now this extra stress with the stupid dog. How could I pile my own problems on top of that? Especially when Mom and Dad looked so proud—something that didn't happen every day where I was concerned.

I thought of my namesake, James Donovan, on the foundering *Titanic*. What would he do—sink or swim?

"Gifted," I said a little louder, as if trying it on for size. "I guess I'd better go to school and clean out my locker."

UNARMED
CHLOE GARFINKLE
IQ: 159

<<*Hypothesis: Being gifted is not a gift.*
A gift you get for nothing. This you have to pay for.>>

O kay, I know it's not a *real* hypothesis—by that, I mean something you can design an experiment to test. But it's true. There's a *price* to being gifted. The cost is your life. You don't die or anything like that. But you don't live either. Free time? Forget it. You go to a special academy that gives you extra work to suck up every spare minute—especially since it probably takes forever to get there. Schools for the gifted are few and far between. Chances are you don't live near one. Friends? Those are the people you slave alongside. They might be awesome, but how would you ever find out? You're too busy for them, and they're too busy for you. Sports? When? And besides, why play when you probably stink?

<<*Hypothesis: Athletic ability exists in inverse proportion to intelligence. Technically untrue—there are plenty of smart athletes. But not many compared with the number of brilliant sofa spuds.* >>

What about TV or video games? Oh, please. You're far too smart for that. Pep rallies? For what—the robotics team? Forget it—and the same goes for school dances, funny-hat day, drama club, charity drives. . . .

"Dances?" repeated Abigail Lee when I brought up the subject in homeroom. "Who do you want to dance with? Him?" She pointed at skinny, needle-nosed Noah Youkilis.

She had a point. Most of the guys at the Academy for Scholastic Distinction weren't exactly what you'd call Hollywood hunks. I didn't expect body-builders, but it would be nice if they could grow a set of shoulders between the lot of them. And it wouldn't hurt to spend a little time outdoors to put some color in those prison-pale faces.

<<Hypothesis: Sunlamp-enhanced computer monitors, perhaps . . . ?>>

Then again—being smart requires you to examine things from all sides—why pick on the guys? We girls weren't exactly homecoming queens either. Abigail was a genius biochemist, but her greatest fashion statement was her white lab coat. She looked like she hadn't combed her hair since 2007. Or me, for that matter. I'd scored a perfect 2400 on every SAT practice test since sixth grade, but who was I to talk? Here I was, almost fourteen, and I'd never danced with a guy who wasn't related to me. I'd never been to a party except for kiddy things with balloons. I wasn't going on the cover of *Seventeen* anytime soon, that was for sure.

"Okay, so it doesn't have to be a dance," I told Abigail. "But why can't it be *something*? Every day millions of kids around this country do millions of normal activities, and they have a great time at it. Why can't we?"

"The statewide robotics meet is coming up," she offered.

Sigh.

I took robotics. I was good at it. I was good at *all* of it. I totally belonged at this school. But why did it have to mean that I couldn't be a regular person too?

Mr. Osborne, our homeroom teacher, who was also head of the robotics program, breezed into the lab. "Let's hurry up and take attendance. We've got a lot to do today."

We were all there. Where else would we be? We were any teacher's dream, yet at that moment it made me sad. I had no desire to cut class—but maybe that was the problem. When was the last time one of us broke the rules? This morning, while checking on my experiment in the growth of hydroponic flax, I'd noticed the paper I'd taped to my desk lamp to concentrate the beam onto the seedlings. It was a certificate of merit I'd received for perfect attendance at school. I'd earned seven of these over the years, and what use were they to me? Makeshift lampshades.

<<*Hypothesis: Is there a point where the robotics student becomes the robot?*>>

When was the last time anybody even showed up late?

"Sorry I'm late." A tall sandy-haired boy appeared at the door. "Is this Mr. Osborne's class?"

"This is the robotics lab," the teacher replied. "And you are?"

"Donovan Curtis," the newcomer replied, waving a

printed form. "I'm supposed to be in this homeroom."

"Right—our fresh blood from Hardcastle Middle." Oz accepted the paper and examined it.

Abigail leaned over to me. "That can't be right! *He's* coming to this school?"

I was intrigued. "You know him?"

"We went to the same elementary. He's the kid who jumped off the roof with one of those Gymboree parachutes."

I sized him up. He was kind of cute in a careless, windblown way. Great eyes—black fringed, pale blue. "Well, he must be smart if he passed all the tests to get in here."

Abigail was unconvinced. "Maybe. But he would have had to change a lot since I knew him."

I bit my tongue. Okay, so Abigail thought he was dumb, but next to her, *everybody* was dumb. *I* was probably pretty dense compared with her. If Donovan Curtis didn't measure up to Lee standards, that hardly made him stupid. There were no dim bulbs at our school. But that's not to say that we didn't range from somewhat bright to superbright—and in a few cases, like Abigail and Noah, supernova.

She was telling me about Donovan getting his tongue frozen to a chain-link fence one winter, but by that time I'd stopped listening. I'd never met this new kid, but I already had him perfectly sized up in my mind.

Donovan Curtis was *normal*.

Normal! We had a lot of talents in our homeroom. Normalcy wasn't one of them. Noah's IQ was off the charts, but he'd yet to hold a conversation with a real human being this year. Most of the time, he didn't even make eye contact. He always seemed to be speaking to the empty space over your left shoulder. Or Jacey Halloran, who had already discovered an uncharted galaxy, but still couldn't figure out how to open a combination lock. Or Latrell Michaelson, our mechanical marvel, who took cars apart and put them together again blindfolded—for fun. He couldn't manage to wrap his mind around the fact that he had to wait in the food line to buy his lunch. Every single day was World War Three in the cafeteria.

We had kids who had set academic records, and published books, and won every conceivable prize and honor. We had kids who could quote you the exact line of dialogue that's spoken 94 minutes and 30 seconds into *The Matrix* or *Return of the Jedi*.

What was missing was somebody—*anybody*—normal.

"I am the great and powerful Oz," Mr. Osborne told the newcomer in a mystical tone—he said that to everybody the first time he met them. "Technically, this is homeroom 107, but you've probably noticed that it looks like a cross between a mad scientist's lair and a garbage dump. We do robotics here. Even if you're not taking robotics this semester, I hope you'll help out with the team. It's a pretty big deal here at the Academy." He turned to the rest of us. "Guys, meet Donovan. Donovan—the guys."

There was a very lukewarm chorus of greeting. Another thing about the Academy—being gifted rarely extended to social skills. My enthusiastic "Hi!" stood out embarrassingly over the murmurs.

Donovan ignored us. Instead, he faced our latest robot, a work in progress for this year's competition. "What's his name?"

We were all stunned.

Noah spoke up. "It's not a *he*; it's an *it*. It's a mechanical device, and, as such, has no name."

Donovan blinked. "Robots have names. Haven't you ever seen *Star Wars*?"

Was he kidding? Half of us could recite *Star Wars*.

"We've been doing this for a long time," Abigail informed him in a superior tone. "We've made the finals three years in a row, and we did it with science, not by calling our entry Harry or Fred."

A few others spoke up in agreement. To be honest, I was on their side. The robot wasn't a toy or pet; it was a machine. I kept my mouth shut, though. Poor Donovan had only been in our class about thirty seconds, and we were already jumping all over him.

It didn't seem to bother the newcomer. "Okay, no name." He turned back to the robot. "Sorry, Tin Man." Oz on the brain, I guess.

He grabbed hold of one of the forks of the lifting assembly and gave it a hearty handshake. With a snap, it came off in his hand.

There was nothing lukewarm about the class reaction to that. A babble of outraged accusations filled the lab. Abigail, our team captain, was on her feet barking, "You broke it!"

Donovan tried to press the broken fork back onto the chain drive. It clattered to the floor.

"All right! Quiet, everybody!" Oz held his arms up for order. "Donovan didn't break anything. The component hadn't been attached properly." He turned to his newest student. "But it's not a bad lesson for your first day in the lab."

"I won't mess with any more of your—stuff,"

Donovan promised, chastened.

The robotics teacher shook his head. "I *want* you to mess with stuff. This is a place of tinkering, fiddling, experimentation. But," he added pointedly, "before you touch, *ask* somebody."

"Especially before you touch Tin Man," Latrell added feelingly.

"He's a delicate piece of equipment," Abigail pointed out. "And he's *not* Tin Man."

I was fascinated. Now everybody was referring to this array of nuts and bolts and circuits as *he*. Was it possible that in *not* naming our robot, Donovan had just named our robot?

<<*Hypothesis: A name changes an "it" to a "he."*>>

Kevin Amari raised his hand. "Even though he's not Tin Man, is it okay if we call him Tin Man for short? 'The robot' is so impersonal."

"Maybe because he's *not a person!*" By this time, Abigail was gritting through clenched teeth.

"He's not actually made of tin," Noah mused thoughtfully. "But I guess Aluminum Man isn't appropriate either, since he's also made of titanium, steel, plastic, various polymers, and silicon computer chips."

"How about Metallica?" suggested Latrell.

"That's good too," Donovan approved. "Anything

but 'the robot.' Poor guy."

"Squarepants," Kevin offered. "You know, because he's so boxy."

"Oh, perfect," Abigail snarled. "Now all our hard work is named after a cartoon!"

"Let's live with it for a while," Oz put in hurriedly. "We don't have to decide right away."

Amazing—in a few minutes we had gone from no name to three. And all because Donovan Curtis had walked into our school.

I kept an eye on him through homeroom. Except for the mishap with Tin Man—or whatever the name was going to be—I saw no sign of the buffoon Abigail had described. If anything, Donovan was trying to be friendly—not that he was getting very far with our crew. Engaging Noah in conversation isn't the easiest thing to do under the best of circumstances. But Donovan was asking him for advice on what to expect in some of his classes.

"Well," Noah replied thoughtfully, "math is easy, and the only thing easier than chemistry is biology or maybe physics. Social studies—easy. And English— well, you get the picture."

Poor Donovan just stared at him. He'd probably

spent his entire life hearing stories about the Academy's killer courses and crushing workload. And here Noah had dismissed them all in the space of about eight seconds.

<<Hypothesis: If you want a realistic assessment of a challenge, don't ask the guy with the two hundred IQ.>>

If Donovan had inquired about unraveling the genetic code, Noah would have said that was easy too.

"Thanks, I guess," Donovan told him. "Is anything in this place—well—hard?"

"You know what's hard?" Suddenly, Noah's face flushed with emotion. "Trying to control your own destiny. It's not just hard; it's impossible."

So Donovan shifted gears and talked to Latrell about the robot, which also backfired. Latrell got weirdly defensive, as if Donovan might be trying to steal his job as the team's top mechanic. And Jacey became so genuinely flustered by the newcomer's presence that she asked him which of the earth's continental plates was his favorite.

Abigail went over to Donovan and put her two cents in. "You know a Gymboree parachute isn't the same as a real parachute, don't you?"

Well, how could I *not* say something? He was going

to think we were all nuts.

I caught up with him in the hall on the way to first period. "Hi, I'm Chloe Garfinkle from homeroom."

I held out my hand, and he shook it lightly. Maybe he expected it to break off like that piece of robot.

"Hey, don't worry about the lift mechanism," I soothed. "The weakness probably came from a bad weld that got jarred loose by the chain drive, or maybe too much compression from the Bimba cylinder."

He looked blank. "What's it for?"

"Oh, the Bimba cylinder provides the pneumatic pressure—"

"I mean Tin Man," he corrected. "What does he do?"

"The robot has multiple capabilities," I enthused. "The electric eye can navigate color-coded tracks on the floor. The forks pick up inflatable rings that the lift mechanism places on various pegs at different heights. And it—uh—*he* can deploy a mini-bot that will climb a pole and strike a bell at the top."

He seemed confused. "Is that how geniuses spend their time? Picking up toys and ringing bells?"

I bristled. "You're here, aren't you? If being smart's such a crime, you're just as guilty as the rest of us!" He

42

had no answer for that, so I went on in a calmer tone, "Noah's the only one who's *really* a genius. Except that the work is a little more challenging, how's the Academy any different from Hardcastle?"

He gave me a half smile. "Seriously?"

"If there's one thing we're good at here," I assured him, "it's being serious."

"Have you ever been to Hardcastle Middle School?" he asked.

"I know we probably take some things for granted—"

"But they're probably not the things you think. If you want to plug in a computer, can you find an outlet with three prongs? Can you find one that even works? Will part of the suspended ceiling come down on your head in the middle of class? Will the cafeteria refrigerators break, so you can't buy lunch for a day, or a week, or a month?"

"Hey, things like that happen at the Academy too," I insisted, almost triumphantly. "Last year the freezers failed so there was no ice for"— the wind went out of my sails as I realized how lame this was going to sound—"the sushi bar."

He nodded sympathetically. "You guys should get T-shirts made. You know: I Survived the Sushi Crisis."

"Hey!"

"All I'm saying is that you brainiacs have a nice racket going here."

I skewered him on that point. "Don't you mean *we* brainiacs? You're one of us now."

"Right," he agreed, flustered. "But—well, I just got here, so you've been riding the gravy train longer."

"Regular school has its advantages, right?" I didn't want to seem dorky, but I was genuinely interested. "Dances, parties . . ."

A shrug.

"Pep rallies, sports—the basketball team is all-city. Wasn't there some kind of huge accident at their last game?"

His eyes narrowed. "What do you know about that?"

"Everybody's talking about it. A piece broke off this statue. . . ." My voice trailed off. Why did he seem so suspicious? I was only trying to be friendly, and he was acting like this was a CIA interrogation under hot lights.

"I don't go to that school anymore," he said very sharply, almost like he was mad at me. "I'm too— smart." And he stormed away, leaving me standing in the hall with my mouth hanging open.

It wasn't his rudeness that struck me. It was this: Ever since I'd started at the Academy, the one thing I'd been yearning for was somebody normal. Now, finally, he was here.

<<*Hypothesis: What if the normal people are even weirder than we are?*>>

UNKNOWING
DONOVAN CURTIS
IQ: 112

When the paper airplane bounced off the back of the driver's head, the man pulled the bus over onto the shoulder. He got out of his seat, picked up the offending aircraft, and waved it at us.

Honest—it wasn't me. The last thing I wanted to do at the Academy was draw attention to myself. But I was so used to getting blamed for stuff that I braced myself for the onslaught.

"Interesting experiment," the driver said in an

approving tone. "The air moves with the bus, so the plane flies normally. An open window would interfere with that. The more open windows, the greater the interference. And if the bus had no roof, the plane would be half a mile behind us."

Whoa, even the Academy bus drivers were gifted! If you chuck a paper airplane at someone, they assume you did it for science. On my old bus, the driver would have held us all hostage until we gave up the person who did it—probably me. And you can bet that "interesting experiment" wouldn't have been what he called it. *Mutiny*, maybe. Or *armed insurrection*.

There was a smattering of applause as a seventh grader, flushed with triumph, reclaimed his plane, and we were under way again.

Soon we arrived at the Academy for Scholastic Distinction, which looked absolutely nothing like a school if you ask me. It was, by far, the most modern building in town. Every inch of the place was covered with solar panels. On sunny days, it was like pulling up to a jewel-encrusted palace. Supposedly, the students had worked with the architects who designed it. The Academy was 100 percent eco-friendly, right down to the bathrooms, where the toilets had different "flush settings," depending on the kind of waste you were getting rid of. There was no button for "cherry bomb," which is what the teachers invested a lot of energy preparing for at my old school.

Mr. Del Rio, the principal, stood outside the automatic sliding doors greeting his students with handshakes. At Hardcastle Middle, you never saw the principal unless you did something wrong—which, in my case, was fairly often. Mom always used to say, "Donnie gets a lot of personal attention at the very highest level at that school." She was so proud that I was at the Academy now. I felt a pang of guilt for the bogus reason behind it.

Determination surged through me. Maybe I could hack it here. After all, half of being gifted was just the fact that everybody *expected* you to be smart. Like that seventh grader on the bus. No way was that any experiment. The guy made a paper airplane, and he couldn't resist flying it. Well, Couldn't Resist was practically my middle name. I wasn't that different from the Academy kids. Obviously, I was never going to star at this place. But with hard work, a little bit of luck, and a lot of good acting, I might just be able to fake it.

If x represents the vector of variables, b *and* c *are vectors of known coefficients, and* A *is a matrix of*

coefficients, determine the maximum value of the
objective function $c^T x$ . . .

I stared at the problem until my liquefied eyeballs were about to drip out of their sockets and roll down my cheeks.

All around the math room, my classmates were working away, calculating and figuring. It went without saying that I couldn't *do* it. Man, I couldn't even *read* it.

In the next row, Noah Youkilis was scribbling away like it was the easiest thing in the world. The kid really *was* gifted—although anybody who looked like Noah and *wasn't* gifted would have a genuine complaint. Picture a four-foot-eleven praying mantis suffering from extreme malnutrition, with a long nose and glasses that were last in style when President Truman wore them.

As he plowed methodically through the page, I couldn't help noticing what a dark pencil he was using. The numbers really stood out against the bright white of the worksheet. Another thing about me—I've been blessed with excellent peripheral vision. Well, what was I supposed to do—sit there while the period ticked away? According to ancestry.com, my great-great-great uncle was a "spotter" during World War One—he floated over the battlefield in a hot-air balloon and peered down into the German trenches. It didn't explain much about me, since he never tried to bungee-jump out of the basket. But it was probably why it was so easy for me to copy the answers off Noah's paper.

I tried to get a few wrong, which was actually pretty tricky. I understood so little that it was impossible to know what a reasonable mistake might be. Even cheating was harder in this place.

Noah scrambled up on scrawny legs and handed his paper to Ms. Bevelaqua. "I'm done."

She glanced at it and then handed it back without so much as notation. "All right, Noah. Do it properly this time."

The praying mantis hunched a little farther forward. "I'm working to the best of my ability! It's not my fault this math is too hard! I'll never get it right!" His lower lip quivered.

The teacher nodded understandingly. "Poor you. It isn't easy to master calculus in middle school."

"This isn't calculus; it's linear programming!" Noah blurted. "Everybody knows that!"

"Right," she said triumphantly. "Including you."

She motioned him back toward his seat.

He looked bummed at getting caught, but he couldn't have been half as bummed as I was. In a class of geniuses, I had copied from the guy who got it wrong on purpose.

Luckily, there were plenty of fish in the sea. I leaned a little closer to Abigail Lee, who was motoring through the assignment at almost-Noah speed. I remembered her from elementary school, where she'd been all-universe at anything that took brains. Her writing wasn't quite as clear, but beggars can't be choosers. At least I had the reasonable belief she wasn't trying to fail. What was up with this Noah kid, I couldn't imagine.

"Hey!" Abigail hunched over, blocking my view of her paper. "What do you think you're doing?"

I played dumb. "What?" I covered my worksheet, like I was preventing *her* from copying from *me*.

"Ms. Bevelaqua!" she bawled. *"Donovan's cheating!"*

"Chill out," I tried to hiss.

"I'm not going to chill out! If we have the same answers we'll both get zero! I've never had a zero in my life! I can't get zero! I work too hard to get zero! What am I going to tell my tutors if I get zero?" She was red in the face, heading for purple.

Noah seemed genuinely bewildered. "Well, if you're

looking for the *right* answers," he asked me, "why don't you just *calculate* them?"

"Big talk from the freak who goes out of his way to put down the wrong ones!" I retorted.

That got Chloe's back up. "Watch who you're calling a freak, you—*troglodyte*!"

"Yeah?" I spat back. "Well, I don't know what that is, so trog-whatever to you too!"

Then this girl Jacey, who said random things at moments of stress, announced, "In Brazil more cars run on ethanol than regular gas."

It had the effect of a referee's whistle, separating the combatants from their clinch.

I learned a few things in that class. First, the regular student code about not ratting people out—that didn't apply at the Academy. Second, nobody knew how to deal with cheating, because it never happened. No one needed to do it. Third, *zero* is a four-letter word.

Amazingly, I didn't really get in trouble, although it was pretty obvious who was copying from whom. I wasn't sent to the office; there was no detention; nobody even yelled at me, which was a first in my educational experience. Instead, my homeroom teacher, Mr. Osborne, came and suggested we take a walk. At Hardcastle Middle, if you're caught off campus during school hours, they've practically got guard towers to gun you down. I was beginning to see that they had two sets of rules in our district—one for the brainiacs, and one for everybody else. Of course, I was living the good life now. But I still took it personally since I knew it was all a mistake.

"Look, Donovan," Mr. Osborne said pleasantly, "at the Academy, we've got kids who are talented at a lot of different subjects. But very few of us are good at *everything*. If you're not up to this math, it's no disgrace to admit it. In fact, it happens all the time. We have regular classes too."

I nodded dumbly.

"This is a period of discovery," he went on. "We're getting to know you, and you're getting to know us. And during that process, we'll explore where your true gifts lie. Are there any fields of study that really turn you on?"

I hesitated. Sooner or later, somebody was going to realize that my presence here was completely bogus. But—also sooner or later—my namesake, James Donovan, would have joined his fellow *Titanic* passengers on the bottom of the ocean. He'd survived by staying afloat until the rescuers could get to him—*by making it later rather than sooner!*

I had to keep swimming.

"I think," I said aloud, "that we should stick with the exploring part a little while longer."

He nodded approvingly. "Very wise. Let's not rush into anything. But promise me you'll join the robotics team and help out with Tin Man. I mean—our entry."

"Last time I touched Tin Man, his hand fell off," I reminded him gently.

He shrugged it off. "You'll watch and learn. That's what the Academy is all about."

"Thanks, Mr. Osborne," I mumbled.

"Call me Oz."

I hate it when adults do that.

The Hardcastle Mall used to be one of my favorite hangouts. Tonight, though, it looked a little drab and in need of a face-lift. It wasn't the mall that had changed. It was just that school was newer, nicer, and cleaner. The Academy, not Hardcastle Middle, obviously. Our cafeteria had better options than the food court, and the prices were lower.

We didn't even have the dumb rules that ruined everything. For example, soda was banned at my old school because of the sugar content. But the Academy lunchroom had a drink machine that was open to everybody. It even sold the extra-sugar, extra-caffeine stuff. It was fine, even necessary to fuel the brainiacs through late-night studying marathons. But if one of the ungifted kids at Hardcastle happened to get a sip, he'd go straight out and rob a bank.

Technically, my six-month ban for swimming in the fountain was still in effect. But the security guard who had busted me wasn't on duty. It was a bum rap. It isn't skinny-dipping if you're wearing boxers. Besides, if the air-conditioning is going to break down on a ninety-degree day, it's management's responsibility to fix it before people start looking for other ways to cool off.

The Daniels had never experienced the Academy cafeteria, so they thought the food court was fine dining. We weren't eating anyway. I was on a bench, trying to ignore the Daniels' whooping and yipping, designed to catch the attention of a couple of girls.

"Do something funny, Donovan," Nussbaum urged. "Chicks eat that stuff up."

I glared at him. "If you want to talk to Heather Mahoney, why don't you walk over there?"

"Because that would be lame," he explained reasonably. "*She* has to come to *me*."

"Jump in the fountain again," Sanderson urged me.

"That's an attention grabber."

"*You* jump in the fountain," I shot back.

He grabbed me under the arms, but I disarmed him with a punch to the gut before Nussbaum could help him wrestle me into the water.

It did the trick, though. Heather and her friend—Deirdre Somebody—were ambling in our direction.

"Hi, Donovan," Heather addressed me. "Haven't seen you for a few days. Were you sick?"

"Donovan's a genius now," Sanderson supplied. "He goes to the gifted Academy."

"Really?" Deirdre was impressed. "Don't you have to take a lot of tests for that?"

"It's no big deal," I put in quickly, studying the floor.

"You're telling me!" Nussbaum exclaimed. "You know how he got picked? He's only there because—"

I stomped on his sneaker hard, silencing him before he could say more.

"Donovan!" came another voice.

It took me a second to recognize her. It was Chloe from the Academy. She said something to a middle-aged woman and headed toward our table.

"Who's that?" Sanderson asked.

"She's in my new homeroom," I replied.

Nussbaum snickered. "Nice lumberjack shirt."

Funny—surrounded by the kids at the Academy, Chloe looked kind of good. Call it the Youkilis factor; the gifted crew wasn't exactly Fashion Week. Yet next to Heather and Deirdre, you could tell she was out of her league. Those two wore skinny jeans and vintage T-shirts that were just—well, *right*. Chloe wasn't ugly or anything like that—in fact, she had a pretty face. But you had to concentrate to notice it. She wore no makeup, and her loose flannel shirt gave her a lumpy appearance. A huge button on her lapel declared: THAT'S OKAY, PLUTO. I'M NOT A PLANET EITHER. It clanked as she walked.

I was surprised to see her at all outside of school. I always thought of her as one of those people who suddenly whooshes into being at the sound of the first bell in the morning, and winks out again when the clock strikes three-thirty.

"Hi, Donovan," she greeted me eagerly. "Do you live around here?"

"Hey, Chloe." She was looking expectantly at the others, so I semi-introduced them. "Meet the guys."

"Hi, Chloe." Nussbaum stepped forward and pumped her hand. The grin on his face was barely this side of idiotic. "How does it feel to have Donovan in the Academy? I mean, is he gifted or what?"

"I think it's 'or what,'" Sanderson said with a smirk.

Chloe could tell they were messing with her, but she had no idea how much. "Donovan's cool," she offered tentatively. She turned back to me. "Sorry about what happened in math today. How did it go with Oz?"

For some reason, I felt I had to defend myself. "I never meant to cheat off Abigail. I was *trying* to cheat off Noah. How was I supposed to know he puts down the wrong answers on purpose? I thought he was this big genius."

"He definitely doesn't feel the need to prove it," she replied with a sympathetic smile. "Abigail's the opposite. If she ever brought home a B-plus, it would be the end of the world."

"She practically tore my head off."

"She's under a lot of pressure," Chloe explained. "She does just about everything, and she's keeping half the tutors in town in business. She pushes herself pretty hard."

"I never thought the gifted kids had problems," mused Deirdre.

"It's those big brains," Nussbaum supplied wisely. "It makes a person top-heavy, out of balance. Like the Atlas statue."

"How crazy was that?" Heather exclaimed. "I was at

the game! The girl at the end of my row was covered in broken glass!"

"They still haven't found the guy who did it," Deirdre added.

"I heard it was an accident," I suggested, looking daggers at Nussbaum. "Wear and tear on the statue. It can't be easy to hold up the weight of the world in the wind and rain year after year—especially when it's attached by one bolt."

"One bolt," Chloe repeated dubiously. "That's pretty shoddy engineering. We put more thought into Tin Man's stress points."

"Tin Man?" Sanderson echoed.

"Our class robot," I answered, and bit my tongue. "I mean the robot that happens to live in the homeroom I got assigned to."

"It's your robot, too," Chloe said generously. "You're on the robotics team now. Maybe you'll put us over the top at the big meet. We've come in second to Cold Spring Harbor three years in a row."

You could just see the Daniels swelling up with joy at this new information. Not only did I go to the nerd school, but I was on the robotics team, which was nerd squared. No way could I ever live this down in only one lifetime.

Chloe waved at the woman she'd arrived with. "Got to go. My mom's done shopping." She beamed at me. "See you tomorrow."

"See you," I mumbled.

"We should hop too," Heather put in. "Our ride will be here any minute."

I hated to see them leave. When it was just me and the Daniels, I knew I was going to get it.

Nussbaum didn't disappoint. "Some girlfriend you've got there, Donovan. Or is she just a regular friend, and you're dating Tin Man?"

"I can't believe Tin Man's cheating on Tin Woman." Sanderson clucked disapprovingly. "She must be hot. She probably doesn't wear her grandfather's plaid shirt."

"Shut up, you guys. Chloe's not my girlfriend and it isn't my robot. I'm only on the robotics team because my homeroom teacher is the coach. I have to try to fit in over there, and believe me, it isn't easy—and not just because I haven't got the brainpower. You heard about the guy who tried to flunk the math test—the teacher had to trick him into admitting he understood it. So he's a genius and a moron all in one. It's a nuthouse!"

"Well, it's not safe to come back to Hardcastle yet,"

Sanderson advised. "We had an assembly today, and that guy Schultz was standing right at the door. He looked at every single face that came into the gym. I'll bet he's searching for you, man! He didn't even stick around. He just watched us file in and took off."

I felt ice-cold tentacles wrapping around my stomach. It was my worst fear coming true, but at least it settled one issue. All day I'd been asking myself what I was doing at the Academy for Scholastic Distinction. Now I knew.

I was hiding out.

UNCREDITED
MR. OSBORNE
IQ: 132

If I didn't know better, I'd swear that Donovan Curtis wasn't gifted at all. I'd bet a month's pay that an eighth-grade boy had been chosen at absolute random and dropped into the top academy for differentiated instruction in the state.

But I did know better. Our selection procedure was ironclad. Students had to pass a battery of tests from the state department of education, not to mention faculty interviews, and even a psychological exam. A mosquito couldn't make it through the screening process.

Our last faculty meeting was essentially a seminar on Donovan Curtis. It turned out to be quite a revelation. All his teachers had realized that he was weak in their courses, and had assumed that his gifts lay elsewhere. But after comparing notes, it became clear that his gifts lay *nowhere*. He was mediocre in English, social studies, French, and computer science, and well below average in math and science. I didn't expect him to excel at *everything*, but Donovan excelled at *nothing*. Which begged the question: What was he doing at the Academy?

"Have you tried getting him involved with the robotics team?" asked our principal, Brian Del Rio.

I nodded. "He's our designated Googler."

"Your what?"

"He has no knowledge of programming, engineering, hydraulics, pneumatics, or even basic mechanics. So he surfs the internet looking for pictures to download and paste on Tin Man. Like Albert Einstein eating a banana."

Brian frowned. "What's Tin Man?"

"The robot. It's short for Tin Man Metallica Squarepants. Donovan's idea."

"You don't think he's putting us on, do you?"

suggested Ellie Shapiro, the department head for social studies. "Some of these bright kids have a warped sense of humor."

"I doubt it," I told her. "To be honest, the other kids love what he does with the graphics. And nobody's ever thought of naming the robot before. I admit I wasn't too crazy about the idea. At first I only went along with it to empower Donovan. But you know what? I'm glad we did it."

"It's very cute," Ellie agreed.

"It's more than cute," I amended. "It's humanized our entire program. The difference between dealing with an *it* and a *him* is a transformative concept."

"Maybe that's our answer," Brian mused. "Dozens of brilliant kids pass through your class, building machines that win prizes at the highest levels. Yet the simplest thing—naming a piece of equipment, or decorating it—gets by everybody except Donovan."

Maria Bevelaqua—math—spoke up. "Or he does it because he can't do anything else. He doodles through my class. He hasn't taken a single note."

I jumped on this. "A photographic memory?"

"He's lucky he can remember his own name," she deadpanned. "I asked him what school he came from, and you know what he said? 'I forget.' If that's a photographic memory, he left the lens cap on."

"Perhaps it's a kind of social intelligence," Brian ventured, really reaching.

"Oh, please," Maria snorted. "He may seem like a smooth operator compared to our usual clientele. But there's nothing special about him in that way either."

"I have to agree," I said wearily. "He alienated Abigail on day one. And he causes a lot of friction in the lab. Latrell feels threatened by him, and Jacey doesn't know what to make of him."

"Jacey doesn't know quite what to make of anyone," Ellie cut in.

"Chloe comes the closest to understanding him, but they butt heads too," I went on. "And as for Noah—"

"Noah's so smart that most of us can't even begin to imagine what's going on in his head," Maria put in.

I sighed. "Maybe. But the reverse is also true. Noah can't understand not understanding. And there's Donovan, who understands *nothing*. To Noah, he's like some exotic space alien who crash-landed in the gifted program."

"Maybe Noah isn't wrong about that," Maria challenged.

Brian's brow furrowed. "What are you saying?"

"What if," Maria went on, "our much-vaunted

selection system broke down and sent us your average knuckle-dragger?"

"Impossible." Our principal was adamant. "All our kids have strengths and weaknesses. We seem to have a good sense of Donovan's weaknesses. It's a start. Now we have to find his strengths. He wouldn't be here if they didn't exist."

As the meeting broke up, he pulled me aside. "There's one more thing." He hesitated. "You're not going to like it."

I sighed. "Let me guess—Donovan again?"

"This time it isn't Donovan. As you may know, all students graduating from middle school are required to complete one quarter of Human Growth and Development."

"Human Growth and Development?" I echoed. "You mean sex education?"

He made a face. "We haven't called it that in decades."

"But what does that have to do with me?" I asked. "They teach that in seventh grade, don't they?"

"Usually . . ." The principal took a deep breath. "Your kids don't have it."

I was horrified. "None of them?"

"None of the big names—Youkilis, Halloran, Garfinkle, Lee. A few transfers took the equivalent at their old schools. And Donovan's okay—he got the instruction at Hardcastle."

"How could we miss that?"

Brian shrugged unhappily. "Robotics has always attracted our best and brightest. Anything new and innovative and exciting is thrown at your group. They're always busy. And the last thing anyone thought they needed was to spend hours drawing diagrams of the human body and watching videos on how babies are made."

"So what happens now?" I asked wearily. "I have to drop what I'm doing, and spend the rest of the year on . . . sex ed?"

He shook his head. "You need a state certification to teach Human Growth and Development. You're not qualified."

"So who is?"

"Nobody," Brian told me. "Beth Vogel has been coming over from Salem to work with our seventh grade, but she's teaching a full schedule this quarter. The whole district is running on austerity. Staffing is cut to the bone. Believe me, Oz, I've been over this every which way with Dr. Schultz. If there were a way out, we would have found it. The state allows us absolutely zero flexibility. Forty hours under a credentialed teacher, with triple time credited for real hands-on experience."

"They're kids, Brian! Where are they going to get hands-on experience of *that*? Would we even want them to?"

"We're still working on a few possibilities," he admitted. "They could take the course after school. Or over the summer."

"Think of the students you're talking about," I pleaded. "They take music lessons, learn languages, intern at research labs, work with private tutors. They're scheduled down to the nanosecond. You're going to make them give up all that for *sex ed*?"

"Human Growth and Development," he amended.

"We ought to be ashamed of ourselves!"

He nodded grimly. "We are."

I was heartsick. "What am I going to tell the kids?"

"Don't tell them anything yet. Not till we've explored every option."

Privately, I was hoping that one of my colleagues might bail me out on the Mission Impossible of Donovan and his hidden talents. Every time another teacher approached me, I expected the eureka moment—"I've got it! He's a brilliant . . ." I didn't care what came next—writer, physicist, harpsichord player, linguist, chess master, infrared astronomer; he has total recall, perfect pitch, a knack for languages, great potential for spelunking. Anything!

It was a cop-out. The answer wasn't going to drop from the sky and land at my feet. I'd watched him in my own classroom. Why would he be different anywhere else?

Actually, he did *less* for me than he did for the other teachers. At least in his core subjects, he tried and failed. In robotics, all he did was search the internet for graphics to stick on Tin Man. Seriously, to justify the time he spent on Google Images, we would have needed a robot the size of a twenty-story building.

A convulsive high-pitched cackling filled the lab. When I went to investigate, I found Donovan at the keyboard and Noah peering over his shoulder—holding on to it, in fact—hysterical with laughter.

Noah *never* laughed. He had a stratospheric IQ with few commonsense skills, and zero sense of humor. His thinking was lightning fast and flawlessly accurate, but also 100 percent literal. I barely recognized him, convulsed with mirth, breathing hard, his face bright pink.

"What is it?"

"Look—" He pointed at the screen, bereft of speech.

On the screen, a brief video clip showed a barefoot man walking along the edge of a pool. He stubbed his toe on a rubber dog bone and tumbled, arms flailing, into the water. Noah pounded on the desk, choking.

Chloe appeared at my elbow. "It's called YouTube, Noah."

"It's the latest thing," Donovan added. "Ten years ago."

"*That's* YouTube?" Noah was incredulous. "I've heard of it, obviously, but I never—who's the actor? He's brilliant! I really *believed* that he fell in the pool by accident."

I sighed. Of course a kid like Noah had never explored YouTube before. When he got on a computer, most of us couldn't imagine what he was capable of. What he *wasn't* capable of were the ordinary things.

"He's not an actor," I explained patiently, "he's a regular person. Anyone can post a home video on YouTube."

He was wide-eyed. "Anyone?"

"And anyone can watch it," Donovan confirmed.

Noah may have started the day a YouTube novice, but by the end of the period, he could have written a doctoral dissertation on it. Such was the power of his intellect. He took Donovan's seat at the computer, and disappeared into the site, reappearing only occasionally to explain the math behind his estimate of the total number of videos—over eight hundred million—or the amount of time it would take to watch them all—more than six hundred years.

"Assuming an average duration of twenty to twenty-five seconds each," he concluded. "I'll be more precise when I've had a few weeks to study it."

"Way to go," Abigail told Donovan savagely. "Noah should be curing diseases and changing the world, not watching some dimwit falling in his pool."

"Give the guy a break from his brain," Donovan argued. "When's the last time anybody saw him so psyched about something?"

I had to give Donovan that. For all Noah's incredible abilities, the boy would fail out of school if his teachers were to let him. Donovan alone had managed to engage him. Could that be a kind of giftedness in and of itself?

Regardless, Donovan had succeeded in running through yet another class without yielding the slightest hint as to why he was at the Academy.

Of all the kids in my homeroom, Chloe was the one most taken with Donovan. It was a crush, not so much on Donovan himself as what he represented—normal middle school life. She peppered him with questions about parties and school spirit and big games and pep rallies.

"I wasn't really into that stuff," Donovan told her.

He was reluctant to talk about his experiences at Hardcastle Middle. Something must have gone on there that I couldn't quite put my finger on. He seemed anxious to put the past behind him—anxious enough to ignore the obvious signs that he wasn't fitting in here. Had he been bullied? A lot of our students had suffered that at their old schools. But Donovan didn't seem like the type.

Chloe would not be put off. "Well, there must have been parties," she reasoned. "You know, dances—that kind of thing."

"I think it's a pathetic waste of time," Abigail chimed in. "Can you imagine having nothing better to do than bounce around a school gym to bad music under cheap streamers and a cheesy rented disco ball? Don't we all have better things to do?"

"No argument from me," said Donovan.

Nothing pleased Abigail less than being agreed with by Donovan.

"Hey, you guys—do something funny," Noah waved

at us from behind a flip video camera. "This is for YouTube."

The kids ignored him, but I felt it was important to support Noah's new interest. For all his brilliance, Noah spent his life in a kind of cocoon. Pointing a flip cam at people was as close as he got to social interaction.

"What about Tin Man?" I suggested. "He looks like a YouTube star to me."

Abigail was horrified. "That's a terrible idea! We'd be showing the other teams exactly what we're working on for the robotics meet!"

I chuckled. "It's supposed to be a friendly competition, Abigail, not a life-and-death struggle."

Never try to tell Abigail to take it easy.

"The results of that meet go on your permanent record," she insisted. "There could be college admissions on the line, maybe even scholarships. If that's not a life-and-death struggle, I don't know what is! This could be the year we finally defeat Cold Spring Harbor and win it all! Do you want to risk that?"

Eventually, we shouted her down. If Cold Spring Harbor found our little clip among six hundred years of video on YouTube, they *deserved* to beat us again. And anyway, some of the kids were already rolling

Tin Man Metallica Squarepants out into the middle of the room.

I had to admit, our latest creation was taking shape. No credit to me—everything had come from the kids. Abigail and Chloe provided the design, and Noah did all the programming. The boy had never watched YouTube, but he could think in computer code. Kevin was our welding and soldering expert. Jacey and Latrell built the body. And there, large as life on Tin Man's "chest," was Albert Einstein eating a banana, courtesy of Donovan. There were other graphics too—a cat with a Mohawk, the fiery eye of Sauron from the *Lord of the Rings* movies, the flag of Mozambique, and a bumper sticker that read OFFICE OF NEW YORK CITY RATCATCHER.

Noah brandished the flip cam, and Abigail worked the joystick, sending our work in progress on its first trial run. The robot was capable of moving on its own, following a route marked by colored lines on the floor. But the most important rounds of the competition required a human driver.

I watched carefully, taking special note of the wheels, which were a new type for us. Last year, Cold Spring Harbor had used Mecanum wheels, which gave them extra maneuverability. But on Tin

Man, I couldn't see much difference.

"Hold it." I got down on all fours and examined the bearings to make sure the Mecanums had a full range of motion.

"The problem's not the wheels," put in Donovan. "It's the driver."

Abigail glared at him. "What do you know about robotics?"

"Nothing," he replied honestly. "But I can use a joystick. Don't you guys play video games?"

"I'd like to see *you* do better!"

And with a casual shrug, he held out his hands for the controller. Eyes shooting sparks, Abigail relinquished it, and Donovan put Tin Man through his paces. I watched in amazement. The robot fairly danced around the lab, the lift mechanism moving easily. The Mecanums worked like magic, changing direction instantly with a flick of Donovan's wrist.

The kids broke into cheers. They mobbed Donovan, begging him to be our operator at the meet—all except Abigail. She stood rooted to the floor, fuming.

"Got it!" Noah lowered the camera and ran for the computer to upload his very first YouTube video.

And me? Well, I was thrilled for the team and tantalized at the prospect of finally giving Cold Spring

Harbor a run for their money. But I also realized that my chief problem was no closer to a solution. Being good with a joystick because of hundreds of hours playing video games was not the kind of talent that got a student into the Academy for Academic Distinction.

What was Donovan Curtis doing in the gifted program?

UNREPAIRED

DONOVAN CURTIS
IQ: 112

The grade glowered at me off the cover sheet of my social studies paper: D-minus.

"Is that graded on a bell curve?" I asked Mrs. Shapiro.

She was almost sympathetic. "No, Donovan. It's just graded."

"Oh."

I wasn't normally grade-obsessed, but this really threw me. The thing is, I had no chance with the kind of math and science they taught in this place. If I was going to have any prayer at all of hacking it in the Academy, I'd have to rock subjects like English and social studies. That's why I was so shocked about the D-minus. I'd worked really hard on this paper. Maybe I hadn't aced it by gifted standards. But I'd figured I'd get a least a B. I would have settled for a C!

The teacher sighed. "Is there anything you want to tell me? Is something wrong?"

Something was wrong, all right. When the biggest effort I'd put into a school project since kindergarten pulled a D-minus, yes, it was pretty fair to say that something was wrong.

She interpreted my silence as an invitation to probe further. "At home, perhaps?"

"Well, it's just that I have ADD." That was pure blind inspiration. Sanderson had ADD, and occasionally he got cut a little extra slack because of it.

Mrs. Shapiro's expression softened immediately. "Why didn't you say so?"

"I guess I was too distracted by other things." She looked a little suspicious, so I added, "I really wanted to make it on my own. ADD doesn't sound very gifted."

"That's nonsense," she reassured me. "You'd be

astounded how often giftedness is accompanied by some sort of learning disability." She handed the paper back to me. "Why don't you work on this for another week?"

I didn't like the sound of that. "Well . . ."

"And we'll see what we can do about raising your grade."

Hmmm, maybe there was more to this learning disability racket than met the eye. After all, ADD was just the beginning. With a little bit of effort, I could work up a case of obsessive-compulsive disorder that would knock your socks off. And what about dyslexia? That could be just the ticket to ward off any D-minuses that might be coming down the pike in English.

I put my all into the social studies paper, and Mrs. Shapiro grudgingly upped me to a C. I fared no better in English class. Dyslexia or not, C-minus was the best I could come up with, and that was a stretch. Have you ever read *Beowulf*? Even the Cliff Notes could kill you.

I expanded my list of disorders. Restless leg syndrome was a good one. It explained all my fidgeting. And my nonspecific bladder issues allowed me to spend as much time in the bathroom as outside of it. I had this recurring nightmare that all my teachers got together and compared notes on my various illnesses, weaknesses, and diseases. At the end of the dream, an ambulance pulls up to the Academy to haul me off to intensive care. But when the attendant takes off his surgical mask, it isn't a paramedic; it's Dr. Schultz. Then I'd wake up, choking and spitting, because Beatrice was sleeping on my face.

Yes, the chow chow was still a fact of life—I should say a fact of *my* life, since she totally loved me. Props to Katie—she tried to help out. But every time she even got in the same room with her husband's dog, Beatrice growled her off. All the mutt wanted was me. She spent her nights in my bed and her days in my dresser drawer, because my scent was on my sheets and clothing—which meant I spent nights *and* days scratching at itchy dog hair. There wasn't a part of my body the chow chow hadn't napped on yet. I should open up for business as a parking lot. I'd make a fortune in dog biscuits.

I would have put a stop to it, except that I was beginning to think Brad's mother was right. Beatrice really *was* sick. Her energy level was absolute zero, and she ate nothing at all, which was amazing, because her stomach seemed fatter than ever. Nussbaum's pet snake had more get-up-and-go. When the cold-blooded animals are livelier than the warm-blooded ones, you know you've got a problem.

Katie was freaking out. "If anything happens to Beatrice, Brad's going to drive his M1 halfway around the world and run me over."

"Not a good idea," I told her. "You're a pretty big speed bump. We don't want to owe the Marines a new tank."

Poor Katie: her belly was expanding, her butt was widening, her ankles were thickening, and her varicose veins looked more like a road map every day. She was almost as big a mess as Beatrice—except that Katie hadn't started peeing on the floor.

That unpleasant surprise came in the form of a warm puddle on the carpet as I made my way downstairs for breakfast.

"That mutt has got to go!" I howled, hopping on the steps, pulling off my soggy sock.

My dad grinned at me from the front hall. "Is that how you support our troops? By evicting their pets?"

"I don't want to live in a chow chow's toilet!" I complained.

He laughed appreciatively. "Good thing you went to charm school before you got picked for the Academy." Even Dad cut me a little slack these days. No wonder the gifted kids were different. They lived in a bubble. "I'm going to pick up a carpet steamer on my way to work this morning. Change your socks. I'll give you a ride."

Outside, my eyes were drawn to the new bumper sticker on Dad's car:

PROUD PARENT OF AN HONOR STUDENT

AT THE ACADEMY FOR SCHOLASTIC DISTINCTION

"I'm not an honor student," I managed, understatement of the year. "I just go there."

He was unperturbed. "Everybody's an honor student at that place. It's an honor just to walk in the door. We're all proud of you, Donnie. Your mother and me, Katie—"

"Right," I snorted. "She said I'm dumber than her bladder-challenged dog."

Dad started the car. "She may not say it in so many words, but don't think she isn't feeling it. These are tough times for our family, what with Brad deployed and the baby coming. And now Beatrice—like we don't have enough stress in our lives already. Then you step in and do something for everybody to feel good about. It's like it was sent from heaven."

I felt as if I was losing my mind. Hiding out in the gifted program, and carrying the emotional well-being of my entire family. No pressure.

At the small appliance shop, I hung back while Dad spoke with the salesman. There was a copy of the town paper lying open on the cashier's desk. I nearly threw up my breakfast when I read the banner headline:

REPAIRS IN LIMBO THANKS TO "STATUE-GATE"

Physical Education classes at Hardcastle Middle and High Schools are being held outdoors despite the frigid winter temperatures. The glass double doors of the athletic facility are still boarded shut, and 25 percent of the floor is badly damaged. The school district is ready to roll on the repairs; a contractor has been hired.

So what's the holdup?

The Parthenon Insurance Group is refusing to pay, arguing that the damage was caused by "engineering negligence" in the statue of Atlas, a portion of which rolled down the hill and smashed into the building. The offending object, Atlas's "globe of the world and heavens"—all 400 pounds of it—was affixed by a single bolt, which corroded over the years. This "design flaw,"

Parthenon argues, is the responsibility of the statue's manufacturer. However, Classical Bronze Foundries, Inc., went bankrupt in 1998, leaving the school high and dry.

The Hardcastle School District has filed suit against Parthenon, but the case is likely to drag on for years, according to Superintendent Alonzo Schultz. In the meantime, the physical education program is out in the cold. All varsity basketball home games have to be relocated, and even the middle school's annual Valentine Dance will take place elsewhere. Dr. Schultz holds out little hope for an early resolution unless he can track down a "person of interest" in the case. . . .

Yikes! If the insurance company stiffed the school district, would this "person of interest" have to pick up the tab? It wasn't my fault Schultz cheaped out and bought a bum statue from a company that went bankrupt! Classical Bronze Foundries probably tried to save a few bucks on bolts and had to pay it all back a hundred times over in lawsuits.

But I'll bet our superintendent was the only genius who put *his* Atlas at the top of a hill overlooking a breakable gym!

With a sinking heart, I watched Dad haggling with

the salesman, trying to save every penny. We weren't poor, but money was tight, especially with an extra mouth to feed—Katie—and a baby on the way. The one good thing about Beatrice's hunger strike was that we weren't blowing a fortune on dog food. There was no way we could afford to fix a busted gym. It didn't take Noah Youkilis or Abigail Lee to do *that* math.

I got to the Academy earlier than usual, which gave me some much-needed extra time to work on my science project. Abigail's was entitled "The Abiotic Synthesis of Organic Compounds"; Chloe's had something to do with the wave/particle duality of light, whatever that is; Noah's, "The Youkilis Constant," was this number he'd developed that supposedly explained the expansion of the universe in the first few seconds following the Big Bang. Mine was called "Chow Chows: A Special Breed." Obviously, it wasn't as impressive as the others, but I was really slaving over it. My plan was this: I was never going to outscience the Academy kids, but I could give it the personal touch. Hey, if I was stuck being hospice nurse to a dying dog, at least I should get a project out of it. I had photographs, and sound recordings of barking, and microscope slides of fur and drool samples. If I loaded up enough stuff, Mr. Holman would have to give me a decent grade on sheer volume. And if he turned out to be a dog lover, I'd be golden.

I stashed my coat in my locker, which was still basically empty. Lockers were huge at the Academy. I'd never seen it, but supposedly one kid kept a full tropical fish tank in his, plugged into the built-in power strip. Unlike Hardcastle Middle with its no-phones-during-school-hours rule, the Academy encouraged its gifted students to have laptops and smartphones charged up and available at all times. "You never know when the research bug might hit," Mr. Osborne was fond of saying. It made me smile that Noah—apex of the IQ pyramid—now used his BlackBerry purely for watching YouTube.

The robotics lab was deserted when I got there. "Hey, Tin Man," I said, greeting him in a low voice, bestowing a very gentle high-five on one of the lifting forks.

Call me crazy, but it sort of pleased me that the robot had a name thanks to me. Just like it pleased me that I was now Tin Man's first-string driver for the robotics meet. I know that must seem pretty stupid coming from someone who was in such big trouble in every other phase of his life.

Standing there next to Tin Man, I happened to glance over to the teacher's cluttered desk. There was an internal memo form on top of the mess. My eyes froze on the subject line: "SUMMER SCHOOL."

It had to be about me. Who else in this class of brainiacs could possibly need summer school? In the interest of self-preservation, I had to read it.

Oz—as we feared, the district has been unable to find a certified teacher to offer Human Growth and Development to your students who have unfortunately missed it. Summer school appears to be their only option. The kids affected are Chloe Garfinkle, Abigail Lee, Noah Youkilis . . .

That was as far as I got before Mr. Osborne came in and caught me snooping.

"Donovan—step away from my desk!"

I was too blown away to worry about whether or not he was mad. "Summer school!" I exclaimed. "For *those* guys?"

"It's none of your business," the teacher interrupted sharply. "It doesn't affect you at all."

"But why would the smartest kids in town need

summer school?" I persisted, bewildered. "What's Human Growth and Development?"

"It's a health course required by the state," he explained wearily. "You took it last year in seventh grade."

Light dawned. "And you were so busy teaching them genius stuff that you missed it." I mulled it over. "That's on you, not them."

He looked like I'd slapped him. "I know."

I would have bet money that I had absolutely nothing in common with my gifted classmates. But here they were just like me, getting jerked around because the school district had messed up. I was on the hook for the damage caused by Schultz's defective statue; they were on the hook for a required course nobody remembered they needed. And the cost was going to be one summer.

"So teach it to them," I concluded. "Those guys, it won't take ten minutes before they know it better than you."

He shook his head gravely. "The teacher has to be state certified. Or it has to come from hands-on experience."

"Hands-on experience?" I repeated, startled. "They want that? Isn't it all about—well, you know?"

"Physiology," he interjected. "Adolescence, body changes . . ."

The seed of an idea began to germinate in my mind. "What else?" I prompted.

"Reproduction."

Katie folded her arms atop her big belly. "You're out of your mind," she told me. "I always knew you were crazy, but this is proof positive."

"Don't be like that," I wheedled. "It won't cost you anything except a few trips to the school. Why should you care? You'll be pregnant anyway."

"It won't cost me anything?" she echoed. "How about my privacy? My dignity? My self-respect? My right to bring a baby into this world without turning it into a science fair project?"

"It isn't even for me," I argued. "These kids really need your help. They're in a jam."

She was adamant. "Well, if they're so gifted, let them find a way out of the jam."

"You have to do this for me," I said stubbornly.

"No way, Donnie. Not in a million years. I'm not crawling into a petri dish for you or anybody."

I sighed. "Well, okay. I feel sorry for Brad, though."

She was wary. "What's Brad got to do with it?"

"You know, there he is, far from home, serving his country. It'll break his heart when he finds out his beloved dog isn't getting the care and attention she deserves." I pointed to Beatrice, who was making another liquid deposit on the rug.

She shrieked so loud that it brought Mom running up the stairs. "What's wrong?"

"Nothing, Mom," I called. "But fire up the carpet steamer, will you? We're going to need it in a few minutes."

Katie was beside herself. "Just what are you saying?"

"Do I have to spell it out for you? If I don't look after Beatrice, Beatrice doesn't get looked after."

"And that's my fault?" she demanded. "She won't let me anywhere near her."

"I totally sympathize," I assured her. "Bad things happen to good people sometimes. Look at the poor Academy kids. It isn't their fault they missed this credit, but they're the ones who have to suffer. Just like it isn't your fault your mother-in-law dumped a dying dog on your doorstep."

"Don't say 'dying'! She's not dying! She can't—" Suddenly, Katie clued in. "You miserable blackmailing slime bucket! This is low even for you."

I nodded in agreement. "Poor Brad."

She was bitter. "What do you care if a bunch of nerds go to summer school? You already took this course. There's nothing in it for you!"

She was only half right. There *was* nothing in it for me—at least nothing I could explain to Katie. If this worked—if following Katie's pregnancy could count as hands-on experience for Human Growth and Development—that would strengthen my ties to the Academy for Scholastic Distinction. It wouldn't make my grades any better, but it might take people's attention off how ungifted I was. The longer I could stay at the Academy, the longer I could keep myself hidden from Schultz's justice.

Selfish? Big-time. And something else, too: It was absolutely what James Donovan would have done. Maybe ancestry.com wasn't such a waste of money after all. The Hardcastle gym may have been my *Titanic,* but we were survivors, James and me.

Aloud, I said, "I'm doing it because a nice person helps his friends."

She rolled her eyes, but I knew I had her.

UNSURPRISED
CHLOE GARFINKLE
IQ: 159

*<<Hypothesis: Donovan Curtis is smarter than
all of us put together.>>*

Okay, probably not. Make that definitely not. Yet
all our spectacular grades, killer IQs, and gang-
buster test scores couldn't keep us out of summer
school. Neither could Oz, Mr. Del Rio, and even Dr.
Schultz. And Donovan managed it with a flick of the
wrist.

The stomach entered the room first. It was enormous,

like someone had stretched a tablecloth over a prize-winning watermelon. We waited for the rest of her to come in. It took longer than we thought because she wasn't moving too swiftly. When I finally saw how petite she was, it seemed like a miracle she was moving at all.

Her name was Katie Patterson, and she was Donovan's older sister. This was kind of like Show and Tell on steroids. She was our Human Growth and Development project, our way out of summer school. We needed final approval from the state, of course. But Oz and the school agreed that she counted as hands-on experience, provided we followed her pregnancy for its final six weeks.

I'd known the minute Donovan showed up in the lab that something important was happening. And here was the proof. He was the cavalry, galloping to our rescue. Can you imagine the top students in the state, and maybe even the whole country, not being allowed to start high school? It would be a huge black eye for the Academy and the whole school district. And what did Donovan get out of this? Nothing. He'd already taken Human Growth and Development, so *he* wouldn't have to go to summer school. And he had a sister who didn't exactly look thrilled that he had volunteered her unborn child as our class pet. So he was probably going to pay for it at home.

Abigail said Donovan was a self-centered jerk, not gifted at all, who was laughing at us behind our backs. I didn't agree. Maybe he wasn't gifted in the way we were, but he had an uncanny knack for making a difference. Take the robotics program. From a scientific standpoint, Tin Man hadn't changed at all since his arrival. Donovan had contributed a name, a few pictures from the internet, and his joystick skills. Yet somehow he'd transformed our entire team. We were focused, excited, united. Cold Spring Harbor had better watch out.

<<*Hypothesis: The whole is greater than the sum of its parts. Especially if one of those parts is Donovan.*>>

"Welcome to the robotics lab, Katie," Oz greeted the newcomer warmly. "We're so grateful to you for helping us out by allowing us into your life."

She glared in her brother's direction, then turned to the teacher. "I have only one rule, and this one's a deal breaker. When you're seven and a half months pregnant, you go to the bathroom every time the wind blows. So when I have to run, nobody had better get in my way."

Oz seized the teachable moment. "What happens is

the growing baby expands the uterus, and puts pressure on the bladder."

"Whatever the reason," Katie continued, "when I've got to go, everything else is on hold. I don't care if I'm performing CPR and have to leave one of you gasping and suffocating. Are we clear?"

<<*Hypothesis: The Belly Rule—whoever has the belly makes the rules.*>>

"First off," Katie told us, "being pregnant is the weirdest thing that's ever going to happen to you. It's like growing a whole extra body part that doesn't seem to do anything except bump into furniture, and slowly get bigger so you can bump into even more furniture."

I raised my hand. "But aren't you excited?"

"I was," she admitted. "But then six months go by, and you stop believing that it's ever going to happen. It's hard to maintain the fever pitch for almost a year." Her expression grew sad. "And it's hard to think that, when this baby is born, its dad won't be there to see it."

"When did he die?" came Noah's nasal voice.

Donovan brayed a laugh right into his face. "He's not dead, wise guy! He's a tank commander in Afghanistan, and he won't be home in time!"

Oz jumped in. "You get used to Noah," he said quickly. "He's not being insensitive, I assure you."

Katie nodded. "Another thing about being pregnant—your body, which used to be your own private business, is suddenly a hands-on theme park for total strangers. Everybody in a white coat pokes, prods, or examines you in some way or another. And for what they can't see, they have plenty of sophisticated machines that can look inside you. I brought a few of my sonogram pictures if anyone's interested in having a look."

We all were. I think Katie was kind of surprised about that. She was used to Donovan and, let's face it, he was pretty different from the average gifted kid. None of us knew anything about pregnancy, or sonograms, but it was natural for us to take everything seriously and to do our best with it. We wanted to know about this because we wanted to know about everything. We were just knowers.

I scoured the black-and-white images, searching for anything that resembled a baby. I think I spotted a set of ribs, and maybe a foot, but I also saw something that looked like a bust of Abraham Lincoln, and that definitely wasn't in there. Abigail thought she'd found the head, but Katie explained that it was just a bubble in the amniotic fluid. Latrell was convinced he saw twins. Kevin and Jacey saw nothing at all.

Donavan wouldn't even try. "I'll have plenty of time to look at it after it's born. It's going to be my niece. Or nephew. Whatever."

Noah stepped forward for a closer look. "If it's a girl," he said finally, "then what's *that*?" And we could all see exactly what he was pointing at.

Katie looked both startled and forlorn at the same time. "We didn't want to know the sex. We wanted it to be a surprise."

"He could be wrong," Oz managed without much conviction.

The rest of us nodded in agreement, but we knew better. Noah was never wrong unless he wanted to be.

"Better start knitting blue bootees," Donovan told his sister.

She looked daggers at her brother. "Wipe that grin off your face, Donnie. I wouldn't even be here if it wasn't for you. So everything that happens is your fault!"

<<*Hypothesis: Brothers and sisters forge family bonds through a complex byplay of accusations and insults.*>>

It wasn't all business. Katie wanted to see the robot, so we gave her a little demonstration. And while Donovan was operating Tin Man, I ended up next to his sister.

"What's he like at home?" I whispered.

"He's a barrel of laughs," she replied. "He drinks orange juice out of the bottle, carpets his room in old socks, watches poker on TV, and has never said the words *thank you* in living memory. Should I go on?"

I felt my face flushing as I stuck up for him. "He's doing an amazing thing bringing you here for our class." She cast me a piercing look that instantly had me on the defensive. "What?"

"Nothing, really." She smiled at me. "It's just— interesting to see your brother through someone else's eyes."

And suddenly, just as Tin Man was deploying the mini-bot, she became very still, her expression far away.

"Are you okay?" I whispered in concern.

"The baby's kicking." She took my hand and placed it on the sweater over her rounded abdomen.

I could feel it tapping against my hand, like little hiccups. It was strange, but also kind of beautiful. I was so much more than just one hour closer to my

Human Growth and Development credit. In those sixty minutes, I'd learned what a brand-new human life felt like.

<<*Hypothesis: And a certain tank commander in Afghanistan will soon find out he's having a son.*>>

UNFAILING

NOAH YOUKILIS
IQ: 206

These were my math test results for the semester so far: 0 out of 20, 1 out of 15, 4 out of 35, and incomplete.

This was my math grade on my progress report: A-plus.

I explained to Ms. Bevelaqua that my score was actually 4.52 percent, a solid F-minus on any reasonable scale. She just laughed, and changed the A-plus to A-plus-plus. Then she wrote in the "comments" section: "Computes averages without aid of calculator."

How unfair was that?

I found a clip on YouTube called "Failing Math." But when I watched it, it was completely unhelpful. They didn't teach you how to fail math; they taught you how to pass! I expected more from YouTube, which usually had great stuff, like wrestling videos, oranges that talk, and people putting out oil-well fires.

There was another video called "Failing Schools," but it turned out just to be this news story about how our education system isn't any good. I could have told them that. And not for the reasons *they* gave. The problem with our education system is if you score one little 206 on one little IQ test, everybody goes nuts about it. You have to go to a special school, only they call it an "Academy," which really just means the same thing. And then the pressure starts: Do better, reach for the stars, live up to your potential, go all out, strive, achieve.

Why?

"You've been blessed with an incredible gift, and you're wasting it!" Oz was constantly telling me. "You should be getting a hundred percent on everything!"

He wanted me to admit that I got 4 out of 35 on

purpose; that I could have gotten 35 out of 35 without breaking a sweat. That was missing the point entirely. To me this stuff was all so easy that 4 out of 35 and 35 out of 35 were really the same thing. It was like kicking puffballs of dandelion seeds as you walk across an open field. You *could* get them all. But why would you? It just didn't *matter*.

Abigail thought I was crazy. I disagreed. And if I was as smart as the IQ test said I was, which one of us was right?

I never asked to be right about everything. It just happened that way. When you have the answers before anybody asks the questions, nothing is very surprising, whether you're in the gifted program or not. You might as well go to the regular school around the corner from your house.

I wanted that *so much*. The students who went to that school laughed a lot. And even when they weren't in the act of laughing, they seemed *unpressured*. I could hear it in snippets of conversation as I waited for my bus to the Academy: "I don't care . . . who cares . . . I couldn't care less . . . ask me if I care . . . like I care . . ."

Everybody said they were less intelligent than us, but I thought those kids were really on to something.

At the Academy, people cared *too much*, which was why we laughed so *little*. And *unpressured* was the last word you'd use to describe us.

So why couldn't I convince my parents to let me transfer? Was that argument beyond even my intellect? Did it require an IQ of 207 or better? I was failing at failing. The teachers were on to me. They'd never let it happen.

There was a conundrum here:

A) Only sheer genius could get me out of the Academy.
B) Anyone showing sheer genius is sent to the Academy.

I used to spend many hours pondering this, back in the days when I had many hours to spend pondering. That all changed when Donovan Curtis told me about YouTube. This was an important revelation for me, because almost everything on YouTube is surprising. I'll never forget when Donovan showed me how to use it. He clicked on a video and, for eleven magical seconds, we watched a cocker spaniel drinking out of a toilet. In those eleven seconds, my world was transformed. What I had just seen could not have been predicted by anyone, regardless of IQ. It was astonishingly simple and utterly random—the brain hiccup of a collective mind seven billion people strong.

I'd been looking for something like this my whole life. And I was infinitely grateful to Donovan for opening that door for me. I almost forgave him for bringing in his sister and spoiling the only chance I might ever have to flunk.

The word had just come in from the state department of education that studying Katie Patterson's pregnancy officially counted as real-life experience in Human Growth and Development. You should have seen the celebration when Oz made the announcement in the robotics lab. Everyone mobbed Donovan, slapping him on the back and cheering. All except Abigail. She actually wept at the news that she wouldn't have to go to summer school. It was a little confusing. She took classes all summer anyway, so wasn't that summer school too? What was the difference between the summer school she went to on purpose and the summer school she'd do anything to avoid?

Speaking of confusing, there was Donovan himself. He clearly didn't belong at the Academy. I knew that after his first twenty minutes in the lab. What was he doing here? I had no idea—and that alone was considerably awesome. There were very few things that I had no idea about. The fact that one of them had landed a few seats away from me in homeroom was wonderful in itself.

Donovan was like a human YouTube video—unpredictable. We could have worked on Tin Man for years, incorporating every refinement allowed by technology. But none of us could have envisioned that the greatest improvement of all would be simply in the way you drove it. Yet when Donovan took over the joystick, the answer was right there for all of us to see.

It also made excellent YouTube footage. Google *Tin Man Metallica Squarepants Exposes Teacher's Underwear* and the clip should come up. It already had more than a thousand page views, making it my greatest hit so far. Picture this: Ms. Bevelaqua was covering for Oz in the lab, and one fork of the robot's lift mechanism got under her skirt. By the time she noticed it, her hem was up around her ears, and everybody was staring at her underpants, which were bright yellow with a pattern of Cartesian geometry.

Ms. Bevelaqua didn't accept Donovan's apology. You'd think a math teacher who wore Cartesian geometry underwear would have a better sense of humor. But she was really mad. Her face looked like she was being tasered—or at least how those people look in YouTube videos.

We were just getting calmed down after that brou-haha when Chloe pounded into the lab, gasping from an all-out sprint. "You won't believe it!" she panted. "They still haven't fixed the Hardcastle gym, so they're moving the Valentine Dance *here*!"

Donovan looked uncomfortable. "What do we care about another school's party?"

"Don't you get it?" Chloe crowed. "It's on our turf, so we're all invited! I've been in the gifted program since I was eight, and you know how many dances we've had? Try zero!"

"Except for 'The Dance of the Electrons,'" I reminded her. "My sixth-grade science project."

Abigail did not share Chloe's enthusiasm. "I can't think of a single thing that interests me less than a school dance."

Chloe stared at her. "But you're *going*, right?"

"Not even at gunpoint."

Chloe was devastated. "But you have to! We may never get the chance to go to another one!"

Abigail was adamant. "That suits me just fine."

"You're a scientist," Ms. Bevelaqua challenged her. "How can you arrive at a conclusion without any data to back it up?"

Chloe jumped on the bandwagon. "Look at this as

an experiment. A *social* experiment. Right, Donovan?"

Donovan shrugged. "Don't ask me. I never go to dances."

"Well, you're going to this one," announced Oz, striding into the room. "I'm making it a class assignment."

Abigail was horrified. "Oz—you can't make us go to an after-school event!"

"No," the teacher agreed, "but I can assign everybody to write an essay about it. And if you haven't been there, you'll have to take a zero."

"*I'll* take a zero," I volunteered readily.

"You couldn't get a zero if you handed in a blank page," Abigail said in a resentful tone.

She was tight-lipped, but I had a feeling she'd be there. I'd kill for a bad grade; she'd kill to avoid one.

Oz panned the room, making eye contact with each student. "This is a good idea, people. We're all so focused on our specialties that we tend to miss out on ordinary experiences. Having fun is part of an education too, you know."

"I don't have time to go to a dance," I complained. "In the three hours it would take me to get there, be there, and get home, I could watch between seventy and one hundred YouTube videos—depending on the duration of each, of course."

"There's more to life than YouTube, Noah," chided Chloe.

"That's where you're wrong," I retorted. "YouTube *is* life, only better. The entirety of human experience is on that little screen. Last night, I watched a modern-day clash of gladiators in bathing suits battling in and out of a roped square, jumping off tables and hitting each other with chairs!"

"It's called professional wrestling, Noah," Donovan announced. "And it's all fake."

"I saw blood!" I respected Donovan, but he didn't know everything. "If my mother hadn't pulled the plug on my computer, I could have watched a steel-cage match!"

Oz put an end to the discussion. "It's settled. We'll all be there. And there's extra credit in it for anybody who can relax enough to have a good time."

"Will you be going?" I asked Donovan as we headed back to our seats.

"I never went to Hardcastle dances when I was a Hardcastle student," he told me. "Why should I start now?"

Oz overheard us. "Extra credit, Donovan," he said

enticingly, dangling the prospect like a fisherman dangles bait.

"So you'll be there?" I persisted.

"What do you care?" Donovan snapped, suddenly angry. "*You* shouldn't even be going. You don't need extra credit. You've got more points than you know what to do with."

"I wish I could give you some of mine," I told him honestly. "But I don't think it works that way."

He stared at me for a moment, and then sighed. "See you at the dance."

UNPASTEURIZED
DONOVAN CURTIS
IQ: 112

"Donnie!"

I was getting ready for school when the blood-curdling scream brought me running out of the bathroom.

"Donnie, get in here this minute!"

I leaped over Beatrice, who was sprawled across my doorway, and ran into Katie's room, preparing to dial 911. But she was alive and well, sitting at her laptop computer, reading her overnight emails from Afghanistan.

From: First Lieutenant H. Bradley Patterson, United States
Marine Corps
Katie—Captain Hunsinger says he saw your stomach on
YouTube.
What gives?
Brad

I reddened. "It was probably Noah. YouTube is his whole life."

"I'm entitled to a life too, you know!" she stormed at me. "That didn't change because you blackmailed me into signing on with your freaky brain trust! I found that video! It's basically a two-minute close-up of my fat belly while 'We Are the Champions' plays in the background!"

"It's a compliment. He's got nothing better to do with his two hundred IQ."

"Cut it out, Donnie. You're not talking to your misfits here—"

"They're not misfits," I insisted. "They're just—different. Supersmart. But dumb in a way, too. Like babies."

It was the wrong word. It reminded her. "My husband is eleven thousand miles away in a dangerous war zone. He shouldn't be hearing about his wife's pregnancy from YouTube. And his captain shouldn't be hearing about it at all."

"I'll get Noah to take the video down," I promised. "He didn't mean anything. You don't understand about him."

She looked curious. "What happened to you, Donnie? You're giving your best friends the cold shoulder, but defending these crazies?"

"I'm not—" I protested.

But she had a point. I *had* been avoiding the Daniels, who were being totally unreasonable about "sharing *our* Valentine Dance with a dweeb army." Sanderson's words, not mine.

"Poor you," I'd told him at the time. "If you're so offended by smart people, don't go."

"Deirdre's going to be there," he'd shot back. "And Heather. She's into you, man."

At that point Nussbaum had punched him in the gut. "Heather's into *me!*"

"Nobody's going to be into anyone when the Academy dorks suck all the coolness out of the air," Sanderson had complained.

That conversation really bugged me. I mean, nobody knew better than me that the gifted kids weren't exactly über-happening. But this was a school dance, not some A-list Hollywood red-carpet event. Like there weren't any uncool people at Hardcastle!

I faced Katie. "They're not crazy—most of them. Don't knock them. These days, they're your biggest fans."

She cast a sour look at Beatrice. "They're not exactly facing stiff competition in that department."

"Show some respect for the almost dead."

"That's not funny," she snarled through gritted teeth. "Did it ever occur to you that my marriage could be on the line over that dog? No, because it's all the same to you so long as your weird classmates get to paw the Incredible Expanding Stomach!"

I sighed. "If they're smart enough to predict supernovas on the opposite side of the galaxy, credit them with the brains to appreciate how you came to their rescue."

Her eyes narrowed. "There's something fishy about this whole gifted thing. It doesn't add up. I'm not saying you're stupid, but you're hardly the type to sniff around for extra work."

"I *didn't* sniff around. The Academy found me, remember?"

"I do remember," she conceded. "That's the fishy part. Anyway, we should get going. My appointment with Dr. Manolo is at nine-thirty."

I was attending Katie's next obstetric checkup—not as her brother, but as a member of Human Growth and Development 101. Mr. Osborne had gotten permission for a field trip, so our whole class was going. I hoped Dr. Manolo had invested in a spacious office.

Driving with Katie was an adventure these days. Her stomach was so huge that she had to set the seat all the way back. Her arms were barely long enough to reach the wheel, and she hunched forward, looking like Jeff Gordon wedged behind a giant beach ball.

We were just waddling in from the parking lot when the minibus arrived. You could tell they didn't get a lot of school buses at the clinic. In obstetrics, the only kids involved were the ones being born. And not too many pregnant women arrived with an entourage of brainiacs.

The doctor was running late, so we had to wait forty minutes, which wasn't exactly pleasant. Noah speed-read through two years' worth of *Mother-to-Be Magazine*, peppering Katie with questions like "Have you eaten any unpasteurized cheeses lately?"

"No," she grumbled. "Have you?"

"What's your opinion of giving the baby solid food before four months?"

"You're bringing back my morning sickness," she warned.

"Really? According to the June 2011 issue, that happens in the first trimester."

She glared at him. "It came back when they saw my stomach on YouTube—in Afghanistan."

Oz quickly stepped between them. "Let's give Katie a little space, Noah. This is *her* doctor's appointment, after all. We're just privileged to be here."

When we finally got called, the nurse said, "I'm sorry. Only immediate family in the examining room."

"They *are* family," Katie informed her with a sigh. "You know how you can't pick your relatives?"

The woman was adamant. "I'm afraid it's a privacy issue."

"I have no privacy," Katie replied wearily. "My stomach is on YouTube."

Oz was ready to back everybody off, but Dr. Manolo was kind of psyched to have an audience. He used to work at a teaching hospital, he explained. He missed having students around.

We kept our distance for the exam, of course, but we watched the sonogram, and we were all invited to put on the stethoscope and listen to the baby's heartbeat.

"Sounds kind of freaky," commented Latrell. "You know, listening to another person who's trapped in there."

Katie made a face. "I can't tell you how thrilled I am that my family planning is contributing to your horror-movie fantasy."

"It's a miracle," Chloe breathed.

Even Abigail's serious expression softened when she had the stethoscope on.

Oz assumed a far-off, dreamy expression. "I remember these appointments from when my wife and I were expecting our own kids. There's nothing quite like it."

The doctor kept Katie a few minutes extra. When she stepped out into the waiting room, the students of Human Growth and Development 101 leaped to their feet and gave her a rousing standing ovation. Their enthusiasm was so infectious that everybody in the reception room joined in—all the other expectant moms and dads and family members.

Katie was so taken aback that she actually did a little curtsy, blushing deep mauve. "I didn't do anything," she insisted. But the smile on her face was 100 percent genuine.

Katie headed home alone, and I got on the minibus

with everybody else for the ride to the Academy.

"How was the field trip?" asked the driver. "Fun?"

Chloe nodded enthusiastically. "We were at a pelvic exam!"

"And we listened to a fetus," added Noah.

The driver seemed bewildered.

"We're gifted," I explained.

UNSUCCESSFUL

DR. SCHULTZ
IQ: 127

Well, my "no screwups" rule was pretty much out the window. My life had become one big screwup after another.

Three weeks had now passed, and not a single repair had been made to the Hardcastle gym. Frankly, no one was doing anything about anything. The insurance company was digging in its corporate heels, and we had no option but to dig in ours. The instrument of destruction, Atlas's detached "globe," was collecting dust in the basement of the administration building, next to old filing cabinets and a lawn tractor that was missing one wheel. What was left of the statue looked incomplete and idiotic. Most maddening of all, I could not for the life of me find the piece of paper on which I'd written the name of the horrible boy responsible for all this.

I'd scoured every millimeter of my office. I'd even gone personally and ransacked Cynthia's desk, in case she'd carried it off by accident. I'd hired a cleaning company to go over the entire administration building with a fine-tooth comb. Nothing. He was out there somewhere, laughing at me, getting off scot-free.

My wife said I was becoming obsessed with this phantom boy. Maybe so. Lately, I'd been finding excuses to visit Hardcastle Middle School in the hope that I would recognize his cocky sneering face somewhere. But I never saw him. It was as if the culprit didn't go to school there anymore. If only I had the name . . .

Irrationally, I began shuffling papers on my desk. It had been right here!

Cynthia tottered in on her high heels. "Dr. Schultz, I have the first progress report on the new Human Growth and Development project at the Academy.

The special expert is named Katie Patterson, and she's the sister of one of the students, a boy named Don—"

"Just put it on my desk," I interrupted, still peering into drawers. Wasn't that the definition of insanity? Doing the same thing over and over again, and expecting a different result?

I had to get a grip on my nerves. I had duties to perform, and bringing this boy to justice was only one of them. Case in point: The relocated Hardcastle Middle School Valentine Dance was tonight. This would be the first time it had ever taken place off campus, *and* the first time that outside students were being included. We were infinitely proud of our high achievers at the Academy for Scholastic Distinction, but many of them weren't the most socially adept young people. I wanted to be on hand to make sure everything ran smoothly.

And I mustn't forget to make contact with this Mrs. Patterson so I could express the gratitude of the entire school district. What a wonderful family they must be—the husband serving our country in the military, and she, selflessly helping that one class in its time of need. If only more people were like that.

UNROCKIN'

CHLOE GARFINKLE
IQ: 159

<<*Hypothesis: I have the perfect wardrobe—*
for milking a cow.>>

No, that was more than a hypothesis. It was cold, hard fact, backed up by the pathetic reality of the contents of my closet. Also feeding chickens, pulling weeds, driving a combine harvester, and other farm chores. What I didn't have was anything to wear to the Valentine Dance.

It wasn't exactly a shocker. Sad to say, I'd never been

to anything like this before. Almost fourteen years old, and the only real party I'd attended was the kind where your parents are there and you have to waltz with your cousin, the bowlegged one with the giant Adam's apple.

Don't get me wrong. I was psyched. I was *beyond* psyched. To me, this was far more than another school's shindig we'd been invited to crash. This was a chance for us to prove an important hypothesis in front of the staff and students of the biggest middle school in town:

<<*Hypothesis: Being gifted doesn't automatically make people social outcasts.*>>

True, some of us *were* social outcasts—Noah Youkilis came to mind. But regular schools had those too. We were no different from the rest of humanity. And we were going to show that we were every bit as capable of having a good time.

All thanks to Donovan Curtis.

Obviously, I understood that Donovan hadn't made any of this happen directly. He couldn't possibly have destroyed the Hardcastle gym, forcing them to move the dance to ours. Nobody was capable of shaping human events like that.

Yet the minute he'd walked into Oz's homeroom

that day, I knew things were about to change. I could feel it in the air; smell it in the wind—of course, that might have been the sulfur fumes from the chemistry lab down the hall. It was almost as if the gods of Normal had sent us their messenger as a sign that our geekdom was coming to an end.

Donovan was almost too normal. I'd heard the rumors around school about an unqualified kid at the Academy. It wasn't hard to identify this newbie who didn't have what it took. It might have been just gossip. Some of us were so hypercompetitive that it killed us to admit anybody else could be the real deal.

From what I'd seen of Donovan, though, there might have been an element of truth to the gossip. It pained me to say it. I liked him a lot, and he'd made a huge contribution to our robotics team, in spite of very limited knowledge of the subject. Best of all, he'd found a way for us to fulfill our Human Growth and Development requirement—something that helped him not at all. He was doing it purely for us.

He was wonderful. But was he gifted?

I wanted to believe it. I tried *so hard*. Yet in my heart of hearts, I knew the answer.

Back to the matter at hand: What to wear? The only guidelines from the school stated that attire couldn't be "inappropriate." That meant no T-shirts with bad language, torn jeans, or miniskirts that could double as headbands. One look in my closet told me that my entire wardrobe was inappropriate. There was nothing that would get me in trouble with the teachers, but everything was so drab. My shirts were all plaid, which doesn't exactly scream party, unless there's a lumberjack theme.

I finally settled on the dress I had worn to my aunt Julie's wedding. It was definitely over the top for a school dance, so I made it more casual by adding a plain black cardigan. I considered wearing sneakers instead of the fancy shoes that went with the outfit, but I couldn't tell if the combination would be funky or just plain stupid. I went to the Academy for Scholastic Distinction, not the one for Fashion Sense.

Makeup was the next hurdle. I thought back to those girls in the mall—the ones hanging out with Donovan and the two boys named Daniel. They'd been wearing tons of makeup. It looked great on them, but if I tried it, for sure I'd paint myself up like Bozo the clown. In the end, I opted for light mascara and a hint of blush—my complexion can be a little pale from too much time in the library.

"You look beautiful!" my dad declared emotionally.

<<*Hypothesis: The compliment loses credibility in direct proportion to how closely related you are to the speaker.*>>

We headed for school. There was a traffic jam on the circular drive. Kids were swarming from all directions, alone and in groups, arriving by car, bike, skateboard, scooter, and on foot. The Academy was small, but Hardcastle Middle had nine hundred students, and it looked like this was going to be a huge turnout. I felt a renewed buzz of excitement, followed by a severe bout of anxiety. By the time we got to the front door, I already knew that my outfit was totally wrong. Most of the girls were wearing either jeans or short skirts, with sneakers or sandals despite the cold weather.

In the end, though, nothing could overpower my exhilaration. Now, barely a few months shy of eighth-grade graduation, I was attending my first middle school dance. I finally had an answer for all those people who said, "Get a life." I was getting one.

Amazingly, I made it into the gym attracting only a few strange looks, so I guess I wasn't as overdressed as I'd feared. The place was about a third full, and kids were pouring in, chattering happily, ready for a good time. The decorations caught the eye first. I don't want to be unkind, but they were really lame—hearts and cupids, lots of streamers, pink, red, and silver everywhere. Hardcastle had done the whole setup—if they'd put us in charge of it, I'm sure we could have come up with something a little more creative. But maybe that was the point.

<<*Hypothesis: Not everything needs to be measured by gifted standards.*>>

Tonight was supposed to be about kicking back and cutting loose a little. Too bad I was doing it in a dorky party dress.

The music was loud—really loud. Feel-it-in-your-molars loud. People were already dancing. Another problem: I didn't know how to do *that* either—not the way they were doing it, anyway.

<<*Hypothesis: The scientific method applies to everything, dancing included.*>>

In other words, if I studied it hard enough, I could catch up.

I only saw a few kids from the Academy, mostly because they seemed to be hiding. They lurked in corners, or in the shadow of the deejay booth. The way they goggled at our guests, you'd think we'd been invaded by Huns who were presently sacking the school. The Hardcastle kids were brasher than us, wilder, and more confident. The boys were a lot more physical—at any given time, 40 percent of them were engaged in shoving one another. And they outnumbered us ten-to-one.

I spotted Oz right away. He wasn't with the other chaperones. He circulated among his own students, urging them to mingle. He would have had a better chance getting Abigail to impale herself on a fence post. I caught her attention, and she gave me a beseeching look—the kind you turn on the helicopter pilot who's coming to save you from drowning. Trying to set a positive example of the sort of hosts Oz expected us to be, I turned to the boy standing next to me and said, "Great turnout. Are all the Hardcastle parties this crowded?"

He didn't hear me. The pounding beat was so loud that my words died less than an inch from my lips. I repeated it, shouting this time.

He shot me a smirk and I leaned in to catch his reply.

"You getting married in that dress?"

And before I could answer, he was yanked away through the crowd by a group of friends.

"Hi, Chloe!"

The voice wasn't any louder than mine, but its piercing quality cut through the music like a fire siren.

If I was worried about being improperly dressed, Noah took all that pressure onto his slender shoulders.

His outfit defied description, but in the gifted program we're encouraged to try. He was shirtless, his upper body covered only by a sparkling sequined vest. His pants were black tights, which made his skinny legs even skinnier. You couldn't see much of them, though, because he had on knee-high red leather boots that must have weighed thirty pounds each. It was a miracle he could even walk. Mirrored sunglasses concealed his eyes, and his unstylish brush cut was covered with a red do-rag.

I was horrified. "Noah, what are you wearing?"

"I borrowed the boots and the vest from my mom," he enthused. "When the Angel of Death fought Kid Nitro at the Royal Rumble, this is just like what he wore."

"Yeah, but this is a dance, not a wrestling match."

He shrugged. "Oz said we had to dress up."

I had no answer to that. But I sure wanted to be there when Oz got a gander at what Noah thought "dress up" looked like.

<<*Hypothesis: As a space fills with people, the air inside warms, approaching 98.6 degrees Fahrenheit, the body temperature of the crowd.*>>

I began to regret my cardigan. I was going to be sweaty, not just overdressed. It was getting really packed, to the point where glimpses of the floor were rare.

Lost in the wall-to-wall students, I was no longer able to survey the entire party. Instead, I'd catch the occasional familiar face amid the forest of heads and shoulders. I located Latrell by the back wall—it seemed like Oz was working on him to ask someone to dance. Kevin and Jacey were hanging together for mutual support in this alien environment. I thought I saw Donovan once, but it turned out to be somebody else. Maybe he wasn't going to show up.

All my nervousness returned in any icy wave. There was something isolating about being smothered by strangers, even in a familiar setting like your own school gym.

As the crush tightened around me, I felt myself swept along with the movement of the crowd. I was afraid at first, until I recognized the strange combination of motions that pushed me back and forth.

Dancing! As far as I could see in every direction, bodies gyrated, heads were thrown back, hands swayed through the air. I tried to bulldoze my way out of the group, but flailing arms and swinging hips jostled me. I kept stumbling—but there was more to it than that.

I was stumbling *in perfect time to the music!*

I raised my hands and moved my feet, following the pounding bass.

<<Hypothesis: Intentional or not, movement to a beat = dancing.>>

I risked a furtive glance at my neighbors. No *What-do-you-think-you're-doing?* glares; no gathering lynch mob. I cranked up the energy level, rollicking at light speed.

I—Chloe Garfinkle of the Academy for Scholastic Distinction—was one of the crowd, letting it all hang out at a major middle school bash.

This was the greatest night of my life!

UNTRUSTWORTHY

DONOVAN CURTIS
IQ: 112

This was the worst night of my life.

Bad enough to be banished to the Island of Misfit Toys without having everybody you know come and visit you there. I'd have given anything to take a pass on this dance. I'd even offered to do an extra-credit project for Oz. He'd just regarded me sadly, as if to say, what could I possibly deliver that would be good enough? Showing up was the only thing I could do every bit as well as Abigail or Noah.

Speaking of Noah, he looked like—holy hamburgers, what *did* he look like? It was almost comforting that I had no idea. If I understood his getup, it might have meant part of me was inside that bizarro world.

I saw the smirks and overheard some of the nasty remarks directed toward kids like Noah and Abigail, who was dressed for the National Spelling Bee. Or Latrell, who had asked at least half a dozen girls to dance, and had been shot down by all of them. If Oz thought this would be confidence building, he was nuts!

"Pa-a-arty!!!"

It wasn't easy to drown out the sound system, but Sanderson bellowed it right in my ear.

Nussbaum was beside him. It was a bad omen. "What a night, huh, Donovan? Lot of hotties in this crowd! Her, for instance."

I followed his pointing finger, expecting to see Heather or Deirdre. No, it was Abigail in the crosshairs. Oz had her dancing, which she was accomplishing with two locked knee joints. I've seen heads of lettuce with more rhythm. She moved like a stilt walker. The things some people do for their straight A's!

"Cut it out," I growled.

"This party rocks!" Sanderson declared. "You can

feel the brainpower buzzing around like radio waves. I'm getting smarter just standing here."

"That's not how it works," Nussbaum scoffed. "The higher up you wear your belt, that's your genius level. If I buckle mine around my forehead, do you think I could go to school here just like the great Donovan Curtis?"

I groaned. "Hilarious, guys. Now, go find—"

My voice trailed off. Mr. Osborne had left Abigail, and was venturing on in search of somebody else to annoy. Now the Daniels were pushing through the crowd, heading right for her.

"Come back here!" Who was I kidding? I'd never make myself heard over the music. And if they did hear me, would they listen? Fat chance.

There were only two Daniels, yet they seemed to swarm Abigail, surrounding her, smiling, being charming, all the while smirking and rolling their eyes. Their audience was everybody—the Hardcastle kids, anyway. The Daniels got her dancing again, comically stiff-legged.

I should have been laughing myself. What did I care about Abigail Lee? The girl hated me, and I wasn't too fond of her, either. But the whole attitude—the idea that the gifted kids were here for the entertainment of the cool people—made me sick. It was bad enough now, with Abigail treating the Daniels like muggers. But if they managed to win her over, convince her that they liked her—*that* would be major-league humiliation.

I blasted through the gathering crowd, outflanked the Daniels, and grabbed Abigail's wrist with a grip that must have hurt at least a little. I don't even know what I said. Something like, "You're dancing with *me* now."

If she viewed the Daniels as muggers, the look she gave me was Voldemort-worthy. I didn't care. She had to be saved, undeserving as she was.

Nussbaum got in my face. "What's your problem, Donovan?"

"She's in my homeroom," I replied through clenched teeth. "I get first dibs."

"Manners, dude! We're guests!"

Abigail was watching all this through her thick round glasses, her uncomfortable expression turning to bewilderment. She was brilliant, but all the IQ points in the world wouldn't help her in a situation like this. It must have seemed like three guys fighting over her—something I guarantee had never happened before. Not on this planet.

She tried to sidestep me and return to the Daniels. Talk about a blow to your self-esteem—I was being *dumped* by Abigail! That had to be an all-time low! I stuck with the plan, though, taking her hand and twirling her around—a maneuver she executed with the grace of someone who was being handcuffed by police.

Luckily, the Daniels saw the chaperones watching and retreated before Abigail could get back to them. Or maybe it was unlucky—it left me dancing with her. I was stuck too. I couldn't very well chase away two guys, and then blow her off the minute they were gone. It was pretty ridiculous, when you think about it. I didn't even like these school parties, and here I'd gone to great lengths to saddle myself doing my unfavorite thing with my unfavorite person. At least the Daniels had retreated. I saw them over by the drink table, now schmoozing some other girl—one who was a lot more their type. She was tall with long legs and a really cute face. A little overdressed, but she made it work. A cut above your standard eighth-grade girl who got caught downwind of the makeup factory explosion.

I did a double take.

That was no hottie; that was *Chloe!* Plaid-flannel

Chloe! I barely recognized her! Man, she looked different! And not just different-different! Different-*awesome!*

It made sense. This party was a huge deal to her. Of course she'd go all out.

And now the Daniels were going to lob a grenade into her night.

I snagged Noah by the sparkle vest, and yanked him over to Abigail. "No problem, Noah. Of course you can cut in. Have a good time, you two."

And I was off like a shot, plowing through the tightly packed attendees. By the time I'd reached Chloe, she was in her glory, basking in the attention of two "normal" guys. Sarcasm intended.

I grabbed each Daniel by the back of the collar and pulled them away from her.

Chloe was horrified. "Donovan, what are you doing?"

I decided to be more honest with Chloe than I'd been with Abigail. "I know these clowns."

"I know them too, remember? From the mall?"

"Beat it, Donovan," Nussbaum urged. "You know when they say 'party pooper?' That's you right now."

I'd never be able to explain it to her—that they were only building her up so they could drop her over a cliff and walk away laughing. So I just kept hold of them by the scruffs of their necks, and marched them through the exit.

Chloe was following us. "What's the matter with you, Donovan? You can't treat people like that!" Her anger was a microclimate. I could feel the heat all around me. Another satisfied customer.

I dragged the Daniels where she couldn't follow us—into the boys' bathroom. The door gonged shut behind us, leaving her in midsentence.

Nussbaum surveyed the plumbing fixtures. "Look at that toilet! That's got to be the smartest toilet I've ever seen. You could come in here an idiot, and leave a genius!"

"And you would have done your business too," added Sanderson helpfully. "You know—if you had to go. It's a win-win situation."

"All right, guys," I sighed. "I get it. You don't like the gifted school very much. Neither do I. But for reasons you know very well, I'm stuck here."

"I pity you," Nussbaum commiserated. "These people! Did you catch that guy with the vest and the boots? What is he—a Christmas tree ornament?"

"That guy," I told him, "is smarter than everybody else at the Academy put together, with the rest of us thrown in for good measure. He could probably devise a way to kill you without looking away from his YouTube videos."

"Him?" Nussbaum hooted. "Don't make me laugh!"

"They're just people," I pleaded. "So what if they're a little nerdier than the rest of us? I know you came here to make trouble. Please don't."

"You're no fun anymore," Sanderson complained. "The old Donovan would be with us a hundred percent. You'd pants the vest guy, and take the kneeless chick on *Dancing with the Stars*. And the good-looking one—"

"She wasn't *that* good," Nussbaum put in critically.

"You could whack her with a branch so that she rolls down and smashes something. It wouldn't be the first time."

I sighed. "Go home. This isn't the place for you."

"Now I'm insulted," Nussbaum drawled. "We come all the way across town to visit your smarty-pants school, and you try to kick us out? Where's your hospitality? You didn't show us your locker. You didn't show us your homeroom. You didn't even show us your famous robot. We deserve better than that."

I looked at him skeptically. "You're interested in the robot?"

"Interested? Man, I'm a robot enthusiast! I saw *The Terminator,* like, twenty times!"

I hesitated. "If I show you Tin Man, do you promise to leave the Academy kids alone?"

Sanderson snapped the two-finger salute. "Scout's honor."

"You were never a scout!" sneered Nussbaum. "They threw you out! They threw us all out when Donovan burned down the tent."

I couldn't suppress a smile. "It said 'fireproof' on the box."

"Maybe that meant the *box* was fireproof," Nussbaum conceded.

We all laughed. At the time, it hadn't been funny, but it was pretty funny now.

"I'll show you the robot."

Homeroom 107 wasn't far from the gym—just two turns down dim hallways past the custodial offices and a couple of science labs. The door was closed but unlocked. I opened it, and turned on the lights to reveal the organized chaos that was the robotics program.

"Whoa!" breathed Sanderson. "Paging Dr. Frankenstein!"

Funny, I was used to the place. But to the Daniels, it might as well have had bubbling test tubes and jagged forks of electricity dancing up Jacob's ladders. Equipment was piled on every surface, components and spare parts lay strewn like candy wrappers, and odd instruments and tools hung from the walls. There were even "cobwebs" of multicolored wires suspended from the ceiling and stretched all over.

"So where's the robot?" asked Nussbaum.

I pointed to Tin Man at the center of it all. "Star of our show."

"What? That?" Sanderson exclaimed in disbelief. "That's just a metal box with a picture of some old guy eating a banana!"

"That's Einstein, Einstein!" Nussbaum exploded.

"He's old, isn't he?"

"No, he's dead! Sheesh! How stupid can you get?"

Sanderson gestured at the jungle of wires and technology that surrounded us. "Donovan, you understand all this . . . stuff?"

"I don't understand *any* of it," I replied honestly. "Even Mr. Osborne doesn't get much more than half. That's why it takes a team. We've got mechanical people, electronics people, computer people, hydraulics people, and pneumatics people."

"Which are you?" Nussbaum prodded.

"I downloaded the pictures," I admitted ruefully. "And I'm good with the controller—years of practice with video games."

They seemed dissatisfied with this explanation, like I was holding something back. "Guys, you of all people know why I'm at this school. Do you think I got into the Academy for my brain, and then busted up the gym on purpose so I'd have a cover story as an excuse to come here every day? I'm hiding! I know it's not going to last forever, but I have to keep it going at least until the heat dies down. My family doesn't have the kind of money it would take to fix that gym. Or to pay for lawyers if we get sued! So please don't make it any harder than it already is."

They took pity on me. It must have been the lab that did the trick. Maybe it finally sunk in how unfun it was to be the only mental turkey in a school of soaring eagles.

By the time we got back to the gym, the dance was completely off the chain. The floor almost moved with the force of hundreds of pounding feet. Bodies were packed in like sardines, the heat and humidity pushing past the tolerance level. The chaperones were trying in vain to thin out the crowd, which had to be far past what the fire marshal would have found acceptable. Whatever food and drink was left had been mashed into a paste and spread as a thin film across the hardwood. The music was so loud that the beat rattled your brain inside the casing of your skull.

Did I mention the smell? Pizza, sweat, and AXE body spray.

Sanderson grabbed Nussbaum. "Let's find Heather and Deirdre!"

"I'll catch up with you guys later," I promised. It was a lie. The only person I intended to catch up with was Mr. Osborne. Once my extra credit was in the bag, I was out of here.

You couldn't push through this crowd any more. You had to be swallowed, the way an amoeba ingests its food. Movement was worth your life. At least twice, the ebb and flow took me out onto the dance floor. At one point, I passed very close to Chloe, who glared at me, still miffed. When I finally spotted Oz, he looked like he now regretted making attendance mandatory for his students. It served him right.

I waved my arm in an attempt to catch his attention, and that was when I recognized the other adult standing beside him, the man who had to be even hotter than the rest of us in his three-piece suit.

Dr. Schultz.

I ducked out of the superintendent's line of sight. He'd never spot me at the crowd's butt level. Being trampled was a small price to pay to remain hidden. Extra credit meant nothing now. All that mattered was escape.

I got down on all fours and crawled, not the most dignified way to leave a party, and definitely not the cleanest. Let me tell you, whether it's the coolest Hardcastle jock, or the dweebiest squint in the Academy, it hurts the same when they're stomping on your fingers. But it was the most efficient way to travel. Pretty soon, I was at the door, home free.

Before I made my break, I gave the madness one last scan. What I saw nearly stopped my heart.

At the very center of the dance floor, the nucleus of the amoeba, a huge tight circle had formed around a small group of dancers. Three of them, to be exact. Daniel Sanderson, Daniel Nussbaum, and Tin Man Metallica Squarepants.

Rage almost blinded me. My "friends" had doubled back to the lab and wheeled the robot right into the riotous pounding heart of the Valentine Dance.

The dilemma was excruciating, and instantly clear. If I went back in there to rescue Tin Man, and Schultz spotted me, my whole world would come crashing down around my ears. What did I care if Tin Man got trashed? It wasn't my robot. It wasn't even my school. The sum total of my contribution to the project was a name and Einstein eating a banana!

No. Not true. I'd made another contribution—the Daniels. If it wasn't for me, those two bottom feeders would never have known that Tin Man even existed. Anything that happened to that poor robot tonight was my fault.

That's when it hit me. I *did* care. Not so much about the robotics team—and definitely not about some bucket of bolts on Mecanum wheels. How many chances did I get to limit the damage of my impulses? Once Atlas's globe is rolling, there's nothing anyone can do to save the gym at the bottom of the hill.

But this was different. Tin Man wasn't wrecked yet. There was still time to make things right.

I pushed back into the gym, jamming my way through dancing torsos. I could see that my trajectory was taking me on a collision course with Oz and—yikes!—Dr. Schultz. The adults had spotted Tin Man and were rushing to the robot. I grabbed a baseball cap off the nearest head, and jammed it low over my face. Why make it easy for the guy to bust me?

Some of my classmates had noticed too. Kevin, Jacey, and Latrell were stuck at various places in the crowd, struggling to reach Tin Man. Abigail was red-faced and screaming, although her cries were inaudible in the general din. Chloe got behind me, riding my wake toward the scene of the crime. We were making progress, but would we get there in time?

At the center of it all, Sanderson was draped over Tin Man's back, rolling the robot to and fro as if slow-dancing with it. Nussbaum had hold of the two forklift arms, and was jitterbugging to his own rhythms. I tackled him to the gym floor, and when he went down, he took one of the arms with him. Triumphantly, he held it over his head, and an enormous cheer rose in the gym.

To my classmates, it meant only one thing: Tin Man was being dismantled.

Kevin and Latrell faced down Sanderson.

"Get away from Tin Man!" Kevin bawled.

Problem was, those guys had never been in a fight in their lives, so their body language was completely unfightlike. Latrell couldn't even make a fist properly—he had his thumb pressed *inside* his fingers.

Sanderson took one look at that and laughed in their faces. He stopped laughing, though, when Abigail booted him in the shins.

"Get out of my school, you"—she struggled for just the right put-down—"you *average person!*"

That's when it got ugly. A shoving match broke out. After a few seconds, it was no longer just the Daniels *vs.* the robotics team. The conflict had widened. It was now Hardcastle *vs.* the Academy.

All the resentment, the jealousy, and the bullying attitude toward the gifted program boiled over at that very spot, turning the dance into a free-for-all, with Tin Man caught in the crossfire.

The bloodcurdling shriek was barely human. We all looked up to see Noah Youkilis, poised atop the dee-jay's giant speaker tower, muscles flexed—at least, they would have been if he'd had any. The bizarre pose left no room for interpretation. It was a ridiculous time to notice it, but I finally understood what his outfit was supposed to be. He was a WWE wrestler, just like the ones he'd seen on YouTube, only fifty times skinnier.

And before everybody's horrified eyes, he did exactly what they do on *SmackDown*. He launched himself off the tower in a spectacular dive into the fray. I figured he was dead meat. But his fall was broken by the people he landed on. The crowd swayed, absorbing his impact. Many figures went down. Tin Man was one of them.

Oz looked like he wanted to tear himself in half. I'm pretty sure he couldn't decide whether he should rush to the aid of his fallen student or his fallen robot.

And then, for the first time all night, something intelligent happened. The fire alarm went off. At first I was kind of surprised it wasn't me who did it. It was very much my style. But when I looked over at the wall, the culprit was standing there, still holding on to the lever.

Dr. Schultz. I guess when you're the superintendent, you don't have to worry about getting in trouble.

In the blink of an eye, several hundred kids swarmed the gym door. Hey, I knew an exit strategy when I saw one. I was gone before Schultz could even glance in my direction.

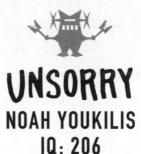

UNSORRY
NOAH YOUKILIS
IQ: 206

For all the eight hundred million videos on YouTube, you had to figure there were at least another eight hundred million that never got filmed.

YouTube had its conundrums too:

A) The best stuff comes when somebody does something awesome.

B) Awesomeness is unpredictable, so it isn't practical to have a camera in hand at all times to capture it.

Me being the hero of the Valentine Dance, for instance.

One day it might be possible to hardwire a person's optic nerve to a tiny memory chip implanted in the base of the skull. You'd just need a simple internet connection to upload the images to YouTube.

With our best minds focused on curing diseases and stuff like that, I wasn't holding my breath.

Speaking of the dance, Friday night had not been kind to Tin Man. Oh, the scratches could be buffed out, the dents repaired, and the broken forklift arm reattached again. But the motor that ran the lift mechanism had suffered permanent damage, and Oz said our budget for new materials was exhausted.

Abigail was distraught. "But if we don't have a lift mechanism, we'll have to withdraw from the competition!"

This prospect had Jacey so stressed out that she started talking about South American butterfly migrations. If anyone knew more random facts than me, it was Jacey.

But today it was getting on my nerves. "My blunt-trauma anterior epistaxis is better, thank you very much!"

"Who cares about your dumb bloody nose?" Abigail snapped.

"*I* care!" I shot back. "It *really* hurt! I didn't see any of you guys single-handedly rescuing Tin Man in the riot." For some reason, I was getting no credit at all for sacrificing my body. If it isn't on YouTube, it might as well have never happened.

"More like you *caused* the riot," put in Latrell sourly. "When you jumped on everybody from the top of the deejay booth."

"It wasn't a jump," I explained through clenched teeth. "It was a takedown. It was a textbook wrestling move."

Chloe turned to Donovan. "Your two friends named Daniel—why did they do that? Why would they want to mess with our robot?"

Donovan shrugged. "A lot of kids have an attitude about the gifted program. And those guys definitely have an attitude now that I'm in it. Look at this place—Hardcastle's an ancient ruin compared to here. They've got about a sixteenth of the stuff we do. They may call us nerds, but it's pretty cool having your own robot."

I didn't agree. A robot wasn't cool; it was just complicated. Like the LEGO Star Wars Imperial Snow Walker. (*Consumer Reports* said that not even a genius could put one together. They were wrong. I'd already assembled six.)

In my opinion, having a robot was a lot less interesting than having a riot. Riots were unforeseeable and chaotic—very YouTube-like.

Oz tried everything to get money for a new motor. He requested funds from the athletic budget, but he couldn't convince them that Tin Man was more important than badminton. He even took apart his own lawnmower in the hope that the engine would be the right size. It wasn't—and now the lawnmower won't go back together again. Latrell has to go to his house to fix it.

"Couldn't we raise the money?" Chloe pleaded. "Sell candy bars or something? We can't drop out!"

Oz shrugged unhappily. "There's simply not enough time to set up something like that. The robotics meet is in three weeks."

Donovan was even quieter than usual during the entire class. Tin Man's outer shell was completely covered with graphics by now, so there was nothing for him to do but drive. And with the lift system inoperable, there was no sense driving the robot anywhere.

Finally, when the period was over, he gathered us in

the hall. "I think I've found us a spare motor."

Abigail began jumping up and down. "What? What? *Where?*"

"In the custodial office," he explained. "It runs one of the floor polishers. You'd know better than me, but I'm pretty sure it'll fit Tin Man."

"How did you reach that conclusion?" I inquired. "Did you measure the unit itself, or are you thinking of the size and location of the key components and connections?"

"I guessed," he admitted a little sheepishly.

We stared at him in amazement. After all, *we* were the ones who had created Tin Man, not Donovan. It had taken design, programming, electronics, hydraulics, pneumatics, and mechanical engineering. No guessing.

Donovan explained. "There are two ways it can go. It can either fit or not fit."

"A probability analysis?" I mused.

He shrugged. "I can't say for sure it'll work. But I *guarantee* that if we don't at least try, that bucket of bolts will have no lift motor. What have we got to lose?"

Chloe had a practical question. "And the custodians are letting us have it? They're always so crabby."

Donovan grinned. "They're really great guys."

He insisted that we had to pick the engine up immediately, even before going to the cafeteria to eat. We'd all learned to trust Donovan for one reason or another, so we went along with it. But when we arrived at the custodial office, it was deserted.

"Where is everybody?" I asked.

"At lunch," Donovan replied.

"But where's the motor?" Abigail persisted.

"It's in the floor polisher," Donovan explained, producing a screwdriver. "Where else?"

It was all beginning to make sense. The custodians weren't *giving* us anything. We were *taking*.

Abigail was furious. "We can't steal their motor!"

"It's not *their* motor," Donovan lectured. "It's the school's motor. It's also the school's robot."

I'd seen things like this on YouTube, but never could I have imagined being a part of it in real life. It took Latrell several tense minutes to dismantle the polisher and remove the engine.

"Put the cover back on," Donovan instructed. "We don't want them to see it's missing."

Abigail was practically hysterical. "Don't you think they're going to notice when they try to polish the floor?"

I was the lookout. It was my job to give the code word if I saw one of the custodians coming.

"Pythagoras!" I hissed.

Donovan yanked the screwdriver out of Latrell's hand and tossed it out of view while kicking the floor polisher under a workbench. In the same motion, he herded everybody into the supply closet, jammed in after them, and slammed the door. I'd never seen anybody move so fast.

"It's okay," I called. "I was just testing."

Donovan came out of the closet and fixed me with twin lasers. "Do that again and they'll be watching your funeral on YouTube."

I admired Donovan, but he scared me sometimes.

Sneaking back to the robotics lab with our prize was the most exciting experience I could remember, even better than my big takedown at the dance. I knew a lot about the effects of adrenaline on the human body, but that was different than actually feeling my heart pounding against my rib cage. Fear mixed with exhilaration, plus the notion that, at any second, we could get caught. It was almost as if I hadn't really been alive until Donovan showed up at the Academy.

Oz was ecstatic. "Where did you guys get this?"

It didn't bother him at all that nobody answered.

The polisher's motor was a little bit bigger than the broken one. "We'll have to reconfigure it to run on battery power," Oz advised. "And the extra weight might slow us down a little."

"But we'll have a lot more juice," Donovan put in.

"We don't need more juice," Abigail pointed out. "The task is to pick up inflatable rings that weigh practically nothing."

Oz had a different opinion. "We had a real problem, and we found a way to solve it. That's what the robotics program is all about."

The next day the floor looked a little dull and neglected. But Tin Man was back online.

The rumor started with Kevin Amari, who dropped the bomb in the cafeteria.

"I overheard Oz telling Mr. Del Rio that they're going to retest Donovan for the Academy."

Chloe choked on a celery stalk. "What? Why?"

"You're kidding, right?" Abigail said flatly. "It's obvious to everybody he isn't gifted. They gave him a few weeks to prove himself, and he didn't."

"He's proved himself a million different ways," Chloe argued.

"Because he stole a motor?" she retorted.

"Maybe," I said defiantly. "If you give the robotics team a motor, we can do anything with it. But if you ask us to *get* a motor, we'd all be dead in the water."

"And what about Human Growth and Development?" Chloe demanded.

"It doesn't matter," Abigail insisted. "They can't just keep on letting him flunk."

"They do it with me," I muttered. "I'd love to be retested. I'd show them the true meaning of *flunk*."

Abigail stared me down. "Come on. You can't seriously be saying that you don't see any difference between Donovan's situation and your personal weirdness. Your IQ is higher than his by at least a whole person."

"We *need* him," I insisted. "He's more important than any of us."

"Please! One of us couldn't learn how to work a controller? Or download stupid pictures to put on him?"

"We could do it," I gritted. "But we'd do it *wrong!*" It was impossible to explain what I meant. Donovan was a human version of YouTube. Click on him, and you might get Einstein eating a banana, or a heisted motor, or a robot driver, or a Human Growth and Development credit. It was like rolling a die with an infinite number of sides.

Chloe looked thoughtful. "Maybe he'll pass the retest."

There was an awkward silence as that idea went down like a lead balloon.

"He's working really hard," she argued. "You know—for him."

"Exactly." Abigail was triumphant. "His grades are *awful*. He might be trying, but what does that mean? That this is the best he can do?"

"You don't have to look so happy about it," I told her.

"What about his science project?" Latrell suggested. "He's burning the midnight oil on that."

"Right," Abigail agreed sarcastically. "Googling dog facts and taking pictures of the family pet."

Kevin had a suggestion. "We could ask Oz to delay the test. At least until after Human Growth and Development. And by then the robotics meet will be done too."

Chloe was annoyed. "A little selfish, don't you think?"

"Besides," Latrell told him, "big-time colleges bench superstars who are household names because their grade point averages drop below 2.0. He's toast."

"*We're* toast," groaned Kevin. "If we go to the meet

without Donovan, Cold Spring Harbor is going to run all over us again."

"Not necessarily," Abigail said defiantly. Even she didn't sound convinced.

Jacey seemed to be bursting with something to say, but when we turned to her, she just mumbled, "Nothing. I was thinking about those subatomic particles that travel faster than light. I guess it doesn't help Donovan to know Einstein was probably wrong."

"He could study," Chloe suggested. And when snorts of laughter greeted this, she added, "We could help him study."

"Or," I put in thoughtfully, "one of us could take the test for him, and make sure he passes."

"Oh, right," scoffed Kevin. "Like no one's going to notice it's the wrong person."

"The test is on a computer, remember? All we'd have to do is gain remote control of his mouse and change just enough of his answers to put him over the top."

Abigail was horrified. "That's cheating! Do you know how much trouble you could get in for that?"

I was intrigued. "How much?" In my case, they'd probably just take the opportunity to give me extra credit. The whole system was against me.

"If you get caught doing something like that,"

Abigail warned, voice rising, "it would go on your permanent record! You'd never get into Stanford or MIT with a black mark like that!"

"Really?" I asked.

Abigail rolled her eyes. "For you, they'd just add twenty grand to your scholarship."

Chloe shook her head sadly. "I feel bad for Donovan. He's a really good person. I got mad at him at the dance, but now I know he was only trying to protect me. I wish we could help him. You know, legally."

I realized something about Donovan then. We were two sides of the same coin. He was struggling to stay in the gifted program, and I was struggling to get out.

UNTESTED
DONOVAN CURTIS
IQ: 112

Noah Youkilis gave Daniel Sanderson a black eye at the dance on Friday night. It happened when Noah did that Wrestlemania dive from the deejay's speaker tower. Somehow, he must have kicked Sanderson in the face with his mother's red leather boots. I'm sure it was an accident. Noah wouldn't hurt a fly.

Technically, it was all my fault. I'm the one who turned Noah on to YouTube, and that's where he discovered professional wrestling. I didn't feel bad, though, because Sanderson totally had it coming. My only regret was that Noah couldn't have gotten Nussbaum with the other foot.

Trust me, I didn't hear any of this from the Daniels themselves. I told my parents and Katie that, if those guys called or came by, I was officially not at home.

"But why, Donnie? They're your best friends."

"I thought they were my friends when I showed them the robot," I replied. "But then they went behind my back and wheeled it into the gym, so a thousand idiots could use it as a punching clown!"

"What do you care about their robot?" Katie challenged.

"I'm the driver," I argued. "We're like the Lone Ranger and his horse."

Her eyes narrowed. "Any idiot can work a joystick. What else did you do on the project? Did you help build it?"

"Part of it."

She was unconvinced. "What part?"

"The exterior," I said stubbornly.

"You can't even make Kraft dinner," Katie accused. "Where would you learn how to build a sophisticated piece of technology?"

"It's not about the robot; it's about the Daniels," I insisted. "Those guys think they can treat the gifted kids like they don't measure up as humans. You can't push people around in front of a dozen chaperones, so they took it out on Tin Man. I'm not talking to them."

Mom respected my wishes but, on Wednesday, Nussbaum took a picture of Sanderson's face on his cell phone, and texted it to Katie. She'd always had a soft spot for the Daniels, if you can imagine Katie having a soft spot for anybody. Anyway, when she showed me the picture, I did a double take. Sanderson looked like he'd been hit by a train, not a half-pint YouTube-obsessed genius. What a shiner! His eye wasn't just black. It was purple and yellow and green, and a few shades I didn't know the names of.

"*Noah* did that?" my sister exclaimed in amazement.

"He comes across like a dork, but he's got killer moves." And his mom had killer footwear.

In the end, my conscience won out, and I headed over to Sanderson's. If the Daniels were texting my sister, they were really angling for a visit. Which meant they probably wanted to apologize. I guess I had to go over there and let them.

Sanderson might have been suffering, but it hadn't

stopped him from milking this injury for all it was worth. He had Deirdre and Heather over there, holding his hand and refreezing ice packs for his poor eye.

Nussbaum was on the scene too, limping a little just in case there was any sympathy spillover from the girls. If I thought I was going to get an apology, I was mistaken. Instead, everyone started talking about the night of the dance, and "that bully." I swear, I had absolutely no idea who they were talking about. The only bullies in that gym had been the Daniels themselves.

"What bully?" I asked finally.

"You know," said Sanderson. "The one who hit me. That bodybuilder in the wrestling outfit."

I was blown away. "With the red boots?"

Sanderson gave me a beseeching look. He was determined to prove in front of the girls that he'd been brutalized by a huge monster, and he expected me to back him up.

He picked the wrong person on the wrong day. "Noah Youkilis could lose a fight to a spiderweb. He's six inches shorter than you, and he weighs about as much as your cat."

"He's a black belt in tae kwon do!"

Deirdre spoke up. "You guys in the Academy may

think you're special just because you're smart. But you can't go around punching people. This Noah delinquent could be kicked out of school for what he did!"

I laughed. "Noah? He couldn't get kicked out of school for murder!"

The Daniels stuck to their guns though. Every time they mentioned Noah, he got bigger and meaner, and trained by a more secret paramilitary organization. As soon as the girls were gone, though, they offered a little remorse for kidnapping the robot—in a Daniels sort of way.

"Yeah, I guess it was kind of uncool," Nussbaum murmured. "But you should have seen the look on your face!"

"*Totally* worth it," agreed Sanderson. "At least till that little ninja cold-cocked me. And by the way, thanks for nothing for having my back with Heather and Deirdre a minute ago."

I laughed mirthlessly. "You'd better pray they never get a look at Noah close up."

"*He'd* better pray he never gets a look at *me*!" Sanderson promised darkly.

"That's quite a crowd you hang with over at the genius school," Nussbaum observed. "You never told us plaid shirt was the normal one."

For some reason, that really got to me. "You know, a few of those kids are so smart that we're not even smart enough to understand how smart they are. So leave them alone. And definitely leave their robot alone."

"We were just fooling around," Nussbaum mumbled. "We used to know a kid who did stuff like that all the time—a kid named Donovan Curtis."

I almost forgave them, because they definitely had a point. What were a few bumps and scrapes on Tin Man compared to the wreckage I'd visited on the Hardcastle gym? They were the same old Daniels. I was the one who was different.

Besides, with my big retest coming up, you had to figure I'd be back at Hardcastle Middle School before too long. I was going to need some friends there.

I approached the upcoming testing the way a death row inmate approaches the date of his execution. Reluctantly, and with feet dragging.

It was kind of touching how many of my robotics classmates offered to help me study, coach me. With the exception of Abigail, who was planning to relish my failure, everyone seemed to be pulling for me. A lot of it might have been because of Katie, or because

I was the best person to drive Tin Man at the robotics meet. But I like to think some of it was because they'd accepted me as one of them—even though I was so far below them intellectually that I needed a telescope to see the soles of their shoes.

Chloe offered to work with me at least twenty times. She was kind of offended that I kept blowing her off. I couldn't make her understand that it was nothing personal. I probably should have just come out and told her, point-blank, that I had even less chance of comprehending what she knew than I had of passing the test. When I finally caved, and let her help me with the math portion, she talked so far over my head that all I could hear was airy whispers. And every time she tried to dumb it down, it became a little bit harder to understand.

When we were done, she looked at me in genuine alarm. "Oh, wow, Donovan. What are you going to do?"

Translation: *Stick a fork in me. I'm done.*

I shrugged. "I'll put in some time tonight. Maybe it'll all click."

She wasn't buying it. "You need more than a click. You need a *miracle.* Maybe we should get Noah to tutor you. He'd do it. Any one of us would!"

I laughed bravely. "If I can't understand you, a study session with Noah would make my head explode."

Funny—even though Chloe was back to her plaid shirts and baggy jeans, I kept seeing her as she'd looked all dressed up at the party. The idea of her finding out exactly how smart I wasn't had become kind of sad to me. I even had a plan for cleaning out my locker after school hours so there would be less chance of her witnessing my disgrace. One day I'd be there, the next I'd be gone. After a few weeks, maybe somebody would say, "Remember that guy who used to go here for a while? What was his name again?" No one would have the answer except Noah, and he would pretend he didn't. Eventually, all that would remain of my time at the Academy would be the faded pictures peeling off of Tin Man. And by then, no one would be able to recall who had put them there.

On the big day, things were quieter than usual in the robotics lab. Nobody would meet my eyes, not even Oz. As my homeroom teacher and faculty advisor, it had to have been him who recommended me for retesting. He probably felt like an axe murderer this morning. Even Tin Man seemed a little slumped over and depressed, although that might have been the extra weight of the floor-polisher motor.

I had one last card to play. I marched up to Oz and placed a thick folder on the teacher's desk. He regarded me questioningly, and I pointed to the title: "Chow Chows: A Special Breed." Below it was a large photograph of Beatrice, flaked out on her side, looking about 90 percent comatose. To my long list of regrets, I should add the fact that I had waited to take the picture until she was too far gone to be alert and alive.

"My science project," I announced.

"Shouldn't this go to Mr. Holman?" he asked.

"I thought maybe you could hand it in for me," I explained lamely, "since I might miss science today while I'm taking the test."

My pathetically desperate Technicolor hope was that he'd see this fabulous project, realize that I was working my butt off, and cancel the retest. But he didn't even open it. "Sure," he said very absently, and glanced at his watch.

Noah drifted by the desk. "Good picture," he commented. "Interesting idea to use a pregnant dog."

The earth lurched. "Pregnant?" I rasped. "Beatrice?"

"Of course." The young genius pointed out the features that had gotten by me and my entire family. "Note the distended belly, the prominent nipples, and the languid posture. Weren't you paying attention in Human Growth and Development when we compared human pregnancies to those of other mammals?"

I couldn't even respond, so rocked was I by this news. Wait till Katie got a load of this one. Her tank commander husband was expecting not one blessed event, but two! Brad's sainted mother must have let Beatrice run wild—and look what had happened! Later, when the dog started acting funny, Fanny had dumped her on us so she wouldn't have to take the blame.

My project—the one that was going to prove I belonged at the Academy—didn't mention a single word about pregnancy. So it was all stupid.

I snatched up my folder. "I just need to make a few last-minute adjustments—"

At that moment, the PA system crackled to life. "Mr. Osborne, would you bring Donovan Curtis to the library. . . ."

"Ten minutes!" I pleaded.

I don't know if the voice heard me, but the announcement continued, "Immediately, please."

That's where it was going to happen—the library. They would sit me down in front of a computer, and feed me questions I didn't have the answers to. In the end, it wouldn't matter that my chow chow project was a disaster. I wouldn't be in the gifted program much longer.

I squared my shoulders to my classmates. "Later, guys." But what I meant was, *Good-bye.*

They looked devastated. Even Abigail seemed a lot less happy than I'd expected her to be. Either that, or she was holding off on the celebration until I was officially out.

The walk to the far side of the building had never seemed shorter.

"The test will be coming over the internet from the state department of education," Oz explained as I took my seat. "Don't be nervous. It's not meant to trick you; it's meant to let you show what you know."

That was not at all comforting.

The state department of education made me cool my heels. I sat in stiff-necked misery, sweating. The bell rang. Homeroom was over. I heard the sounds of moving feet in the hall. Life was going on for everyone but me.

Oz gripped my shoulder. "We're all rooting for you, Donovan."

"Thanks," I said in somebody else's voice as he abandoned me to my fate.

The first question appeared on the screen. I read it over—once, twice, three times. No idea. None. Zero. Zilch. *Nada*. Of course, I had known this was coming. But somehow you always hold out hope. Nobody was perfect. Maybe they'd give me the wrong test—like for second grade remedial. It was possible.

But, no. This was the real thing. And as I looked into those words and numbers and symbols that meant absolutely nothing to me, I could almost see Dr. Schultz waiting at the front door of Hardcastle Middle School. It wouldn't take long for him to find me there.

I felt the icy water that had surrounded James Donovan in 1912, and the suction of the sinking *Titanic* pulling him under. James had resisted, but I didn't have the strength. I was going down.

There was one final chance. The test was multiple choice. I had a one-in-five shot at being right. It wasn't much, but at least it was something.

I took hold of the mouse to make my first fatal selection. And then something strange happened. As I moved the pointer toward box B, the small arrow changed direction and traveled on its own to check box C.

I stared, thunderstruck. Was there a problem with

the computer? Just my luck! On top of all the things that were stacked up against me, I was taking the test at a broken workstation. Although, come to think of it, I was just as capable of getting the wrong answers on my own, without any help from a malfunction. I considered changing C to B. But C was just as likely to be correct. So I left it, and clicked *Next*.

Question 2 seemed to have something to do with chemistry. But again, way out of my league. This time I settled on A, because—well, did there have to be a reason? I clicked it, and then it happened again. I lost control of the pointer. It deselected my choice, and immediately checked box E.

Then, without any action from me, it hit *Next,* and question 3 appeared.

Maybe I wasn't gifted, but I had the brains to know that this was no electronic glitch. There could be only one possible explanation for it. My computer had been hacked! Somebody was taking the test for me!

My first reaction was an emotional one. Another human being cared enough to want to keep me at the Academy! Most of my classmates were so wrapped up in their own skills and talents that they barely noticed anybody else existed. Yet someone had noticed me, and this person was going to great lengths, and risking big trouble, to bail me out.

For a second there, my eyes actually filled with tears, and I almost missed my remote angel answering question 3. I would have bet money that I had no friends in this place. But somewhere in this building—or even outside of it—hunched over a laptop, was the greatest friend I never knew I had. Would the Daniels do something like this for me? Okay, the Daniels couldn't pass this test if an alien microcomputer crash-landed inside their skulls. But even if they could, would they go out on a limb for me? I sincerely doubted it.

Who was doing it? They were all smart enough, but it took more than smarts. It took guts, and that was in short supply at the Academy. It could even be a teacher—Oz or Bevelaqua, trying to prove that the gifted program didn't make mistakes.

I noticed the librarian looking at me curiously, so I took hold of the mouse, and pretended to be busy at work. By that time, "I" was on question 11, and cruising. My bewilderment was beginning to morph into relief. My date with Dr. Schultz, and the consequences of the Atlas incident, had been put on hold. I was dogpaddling again. This time it took a little help—okay, a lot of help. But I was still afloat, just like James Donovan.

The librarian shot me an encouraging smile. What she saw was a student who had all the answers.

And I did. Except one.

Who was doing this for me?

UNFORGIVABLE

MS. BEVELAQUA
IQ: 140

It makes perfect sense that a class with a teacher named Oz would call their robot Tin Man. The parallel to *The Wizard of Oz* doesn't stop there. In the famous story, the Tin Man lacks a brain; what he gets instead is a diploma.

I'm beginning to suspect that's what happened with Donovan Curtis.

He passed the test with flying colors. It was wonderful. We were all really happy for him. Except that it meant exactly as much as the words printed on the Tin Man's parchment. He was still failing my class quite spectacularly. In science, his average was below 50 percent and below 40 in the chemistry and physics portions. He was passing English, but just barely. His C-minus in social studies was the jewel in his crown, except for robotics. He was running a B average there, but only because he was handy with a joystick—a mark of someone who has taken on a life of solemn worship at the altar of Xbox or PlayStation.

Does this sound like Academy material to you?

"He passed the test, Maria," Brian Del Rio, our principal, reminded me. "What more can we ask of him?"

"A decent grade would be nice," I retorted. "Or some faint trace that might indicate mastery of a subject."

"We cut Noah Youkilis a lot of slack," Brian challenged her. "Why shouldn't Donovan deserve the same consideration?"

I sighed. "You're comparing apples and oranges. Come to think of it, pumpkins and raisins." A more appropriate contrast might be Betelgeuse and the nucleus of a carbon atom. "Noah is the kind of mind that comes along once in a teaching career, if you're lucky."

"But the test—" the principal insisted.

"If I buy a dog, but when I open the carrier I find a hamster inside, is it a dog because that's what it says on the bill of sale? My powers of observation and reasoning trump words on a piece of paper. I don't know how he passed the test. I only know that he couldn't have."

Brian was adamant. He ran this place by the book. Donovan had passed and he was in. Everybody was covered—especially the principal. If there was blame to be assigned somewhere down the line, none of it was going to fall on him.

And it had to be in Brian's mind that Donovan had solved the Human Growth and Development problem by providing his pregnant sister as a lab rat. Now, there was an oversight that would have resounded with the parents. I couldn't fault him for being grateful for a solution. Parents can get ugly; parents of the gifted can be positively militant. What I *did* fault him for was allowing that gratitude to blind him to the truth about Donovan. Perhaps he thought it was harmless to harbor a mediocre student in the Academy. But that student was diluting the standards of the gifted program for everybody. Not to mention that Donovan was learning absolutely nothing here. He was entitled to a real education at his own level.

My colleagues seemed to be taking their lead from Brian. If the principal wasn't worried, what concern was it of theirs? Of course they knew that Donovan wasn't exactly acing their classes. But, hey, he'd passed the test. The test! It was as if they believed the test was an infallible superbeing that had descended to earth on a great space ark surrounded by thunderbolts of perfection.

Oz was the last bastion of sanity left in the building. He'd known from the beginning that something wasn't right about Donovan. He was the one who'd asked for the retest. Surely he wasn't complacent enough to put aside his teacher's instinct just because of a test score.

When I barged into the robotics lab, at first I thought it was deserted because the lights were out, and I couldn't see any people.

Then I looked down. There they all were—including Oz—lying flat on the floor with Katie Patterson, their pregnant lab rat. Loud, gasping, wheezing breaths issued from every throat.

"What's going on here?" I exclaimed, shocked, scanning the room for a chemical leak.

"We're breathing," Oz panted.

"I can hear that. Why can't you do it standing up with the lights on?"

"It's a new variation on Lamaze," Chloe explained. "Noah developed it. It's much better than the original."

And would you believe that my colleague made me wait until the end of the class before he managed to find time for me? I stood in the hall, fuming, listening to the scuba-respiration sounds coming from inside the lab. It took a while to resuscitate Noah, who had passed out from his own breathing technique. They were all red-faced and panting as they filed past me, but they looked vaguely pleased with themselves, as if they were accomplishing something. Maybe they were. Very little was beyond Noah's capabilities when he wasn't mounting a concerted effort to flunk.

I noted that they were grateful to their lab rat—but most of that gratitude was heaped on Donovan himself. And it wasn't only gratitude. It was genuine affection. Noah regarded him with nothing less than worship. Chloe cast him soulful glances that might have indicated a crush. Even Abigail seemed to have softened her attitude toward him.

Oz was practically glowing with triumph, mopping at his face with a paper towel. "I have to admit I had my doubts about this project," he said after his students had moved on. "But we've taken a course that was ninety percent giggling at the names of body parts and made it meaningful, and beautiful, and rooted in the real world! I'm going to write an article for *American Teacher*."

That would be a must-read—all about how every class should adopt its own pregnant woman. "We need to talk about Donovan."

He nodded. "Where would we be without him?"

"I'm not talking about Baby 101, Oz. I'm talking about Donovan as an Academy student. Have you noticed any improvement in his performance?"

"Oh, sure, he . . ." His voice trailed off.

"I didn't think so," I said crisply. "He's bailed you out on Human Growth and Development and he's the Mario Andretti of the robot-driving circuit. But his academics are no better than they ever were."

"Well then, how did he pass the test?" Oz demanded with growing defiance.

"Maybe he didn't," I mused, voicing for the first time a thought that had been nagging at me over the past few days.

"Are you saying he cheated?" he sputtered. "Impossible! He took that test over a secure internet connection directly from the state department of education. He was alone in the library with a staff member's eye on him every second."

"It's impossible for Donovan," I agreed. "But what about the others?"

His incredulous expression slowly settled into one of alarm. Of course the others were capable of hacking into a secure connection, some of them without breaking a sweat.

"Why would they do it?" he managed at last. "Why help him pass?"

"Open your eyes, Oz. They *love* him. And it isn't just because of his sister and the way he drives the robot. He's normal, he's casual, he's capable of having a good time. He's everything they can't seem to master, despite all their brains."

He looked melancholy. "I like him, Maria. Maybe he doesn't belong, but he's good for these kids. He completes them."

"He turned one of them into a cheater," I reminded him.

"Hey, we have no evidence of that."

And that was the whole problem. If one of Oz's superachievers had found an undetectable way to take control of a secure computer and do the test for Donovan, who would ever be smart enough to prove it?

CHEATING INVESTIGATION
INTERVIEW WITH DONOVAN CURTIS

MS. BEVELAQUA: Your score on the retest was remarkable, Donovan.

DONOVAN: Thanks.

MS. BEVELAQUA: It far outstrips any work that you've done in class. How do you explain that?

DONOVAN: I studied really hard.

MS. BEVELAQUA: Come, now. You know this isn't the kind of test you can study for.

DONOVAN: Maybe I got lucky. Some people are just good test takers.

MS. BEVELAQUA: Or maybe someone helped you.

DONOVAN: I was all alone. Ask the librarian.

MS. BEVELAQUA: It's possible to take control of a computer remotely. In that case, someone would be able to do the test for you.

DONOVAN: I wouldn't have a clue how to do that.

MS. BEVELAQUA: I believe you. In fact, you've just proved my point. You could never accomplish such a thing. But the person who achieved that score could.

DONOVAN: I don't know what you're talking about.

MS. BEVELAQUA: Yes, you do. I want the name, and I want it now.

DONOVAN: I'm late for robotics.

MS. BEVELAQUA: You realize that we're talking about cheating here.

DONOVAN: You know the kind of kids in my class. Who'd risk that kind of trouble to help someone like me?

MS. BEVELAQUA: Perhaps nobody. But to help the brother of a living, breathing Human Growth and Development credit . . .

UNREAL
KATIE PATTERSON
IQ: 107

Well, it was official, confirmed by the vet. Beatrice wasn't dying. She wasn't even some evil demon dog dumped into the world for the purpose of ruining my life. She had a reason for her nasty behavior. The chow chow was as pregnant as I was. I never thought I'd say this, but she had my sympathy.

And that was pretty pregnant. Dr. Orsini said Beatrice might even whelp before I did. That came out wrong. Beatrice was the one who would be whelping. *I* would be giving birth. And while I knew exactly who the father was, the jury was still out on Beatrice. Odds were, we were about to welcome a litter of serious mongrels. And if you've ever seen a chow chow, you'll know they don't mix well with any other breed. So the Westminster Kennel Club was out.

I still hadn't worked up the nerve to tell Brad—even though the whole fiasco was his mother's fault, not mine. To be honest, I didn't like to distract him with the kind of problems that would seem silly to someone fighting a war. Plus, he'd been emailing me about how relaxed and happy I seemed lately, and I didn't want to spoil it by dumping this big matzoh ball in his lap.

From: First Lieutenant H. Bradley Patterson, United States Marine Corps
Honey, you're the best! I know this has been a stressful time with me away and the baby coming. What's your secret? . . .

My secret?

Reality check—I felt like I'd swallowed an anvil and it was lodged behind my belly button. I'd gained thirty-two pounds. A stiff wind was enough to knock me off balance. I had to sit so far back from the dinner table, I needed a telescope to see my food. My legs were covered with varicose veins. My back ached. My skin had broken out, thanks to my raging hormones. I couldn't allow myself to be more than sixty feet from a bathroom. Yeah, I felt wonderful.

Was it the news that the dog wasn't dying? Ha! Just because Beatrice was okay didn't mean she wasn't driving me nuts. For the past month she'd had no appetite at all; now she was eating us out of house and home. She had no bladder control, so the carpet was a minefield. She was antisocial to everyone except Donovan. And her new hobby was disappearing. The last time she vanished it took an hour to find her curled up inside a bale of pink insulation in the furnace room, and longer than that to pick the fiberglass fragments out of her coat.

I'd moved back in with my parents and kid brother, a world away from my husband, who was fighting in a war zone. My life stunk, no doubt about it.

But Brad was right. He had read between the lines of my emails. I *was* relaxed, even happy. Positively serene.

Why?

It had to be Human Growth and Development. For

some reason it was like therapy. Only instead of telling my innermost secrets to some high-priced shrink, I was spilling my guts to Donnie's geek patrol. For free!

Trust me, I could have killed my brother when he blackmailed me into serving as their class pet like a lizard in a glass terrarium. It would have been uncomfortable enough in front of normal kids. But to be stared at by these geniuses with their Coke-bottle glasses and analytical frowns—it was like being dissected and having your vital organs spread out on slides. At first, I had to pretend I was floating above my body, and that was somebody else down there being studied.

But then there was this one morning when I got out of bed and stepped right into one of Beatrice's puddles. By the time I got that sopped up, my spine felt like the disc spaces were filled with lava, but my mother only wanted to talk about the wonky pilot light in the furnace. So I wrote an email to Brad that was so full of whining and complaining, you could have set it to music. I deleted it without sending. Reality check— the poor man was risking his life every day. He didn't need to hear my problems.

That was when I glanced at my watch and realized that I was counting the minutes until I could go to the Academy and lay out my complaints to the only people who seemed to be interested. Chloe, Abigail, Latrell, Jacey, Kevin, even Noah—they'd understand because they understood *everything*. They knew more about me than my husband; they knew more about my pregnancy than my doctor—and they were a lot easier to reach than either of them.

When friends took me out to dinner, and I was unsure whether or not it was safe to eat oysters, I texted Chloe. I had the answer I needed—cooked, okay; raw, never—within thirty seconds. When I noticed an odd chemical on the ingredient list of my shampoo, I emailed Abigail, who was able to tell me it was just a harmless preservative. When I became alarmed by a strange rash on my belly, I had the perfect resource to turn to. I watched Noah's YouTube video "Stomach of Champions," which proved that the skin had been like that for weeks.

How had I survived without those guys?

Until Human Growth and Development I hadn't realized how *alone* I was, even among my own family. Going to those medical appointments was like walking the Tour de France route, up steep hills and over broken roads, all by myself. But when I saw the mini-bus parked outside the clinic, my spirits soared because

I knew I had a team with me—even if it was a robotics team. One day, the bus broke down on the way to the office. Dr. Manolo wouldn't start the appointment until the kids had arrived. He forwarded Oz Listserv emails from the American Congress of Obstetricians and Gynecologists. This class wasn't just going to pass Human Growth and Development. They were going to be qualified to teach it. All except Donnie. If there was one of them who didn't have a clue, it was my lunkhead brother.

What was he doing with these brilliant, motivated students? That was the biggest reality check of them all. Was it that, as his sister, I couldn't see how gifted he really was? Or did he just not care about this course because he already had the credit?

We were replaying the results of my fetal echocardiogram, watching the image of my baby's tiny heart beating on the Smart Board. It was entrancing. Chloe was almost in tears at the beauty of it. Abigail scribbled pages of notes, all without looking away from the screen. Noah had the flip cam trained on the monitor, so I knew this would be on YouTube in Kandahar before I got home that day to warn Brad that it was coming. The whole class, including the teacher, was fascinated.

All but Donnie. He was bored out of his mind, struggling to keep his butt in his chair. And he lost the struggle, jumping up and mumbling, "Going to the bathroom." He practically galloped out of the room.

A few minutes later, a couple of visitors walked into the lab, and Oz paused the video. I knew one was the principal, Mr. Del Rio. The other looked like a congressman, or some other kind of big shot, an older guy in a very snazzy suit.

He walked right up to me, smiled warmly, and held out his hand. "I'm Dr. Schultz, superintendent of the Hardcastle schools. I came specifically to meet you, Mrs. Patterson, and thank you for what you're doing for this class."

That's why he looked familiar. He used to be the principal at North High when I was a cheerleader at Hardcastle. He's the jerk who lodged a complaint that our uniforms were too "minimalist." He'd been a stuffed shirt back then, and it didn't seem as if that had changed now that he had the top job.

But all that was in the past, especially my cheerleading career. I was a mature adult, almost a mother. I shook his hand. "I'm happy to do it. They're great kids."

Dr. Schultz went on for a while—how selfless I was,

people should follow my example, my brother was so grateful, blah, blah, blah. He seemed to think that a) Donnie needed the credit I was providing, and b) Donnie was actually *here*, and not in the bathroom. Neither Oz nor Mr. Del Rio corrected him, though. I guess you don't interrupt a superintendent, even when he hasn't got his facts straight.

Then Donnie made his return—at least he started to. His head poked in through the doorway. His eyes widened in horror at the sight of Dr. Schultz—like I was standing with Count Dracula, not the superintendent of schools. Donnie backed up and was gone in a heartbeat. No one else noticed him. For sure Schultz didn't.

I don't claim to be an expert, but I knew my brother. He was scared to death of the guy. Something was up.

The class went on to show Dr. Schultz some of the work we'd been doing. He seemed impressed by the echocardiogram and the sonogram footage, but he didn't have much patience for Noah's new breathing technique. The superintendent had begun glancing impatiently at his watch.

Noah wasn't offended. "That's okay. You can watch it on my personal YouTube channel, Youkilicious."

"Let us introduce you to Tin Man at least," Oz

offered. He looked around for his designated driver. "Where's Donovan? Not on another one of his extended bathroom breaks?"

"Some other time," Dr. Schultz said briskly. He turned to me. "Thank you once again, Mrs. Patterson. You're a credit to the Hardcastle community." And he and the principal slipped out of the lab.

I waited a few minutes and then took a bathroom break of my own. Once in the hall, I headed straight for the boys' room, figuring my brother would be holed up there.

I threw open the door and broadcast a warning. "Big stomach waddling in."

"There's nobody here but us toilet paper" was the timid reply.

"You can come out now, Donnie. The guy's gone."

He emerged from a stall, wearing a guilty look that I'd seen a million times before.

I folded my arms, resting them on the shelf that my stomach now formed. "All right, out with it."

He looked haunted. "You don't want to know."

"Of course I don't want to know. But I think I have to."

Not even growing up in the same house with Donnie could have prepared me for the story I heard next.

Donnie—the Atlas statue—the Hardcastle gym. As reality checks go, this one had me pinching myself to see if I was hallucinating. It wasn't impossible, you know. On rare occasions, the chemical changes of pregnancy have been known to bring on psychotic episodes. I got that from Noah himself.

I heaved a sigh. "And you had the nerve to blackmail me over something as insignificant as a sick dog who wasn't even sick. That's low."

He shrugged miserably. "I'm sorry, but I'm trying to make myself a part of this class. They need you, so they're stuck with me, regardless of how ungifted I am."

"Your teachers are going to notice that you don't measure up," I pointed out gently.

"They already noticed. They had me retested. I passed."

"No way!"

He reddened. "Well, it wasn't really me. Somebody hacked into the computer I was using and did the test for me. Honest, I had nothing to do with it! I don't even know who it was."

I groaned. "That's worse. You've taken one of those brilliant students and corrupted him. Or her." I thought of Chloe, who seemed to be my brother's biggest fan.

"Well, what choice did I have?" he demanded, practically whining. "Bevelaqua already raked me over the coals, trying to get me to confess!"

"Did you ever consider going to Dr. Schultz and owning up?"

He was outraged. "Oh, sure! And Mom and Dad will collect soda bottles to get the money to fix the gym!"

I was astounded. "Who said we'd have to pay?"

"Come on, Katie. I may not be gifted, but I read the papers. The district is getting stiffed by the insurance company. Somebody has to pick up the tab—why not the guy who did it? I can't lay all that on Mom and Dad—not with money so tight, and Brad out of the picture, and you moping around, big as a whale. Even the dog went and made more problems. This is the worst possible time for me to add to all that."

I was thunderstruck, staring at my idiot brother with a new respect. This was the first indication I'd ever had that Donnie was aware of anybody besides himself. It jarred me down to my swollen ankles.

"Give me some time to mull this over," I told him. "I'd like to get Brad's opinion. Maybe he'll have an idea how we can explain all this to Dr. Schultz."

"Tell him to come quick," Donnie advised. "And bring his tank."

And right there, in the bathroom where *I* didn't belong, in the Academy where *he* didn't belong, the two of us shared a brother–sister hug.

Reality check—Dad kept a picture on his desk of the last time *that* happened—Disney World, 2002. I was sixteen. Donnie was three.

UNMASKED

DR. SCHULTZ
IQ: 127

I was in my car heading back to the office, but something didn't sit well with me. I couldn't quite put my finger on it. Expressing my appreciation to Mrs. Patterson had been the right thing to do. We all had dodged a bullet, thanks to her. She had saved the district an enormous amount of aggravation. Irate parents; frantic phone calls; summer plans changed; complaints to the school board and maybe even the state. It would have been the biggest screwup of the year—well, second biggest.

Perhaps it was the Academy itself that had unnerved me. That place always made me uneasy. Don't get me wrong—gifted programs are an essential resource for a school district. The trouble with them is they attract so many know-it-alls!

I stopped at a light, frowning. Something Kyle Osborne had said was still rattling around my head: "Where's"—I couldn't recall the name; Dominic? Donnelly?—followed by: "Not on another one of his extended bathroom breaks?"

Extended bathroom breaks . . .

That was the answer. It was common enough for an unmotivated student to kill time in the bathroom, hoping to make the days speed by. But not at the Academy. There were no mediocre students there. And if one of our best and brightest had decided to squander his placement, he should step aside in favor of someone who wouldn't waste the opportunity.

As soon as I was back at my desk, I called Brian Del Rio. Maybe he could identify this missing kid.

He was out of the office. "Page him, please," I said, and sat back to wait.

As my eyes passed over the screen saver on my computer, it occurred to me that Brian might not be my only source of information about that class. There was also Noah's YouTube channel—I winced—Youkilicious.

Not the easiest name to spell, but I found it soon enough and stared in amazement: 114 featured videos? Noah had the highest IQ in the history of the district, but from the looks of this, all the boy did was run around with a flip camera!

My attention was instantly drawn to "Tin Man Metallica Squarepants Exposes Teacher's Underwear." God bless America, it had already been viewed more than six thousand times! That wasn't good. What could be a bigger screwup than a lawsuit over the misconduct of a robot?

I clicked on the link and the clip began to play. It showed Maria Bevelaqua laying papers on a semicircle of desks. As she moved, Tin Man rolled into the picture, falling in behind her, matching her pace almost perfectly. The forklift mechanism began to rise, catching the hem of her full peasant skirt. Up it went, until there was more of Ms. Bevelaqua on the screen than I cared to see. Judging by the giggles in the background of the video, the last person to notice this was Maria herself. When she finally did, the screech prompted my computer to warn me that my speakers were in danger. And right before the clip ended, the camera swung around and focused on the student who was operating the robot's joystick controller.

My blood turned to ice in my veins.

It was—it was—

I had a vision of an upturned face staring wide-eyed into the wreckage of the Hardcastle gym. That nameless face was the first thing I saw every morning, and the last thing I saw at night. It had starred in my wildest nightmares, taunting me, driving me crazy for weeks.

Dominic . . . Donnelly . . . *Donovan*.

It was *him*.

CHEATING INVESTIGATION
INTERVIEW WITH CHLOE GARFINKLE

MS. BEVELAQUA: I've noticed that you and Donovan are pretty good friends.

CHLOE: I guess.

MS. BEVELAQUA: It would bother you if he had to leave the Academy, wouldn't it?

CHLOE: Why would he have to leave?

MS. BEVELAQUA: You have a brilliant mind, Chloe. You must have noticed that Donovan doesn't share your academic abilities.

CHLOE: He's good at a lot of things I'm not.

MS. BEVELAQUA: You know as well as I do that operating a video game joystick doesn't compare to the kinds of strengths we value here.

CHLOE: Well, maybe. But he passed the test.

MS. BEVELAQUA: Did he?

CHLOE: You'd know better than I would. The scores were reported to the school, not to me.

MS. BEVELAQUA: We're beginning to suspect that someone helped Donovan. Was it you, Chloe?

CHLOE: How could I possibly—you mean a hacker?

That would be hard. You'd have to override the encryption of a secure internet connection from the state!

MS. BEVELAQUA: Exactly. I see you know how it's done.

CHLOE: Yeah, but that doesn't mean I'd do it! Not for my own mother!

MS. BEVELAQUA: But for your boyfriend?

CHLOE: Donovan is not my boyfriend! I don't have a boyfriend!

MS. BEVELAQUA: Calm down. No one is making any accusations—yet.

CHLOE: Honestly, Ms. Bevelaqua, we knew Donovan was in trouble with the test. We offered to help him study, but he just couldn't—it didn't work out.

MS. BEVELAQUA: Define "we." You and who else?

CHLOE: Are you asking me to rat out my friends?

UNWELCOME
DONOVAN CURTIS
IQ: 112

I was pretty good at video games, but never had I felt more comfortable with a joystick in my hand than when I was driving Tin Man. The robot was like an extension of my will. The slightest twitch of my finger and he was instantly obedient to the controller. It was as if my every thought could make him dance.

For once, we weren't in the lab. With the state robotics meet barely a week away, it was time to simulate competition conditions. The team had spent all morning converting the gym into a perfect copy of the Dutchess Auditorium, where the tournament would take place. Tin Man moved back and forth, accepting inflated rings from Abigail and placing them on the pegs we had attached to the gym's climbing apparatus. We'd even set up the "pit," which would serve as our headquarters at the meet. It supplied everything from tools and spare parts for Tin Man to a cooler of "YoukilAde"—a high-energy drink that, according to Noah, hydrated faster than Gatorade.

Most of the team was gathered around Oz, their eyes panning back and forth from the robot to the teacher's stopwatch. They let out an audible groan when I raised one of the rings too high, and had to stop the robot to lower the mechanism down to the peg. That cost us time for sure.

"Easy, Donovan," the teacher cautioned. "Remember, you've got a stronger motor in the forklift."

At last, Tin Man placed the final ring, swung around, and headed for the starting position. The stopwatch beeped and Oz called out our time. "Best we've ever done, people. Even with a few hiccups."

"This is going to be our year!" Latrell crowed.

We broke out the YoukilAde and toasted Tin Man and one another. Chloe had brought brownies, so it was kind of a party. It actually reached the point of some good-natured trash talk directed toward Cold Spring Harbor, and how Tin Man was going to leave their robot lying in the dust.

Of course, our team members were too polite for *real* trash talk, so I had to show them how it was done: "Their hunk of junk doesn't stand a chance against Tin Man! Their hunk of junk wouldn't stand a chance against Tin Man's *grandmother*!"

"Tin Man can't have a grandmother," Noah interjected. "A machine is not a living entity, and has no familial line."

Probably why I never ran into any robots on ancestry.com.

"We get the point," Oz put in, grinning. "Let's keep it to ourselves. It's a little premature for a victory celebration."

"There's no way Cold Spring Harbor can match the kind of times we're putting up," Kevin enthused. "Not unless they're running their robot on rocket fuel."

I'd never been much of a joiner, so this was my first taste of how it felt to be part of a team that was a real contender. And not just a part. With the robot completed, I was more important than any of them. All those geniuses, and the one person who could make Tin Man perform at championship level was the dummy who got stranded in the gifted program by mistake. I didn't have a clue how to design, build, or program a robot. But it was up to me to bring home the gold.

For the first time since I'd landed at the Academy, I truly *belonged*.

The heavy metal gym door was thrown open with such violence that it pounded against the cinder block wall. There, framed in the light from outside, was nothing less than an avenging angel.

Dr. Schultz.

I swear he crossed the gym in three gigantic strides, shooting sparks from his eyes. I considered running, but what for? Even if I could manage to escape, where did I think I could go? I was completely and totally busted.

"Dr. Schultz—what a surprise," said Oz. "You're just in time to see us put Tin Man through his paces."

"That will have to happen some other time." The superintendent's voice was colder than his expression, if possible. The eyes fell on me. "Donovan Curtis—your parents are on their way."

Chloe was the first to clue in to the gravity of what was going on. "Donovan might not be gifted in the same way as the rest of us, but he's the heart and soul of our team! He's the heart and soul of our *class*!"

Dr. Schultz regarded her sternly. "Donovan's problems go far beyond trying to be what he's not."

I followed him out of the gym, while the squawking and protesting of my teammates rang off the rafters.

"He drives the robot!"

"We're dead without him!"

"He is *so* gifted!"

"He brought us Katie!"

"He showed me YouTube!"

"He's one of us!"

Their support would have made me feel good if I hadn't been on my way to the end of the world.

I scrubbed hard with the polishing cloth, and Madagascar got a little shinier. Maybe. It was so dark in the subbasement of the administration building that it was hard to tell Africa from South America.

I was in the dungeon—or at least the closest thing they had to a dungeon in the Hardcastle school district. My sentence was to polish up the bronze world I had knocked off Atlas's shoulders all those weeks ago. The worst part wasn't the polishing; it was chipping off years of bird droppings that had ossified by a chemical process I'll bet even Noah Youkilis couldn't explain.

It was all useless, of course. There was no way Schultz was going to put this thing up again. Not after what had happened. But he wanted it perfect and gleaming in its hiding place. Actually, what he really wanted was for me to suffer. Believe it or not, cleaning the celestial sphere—as part of twenty hours of community service—was my only punishment for everything that had happened. My family was not going to have to pay for repairs to the Hardcastle gym. I was off the hook—a survivor, just like my ancestor, James Donovan, when he climbed out of the icy North Atlantic and into the lifeboat. Whacking the statue with a branch had been a dumb thing to do, but, in the end, it fell within the range of normal wear and tear. The rusted bolt was at fault, not me. Now the only question was, would the insurance company pay for a design flaw from a foundry that no longer existed?

"You got off easy, Donovan Curtis," the superintendent had told me sternly at the meeting with my parents. "I hope you realize that this could have gone a lot harder on you."

He called me by my full name, almost as if he was afraid he might forget it again. I couldn't blame him. These past weeks must have been like chasing a ghost.

That's probably why he was so animated when he added, "I suppose I don't have to tell you that you're no longer a student at the Academy for Scholastic Distinction."

Seated between Mom and Dad, I'd recoiled as if he'd slapped me. I didn't much care about the Academy—I'd never belonged there in the first place. But it hurt to be off the robotics team.

My mother cried, but that wasn't exactly breaking news. She cried whenever anyone got voted off the island on reality TV. I understood her disappointment. As of today, I wasn't gifted anymore. Not only that, but I was responsible for the biggest town disaster since the famous gas-line explosion of 1986, which ruptured a drainage pipe and filled the Hardcastle Public Library with raw sewage up to the second floor.

Worse still was how Dad took it in stride. Some of that might have been his good mood at finding out he wasn't going to have to foot the bill for a new gym. Mostly, though, it said he had never truly believed I was gifted in the first place.

His only comment was, "Do you think turpentine will take that bumper sticker off the car?"

I never gave much thought to the fact that me being

at the Academy had been such a big deal to him. But for some reason, it bugged me that he wasn't more upset to learn that the whole thing was a sham.

"You always suspected, huh, Dad?"

He was quiet for a moment, then, "You know that website you like—the one about the ancestors and great-granduncles and old-time relatives? Well, I did my share of that kind of poking around when I was your age."

That didn't make sense. "They had ancestry.com when you were a kid?"

"Well, back then they called it the library. But if you go through enough microfiches, you can learn the same things. The names you dig up, I've heard most of them before—Irish forebears who moved to America, Canada, England, Australia—places like that."

Amazing! I still couldn't explain why I did the things I did. But at least now I understood why I turned to ancestry.com to look for answers.

"All those people went on to different jobs," he continued. "Teacher, construction worker, lawyer, grave digger—even a mayor and a couple of city councilmen. As far as I can tell, they all lived satisfying, happy, productive lives, but you know what? Not one of them was especially gifted. Think about that, and maybe you'll see why I'm not so crushed about this. What matters—the only part I really care about—is that you're happy."

It was an impressive speech for a normally quiet guy like my dad. There was only one problem: I *wasn't* happy. In fact, I was pretty far from it.

It was completely outside my control, but I felt like I was letting the robotics team down. For sure Tin Man wasn't going to win anything with Abigail at the joystick. Worse, Katie was quitting Human Growth and Development.

"If they boot my brother, they boot me too," she said stoutly. "Who says you're not gifted?"

"*You* do," I replied honestly. "And it's the truth. Come on, Katie, it wasn't the kids who kicked me out. They're still fourteen hours short for their credit. They'll have to go to summer school!"

"That's tough!" she snapped. "Summer school will be good for them. Let them see how the other half lives!"

What could I say? She was supporting me. Strange she should choose to start now. I felt bad, but I had to let it go. Dr. Schultz had spelled it out. That place wasn't my life anymore. In the real world, it never had been.

***

My locker was gone. I mean, it was still there. But while I was at the Academy, the administration had hacksawed my lock off, and all my stuff had vanished. At the office, they told me to make a list of the missing items. I tried, but the only thing worth more than three cents was one combination lock. So I gave up.

I kept seeing my locker at the Academy—spacious, freshly painted, its built-in power strip waiting to help me by keeping my devices charged—not that I had any devices. By comparison, my Hardcastle locker was about the size of a tiny apartment mailbox. It smelled like feet.

The whole building was an extension of my locker—shabby, crumbling, depressing. The Academy was a palace by comparison. I don't know if I appreciated it when I was there, but I definitely appreciated it now, surrounded by broken drinking fountains and crumbling plaster. Week-old lunches overflowed out of every garbage can. The halls rang with the voice of an assistant principal, chewing out some poor kid over a random offense. Nobody took you for a cooling-off walk and a philosophical discussion at Hardcastle. Here, a paper airplane was not an experiment in aerodynamics. It was an act of war.

I tried to work up more gratitude for being off the hook for the Atlas incident. This place just crushed it out of me. I doubt James Donovan ever stood on the deck of the *Carpathia* and yearned to return to the icy water, but I couldn't stop itching for a rewind button to whoosh me back to the Academy. It was stupid, I know. I never said I was gifted. I just wish I'd been better at faking it.

The Daniels arranged a homecoming for me that I'm not soon going to forget. In front of the entire lunch crowd in the cafeteria, they presented me with the 2012 Moron of the Year Award, which looked suspiciously like the missing toilet from the upstairs boys' room. On the bowl, in dribbling red paint, was written: WELCOME HOME, STUPID. It weighed a ton and a half.

"Here he is, back from a very limited engagement at the Academy for Scholastic Dork-stinction, the man who turned out to be just as lamebrained as the rest of us—give it up for *Donovan 'The Dummy' Curtis!*"

I didn't die of humiliation. I only wanted to. There were a few lukewarm cheers, but most of the kids didn't know quite what to make of it. I'd only been gone a few weeks. Half of them might have figured I took a long trip, or had mono, or got suspended or something. Probably a lot of them thought: Who's Donovan Curtis?

"Come on, you guys!" Sanderson goaded the crowd. "If it isn't loud, he won't understand it!"

I hefted my "award"—which must have tipped the scale at thirty-five pounds—and swung it at the Daniels. The seat came off, whacking Nussbaum in the back of the head before cracking on the floor. That got a bigger response than the announcement of my award. My one consolation was that Chloe wasn't here to witness this. I didn't know for sure, but she struck me as a pacifist. At any rate, toilet fighting was probably a no-no. This might have cured her of her longing to be "normal." If it didn't, she was nuts.

"Come on, man," Nussbaum offered. "We'll buy you lunch."

"I brought my lunch," I said stubbornly.

"Then grab a table," Sanderson instructed, rubbing the back of his head. "And don't forget your award—what's left of it."

I was wary. "I'm not going to get blamed for stealing this, am I? I'm running low on schools I haven't been kicked out of yet."

"See, that's what's been missing around here," Nussbaum noted. "That Donovan sense of humor.

Welcome home, bro. The place wasn't the same without you."

We had lunch with Heather and Deirdre. Apparently, those four had been eating together for weeks. That made me the party crasher. I'd thought the one good thing about coming back to Hardcastle was at least I'd fit in. Guess again.

As it turned out, I had to throw my sandwich away. It had spent the morning in my locker, and now the mayonnaise tasted like feet. I took handouts from my four companions.

Girls put avocado in everything.

I was back with friends, or what passed for that. Funny—I'd been convinced I was friendless at the Academy. But I'd felt more a part of things in Oz's robotics lab than anywhere here at Hardcastle. How could I compare the Daniels and their jokey, in-your-face version of friendship to the guardian angel/hacker who had risked everything to pass that test for me? Now, with the Academy permanently in my rearview mirror, I still had no idea who it was. I would have liked to say thank you. In a weird way, though, that person was even more ungifted than me. It made no sense to believe that a test score could make me into something I wasn't.

Classes at my new old school weren't better, exactly, but at least I understood what was going on. I'd been faking it for so long at the Academy that it was startling to suddenly know actual answers. I even raised my hand a few times in math, until Sanderson bounced a spitball off my skull and hissed, "Dude—this isn't the Academy!"

And I couldn't help thinking, No, it sure isn't. You can see it in the paint job, and taste it in the bad cafeteria food. You can hear it in the dead air that hangs in the classroom when the teacher asks a question. You can smell it in the sweaty gym socks—so different from the synthetic-oil aroma of a set of Mecanum wheels.

While I was in the bathroom, someone stole my toilet—the award one, not the one I was using.

I made a mental note to buy Febreze for my locker.

On the way home, the Daniels and I passed by the statue of Atlas. I hadn't been there for a while, not wanting to revisit the scene of the crime. The titan was still oddly bent, with no celestial sphere to weigh him down. And, at the bottom of the hill, the entrance to the high school gym remained boarded shut. I'd been so wrapped up in my own weird predicament that I hadn't given much thought to the mess I'd made over here. The wave of remorse was stronger than I'd anticipated. Suddenly, twenty hours of scraping pigeon poop off a bronze sphere seemed like no more than I deserved.

"You've done a lot of crazy stuff," Nussbaum sighed, "but this was your finest hour."

"It wasn't so fine for the gym," I said bitterly. "Or for me."

Sanderson nodded thoughtfully. "You're right. It would have been better if the globe had gone crashing into the parking lot. It could have smashed, like, ten, fifteen cars."

I glared at them. "You guys deserve the toilet award more than me."

Nussbaum grinned appreciatively. "Good to have you back where you belong."

Where I belong. I looked at the gray, dreary hulk of Hardcastle Middle School, and felt deeply bummed that he was probably right.

CHEATING INVESTIGATION
INTERVIEW WITH ABIGAIL LEE

MS. BEVELAQUA: You're aware, of course, that Donovan Curtis has left the school for good.

ABIGAIL: He never should have been here. I knew that from the first day.

MS. BEVELAQUA: As did I. Which brings up the question of how he managed to pass the retest. We believe that someone took control of his computer, and helped him cheat. Was it you?

ABIGAIL: You must be joking! I'm the last person who would help that guy! His presence lowered Academy standards for every one of us. Why would I want to help him stay?

MS. BEVELAQUA: Well, for one thing, his sister was providing you with a Human Growth and Development credit. Then there's the robotics team, in which he had taken a key role.

ABIGAIL: Oh, please. He worked a joystick like any other half-witted gamer.

MS. BEVELAQUA: Except that a better driver could have meant the difference between winning and losing. It's been my observation that you're not too keen on losing.

ABIGAIL: Nobody likes to lose.

MS. BEVELAQUA: I know how you think, Abigail. For you, education is more than learning. It's a high-stakes chess match. The state robotics meet is a resumé builder. A better resumé means a better college. A better college means a better future. Just how far would you be willing to go to assure all that?

ABIGAIL: Part of strategy is risk *vs.* return. Why would I risk getting busted for cheating over a jerk I can't even stand?

UNBELIEVABLE

CHLOE GARFINKLE
IQ: 159

<<*Hypothesis: Truth is stranger than fiction.*>>

Make that *way* stranger.

At the Academy, we're taught to think outside the box. But to guess this, you'd have to be so far outside the box that you couldn't find your way back with a GPS.

The disaster at the Hardcastle gym—that was Donovan. And by some misunderstanding growing out of it, he'd been sent to the Academy and parachuted into our lives.

Abigail had been right, as usual. He didn't belong. She'd said it first, but since then, every one of us had at least thought it. He'd *never* belonged. There was not a single imaginable reason why Donovan Curtis should ever again set foot inside the Academy.

<<Hypothesis: I don't care.>>

"I miss him too, Chloe," Oz admitted when I finally cracked in front of him. "I think we all do. But there's no way he can ever come back."

"Why not?" I demanded.

"For starters, because it comes from Dr. Schultz himself, and his word is law in this district. And second, because there are dozens of requirements for admission into the Academy, and Donovan meets none of them. Besides, what would he do here?"

"What did he do when he *was* here?" I countered. "He brought us to life! He turned Tin Man from a nameless machine into a part of the family! We got a spirit from him that we don't have anymore! And next week we're going to sleepwalk into that robotics meet and finish dead last when we could have won it all! I don't know if I even want to go to this school anymore!"

He was horrified. "Chloe! You need the level of

220

academic challenge—"

"That academic challenge landed me in summer school!" I snapped. "And in case you forgot, Donovan had a solution for that too. And we threw him out."

"Katie had a choice," Oz argued. "She could have stayed with us and finished the course."

"Why would she, after the way we treated her brother? I don't blame her a bit. I blame us."

<<*Hypothesis: Desperate times call for desperate measures.*>>

I was so upset that I did something I'd never done before. I cut school that afternoon. Not just a class or two; all of it. I hopped on a crosstown bus, and rode east toward the one person who could help, if anybody could. I was going to Hardcastle Middle School to find Donovan.

The ride was endless, slow, stopping at every tiny un-street along the way. I kept checking the time on my phone, but it didn't move the bus any faster. I wasn't sure what the schedule was at Hardcastle, but dismissal had to be coming up pretty soon. To commit my first act of truancy in a spotless school career only to miss Donovan would be too much to bear.

I got off at the high school and started running up

the hill. There he was, Atlas, *sans* globe, overlooking the boarded-up gym. I took heart—this was definitely the right place. But my first sight of the middle school almost took my breath away. They were already coming out, swarming all over the campus, crowding onto buses.

I ran into the midst of the crowd, frantically scanning faces on the off chance I'd find the one I was searching for out of more than nine hundred. They all seemed familiar and unfamiliar at the same time. I'd probably seen many of them at the dance. But that didn't matter. Nobody was familiar *enough*.

I was beginning to get some strange looks. "Is Donovan Curtis around?" I asked one boy.

His response was a blank stare.

His companion shoved him. "The dude who dissed the basketball team."

"You know him?" I prompted.

"Not really."

<<*Hypothesis: Donovan made a bigger impression in just a few weeks at the Academy than in nearly three years here.*>>

I caught a glimmer of how someone could disappear among a student body of more than three hundred at each grade level. It could never happen at my school. You were famous for what you knew, or what you could do, or what you might become. Or, in Donovan's case, even for what you didn't know.

I tried another kid, a girl this time. "Do you know Donovan Curtis?"

She shrugged. "I heard he transferred to the Academy."

"I think he's back," piped up the boy behind her. "Isn't he the guy who won the toilet award?"

Probably. It sounded like him. "Have you seen him anywhere?"

Another shrug.

<<*Hypothesis: Non-Academy kids are very loose in the shoulders.*>>

I'd always envied them their relaxed casual attitude—something that never came naturally to us in the gifted program. But right now, I felt like I was drowning, and nobody cared enough to throw me a life preserver.

By this time, some of the school buses had taken off, and the crowd was thinning out. An ugly truth began weighing me down like a heavy meal. I wasn't going to find him. I'd come all this way for nothing. Worse,

I was going to have to get back on that crosstown bus and jounce my way home. I wasn't even really sure what I'd been planning to say to the guy. I just knew for certain that the mere sight of him would have settled me down.

Suddenly, a too-loud voice behind me announced, "Hey, isn't that the plaid chick?"

I wheeled. There they stood, staring at me, Donovan's two friends named Daniel. I ran over to them. "I'm so glad to see you guys—"

"Whoa—" One of them held out a hand. "Not too close! Your brain waves might fry my cell phone!"

"Guys, is Donovan still here?"

The taller Daniel sneered down at me. "Look who needs Donovan all of a sudden! You should have thought of that before you threw him out of your smarty-pants school!"

"Woulda, shoulda, coulda," put in the other one.

I ignored their baiting, and plowed forward. "I totally agree with you. If it was up to me, Donovan would still be at the Academy. That's what I came here to talk to him about. Has he left yet?"

"He wasn't in school today," the taller Daniel said finally. "Schultz took him to meet with the school district's insurance company. You know he's the guy who busted the gym, right?"

"We were eyewitnesses," added the other one. And he went into this ridiculous story about how Donovan had, for no reason at all, whacked the statue on the rump with a tree branch, and all the damage had happened because the globe had disconnected and rolled down the hill.

I was just about to say, "How stupid do you think I am?" when it dawned on me—that story was *totally* Donovan! It was exactly why he was so needed at the Academy. None of us ever did anything without thinking it out in detail, making an elaborate plan. Donovan *acted*—whether it was hitting a statue, or naming a robot, or stealing a motor, or finding someone to teach Human Growth and Development because she *was* Human Growth and Development. For Donovan, it was all as natural as breathing.

"Well," I stammered, "can you give me his phone number? I really need to talk to him."

Taller Daniel was indignant. "And give you brainiacs another chance to make him feel stupid? No way! He's miserable enough!"

And then, as if I hadn't sufficiently humiliated

myself, I began to sob like a heartbroken child. Part of it was pure frustration with this wild-goose chase—the fact that these two jerks could easily have put me in touch with Donovan, but they wouldn't. And part of it was this: I'd been so wrapped up in what *we'd* lost, how *we'd* suffered, the fact that *we'd* have to go to summer school; I'd never even wasted a thought on how Donovan must have felt about all this. How selfish was I?

<<*Hypothesis: We don't deserve Donovan at the Academy.*>>

"Hey, wait a minute!" the other Daniel exclaimed. "What are you doing?"

"Go ahead!" I sniffled. "Let me have it! Make fun of the Academy nerd crybaby! All I wanted to do was let him know how much we miss him, and how we've all been like zombies since he left! Next week is the robotics meet we've been preparing for all year, and now nobody even wants to go! I didn't come here to make him feel bad! I came to tell him how sorry we are!"

I fell silent, catching my breath, and waiting for them to laugh in my face. This was one more thing to regret for poor Donovan: He had such lousy friends.

The shorter Daniel took something out of his pocket

and began unfolding it meticulously. It was a T.G.I. Friday's napkin, crushed for who knows how long in a linty pocket. He handed it to me, and I blew my nose gratefully. Neither of them spoke. It was the first time I'd ever seen those guys at a loss for a snide remark.

Finally, the taller Daniel spoke up. "When did you say that robotics meet was?"

CHEATING INVESTIGATION
INTERVIEW WITH NOAH YOUKILIS

MS. BEVELAQUA: No, you may not film this interview. I've already made enough appearances on your YouTube channel. But we'll have that conversation on another day.

NOAH: We should reach ten thousand hits sometime next week. You know, based on the rate of increase of daily views. It's simple calculus—

MS. BEVELAQUA: I know that. I'm a math teacher. Please pay attention, Noah. Would it be possible for someone to take control of a computer that's transmitting over a secure internet connection?

NOAH: Oh, sure. You just have to create an application to decrypt the data. It's boring stuff.

MS. BEVELAQUA: And did you do it to make sure Donovan passed his retest?

NOAH: I thought of it, because we really need him around here. But it wouldn't have done any good, because he got kicked out anyway. You know that statue thing? That was Donovan. What a YouTube video that would have made . . .

MS. BEVELAQUA: Back up. You thought of it?

NOAH: Sure. I was going to do it. But I forgot.

MS. BEVELAQUA: And I'm supposed to believe that?

NOAH: I got busy shooting a video and, by the time I remembered, the test was over. Donovan was back in class, and he didn't seem upset, so I assumed he aced it. It is pretty easy, you know.

MS. BEVELAQUA: I can't believe you're being so casual about something this important. Cheating is a very grave offense, whether you do it for yourself or somebody else. You could get expelled from the Academy for that.

NOAH: Really?

UNSCHOOLED
DONOVAN CURTIS
IQ: 112

According to ancestry.com, James Donovan went to Washington to testify as a witness at the Senate hearings into the sinking of the *Titanic*. That was what I had to do, only it was more like I was saying that I deliberately picked up the iceberg and sliced open the boat with it. According to Schultz, the insurance guys needed to hear the real story straight from the mouth of the person who did it. The executives looked like they were all going to go home and yell at their kids, just to keep them from turning out like me.

The worst part wasn't the testimony, but the one-on-one time with Schultz in his car. The guy hated me basically because *he* had made a mistake. Plus, he was such a slow driver that the trip took twice as long as it should have. And trust me, the conversation wasn't flowing. The only upside was, when he dropped me at home, Beatrice climbed into the car and peed on the floor mat. Believe it or not, I was starting to appreciate that dumb dog.

These days, the chow chow was kind of my soul mate around home. She moped; I moped. She hid in the basement and refused to talk to anybody; me too. We lay side by side on the furnace room floor, gazing up at the spots where the ductwork disappeared into the ceiling. Her belly was even more swollen than Katie's now. Sometimes you could actually see the skin rippling as the unborn puppies wriggled inside.

My mom tried to pretend she wasn't devastated by my new ungifted status. But I could read between the lines no matter what she said.

"I'm every bit as proud of you as I was the day before we got that letter." See the problem? Think about it. It'll come to you.

Katie was already nostalgic. "Strange but true, I miss

those geniuses. They're getting restless in Afghanistan. My stomach hasn't been on YouTube for a whole week."

My dad reported that the turpentine had worked, and he no longer was the proud parent of an honor student.

School was the worst. I couldn't hack it in the gifted program, but the work at Hardcastle was just too easy. Crazy as it seemed, all my fruitless studying at the Academy had stuck with me. Now I was getting straight A's—and instead of being happy about it, my good grades served as yet another reminder of the place I'd been kicked out of. It was like I had a foot in two different worlds, and they were moving apart. I was going to crack up the middle like a wishbone, and I didn't much care.

The Daniels kept trying to cheer me up. But their plans always involved doing something that would get me into trouble for their entertainment. One day they brought a stink bomb for me to set off in the cafeteria, and they were genuinely amazed when I said no. Believe me, it had nothing to do with following the rules. I just wasn't that guy anymore. I felt the presence of that bent-over Atlas, and I couldn't work up a stink-bombing mood.

It was the same with the vampire teeth for the skeleton in the science lab on Tuesday and the latex vomit for the teachers' dining room on Wednesday.

So when I got to school on Thursday, and saw the Daniels coming at me in the hall, I was wary. "What is it this time? Itching powder for the soap dispensers? Nerve gas for the ceiling fans? Cyanide for the salsa?"

"Better than that," Nussbaum promised. "You need a mental health day off from school."

"Be serious, you guys," I complained.

"Trust us," said Sanderson.

They wouldn't take no for an answer. I swear, I thought they were kidding, because they were always kidding. And besides, where could they possibly want to take me in the middle of a weekday, when it would be obvious to everyone that we were ditching?

They shoved me out the double doors at the side entrance. I was just about to fight my way back in when I recognized the car parked at the curb, waiting for us. The front seat was pushed all the way back to make room for the burgeoning stomach of the driver.

Katie.

"What's going on?" I demanded.

Nussbaum grinned. "Shut up and get in the car."

"Hey, Donnie." Katie greeted me as I got into the passenger seat and the Daniels crawled into the back. "Up for a road trip?"

I was mystified. "Where are we going?"

"Dude, it's a very special day," Sanderson reminded me, sitting forward until he was breathing down my neck.

"What day?"

"Well, let's work it out," Nussbaum pondered. "It's not my birthday, and it's not Cinco de Mayo. Christmas? No, that's already past. It's not the Fast of Gedalia, or Bastille Day—"

"Cut it out!" I snapped.

Katie was laughing. "Put him out of his misery. Tell him, already!"

"I can't believe you forgot," Sanderson scolded. "Your girlfriend is going to be really mad."

"What girlfriend?"

"You know—plaid Chloe with the big brain."

I bristled. "She's not my—" But the thought of Chloe made me remember. Today was the state robotics meet at the Dutchess Auditorium in St. Leo!

They were taking me to watch Tin Man.

My first thought was *I don't want to go*. Yet before the words made it out of my mouth, I realized that I *did* want to go. Possibly more than anything I'd ever wanted in my life. It would hurt to be sitting in the audience instead of in the pit with the joystick in my hand. But it was better than not being there at all. Tin Man was going into competition against Cold Spring Harbor and the top robots in the whole state. I should be there to cheer him on.

"I love a good robotics meet," Nussbaum enthused. "It's just like the Super Bowl, only nobody cares, and it's way more boring."

I shook my head. "How did you guys even know about this?"

"Don't look at me," Katie put in. "I'm just the driver. Your buddies put together the whole thing."

"Your girlfriend told us," Sanderson supplied. "She showed up looking for you, and she was all moaning and groaning, and a total downer pain in the butt. In other words, exactly like you've been lately. So we figured the only way to shut the two of you up was to get you together at a good old-fashioned robotics meet."

"Thanks—I think." But I didn't just think; I knew.

Who would have dreamed that there were real hearts hidden under all that baloney? Not even the gifted program could have predicted it.

St. Leo was forty-five miles from Hardcastle, but Katie needed two bathroom stops on the way, so it took more than an hour to get there. I was amazed at the size of the Dutchess Auditorium, which was a huge rambling building on the edge of town. The team had always said that the robotics meet was a big deal, but I guess I'd never really believed them.

"Maybe it *is* the Super Bowl," Nussbaum mused.

Inside, grandstands ringed the vast floor. On one side, a checkerboard of pits was laid out in an orderly fashion, providing home bases for the teams. I counted thirty-six of them. On the other side was the course, looking remarkably similar to what we'd laid out in the gym for Tin Man. Even though I wasn't a part of it anymore, I felt a jolt of excitement. My teammates had told me about this, had described it in such detail that I felt like I'd already seen it.

Katie, who had trouble standing for long periods of time, settled her awkward bulk into a seat, and reserved three more for the rest of us.

Sanderson leaned back in his chair and tipped the

peak of his baseball cap over his face. "If anything happens in the next four hours," he murmured, "wake me up."

"Are you kidding?" Nussbaum crowed. "It's like a nerd city down there! One good wedgie could start an epidemic!"

"Can it," I ordered. I had just spotted the Academy pit. I saw Latrell first, lying on his back, working on Tin Man's undercarriage. Tin Man! There were a lot of robots, but I only had eyes for ours. I hadn't built him, and I wouldn't be driving him, but the pride of ownership was electric.

"Hey"—Nussbaum nudged his fellow Daniel—"isn't that the little shrimp who kicked you in the face?"

Sanderson sat up and followed his pointing finger. "He's not so small. We're just high up, that's all."

I had to laugh. "Save my seat. I'm just going to run down for a minute and say hi to the team."

I worked my way through the crowd, which was made up mostly of parents and siblings of the contestants, mixed in with an assortment of teachers from the various participating schools. I stepped around a large cardboard sign that said GREAT NECK SOUTH ROBOTICS and jumped down to the floor. As I snaked through the grid of pits, I checked out a few robots. They were nothing special but, of course, I hadn't seen them in action yet.

I didn't know any of the contestants from other towns, but in a way they were familiar to me. They looked like the Academy kids. The brilliant dweebs, like Noah. The psycho overachievers, like Abigail. The hands-on engineers, like Latrell. The all-purpose brainiacs, like Chloe. There was even the occasional kid who reminded me of me—some average ungifted slob who happened to get taken along for the ride. Some of the teams were tinkering and fine-tuning; some were greeting old friends and competitors; a few pits had music playing—one group was dancing, doing "the robot."

Right. We get it.

The school banner read COLD SPRING HARBOR, but I would have known this team anywhere. Their pit was better equipped and better organized than anybody else's, from the easy-access tool rack to the stacked hammocks for relaxing between rounds. Their robot looked like it had just rolled off an assembly line in a high-tech factory. It had none of the homemade, cobbled-together appearance of Tin Man and most of the others. The shape reminded me of my grandma's giant stew pot if you added wheels and mechanical arms. But it was huge—Pot-zilla, Lord of the Robots.

Cold Spring Harbor were the defending champions, and the kids wore their arrogance like a uniform. Come to think of it, they had a real uniform—custom T-shirts that blazoned their achievements not just at this meet but at others around the country. To look at them was to want to ram their robot down their throats. But that might have been my team spirit. If my time in Oz's room had hammered one thing into my head, it was that Cold Spring Harbor was the enemy.

I passed Pot-zilla and headed down the narrow aisle for the Academy's pit, the smile already transforming my face. It had only been a week, but I could hardly believe how glad I felt at the prospect of seeing my former teammates again.

The smile didn't last. I was close—so close that I was about to call out to Oz—when a tall figure in a three-piece suit crossed my line of vision.

Schultz.

I did the fastest about-face in the history of direction changes. I couldn't let him see me! I was supposed to be in school right now! He'd had to let me off the hook for Atlas because it made him look bad too. But if he caught me here, cutting class to attend an event

239

of the gifted program he'd just yanked me out of, I'd get no mercy.

I returned to the seats, heart pounding in my ears.

"Is it over yet?" Sanderson mumbled, half asleep.

"How are the dorks?" Katie asked fondly. "Do they look nervous?"

"They're fine," I assured her.

I wish I could have said the same thing about myself.

UNSEEN

MR. OSBORNE
IQ: 132

The state robotics meet.

It was my favorite day of the year. There was nothing quite like it for our kids at the Academy. Schools have so many outlets for athletes to shine. But for the gifted program, robotics was ideal. It combined creativity, design, engineering, mechanics, electronics, pneumatics, and computer science, all in an atmosphere of healthy competition. It was sent from heaven.

This year? Not so much.

The team I brought to St. Leo was distracted and dispirited. And I hated to admit it, but I was too.

He should have been here. Donovan. And not just because he drove Tin Man better than anybody else. My group was unmatched in ability level, but it took Donovan to make them a team. On the surface, he contributed very little. But without him, nothing worked.

I should have been furious with that kid. He had committed an atrocious act of property damage. He had got into the gifted program under false pretenses, and had used it as an opportunity to hide from the consequences of his actions. He had cheated on the retest. Or, at minimum, he had let somebody cheat for him, which was even worse. He was barely from the same planet as my students.

If I had been a better teacher, I would have shouted down the class's complaints about Donovan's sudden departure from the Academy. When the bellyaching continued, I would have set a strict rule for our class: the name of Donovan Curtis was no longer to be mentioned within those walls. And if that hadn't worked, I would have told them a few home truths about misplaced loyalty, and people who lie and cheat to get their way. I had considered doing all those things. But I didn't. Because, deep down, I missed Donovan just as much as they did.

Maybe even more. I kept seeing him around the auditorium, as if wishful thinking might produce him in front of me. One time the illusion was so real that I actually began to wave before I looked again, and he wasn't there. That's the kind of impression the kid made.

Dr. Schultz shook my hand and nodded affably to the students. "Good luck, everybody. Make me proud."

If looks could have killed, he'd have been pinned to the wall by a volley of arrows. The last time they'd heard from their superintendent, he'd been pulling Donovan out of the gym, and out of their lives.

The first phase of the competition was the autodirected portion, where the robots navigate by electric eye, following a course of varicolored lines painted on the floor. By the time Tin Man's heat came up, Cold Spring Harbor was already in first place with a comfortable lead over Orchard Park in second. I watched, the team crouched around me, following the stopwatch in my hand, as Tin Man ran that course to perfection. My number was unofficial, of course, but I was certain our time was right up there with Cold

Spring Harbor's mechanical monster. And when the final scores went up, Tin Man Metallica Squarepants was ahead of the pack with a two-second lead over last year's champions. The performance held up, and we headed into phase two with a ten-point advantage.

We had a long break before our next event, and experience had taught me that that wasn't always a good thing, especially for front-runners. I tried to keep the kids busy, checking things that didn't need checking. But soon Noah came back from the bathroom with huge black thumbprints on the lenses of his glasses.

"What happened to you?" I asked anxiously. "Is that paint?"

"It was a stamp pad," he replied, annoyed and embarrassed. "Those Cold Spring Harbor guys did it to me. They were waiting in the bathroom."

I frowned. This was something you could expect from Cold Spring Harbor that you didn't get from any other team. They traveled with a large group, and two or three of them were big sullen boys who didn't seem to have much to do with their robot. I think they were there as intimidators. They had certainly done a pretty good job of intimidating Noah.

Abigail was angry. "We have to complain to the judges! They shouldn't get away with this!"

"Take it easy," I soothed, handing her a cup of YoukilAde. "They're just trying to get into our heads. And see? It's already worked. Forget about Cold Spring Harbor. We'll let Tin Man do our talking."

But as the competition progressed, the human element became a bigger factor. Abigail was at the controller, and she was darn good. But it was impossible to avoid comparisons with the way Donovan had handled the joystick. He couldn't make Tin Man go any faster, of course. But there was a nimbleness to his driving, an economy to the robot's maneuvers. Every cut and turn seemed to be an inch or two wider than it needed to be without Donovan at the helm. And all that extra motion added up to lost time. Before you knew it, Cold Spring Harbor had retaken the lead. Soon after that, we dropped to third position, and then fourth. That was a cause for worry, because if Tin Man fell one more place, we'd fail to qualify for the final round.

In the pit, we slaved over our robot. Noah ran a software diagnostic, and Latrell and Kevin agonized over each physical connection and bearing. We had to coax every microgram of performance out of Tin Man to keep our hopes alive.

I could see Abigail's fingers trembling as she worked the joystick. I can't say for sure if she was rattled before, but right now she was scared to death. I looked down at the stopwatch in my hand, and realized that I'd forgotten to start it. The atmosphere was that tense.

Tin Man had a big lead on the other three robots, but we knew that meant very little. None of the competition in this heat was battling us for that last spot in the finals. At this point, our opponent was the clock.

Tin Man reached the pole, and Abigail pressed the control to deploy the mini-bot. We held our breath as the magnet locked onto the metal of the pole. With a high-pitched whirring sound, the wheels engaged, and the small unit climbed the pole.

Ding! The bell sounded as the mini-bot reached the top.

The round was over, but the uncertainty had just begun. Had our time garnered enough points to keep us in the all-important fourth spot? Or had we dropped to fifth, out of the finals? We stood in a circle, holding hands and watching the scoreboard.

One by one, the names of the finalists began to appear.

1. Cold Spring Harbor
2. Orchard Park
3. Abercrombie Prep
4. Academy for Scholastic Distinction

We were in.

UNCONTROLLED
DONOVAN CURTIS
IQ: 112

I leaped up out of my seat, fists punching at the air. *"Yeah! Go, Tin Man!"*

At that, I was several seconds behind the Daniels, who were whooping and high-fiving like madmen, drawing annoyed looks from the spectators around them. Even Katie, who was not much of an athlete these days, was on her feet, cheering.

I couldn't help wondering what it must have been like to be in the pit just then—all those guys going nuts as they got ready for the final contest. I could see Oz talking to Abigail, plotting strategy for the battle that lay ahead. She was the driver. Everything depended on her. I knew how it felt when the controller was in your hand.

The Daniels were analyzing the upcoming showdown like it was the pitching matchup for game seven of the World Series.

"Obviously, Tin Man is the best robot," Nussbaum expounded. "If he wasn't, we couldn't have won the autodirected competition."

"Yeah, but Cold Spring Harbor has been pulling further ahead of us every round," Sanderson worried. "If we can't pick up our driving, we're toast!"

Considering those guys had come to make fun of the parts of the meet they didn't sleep through, they seemed pretty involved in it now.

It took about twenty minutes to set up the grand finale, which involved having the robots place inflated rings of different sizes onto strategically placed pegs. It was the bread and butter of any meet, and we had practiced it endlessly. Each ring carried a different point value. Also, the round would be timed, with bonuses for early completion. It would be tough driving, but there was reason to be hopeful. You had to be constantly aware of what balance of speed and accuracy would get you the most points. A guy like Noah could spit out calculations like that faster than a computer.

A tense silence fell in the auditorium as the four robots were moved into their positions on the floor. Standing beside Cold Spring Harbor's gleaming Pot-zilla, poor Tin Man looked like a soapbox racer next to an Indy car. Albert Einstein's banana barely reached the lowest position of the front-runner's lifting arm. Tin Man *vs.* Pot-zilla; David *vs.* Goliath.

The whistle blew, and they were off. Chloe slipped a green ring around one of Tin Man's lifting forks, and our robot started across the course. The four competitors placed their first rings successfully, but Abercrombie Prep was beginning to fall behind as they came back for more.

"Let's go, Tin Man!" barked Sanderson.

"You can do it, dude!" Nussbaum added.

I held my breath when I saw the next ring. It was one of the black ones—small ring, small hole. Harder to handle, but with the highest point value. Orchard Park wasted precious seconds tightening a loose wheel. Tin Man lumbered back toward the pegs. The lift mechanism rose almost to its apex. It was going to be tricky—one false move, and that ring would hit the floor, taking the Academy's hopes with it.

The tiny ring found its place. The auditorium burst into applause, and Tin Man swung around for the next pass. Pot-zilla was hot on his heels, but with our hardest ring already in place, it was: advantage, Tin Man.

Our next ring was pink, the largest. That was when it happened. As Tin Man crossed the floor, Pot-zilla put on a sudden burst of speed. The swerve seemed completely natural, but it was just enough for one of the arms to sweep into Tin Man's path. It bumped lightly into the pink ring, knocking it off Tin Man's fork. It made no sound when it hit the floor, but it might as well have been a bomb blast.

A gasp went up in the auditorium.

"No-o-o-o!" chorused the Daniels.

Oz was on his feet, shouting at the judges, who were waving him off.

Abigail was panicking, fumbling to pick up the dropped ring. Pot-zilla motored past. Soon after, Orchard Park and Abercrombie followed.

I jumped up. "That was on purpose!"

Katie shot me a sharp look. "Donnie, don't you dare!"

But I was already running. I don't know what I

thought I could accomplish. At minimum, I had to calm Abigail down, talk her through the operation of picking up the fallen ring, get everything back on track.

I pounded down the stairs, and leaped to the floor.

Chloe was the first to notice me. "Donovan?"

One by one, the team members recognized me. Faces lit up. Cries of greeting rang out. But this was no time for a reunion. Our chance of winning the robotics meet was slipping away with every tick of the clock.

"Donovan!" Abigail was last. Her eyes were huge, her expression desperate.

I started shouting instructions, struggling for calm myself. "Take the joystick and—"

She had a better idea. She thrust the controller into my hands, and backed away, panting.

What could I do? I lowered the lift mechanism, tipped up the ring and skewered it with one of the forks. Then I delivered it to its destination, deftly raising it, and placing it onto the peg.

Wasting no time, I wheeled Tin Man around and headed back toward Chloe. She looked devastated, shaking her head tragically. I understood the message instantly. I was too late. Pot-zilla had already picked up the final ring and was headed toward the peg and victory.

I saw red. After sabotaging us, Cold Spring Harbor was *not* going home with first prize. Not while I had the joystick in my hand. I drove Tin Man right into the path of the big shiny pot.

"Donovan!" shouted Oz. *"Stop!"*

Pot-zilla was bigger and heavier, but Cold Spring Harbor didn't know that Tin Man had a secret weapon—a powerful motor in the lift mechanism, one that had polished every floor in the Academy for Scholastic Distinction.

A split second before impact, I engaged the forklift. Tin Man picked up Pot-zilla bodily, the larger robot's Mecanum wheels spinning without traction.

Absolute pandemonium broke out. The Cold Spring Harbor kids were screaming, but my team was matching them in volume. The head judge was blowing his whistle, but it could not be heard over the general din. Neither could Schultz, who was shouting at me from behind Chloe. Anyway, I couldn't stop now. Tin Man was a bundle of circuits, incapable of revenge fantasy, but I was all too human.

Cold Spring Harbor's driver was trying to free Pot-zilla by thrashing with its lifting arms. I needed to act fast. Tin Man had been designed for competition, not combat, so I had to improvise a little. I swiveled ninety degrees and, using Pot-zilla as a battering ram, I charged the scorer's table.

Oz hollered, *"Do-o-o-on-o-o-o-va-a-an!"* It came out a ten-syllable word.

But I was committed. The judges scrambled for cover as I slammed that big pot right into the steel-reinforced corner of the table. Pot-zilla bounced off, dented. One lifting arm hung limply by its shiny bulk. The other reached for Tin Man with evil intent. I backed my robot away.

A shriek behind me penetrated even the chaotic noise of the crowd. Noah bounded onto the scene. He snatched up one of the judges' abandoned chairs, and brought it down, WWE style, on Pot-zilla's polished crown.

Wham! And then again. *Wham! Wham! Wham!*

If the cybernetic pot hadn't been finished before, it was finished now. It wobbled once, and keeled over, lying there, an upended cockroach, wheels turning like struggling legs.

The auditorium had been rocking with excitement, dismay, horror, laughter, and outrage. But now that the action seemed to be over, a strange hush fell as people waited to see what would happen next. Considering the craziness of the situation, it was a strangely familiar moment to me. The impulsive act was over, but the consequences had not yet descended on my head. It was as if time had ground to a halt, and we were all frozen there. What the future held I couldn't predict, but I had a sense that it had something to do with Dr. Schultz, pushing through the throng toward me, his face a thundercloud.

A high-pitched voice suddenly cut through the eerie silence. *"Donnie—"* It was Katie, struggling down the grandstand steps. *"Donnie—it's time!"*

I was so wrapped up in the insanity that I wasn't thinking straight. "Time for what?"

Chloe wasn't like me. She was in the gifted program for real. "The baby!" she exclaimed. "Katie's having the baby!"

UNEXPECTED
CHLOE GARFINKLE
IQ: 159

<<*Hypothesis: The speed of the drive is directly proportional to the acuteness of the crisis.*>>

The yellow minibus squealed up to the emergency entrance of St. Leo Medical Center, and the disqualified Academy robotics team piled out, bearing Katie Patterson with us. While Oz and Donovan handled the patient registration, Katie and the rest of us lay on the waiting-room carpet, practicing Noah's breathing technique.

"Don't worry," Katie assured the two bewildered Daniels. "This pregnancy is a group effort."

"Cool," said the taller one, but he looked a little unnerved.

A door swung open, and an orderly appeared, pushing a wheelchair. "Mrs. Patter"—he gawked at us on the floor—"what's going on down there?"

"It's okay," Latrell told him. "We're the birthing team!"

"We only do robotics in our spare time," Noah explained.

Katie was loaded into the chair and brought to a case room. We followed, every last one of us. The staff wasn't too keen on that, but they had no choice. We were all her coaches, except for the Daniels, and they kept their mouths shut for a change. I'd never seen them so well behaved.

We were in there forever, breathing and timing contractions with our robotics stopwatch. We studied the final sonogram, and kept a close eye on the fetal heart monitor that Katie wore. Everything was fine, but Donovan seemed really scared, even more than his sister, and she was the one having the baby. He spent most of the time on the phone, trying to locate his parents to let them know what was going on. We all

257

took turns calling home to inform our families that this robotics meet was going on a lot longer than usual.

Finally, the doctor decided it was time to take his patient into delivery. As the brother, Donovan went too. The rest of us congregated in the waiting room to—well—wait.

You could tell the two Daniels were pretty cowed by the whole adventure.

"So is this, like, business as usual for the gifted program?" the taller one asked. "I mean, do you do this kind of stuff a lot?"

Oz favored him with an exhausted chuckle. "You mean trash a robotics meet and have a baby? No. It's fair to say this is a big day even for us."

"What's going to happen to us?" Abigail wondered anxiously. "Do you think we might be banned from future competition?"

Oz shrugged miserably. "I don't know. Interfering with another robot is a very serious offense. There are bound to be consequences."

"It was worth it!" the shorter Daniel exploded. "I've known Donovan since first grade, and that was him at his best! Real gladiator stuff!"

"It was WWE," Noah amended.

"You were great too, kid," the other Daniel assured

him. "Mess with you and pay the price. I learned the hard way."

I spoke up. "What Donovan did was against the rules, but it was *right*. Cold Spring Harbor interfered with our robot before he interfered with theirs."

Our teacher sighed. "That's assuming the judges noticed. If they didn't, they'll see the attack as unprovoked."

"But effective," Noah put in.

Kevin rubbed his hands together. "It was beautiful to see that tin pot with a big dent in it."

"I was hoping the arm would fall off," Latrell added wistfully.

"Well, they definitely didn't deserve to win," Abigail said reluctantly. "Even if that means we can't win either."

Jacey opened her mouth to speak, and I braced for one of her odd random comments. Instead, she said softly but with conviction, "Way to go, Donovan."

It hit me just then how different we all were since Donovan had been mistakenly sent to the Academy. The mayhem that had ended the robotics meet would have freaked us out a few weeks ago. Now we were gloating over having destroyed our enemy. If Oz had hoped Donovan would become more like us, here was proof that the opposite was true. *We* had become more like Donovan.

I love my school, but I'd always yearned for us to be a little more normal.

<<Hypothesis: Today we finally got there.>>

We'd been cooling our heels for about an hour when Dr. Schultz came into the waiting room. The superintendent's hair was wild, his tie undone, his normally immaculate suit rumpled.

Spying us, he rushed over. "Any news?"

"Nothing yet," Oz informed him.

He looked frazzled. "I've got your robot in the trunk of my car, but the rest of your equipment is in the storage room at the auditorium. All except the YoukilAde. That got spilled out in the . . . confusion."

"What did the judges finally decide?" asked Oz, and I could tell he wasn't sure he wanted to hear the answer.

"You were disqualified and so was Cold Spring Harbor," the superintendent reported. "Orchard Park were the winners, but I don't think that means much this year. The whole thing was a major fiasco. This is supposed to be a friendly science competition, not a gang rumble."

"Are we in really big trouble?" Abigail asked in a small voice.

"I'm honestly not sure," replied Dr. Schultz. "I inquired several times, but no one would give me a straight answer. The judges have never dealt with this kind of misconduct before. That might work in our favor."

"We should probably keep a low profile in the robotics association for a while," Oz suggested, and we all chimed in our agreement.

Low profile or not, this was one robotics meet I'd never forget. The image of Donovan working the joystick, exacting Tin Man's revenge, would forever be burned onto the inside of my eyelids. I'll bet the others—even Abigail—felt the same way.

<<Hypothesis: To take a robot designed to place rings on pegs and turn it into an instrument of destruction requires a kind of giftedness that none of us have.>>

It was then that the heavy swinging door was flung wide and Donovan staggered out to the waiting room, wide-eyed and white-faced. He was quite a sight in green scrubs and a surgical cap. "It happened," he rasped.

"And?" I prompted eagerly.

"It's a girl," he managed. "Katie had a baby girl!"

The waiting room erupted in cheers and we mobbed him with backslaps and congratulations.

<<Hypothesis: !!!!!!>>

Okay, that wasn't a hypothesis. It was just awesome.

"Dude, you're an uncle!" the taller Daniel exclaimed. "You did it!"

"*Katie* did it," I amended. I threw my arms around Donovan and gave him a big hug.

He seemed startled, and I admit it was a little closer than any of the others got. But I was just so happy for Katie. I *knew* the day Donovan stepped into the robotics lab that there were great things ahead. And this was the greatest of them all.

Donovan worked his way through the well-wishers and nearly jumped out of his scrubs at the sight of Dr. Schultz.

"You can't blame Donovan," I jumped in. "Cold Spring Harbor started it."

The entire team burst into a babbling description of how our opponents deliberately knocked the ring out of Tin Man's control.

"I couldn't let them beat us," Donovan finished. "Not that way."

"I don't appreciate rule breaking," the superintendent said gravely. "School spirit, however, is something I appreciate very much. Whatever else you are, Donovan Curtis, you're a loyal teammate." He smiled. "And please pass on my congratulations to your sister, her husband, and their new daughter."

"Wait a minute!" Noah's brow furrowed. "It can't be a daughter. The sonogram clearly showed a boy."

Oz laughed. "Well, I guess you were wrong about that."

The look on Noah's face as he took in the enormity of that statement was sheer wonder. "Wrong . . ." he repeated, dazed. "I was . . . wrong."

"It's no big deal, Noah," I told him gently.

"It's a colossal deal. I'm *never* wrong." All at once, his normally serious expression dissolved into a large goofy grin. "This is the greatest moment of my life!"

"Maybe, if you get really lucky, you can be wrong again someday," Donovan teased.

Noah considered this. "I'll work on it in summer school."

"No, you won't." Oz was jubilant. "This class was short fourteen hours of Human Growth and Development instruction. But remember, real-life experience counts as triple time—"

I snapped to attention. "We've been with Katie four hours already. One more hour and—"

A flicker of hope animated Abigail's features. "No summer school?"

Dr. Schultz smiled. "Perhaps some good has actually

come out of this horrendous experience. I will personally sign your credit."

"But we have to put in the final hour," Oz added.

"I wouldn't leave anyway," I announced. "Not till I've seen our baby!"

<<*Hypothesis: Maybe the Human Growth and Development requirement isn't so pointless after all.*>>

UNBURDENED

ABIGAIL LEE
IQ: 171

I refuse to let this mess leave a hole in my record.

I spent hours, days even, trying to draft the perfect line to take credit for being on the robotics team without taking blame for what the robotics team had done. *Disqualified* was such an ugly word; *banned* was even worse. *Conduct unbecoming a scientist*—no, don't even go there.

I finally went with: *2012 State Robotics Meet, First-Place Power Ranking (DNF).* Maybe no one would look into the definition of DNF (Did Not Finish), or realize that there was no such thing as a first-place power ranking—which just meant that our robot beat the snot out of Cold Spring Harbor's robot. I don't think Harvard's admissions department would be too impressed by that. It wouldn't hurt someone like Noah. He would get into college wherever he wanted. Sadly, he would probably go nowhere at all. I never thought I'd say this: There was such a thing as being too smart. Confession: I was jealous of Noah. I'd give anything to spend an hour inside his head, to take a mind like that out for a test drive. But I wouldn't want to be him—even though he'd always be above a black mark like the robotics meet, which would be an Ivy League deal breaker for the rest of us.

Another thing Harvard could never be allowed to find out about: how close I came to going to summer school for Human Growth and Development. Do you think their admissions department would care that it wasn't my fault? Of course not. Everybody knows who goes to summer school: People who can't pass in the fall, winter, and spring. People who actually have to open up their report cards to find out their grades. People who think a Rhodes scholarship is Driver's Ed. At least I'd been spared *that* black mark—thanks to Donovan Curtis.

Yes, I know I was really hard on Donovan, and said a lot of terrible things about him. And I stand by my original opinion that he never should have been in the gifted program. But that doesn't mean that we all weren't really lucky for the Atlas incident that put him in Oz's class.

Which brings up the final piece of information that Harvard could never be permitted to learn. Ditto Yale, Princeton, Columbia, Brown, Dartmouth, Stanford, Penn, and Cornell. If anyone accuses me of this, I'll deny it. I might even sue.

I was the one who hacked into the library computer and helped Donovan cheat on the retest.

Surprised?

Me too.

UNCHALLENGED

NOAH YOUKILIS
IQ: 206

'm not sure how the clip made it to YouTube.

The organizers said that the official video of this year's state meet would never be released because our "disgraceful thuggish behavior degraded school robotics programs everywhere."

Somehow, though, the video of Tin Man vanquishing the competition appeared the very next day under the title "Robots Behaving Badly."

I would have called it "The Second-Most Fantastically

Awesome Blow for Justice Ever Struck by an Automaton (after the Terminator Turned Good)." But that might have been too long. People on YouTube don't want to *read*; they want to *watch*. You have to keep it simple to generate traffic. Example: "Robots Behaving Badly" had already surpassed "Tin Man Metallica Squarepants Exposes Teacher's Underwear" in barely a week online.

I felt a little insulted that this new clip had so easily bested my most popular video. But it was okay, since I was the costar of "Robots Behaving Badly," bounding onto the scene at the end to beat the Cold Spring Harbor entry into submission with a folding chair.

It was a great action sequence, every bit as exciting as the real steel-chair battles in WWE videos. I could be wrong, though.

After all, I've been wrong before.

The old-fashioned dot-matrix printer in the main office made a screeching noise as it spat out my class schedule. It sounded like victory. The secretary tore off the page and placed it on the counter along with my student card and locker information.

She smiled at me. "New in town?"

"I've lived here all my life," I told her. "It just took

me this long to get thrown out of the gifted program."

This great day never could have happened if I hadn't been wrong about the sex of Katie Patterson's baby. Just the thought that when I calculate, interpolate, extrapolate, infer, deduce, adjudge, analyze, derive, figure, reason, or surmise something, there's a chance that I might not be right filled me with a sense of infinite possibility. Surprise didn't come exclusively from YouTube anymore. It was a gift.

I owed this, too, to Donovan. Without him, I never would have crossed paths with Tina Mandy Patterson, seven pounds, fourteen ounces. I'd suggested Marie Curie Patterson, but Katie said no. Tina would be named after the star of the day of her birth—Tin Man.

I pointed out that, since Tin Man had been disqualified, he wasn't technically the star of the robotics meet or anything else. But Katie overruled me. And anyway, Orchard Park Patterson was a really stupid name for a baby girl.

I'm not big on babies, but I had to admit that Tina was a very cute specimen of one. Subscribe to my YouTube channel to see what she looks like. There's a clip of her spitting up on my shoes that's particularly excellent. It's my favorite because I got to hold her.

Katie gave each of us a turn so long as we promised to wash our hands for three minutes uninterrupted. One minute would have been plenty given the strength of the antibacterial soap in the maternity ward, but I kept my mouth shut because I didn't want to miss my chance.

Chloe got in trouble for hogging the baby.

I thanked the secretary, gathered my things, and left the office.

I was wrong. It still tickled me to think about it. And for sure that's what had given me the confidence to do what needed to be done to make this glorious moment possible.

"*Noah?*" came a voice behind me in the hall.

I wheeled, and there he was, the author of all my good fortune. My former schoolmate and now my schoolmate again.

Donovan. "What are you doing here?" he asked.

I felt my chest swell with pride. "This is my new school."

He was shocked. "They kicked you out of the Academy? Because of the chair?"

"Oh, no," I replied. "They didn't even mention that. It was because I helped you cheat on the retest."

First he looked surprised, then angry. "I knew it! If you weren't a genius, you'd be an idiot! You shouldn't have done that, Noah! I wasn't going to be able to hang on in there much longer anyway, test or no test. Why would you risk your whole school career to cheat for me?"

"I didn't," I informed him cheerfully. "I just *said* I did."

His voice was rising. "But why?"

"Ms. Bevelaqua told me cheating was a serious offense, and whoever did it would be expelled. How could I pass up an opportunity like that?"

Donovan groaned. "You're crazy. And the worst part is, now I'm never going to know who really did it."

I shrugged. "Sure you are. It was Abigail."

"No way!" His eyes bulged. "Abigail hated me from the first day I walked into the lab! Why would she help me?"

It's strange to me how often I have to explain the obvious to people. "For your robot-driving skills and your sister. Abigail has always been about one thing—Abigail."

"I don't believe it," Donovan said stubbornly.

"Believe it," I recommended. "I had to erase all the

computer evidence that she did it when I created the fake evidence that *I* did it."

He took this in with a mixture of amazement and resignation. "You're crazy."

"I don't care," I replied readily. "See, now that I go here, I can say that. Who cares? Not me! I could not possibly care less! What do I care?" It felt good, like I was unburdening myself of a great weight.

He heaved a sigh. "Well, congratulations, I guess. You got your wish. You managed to get yourself booted out of the only school with half a chance of challenging you."

I was honest. "The Academy wasn't very challenging either."

"More challenging than here," he shot back. "This place is a slumber party for a guy like you. Maybe even a morgue."

I shook my head earnestly. "I was *wrong* about Katie's baby, and that means I can be wrong about anything. Challenge isn't going to come from any curriculum, no matter how hard they make it. It's going to come from life."

That sounded pretty good, even to me. I felt the exhilaration of facing the unknown. I wasn't just heading into the future; I was taking it down, WWE-style. I was Noah Youkilis, version 2.0, and the best was yet to come!

Then again, I could always be wrong.

How awesome was that?

UNLITTERED
DONOVAN CURTIS
IQ: 112

The image was fuzzy at first. Noah pounded the keyboard of his laptop and the picture solidified into a rugged face, obscured by goggles, a chin-strap, and a heavy black helmet. Interference crackled over the audio, and a loud motor roared in the background.

"Lieutenant Patterson?" Noah ventured timidly. Louder: "Lieutenant Patterson?"

My brother-in-law looked around in confusion.

"Who's saying that?"

Another member of the tank crew came into view, pointing out at us. "Look, Brad, it's that kid from YouTube! The one your baby puked on!"

Noah seemed pleased to be recognized. "Nice tank. How's Afghanistan?"

"Brad, it's Donovan," I piped up. "We've got something to show you."

Brad squinted through the goggles. "Is Katie there? Is it happening?"

Katie leaned in front of the laptop. "Hi, Brad. It won't be long now."

The tank commander was excited. "Turn the computer! I want to watch!"

Noah swiveled the laptop, giving Brad a view of the sterile white walls of the clinic, and also of Chloe, Abigail, Latrell, Jacey, and Kevin. At last, the image stopped on Dr. Orsini in his surgical mask.

The other soldier opened his eyes wide. "What's going on, Brad? Didn't this happen last week? Don't tell me they're going back in for the twin they missed!"

Noah made a final adjustment, providing a view of the patient—Beatrice the chow chow, fat and round, about to litter.

"Beatrice!" Brad cried, his voice choked with

emotion. "It's Daddy! Hang in there, girl!"

And as his tank jounced along the Afghan terrain, Lieutenant Patterson watched, tears squeezing out from under the goggles, as his beloved pet deposited six tiny puppies onto the operating table. Compared to the four hours Katie had spent in labor, Beatrice had it easy: The whole thing was over in ninety seconds.

"They make dogs really fast," commented Noah.

"They're beautiful, Brad," said Katie in a husky voice. "You missed Tina being born, but I'm so glad you got to see these little guys."

Noah spoke into the laptop's condenser mic. "Your signal is getting weaker. Are you near a mountain or something?"

"That's classified, kid," Brad replied. "I don't know who you are, but I owe you. Anybody who can Skype a tank in action has really got it going on."

"And I loved you in 'Robots Behaving Badly,'" the other soldier added admiringly.

Then, with a burst of static, Afghanistan went dark.

"Transmission lost," Noah reported. "Should I hack into another satellite?"

"No," Katie decided. "Leave them alone. They're working."

That was how our Human Growth and Development class turned into Canine Growth and Development—at least for one afternoon. The decision was made to keep a puppy for baby Tina, and find good homes for the others. Chloe adopted one dog. I was kind of glad about that. It gave me an excuse to stay in touch with her—you know, just to keep an eye on how Beatrice's kid was getting along.

Noah fit in better than I expected at Hardcastle Middle School. Some of that might have been because I recruited the Daniels, and the three of us formed a bodyguard unit to keep him from being wedgied to death. Who knows what would have happened without us. We liked him, and Sanderson was convinced he was a master of "Dorkido," a secret martial art practiced only by geniuses. But Noah *was* the biggest dweeb who'd ever walked the face of the earth. And while he insisted he could be wrong again at any moment, it hadn't happened so far.

By special request from Oz, both Noah and I traveled by minibus to the Academy three times a week for robotics. The plan was approved by Dr. Schultz himself, who was in a good mood because the insurance company had finally paid up and the gym was being repaired. What was left of Atlas had joined its celestial sphere in the administration building's sub-basement. I hoped I didn't have to polish that piece too. I still had five and half hours of community service to go.

Dr. Schultz had put boxes in all the schools, soliciting suggestions for a new statue. I filled out a card for a *Titanic* memorial—a quiet nod to my ancestor and fellow survivor, James.

Noah didn't mind spending a little time back at the Academy because I was going too. And I loved the change of scenery, and the chance to hang out and ply my joystick in the lab. I never confronted Abigail about how she had cheated for me on the retest. She definitely still hated me, but I had a sense that my reading on her personal grudge-o-meter had gone down a little. Maybe she was more comfortable now that all the cards were on the table. She was still smart, and I was officially ungifted—except for robotics, part-time.

We were working on Heavy Metal, our robot for next year's competition. We'd be in the high school division then, and hopefully no one would remember whose entry had busted up the middle school meet. Tin Man's rampage would live forever in infamy, but maybe the team behind him would fade into the background. Soon the riot would belong to Tin Man alone, and all that remained would be the question, What made the robot go berserk like that?

Hey, I had *that* answer. It was the same wild impulse that could make a guy whack a statue in the butt, setting off a chain of events that reshaped the world—or at least my little corner of it. It was the part of me that ancestry.com couldn't explain. I was working to control it, but sooner or later it would show up again and get me into twice as much trouble.

You don't have to be gifted to know that.

GORDON KORMAN

has written more than seventy middle-grade and teen novels. Favorites include the *New York Times* bestselling *The 39 Clues: Cahills vs. Vespers Book One: The Medusa Plot*; *Pop*; *Schooled*; *No More Dead Dogs*; *Son of the Mob*; and *Born to Rock*. Gordon lives with his family on Long Island, New York. You can visit him online at www.gordonkorman.com.

THE
REHEARSAL

THE
REHEARSAL

ELEANOR CATTON

A REAGAN ARTHUR BOOK

LITTLE, BROWN AND COMPANY

NEW YORK   BOSTON   LONDON

Reagan Arthur Books/Little, Brown and Company
Hachette Book Group
237 Park Avenue, New York, NY 10017
www.hachettebookgroup.com

First American Edition: May 2010
First published in Great Britain by Granta Publications, 2009

Reagan Arthur Books is an imprint of Little, Brown and Company, a division
of Hachette Book Group, Inc. The Reagan Arthur Books name and logo
are trademarks of Hachette Book Group, Inc.

Library of Congress Cataloging-in-Publication Data
Catton, Eleanor.
    The rehearsal / Eleanor Catton. — 1st ed.
      p. cm.
    ISBN 978-0-316-07433-9
    1. High school students — Fiction.   2. Teenage girls — Fiction.   3. Music
teachers — Fiction.   4. Sex scandals — Fiction.   5. Theater — Fiction.
6. Teacher-student relationships — Fiction.   7. Adolescence — Fiction.   I. Title.
    PR9639.4.C39R45 2009
    823.92 — dc22   2009038596

10 9 8 7 6 5 4 3 2 1
RRD-IN

Printed in the United States of America

For Johnny

THE
REHEARSAL

ONE

Thursday

"I can't do it," is what she says. "I simply can't admit students without prior musical training. My teaching methods, Mrs. Henderson, are rather more specific than I think you understand."

A jazzy pulse begins, just drums and double bass. She swirls her spoon and taps it once.

"The clarinet is tadpole to the sax, can you see that? The clarinet is a black and silver sperm, and if you love this sperm very much it will one day grow into a saxophone."

She leans forward across the desk. "Mrs. Henderson. At present your daughter is simply too young. Let me put it this way: a film of soured breast milk clutches at your daughter like a shroud."

Mrs. Henderson is looking down, so the saxophone teacher says rather sharply, "Do you hear me, with your mouth like

3

a thin scarlet thread and your deflated bosom and your stale mustard blouse?"

Mrs. Henderson nods imperceptibly. She stops fingering the sleeves of her blouse.

"I require of all my students," the saxophone teacher continues, "that they are downy and pubescent, pimpled with sullen mistrust, and boiling away with private fury and ardor and uncertainty and gloom. I require that they wait in the corridor for ten minutes at least before each lesson, tenderly nursing their injustices, picking miserably at their own unworthiness as one might finger a scab or caress a scar. If I am to teach your daughter, you darling hopeless and inadequate mother, she must be moody and bewildered and awkward and dissatisfied and wrong. When she realizes that her body is a secret, a dark and yawning secret of which she becomes more and more ashamed, come back to me. You must understand me on this point. I cannot teach children."

Kiss-kiss-kiss goes the snare drum over the silence.

"But she wants to learn the saxophone," says Mrs. Henderson at last, sounding ashamed and sulky at the same time. "She doesn't want to learn the clarinet."

"I suggest you try the music department at her school," the saxophone teacher says.

Mrs. Henderson sits there for a moment and scowls. Then she crosses her other leg and remembers that she was going to ask a question.

"Do you remember the name and face of every pupil you have ever taught?"

The saxophone teacher seems pleased to be asked.

"I remember one face," she says. "Not one individual student, but the impression left by them all, inverted like a photographic negative and stamped into my memory like an acid hole. I'd recommend Henry Soothill for clarinet," she adds, reaching for a card. "He's very good. He plays for the symphony orchestra."

"All right," says Mrs. Henderson sullenly, and she takes the card.

Thursday

That was at four. At five there is another knock. The saxophone teacher opens the door.

"Mrs. Winter," she says. "You've come about your daughter. Come in and we'll discuss carving her into half-hour slices to feed me week by week."

She holds the door wide so Mrs. Winter can scuttle in. It's the same woman as before, just with a different costume—Winter not Henderson. Some other things are different too, because the woman is a professional and she has thought about the role for a long time. Mrs. Winter smiles with only half her mouth, for example. Mrs. Winter keeps nodding a few seconds too long. Mrs. Winter inhales quietly through her teeth when she is thinking.

They both politely pretend not to notice that it is the same woman as before.

"To start off with," says the saxophone teacher as she hands her a mug of black-leaf tea, "I don't allow parents to sit in on private lessons. I know it's a bit of an old-fashioned policy—the reason is partly that the students are never at their best in that sort of environment. They become flushed and hot, and they laugh too easily and their posture changes, folding up tight like the lips of a blossom. Partly also, I think, the reason I like to keep things very private is that these little half-hour slices are *my* chance to watch, and I don't want to share."

"I'm not that sort of mother anyway," says Mrs. Winter. She is looking around her. The studio is on the attic level, and the view is all sparrows and slate. The brick wall behind the piano is chalky, the bricks peeling white as if diseased.

5

"Let me tell you about the saxophone," says the saxophone teacher. There is an alto saxophone on a stand next to the piano. She holds it up like a torch. "The saxophone is a wind instrument, which means it is fueled by your breath. I think it's interesting that the word for 'breath' in Latin is where we get our word 'spirit.' People once had the idea that your breath and your soul were the same thing, that to be alive means, merely, to be filled with breath. When you breathe into this instrument, darling, you're not just giving it life—you're giving it *your* life."

Mrs. Winter nods vigorously. She keeps nodding a few seconds too long.

"I ask my students," the saxophone teacher says, "is your life a gift worth giving? Your normal, vanilla-flavored life, your two-minute noodles after school, your television until ten, your candles on the dresser and facewash on the sink?" She smiles and shakes her head. "Of course it isn't, and the reason for that is that they simply haven't suffered enough to be worth listening to."

She smiles kindly at Mrs. Winter, sitting with her yellow knees together and clutching her tea in both hands.

"I'm looking forward to teaching your daughter," she says. "She seemed so wonderfully impressionable."

"That's what we think," says Mrs. Winter quickly.

The saxophone teacher observes her for a moment, and then says, "Let's go back to that moment just before you have to refill your lungs, when the saxophone's full of your breath and you've got none left in your own body: the moment when the sax is more alive than you are.

"You and I, Mrs. Winter, know what it feels like to hold a life in our hands. I don't mean ordinary responsibility, like babysitting or watching the stove or waiting for the lights when you cross the road—I mean somebody's life like a china vase in your hand"— she holds her saxophone aloft, her palm underneath the bell —"and if you wanted to, you could just...let go."

Thursday

On the corridor wall is a framed black-and-white photograph which shows a man retreating up a short flight of stairs, hunched and overcoated, his chin down and his collar up and the laces on his boots coming untied. You can't see his face or his hands, just the back of his overcoat and half a sole and a gray sock sliver and the top of his head. Onto the wall beside the staircase the man casts a bent accordion shadow. If you look closer at the shadow you will see that he is playing a saxophone as he ascends the stairs, but his body is hunched over the instrument and his elbows are close in to the sides of his body so no part of the sax is visible from behind. The shadow peels off to one side like an enemy, forking the image in two and betraying the saxophone that is hidden under his coat. The shadow-saxophone looks a little like a hookah pipe, dark and wispy and distorted on the brick wall and curving into his chin and into his dark and wispy shadow-hands like smoke.

The girls who sit in this corridor before their music lessons regard this photograph while they wait.

Friday

Isolde falters after the first six bars.

"I haven't practiced," she says at once. "I have got an excuse, though. Do you want to hear it?"

The saxophone teacher looks at her and sips her black-leaf tea. Excuses are almost her favorite part.

Isolde takes a moment to smooth her kilt and prepare. She draws a breath.

"I was watching TV last night," she says, "and Dad comes in with his face all serious and his fingers sort of picking at his tie like it's strangling him, and eventually he just takes it off and lays it to one side—"

She unhooks her saxophone from her neckstrap and places it upon a chair, miming loosening the neckstrap as if it has been very tight.

"—and says sit down, even though I'm already sitting down, and then rubs his hands together really hard."

She rubs her hands together really hard.

"He says, your mother thinks that I shouldn't tell you this just yet, but your sister has been abused by one of the teachers at school." She darts a look at the saxophone teacher now, quickly, and then looks away. "And then he says 'sexually,' just to clarify, in case I thought the teacher had yelled at her at a traffic light or something."

The overhead lights have dimmed and she is lit only by a pale flicking blue, a frosty sparkle like the on–off glow of a TV screen. The saxophone teacher is thrust into shadow so half her face is iron gray and the other half is pale and glinting.

"So he starts talking in this weird tight little voice about this Mr. Saladin or whatever, and how he teaches senior jazz band and orchestra and senior jazz ensemble, all on Wednesday morning one after the other. I won't have him till sixth form, and that's if I even want to take jazz band, because it clashes with netball so I'll have to make a choice.

"Dad's looking at me with this scared expression like I'm going to do something insane or really emotional and he won't know how to deal with it. So I go, How do you know? And he goes—"

She crouches down beside the chair, speaking earnestly and spreading her hands wide—

"Honey, from what I understand of it, he started off real slow, just resting his hand really lightly on her shoulder sometimes, like *that*."

Isolde reaches out and touches her fingertips to the upper end of the saxophone, which is lying on its side upon the chair. As her fingers touch the instrument a steady pulse begins, like a heartbeat. The teacher is sitting very still.

"And then sometimes when no one was watching he would lean close and breathe into her hair—"

She puts her cheek against the instrument and breathes down its length—

"—like that, really tentative and shy, because he doesn't know if she wants it yet and he doesn't want to get done. But she's friendly because she kind of likes him and she thinks she has a crush on him, and soon his hand is going down, down—"

Her hand snakes down the saxophone and trails around the edge of the bell—

"—down, and she sort of starts to respond, and she smiles at him in lessons sometimes and it makes his heart race, and when they're alone, in the music cupboard or after school or when they go places in his car, which they do sometimes, when they're alone he calls her my gypsy girl—he says it over and over, my gypsy girl, he says—and she wishes she had something to say back, something she could whisper into his hair, something really special, something nobody's ever said before."

The backing music ceases. Isolde looks at her teacher and says, "She can't think of anything."

The lights come up again, as normal. Isolde scowls and flops down on to an armchair. "But anyway," she says angrily, "she's run out of time, it's too late, because her friends have started to notice the way she is sometimes, the way she puts her chin down and to the side like she's flirting, and that's how it all starts to come undone, crashing down on itself like a castle of cards."

"I see why you haven't had time to practice," says the saxophone teacher.

"Even this morning," Isolde says, "I went to play some scales or whatever before school, but when I started playing she was all like, Can't you at least be *sensitive*? and ran out of the room with this fake sob noise which I knew was fake because if she was really crying she wouldn't have run off, she would have wanted me to see." Isolde digs the heel of her kilt pin into her knee. "They're treating her like a fucking artifact."

"Is that so unusual?" the sax teacher asks.

Isolde shoots her a vicious look. "It's *sick*," she says. "It's sick like when kids dress up their pets like real people, with clothes and wigs and stuff, and then make them walk on their back legs and take photos. It's just like that, but worse because you can see how much she's enjoying it."

"I'm sure your sister is not enjoying it," the saxophone teacher says.

"Dad said it would probably be years and years before Mr. Saladin gets properly convicted and goes to jail," Isolde says. "All the papers will say child abuse, but there won't be a child any more, she'll be an adult by then, just like him. It'll be like someone destroyed the scene of the crime on purpose, and built something clean and shiny in its place."

"Isolde," the saxophone teacher says, firmly this time, "I'm sure they are scared only because they know the sin is still there. They know it snuck up inside her and stuck fast, wedging itself into a place nobody knows about and will never find. They know that *his* sin was just an action, a foolish deadly fumble in the bright dusty lunchtime light, but hers—her sin is a condition, a sickness lodged somewhere deep inside for now and for always."

"My dad doesn't believe in sin," Isolde says. "We're atheists."

"It pays to be open minded," says the saxophone teacher.

"*I'll* tell you why they're so scared," Isolde says. "They're scared because now she knows everything they know. They're scared because now they've got no secrets left."

The saxophone teacher gets up suddenly and goes to the window. There is a long pause before Isolde speaks again.

"Dad just goes, I don't know how it happened, honey. What's

important is that now we know about it, it won't happen any-more."

Wednesday

"So they called off jazz band this morning," Bridget says. "They go, Mr. Saladin can't come in this afternoon. He's helping with an investigation."

She sucks her reed noisily.

"You know it's something really serious," she says, "when they cross between not enough information and too much. Normally, see, they would have just gone, Listen up, you lot, jazz band's canceled, you've got three minutes to get your shit together, get out and enjoy the sunshine for once, come on, I said move."

This girl is good at voices. She actually wanted to be Isolde, because Isolde has a better part, but this girl is pale and stringy and rumpled and always looks slightly alarmed, which are qual-ities that don't quite fit Isolde, and so she plays Bridget instead. In truth it is her longing to be an Isolde that most characterizes her as a Bridget: Bridget is always wanting to be somebody else.

"Or," she says, "they would have gone the other way, and told us more than we needed to know, but deliberately, so we knew it was a privilege. They would have done the wide-eyed solemn holy thing that goes, Come on everyone, we need your full attention, this is really important. Mr. Saladin's had to rush off because one of his family has fallen ill. Okay, now this could be really serious and it's really important you guys give him the space and consideration he needs if and when he comes back to class."

This is a theory that Bridget has been thinking about for some time, and she gleams with the pleasure of it. She screws down her reed and blows an experimental honk.

"Helping with an investigation," she says contemptuously,

returning to readjust the mouthpiece. "And they all came in together to say it, all in a pack or whatever, breathing together, quick breaths in and out, with their eyes back and forth sideways, and the principal at the front to break the wind, like the chief goose at the front of the V."

"Geese usually rotate, I think," the saxophone teacher says absently. "I gather it's quite hard work breaking wind." She is rifling through a stack of sheet music. The bookcase behind her is stuffed with old manuscripts and bleeding stray leaves on to the floor.

The saxophone teacher would never interrupt Isolde in such a dismissive fashion: that was one of Bridget's reasons for wanting the role. Bridget remembers all over again that she is pale and stringy and rumpled and thoroughly secondary, and then flushes with a new determination to reclaim the scene.

"So they shuffle in," she says, "in their V formation or whatever, this gray polyester army all trying really hard not to look at anybody in particular, especially not the big gaping hole next to first alto which is where Victoria usually sits."

Bridget says "Victoria" with emphasis and evident satisfaction. She looks at the saxophone teacher for effect, but the saxophone teacher is busy shuffling papers with her big veined hands and doesn't flicker.

"The doors to the practice rooms have little windows of reinforced glass so you can see in," Bridget says, trying harder this time. Her voice gets louder the harder she tries. "But Mr. Saladin pasted the booking sheet over his, so all you can see is the timetable and little slivers of white light all around the edge if the light's on inside. When Victoria had her woodwind tutorial all the slivers would go out."

"Found it!" says the saxophone teacher, and she holds up a handful of sheet music. "'The Old Castle' from *Pictures at an Exhibition*. I think you'll find this interesting, Bridget. We can talk about why the saxophone never really caught on as an orchestral instrument."

The saxophone teacher sometimes feels disgusted with herself for baiting Bridget in this way. "It's just that she tries so desperately hard," she said once to Bridget's mother. "That's what makes it so easy. If it wasn't so obvious that she was trying, I might be tempted to respect her a little more."

Bridget's mother nodded and nodded, and said, "Yes, we find that's often the trouble."

Now the saxophone teacher just looks at Bridget, standing there all stringy and rumpled and trying so desperately hard, and raises her eyebrows.

Bridget reddens with frustration and deliberately skips all the possible lines about Mussorgsky and *Pictures at an Exhibition* and Ravel and why the saxophone never really caught on as an orchestral instrument. She skips all that and goes straight for a line she likes.

"They treat it like a dosage," she says, even louder this time. "It's like a vaccination where they give you a little slice of a disease so your body can get a defense ready for the real thing. They're frightened because it's a disease they haven't tried on us before, and so they're trying to vaccinate us without telling us what the disease really is. They want to inject us very secretly, without us noticing. It won't work."

They are really looking at each other now. The saxophone teacher takes a moment to align the pile of papers with the edge of the rug before she says, "Why won't it work, Bridget?"

"Because we noticed," says Bridget, breathing hard through her nose. "We were watching."

Monday

Julia's feet are always scuffing, and she has a scab around her mouth.

"They called an assembly for the whole form this morning,"

she says, "and the counselor was there, all puffed up like he'd never felt so important in his life."

She talks over her shoulder while she unpacks her case. The saxophone teacher is sitting in a slice of cold sun by the window, watching the gulls wheel and shit. The clouds are low.

"They started talking in these special quiet honey voices like we'd break if they spoke too loud. They go, You're all aware of the rumors that have been circulating this past week. It's important that we talk through some things together so we can all be sure of where we're at."

Julia turns on her heel, fits her sax to her neckstrap, and stands there for a moment with her hands on her hips. The sax is slung across her body like a weapon.

"The counselor is a retard," she says definitively. "Me and Katrina went once in third form because Alice Franklin had sex in a movie theater and we were scared she'd become a skank and ruin her life by having kids by accident. We told him all about it and how scared we were, and Katrina even cried. He just sat there and blinked and he kept nodding and nodding, but really slowly like he was programmed at a quarter speed, and then when we'd run out of things to say and Katrina had stopped crying he opened his drawer and got a piece of paper and drew three circles inside each other, and wrote *You* and then *Your Family* and then *Your Friends*, and he said, That's the way it is, isn't it? And then he said we could keep the piece of paper if we wanted."

Julia gives a mirthless snort and opens her plastic music folder.

"What happened to Alice Franklin?" asks the saxophone teacher.

"Oh, we found out later she was lying," Julia says.

"She didn't have sex in a movie theater."

"No."

Julia takes a moment to adjust the spidery legs of the music stand.

"Why would she lie to you?" the saxophone teacher asks politely.

Julia makes a sweeping gesture with her hand. "She was probably just *bored*," she says. In her mouth the word is noble and magnificent.

"I see," says the saxophone teacher.

"So anyway they go, Maybe we could start the ball rolling by asking if anyone's got something they want to get off their chest? And one of the girls started crying right then, before anything had even happened for real, and the counselor just about wet his pants with joy, and he goes, Nothing anybody says this morning will go further than this room, or some shit. So this girl starts saying something lame, and her friend reaches over and holds her hand or something sick like that, and then everyone starts sharing and saying things about trust and betrayal and confidence and feeling all confused and scared . . . and it's going to be one fuck of a long morning."

Julia darts a glance over toward the saxophone teacher to see if the word has any effect, but the saxophone teacher just gives her a wintry smile and waits. Bridget would have balked and fluttered and turned scarlet and wondered about it for a long time afterward, but Julia doesn't. She just smirks and takes unnecessary care in clipping the slippery pages to the edge of the music stand.

"So after a while," Julia says, "the counselor goes, What is harassment, girls?, looking at us all eager and encouraging like when teachers are torn between really wanting you to get the right answer but also really wanting you to be wrong so they can have the pleasure of telling you themselves. Then he goes, speaking softly and solemnly like he's revealing something nobody else knows, Harassment doesn't have to be touching, my darlings. Harassment can also be watching. Harassment can be if someone watches you in a way that you don't like.

"So I put up my hand and I go, Does it become harassment

because of what they watch? Or because of what they imagine while they're watching? They all looked at me and I went really red, and the counselor touched his fingertips together and gave me this long look like, I know what you're doing, you're trying to sabotage the trust thing we've got going here, and I'm going to answer your question because I have to, but I'm not going to give you the answer you want."

The saxophone teacher stands up finally and picks up her own saxophone as if to say "enough." But Julia is already saying it, thrust on by a strange sort of red-cheeked momentum.

"*I* imagine things when I watch people," is what Julia says.

Friday

Isolde is waiting outside in the hall. She can hear the faint rumble of the saxophone teacher's voice through the wall as the 4:00 lesson draws to a close. Here in the deserted hallway Isolde takes a moment to enjoy the backstage silence before she is cued to knock and enter. She inhales and with her tongue she tastes the calm and careless privacy of a person utterly unobserved.

Normally she would be flooded with pre-tutorial dread, leafing through her sheet music, practicing in mime, her eyes following the music on her lap and her splayed hands moving on the empty air. But today she is not thinking about her lesson. She is sitting still and with all her mind trying to preserve and capture a private swollen feeling in the deep well of her chest.

It is like a little pocket of air has rushed into her mouth and sent a little shiver down her back and tugged at the empty half-basin of her pelvic bone. She feels a prolonged and dislocated swoop in her belly and a yank of emptiness in her rib cage, and suddenly she is much too hot. Isolde feels this way sometimes when she is in the bath, or when she watches people kiss on television, or in bed when she runs her fingertips down the soft curve of her belly and imagines that her hand is not her own. Most often the feeling descends inexplicably—at a bus stop, perhaps, or in the lunch line, or waiting for a bell to ring.

She thinks, Did I feel this when I saw my sister for the first time as a sexual thing? After Dad touched my head and said, This is going to be hard time, these next few weeks, and then left me to watch TV, and after a while Victoria came in and sat down and looked over at me, and then she said, Fantastic, so now everyone knows. And we sat and watched the tail end of some C-grade thriller on the Thursday night special, except I couldn't concentrate and all I could think was, How? How were you able to turn your head and look hard at him and crane up and kiss his mouth? How were you not paralyzed with fear and indecision? How did you know that he would receive you, gather you up and press hard against you and even give out a little strangled moan like a cry, like a cry in the back of his throat?

Here in the hallway Isolde is thinking, Did I feel this feeling then, that night? Did I feel this jangled swoop of dread and longing, this elevator-dive, this strange suspended prelude to a sneeze?

Later maybe she will identify the feeling as some abstracted form of arousal, an irregular toll that plucks at her body now and again, like an untouched string vibrating in harmonic sympathy with a piano nearby. Later she might conclude that the feeling is a little like a hunger-stab, not the gnawing ever-present lust of real hunger, just a stab that strikes like a warning—here and gone. But by then, that time in years to come when she has come to know her body's tides and tolls and can say, *This is frustration* and *This is lust* and *This is longing, a nostalgic sexual longing that draws me back to a time before*, by then everything will be classified, everything will have a name and a shape, and the modest compass of her desires will be circumscribed by the limits of what she has known, what she has experienced, what she has felt. So far Isolde has experienced nothing and so this feeling does not mean *I must have sex tonight* or *I am still full from last night, still brimming.* It does not mean *Who must I be in love with, to feel this pull?* or *Again I am wanting the thing I cannot have.* It is not yet a feeling that points her in a direction. It is just the feeling of a vacuum, a void waiting to be filled.

You can't tell any of this from Isolde's face: she is just sitting in the gray half-light, her hands in her lap, looking at the wall.

Monday

"I am never quite sure," the saxophone teacher says, "what is truly meant when the mothers say, I want my daughter to experience what was denied to me.

"In my experience the most forceful and aggressive mothers are always the least inspired, the most unmusical of souls, all of them profoundly unsuccessful women who wear their daughter's image on their breast like a medal, like a bright deflection from their own unshining selves. When these mothers say, I want her to fully experience everything that was denied to me, what they rightly mean is, I want her to fully *appreciate* everything that was denied to me. What they rightly mean is, The paucity of my life will only be thrown into relief if my daughter has everything. On its own, my life is ordinary and worthless and nothing. But if my daughter is rich in experience and rich in opportunity, then people will come to pity me: the smallness of my life and my options will not be *incapacity*; it will be *sacrifice*. I will be pitied more, and respected more, if I raise a daughter who is everything that I am not."

The saxophone teacher runs her tongue over her teeth. She says, "The successful mothers—musical women, sporting women, literate women, content and brimful women, women who were denied nothing, women whose parents paid for lessons when they were girls—the successful mothers are the least forceful, always. They do not need to oversee, or wield, or pick a fight on their daughter's behalf. They are complete in themselves. They are complete, and so they demand completeness in everyone else. They can stand back and see their daughters as something set apart, as something whole and therefore untouchable."

The saxophone teacher goes to the window to let down the blinds. It is almost dusk.

Tuesday

Mrs. Tyke waits in the corridor for ten minutes before the saxophone teacher opens the door.

"I just wanted to touch base, really," she says once they are inside, "in light of this dreadful scandal up at the school. I'm thinking of the girls."

"I understand," the saxophone teacher says, pouring out two mugs of tea. One of the mugs has a picture of a saxophonist on a desert island and the words "Sax on the Beach." The other mug is white and says "Let's Talk About Sax." The saxophone teacher returns the jug to its cradle and carefully selects a teaspoon.

"Mrs. Tyke," she says, "you would very much like, I think, to sew your children's hands to your waistband, just to keep them with you always, their little legs swaying when you hurry and trailing on the asphalt when you stroll. If you turned on your heel very fast your children would fan out around you like a sunburst pleated skirt. You would be a goddess in a corset and a bustle, your children radiating out from you like so many graceful little spokes."

"I'm thinking of the girls, that's all," says Mrs. Tyke. She holds out both hands to receive her mug of black-leaf tea. The saxophone teacher lets the silence creep until Mrs. Tyke bursts out, "I'm just worried about some of the *ideas* she's bringing home. They're ideas she didn't have before. They stick in the side of her mouth like a walnut, and when she talks I can see glimpses of these ideas—just a flash every so often when she opens her mouth wide—but it's enough to make me very nervous. It's like she's tasting them, or poking them around her mouth with her tongue. They're ideas she didn't have before."

She blinks dolefully at the saxophone teacher, then shrugs in a helpless fashion and ducks her head to sip her tea.

"Can I tell you what I think the problem is?" says the saxophone teacher in a special quiet honey voice. "I think you feel a little bit as if that horrible man up at the school, that vile and disgusting man, has left a big fat fingerprint on your glasses, and it doesn't matter what you're looking at, all you see is his fingers."

She stands up to pace.

"I know you wanted your daughter to find out about it all the ordinary way. You wanted her to find out behind the bike sheds, or underneath the bleachers on the rugby field, or in Social Studies, the facts written on the whiteboard with a felt-tipped pen. You wanted her to sneak glances at magazines and at movies she wasn't allowed to see. You wanted her to start off with some sort of blind sticky grope in her mate's front room on a Saturday night while her friends are outside being sick into flowerpots. That might happen more than once. It might become a phase. But you'd be prepared for it."

As Mrs. Tyke watches the saxophone teacher she lets something steal across her face, not something as crude and bold as realization or awakening, but something which registers only as a slackening of her features, a tiny release. It's such a good performance the saxophone teacher almost forgets she's acting.

"You wanted her to finally get a boyfriend in sixth form maybe, some prancing, empty sort of boy you didn't really like, and you wanted to catch her with him eventually, coming home early because you had a funny feeling, and seeing them on the couch, or on the floor, or in her bedroom among her teddy bears and her frilly pink cushions that she doesn't really like but she'll never throw away.

"I respect these things that you wanted for your daughter," the saxophone teacher says. "I imagine they must be the things that every good mother wants. It's a terrible thing that this venomous little man should have stolen your daughter's innocence so slyly, without ever having laid a finger on her, shoving his dirty little secrets down her throat like candy from a brown paper bag.

"But what you need to understand, my darling," she whispers, "is that this little taste your daughter has had is a taste of what could be. She's swallowed it. It's inside her now."

TWO

February

"The first term," they said, "is essentially a physical and emotional undoing. You will unlearn everything you have ever learned, peeling it off skin by skin, stripping down and down until your impulse shines through."

"This Institute," they said, "cannot teach you how to be an actor. We cannot give you a map or a recipe or an alphabet that will teach you how to act or how to feel. What we do at this Institute is not teaching by accumulation, collecting skills as one might collect a marble or a token or a charm. Here at this Institute we teach by elimination. We help you learn to eliminate yourself."

"You may break or be broken," they said. "This happens."

The fat one on the end leaned forward and said, with emphasis, "A good actor makes a gift of himself."

"An actor is someone who offers up his body publicly," they said. "This can happen in one of two ways. The actor can exploit himself, treat his body as a ready and obedient instrument, a product to be sold. At this Institute we do not favor this approach. We do not breed confectioners or clowns. You are not here to sell your body: you are here to sacrifice it."

And then they said, "You're not at high school anymore."

February

"I graduated from the Institute in December," said the golden boy, his gaze passing from face to face with calm disinterest. "They asked me to come and talk to you guys today about my experience of the program and where I'm headed now and maybe you can ask some questions if you have any."

He sat cross-legged on the gymnasium floor like a prophet.

"God, I envy you guys," he said, and then he smiled and smiled. "Not too virginal, not too defiled. Sitting there all shiny and pregnant with the best still yet to come."

The golden boy looked at them, the tight pale ring of nervous faces and black tee-shirts still creased down the middle with newness.

"The three years I spent at this Institute didn't just shape me as an artist. They shaped me as a person," he said. "This place woke me up."

He flushed brightly as if he were describing a lover he had lost.

"Everything you've ever slammed shut gets reopened here," he said. "If none of you had auditioned and been accepted you would all have become cemented, cast in plaster and molded for the rest of your adult life. That's what's happening to everybody else, out there. In here you never congeal. You never set or crust over. Every possibility is kept open—it *must* be kept open. You learn to hold all these possibilities in your fist and never let any of them go."

There was a silence. The golden boy smoothed the knees of his corduroy pants and said, as if he had just thought of it, "Remember that anybody who is clever enough to set you free is always clever enough to enslave you."

October

Stanley was disappointed with his life so far. Here, on the eve of his eighteenth birthday, he stood in the rich dusty quiet of the shuttered foyer in a paralysis of bitterness and dissatisfaction. He was thinking about everything he was not.

Stanley had expected to be savage and dissenting and righteous as a teenager—he had yearned for it, even—and grew more and more dissatisfied as his high-school years passed politely by. He had expected to drink whisky from a paper-bagged bottle by the river, and slip his cold hands up a girl's skirt in the patch of scrub beyond the tennis courts, and take shots at passing cars with a potato-gun from a neighbor's garage roof. He had expected to drink himself blind and vandalize the bus shelters in the suburbs, to drive without a license, to retreat from his family, to turn sour, and to frighten his mother, maybe, by refusing to eat or leave his room. This was his entitlement, his rightful lot, and instead he had spent his high-school years playing gentlemanly sport and watching family television, admiring from a distance the boys brave enough to fight each other, and longing for every girl he passed to lift her head and look him in the eye.

Stanley heard the voice of the Institute tutors in his mind. "The real thrill of the stage," they said, "is the thrill of knowing that at any moment something might go wrong. At any moment something on the stage might break or fall over; someone might miss their cue, someone might botch the lighting, someone might forget their accent or their lines. You are never fearful watching a film, because what you are watching is always complete, always the same and always perfect; but you are often fearful watching a play, in case something goes foul and you must then suffer the private embarrassment of watching the actors flounder and repair themselves. But at the same time, in the silky dark of the auditorium, you ache for something to go wrong. You desire it utterly. You feel tender toward any actor whose hat falls off, whose button breaks. You gasp and applaud when an actor trips and rights himself. And if you see a mistake that others in the audience miss, then you feel a special privilege, as if you are glimpsing a seam of a secret undergarment, something infinitely private, like a scarlet bite-mark on the inside of a woman's thigh."

Stanley stood in the foyer of the Institute and looked about him. Here was another possible life that was in his power to claim, another life he wanted, just as he had wanted, as a shy and useless teenager, to be unfeeling and disrespectful and casual and vile. Now, as then, he felt the weight of a terrible inertia pin him to the foyer floor. He suffered all over again the disappointing and quotable truth that the world would not come to him, or wait for him, or even pause: if he waited, this life would simply pass him by. Stanley thought about this and felt deflated and terribly short-changed.

In his sixth-form school production he had been cast as Horatio, a part which pleased him—Horatio was a memorable name, at least, the only one he had heard of before he encountered the play. Everyone remembered Horatio. It was a name that stuck. Horatio it was who endured, critical and strident in the cultural memory, as the less resonant, less pronounceable characters peeled off and dropped away. Stanley's part was pared almost to nothing by the sharp-nosed drama teacher who said, "People don't want to sit here for three and a half hours," and in rehearsals remarked, "You *are* a bit of a Horatio, aren't you, Stanley?

You're a Horatio through and through." Stanley nodded and smiled and mouthed "Thank you" and felt a private happy-thrill, and didn't truly apprehend her meaning until several months later when he realized that the comment had been less than kind. Even on stage as he trotted about in Hamlet's brooding shadow, flaring his doublet and flexing his hose, he had not really understood that his part existed merely to throw other, more interesting characters into greater profundity and sharper relief. His mother called him "Wonderful," and in the exhilarated lineup of the curtain call he had been close as he could be to the center: by Hamlet's side, holding Hamlet's sweaty hand.

At the end of seventh form Stanley had seen the ragged call for auditions stapled to the pin-board in Careers Advice and simply fished for a pen and written his name. He supposed that he had wanted to be an actor since he was a child. Acting was part of a child's primary lexicon of adult jobs: teacher, doctor, actor, lawyer, fireman, vet. Choosing to become an actor did not require originality or forethought. It was not like choosing to be a jockey, or a greengrocer, or an events manager for a local trust, where part of the choosing meant seeking and creating the choice; it did not depend on opportunity or introspection. Choosing to become an actor was simply a matter of reaching for one of these discrete and packaged categories with both hands. Stanley did not think about this as he wrote his name. The auditions sheet was watermarked and heavy, and the emblem of the Institute was stamped in bronze.

Later, wishing to amplify the memory of this unremarkable decision, he imagined that it was this moment, when he lifted his pen up to the paper and pressed hard to unstick the ink in the roller-ball tip so that for an instant his fingertips were white and bloodless and hard—this moment, he imagined, was the moment when he seized an opportunity to transform from a Horatio into something utterly new.

October

"Welcome to the first stage of the audition process," said the Head of Acting, and he briefly smiled. "We believe here that an untrained actor is a liar merely." He was standing behind the desk with all his fingertips splayed upon the green leather. "As you are now," he said, "you are all liars, not calm persuasive liars but anxious blushing liars full of doubt. Some of you will not gain entrance to this Institute, and you will remain liars forever."

There was scattered laughter, mostly uncomprehending and from the ones who would not gain entrance. The Head of Acting smiled again, the smile passing over his face like a shadow.

Stanley was sitting stiffly at the back. He knew some of the boys from high school, but sat apart from them just in case they betrayed or encouraged some aspect of him that he wished to leave behind. The room was tense with hope and wanting.

"So," the Head of Acting said. "What happens at this Institute? How do we carve up the strange convulsive epileptic rhythm of the days? What violence is inflicted here, and what can you do to minimize the damage?"

He let the question settle like dust.

"This weekend is a virtual simulation of the kind of learning environment that students at the Institute encounter daily," he said. "Today we are holding classes in improvisation, mime, song, movement and theater history, and tomorrow you will extensively workshop and rehearse a text in collaboration with a small group of others. You are all expected to participate fully in these lessons and to try your hardest to demonstrate to us the level of commitment you are prepared to offer us should you be invited to study here.

"We will be watching you over the course of the weekend, patroling the edges of the rooms and taking notes. If you are successful after this first audition weekend, we will invite you back for an interview and a more formal audition. Does anyone have any questions about how the weekend will be run?"

They all had paper numbers pinned to their chests like marathon runners. Number 45 raised his hand.

"Why don't you just hold ordinary auditions like the other acting schools?" he said. "Like where you prepare two monologues, one modern and one classical."

"Because we do not want to attract that kind of student," said the Head of Acting, "the kind of student who is good at self-advertisement, who will choose two contrasting monologues that perfectly demonstrate the range of their skill and the depth of their cunning. We do not care about the difference between modern and classical. We do not want students who color-code their notes and start their essays weeks in advance."

Number 45 blushed, feeling that he had been implicated as a student who color-coded his notes and started his essays weeks in advance. The other hopefuls looked at him with pity and privately resolved to keep their distance.

"Acting is a profession which requires a kind of wholeness," the Head of Acting said. "My advice to you today is this: your ideas about talent count for nothing here. The moment when we decide to move you to the Yes list—the moment when we decide you deserve a place at this Institute—might not be a moment when you are actually acting. It might be a moment when you're supporting someone else. It might be when you yourself are watching. It might be when you're preparing yourself for an exercise. It might be when you're standing by yourself with your hands in your pockets and looking at the floor."

The strategists among them were nodding gravely, already planning to let themselves appear to be caught unawares as frequently as possible. They made a mental note to remember to stand for a moment with their hands in their pockets, looking at the floor.

Stanley looked around at his rivals, all of them eager and fervent like candidates for martyrdom, the Head of Acting looming above them, swollen with the wonderful honor of choosing the first to die.

"Let me hand over to the Head of Improvisation," the Head of Acting said. "Good luck."

October

The longest corridor at the Institute bordered the gymnasium for its entire length. The corridor was glassed on one side with long curtained windows and recessed doors, and on the other side the wall was uninterrupted save for the heavy double doors into the gymnasium that swung out halfway down. On this long wall were fixed a number of costumes preserved and flattened against the high brick, their empty arms spread wide, like ghosts pinned by a sudden and petrifying shaft of light.

Stanley paused to look. He supposed that the costumes had been retained to mark notable performances, and he moved forward to read the first brass plaque mounted underneath a pair of limp tartan trousers and a jaunty ruffled shirt. It bore neither the title of the play nor the name of the actor, but merely the name of the character and a date, engraved as if on the side of a tomb. Belville. 1957. The plaques continued neatly down the wall. Stanley walked along the corridor as one paying respects to the dead, looking up at the stiff splayed arms and limp trouser-legs and tattered lace, the older costumes ragged and flecked with mold. Vindici, Ferdinand, Mrs. Alving, The Court Envoy. He paused at a heavy royal costume, brocaded in silver and satin lined. One of the splayed kingly sleeves had fallen away from the wall and hung limply by his side, so the effigy seemed to be pointing toward the foyer, the fabric of the fallen arm dragging his shoulder painfully down. The War Minister. Hal. The solemn procession of costumes down the wall was like an eerie trickle of spirits from a leak in the bounds of the underworld. He shivered. Perdita. Volpone. The Toad.

November

"They'll do terrible things to you there," Stanley's father said. "You'll get in touch with your emotions and your inner eye and worse. I won't recognize you this time next year. You'll just be this big pink ball of feeling."

"Look at all the famous people who've come through," said Stanley, taking the brochure off his father and pointing to the list inside the back cover, where all the television and film stars were asterisked in red. The pages of the brochure were already soft from being turned and turned.

"I look forward to seeing you on daytime television," said Stanley's father. "That's my son, I'll say out loud, to nobody. There on screen with the airbrushing and the toupee. That's my son."

"Did you see the photos of the grounds?" Stanley said, flipping back through the brochure until he found them. "It's in the old museum building. It's all stone and mosaic floors and stuff, and big high windows."

"I see that."

"Three hundred people audition."

"That's great, Stanley."

"And only twenty get in."

"That's great."

"I know it's just a beginning," Stanley said.

A waiter arrived and Stanley's father ordered wine. Stanley leaned back and looked around. The restaurant was starched and shadowy, full of murmuring and quiet laughter and cologne. The ceiling was strung with little red lanterns glinting back and forth above them.

The waiter bowed and moved off. Stanley's father shook out his cuffs and smiled his therapy smile. He pushed the glossy brochure back across the tablecloth.

"I'm proud of you," he said. "It's going to be great. But you know, we're working for opposing teams now."

"What do you mean?" Stanley said.

"Theater is all about the unknown, right? Theater has its roots in magic and ritual and sacrifice, and magic and ritual and sacrifice depend on some element of mystery. Psychology is all about getting rid of mystery, turning superstitions and fears into things that we can understand." He winked and speared an olive with a toothpick. "We're practically at war."

Stanley felt stumped, as he often did when his father said something clever. Each year after this meal was over Stanley lay in bed and thought for hours about what he could have said back that would have been cleverer. He chased the oily bubbles of vinegar around his dish with his finger.

"Do you disagree?" his father asked, looking at him sharply as he chewed.

"Sort of," Stanley said. "I guess I thought...I guess for me acting seems like a way of finding out about a person, or getting into a person. I mean, you have to understand sadness to be able to act it. I don't know. That seems kind of similar to what you do."

"Ah-ha!" said Stanley's father with the unpleasant greedy quickness of someone who likes to triumph in an argument. "So do you think actors know more about ordinary people than ordinary people know about themselves?"

"No," Stanley said, "but I'm not sure that psychologists know more about ordinary people than they know about themselves either."

His father burst out laughing and slapped the table.

"Aren't you supposed to be giving me life advice and passing on a torch or something?" Stanley asked, to change the subject.

"Shit," said his father. "I would have come prepared. How about you just tell me all the new cuss words, and we can swap dirty jokes. I've never been to drama school. Don't ask me about my feelings."

"I don't know any new cuss words," said Stanley. "I think all the old ones are still current."

There was a small pause.

"I've got a joke for you," said Stanley's father. "How do you give a priest a vasectomy?"

"I don't know," said Stanley.

"Kick the choirboy in the back of the head."

Stanley laughed and felt disgusted that his own father was more outrageous than he was. He started flicking through the brochure again just in case he'd missed something.

The wine arrived. Stanley's father made a great performance of tasting it, rolling it around in the bottom of his glass and inspecting the label on the bottle. "That's fine," he said to the waiter at last, nodding briefly at their glasses, and then switching his smile back to Stanley. "So, you want some life advice," he said.

"Not really," said Stanley. "I just thought you were going to do the big 'now you're all grown up' thing."

"You want psychobabble?"

"No."

"Kid, you got good blood and a fine pair of shoes."

"It doesn't matter."

"Did I tell you about my client who set herself on fire?"

"I heard you telling Roger."

"Life advice," said Stanley's father, holding up his glass for a toast. "Right. I've got something good and nasty. Stanley, to mark your rite of passage I am going to tell you a secret."

They touched glasses and sipped.

"Okay," said Stanley reluctantly.

His father stroked his lapel with his fingertips, his glass

poised and careless in his other hand. He looked rich and camp and deadly. "I am going to tell you how to make a million dollars," he said.

Stanley had the hot frustrated feeling again, but all he said was Okay. He even smiled.

His father said, "Okay. I want you to think of your time at high school. Five years, right? During those five years, same as during anyone's five years at any high school, there was one kid in your year who died. Yes?"

"I guess so."

"Maybe he drove too fast, drank too much, played with guns, whatever—there is always one kid who dies. Did you know, Stanley," he said, "that you can take out life insurance on a person without them knowing?"

Stanley just looked at him.

"And the premiums on school kids," his father continued, "are really, *really* low. Provided they don't have any reasons to think these kids are going to die. You can take out a million-dollar life insurance policy on a kid for something like two hundred a year."

"Dad," said Stanley disbelievingly.

"All you'd need to do is pick it. All you'd need to do is to get in there and do some research and get some information that would give you the edge."

"Dad," Stanley said again.

His father put his hands up like an innocent man, and laughed.

"Hey, I'm giving you gold here," he said. "Think of your kid. The one who died at your school. Could you have picked it beforehand? If you could have predicted it, then you could have got in there and made something good of it. Here's your life advice, Stanley: that is how people get rich. That's the only secret. They see things are going to happen before they happen, and they pounce."

Stanley's father was smiling his therapy smile.

"I couldn't have picked it," Stanley said at last. "The boy at my school. He was hit on his skateboard coming home from the shop. Out of all of them, I'd never have picked him."

"Shame," his father said. He didn't say anything further. He toyed with his fork and reached for his wine and watched Stanley over the frail rim of the glass as he drank.

Stanley fingered the drama school brochure unhappily. He was hot and uncomfortable in his suit jacket, like a chicken trussed up to roast. "What about me?" he said. "Can you see what's going to happen before it happens?"

His father leaned forward and stabbed the tablecloth with a bony white finger.

"I can see," he said, "you are going to have a great year. You're going to be great."

October

"Acting is not a form of imitation," the Head of Improvisation said briskly, after the hopefuls had assembled in a ragged cross-legged ellipsis on the rehearsal-room floor. Near the door the Head of Acting was hovering with his clipboard, watching with a studied indifference and pinching his pen in his fingers as he measured the worth and quality of each student against the next.

The Head of Improvisation said, "Acting is not about making a copy of something that already exists. The proscenium arch is *not* a window. The stage is *not* a little three-walled room where life goes on as normal. Theater is a *concentrate* of life as normal. Theater is a *purified version* of real life, an extraction, an essence of human behavior that is stranger and more tragic and more perfect than everything that is ordinary about me and you."

The Head of Improvisation plucked a tennis ball from the

canvas bag at her side and tossed it across the group at one of the hopefuls. The boy caught the ball in the heels of both hands. "Don't look at the Head of Acting," the Head of Improvisation said. "Pretend he isn't there. Look at me."

She held her palms open and the boy tossed the ball sheepishly back. The Head of Acting made a savage little note on his clipboard with his pen.

"Let's think about the ancient world for a second," the Head of Improvisation said, shifting to tuck her legs underneath herself. "In the ancient world a statue of Apollo or Aphrodite did not exist to trick people into thinking that the statue really *was* the god, or even that the statue really was a true *likeness* of the god. The function of the statue was simply a site of access. The statue existed so people could approach or experience the god *at that site*. Yes? Is everyone with me?"

She tossed a tennis ball to another hopeful, who flinched but managed to catch it and lob it carefully back. The Head of Improvisation caught it and held it in both hands for a moment, pushing thoughtfully at the balding fur, indenting the hard rubber of the ball and letting it snap back against her hand.

"So this statue is definitely not the *real thing*," she continued. "The statue is not Apollo himself—anybody would agree with that, right? And it's not a facsimile of the real thing either. It's not a likeness of Apollo, a clue to what Apollo might *actually* look like, or what clothes he might *actually* wear. It's neither of those things. The statue is only a site which makes worship possible. It is a site which makes it unnecessary to seek that particular connection elsewhere. That's all. Why is what I'm saying important?"

She tossed the tennis ball at a girl across the group.

"Is it because that's what theater is?" the girl said quickly, catching the ball neatly with her fingertips and pausing to answer the question before lobbing it back. "Theater isn't real life, and it isn't a perfect copy of real life. It's just a point of access."

35

"*Yes*," the Head of Improvisation said, catching the ball and slamming it decisively into the palm of her other hand.

The girl smiled quickly and darted a look at the Head of Acting to see if he had seen her triumph. He wasn't watching.

The Head of Improvisation said, "The stage is not real life, and the stage is not a copy of real life. Just like the statue, the stage is only a place where things are *made present*. Things that would not ordinarily happen are made to happen on stage. The stage is a *site* at which people can access things that would otherwise not be available to them. The stage is a place where we can witness things in such a way that it becomes unnecessary for us to feel or perform these things ourselves. What am I talking about here?"

The question was too specific, and the hopefuls frowned at her in silence and pursed their lips to show they didn't know. The Head of Improvisation was almost quivering. She scanned their faces quickly but without disappointment, already pursed and half-smiling as if the answer was waiting to bubble up and out of her in a kind of overflow of joy.

"Catharsis," she said at last, crowing out the word. "Catharsis is what I am talking about. Catharsis is a word that all of you should know. Catharsis is the thing that makes *your* job worthwhile."

October

In the foyer there were two porcelain masks rising like glassy conspirators out of a porcelain basin filled with water. Comedy was turned away, staring with gleeful dead eyes down the corridor past the secretary's office and the trophy cabinet and the loos. Tragedy craned upward. The tragic mask was supported by two brass pipes that ran up out of the water behind the jaw and the cheekbone and into the porcelain under-rim of each staring tragic eye. When the fountain was turned on, these pipes sucked the water up out of the basin and forced the tragic mask to cry.

There was a film of brassy grime around the waterline and at the bottom of the basin a few hopeful silver coins. On the pedestal underneath the basin was a plaque which said:

The Mind Believes What It Sees
and Does What It Believes:
that is the secret of the fascination

October

When he saw the pair of masks Stanley's first thought was that some people turned the corners of their mouth down when they smiled and some people smiled when they were very unhappy. He was not looking at the masks now. He stood by the fountain with his hands in his pockets and frowned into the basin as he tried to dull the sick thump of his heart. The water had not yet been switched on and the surface was tight and smooth like the skin of a drum, the blue-veined porcelain masks dry and discolored in the still of the morning.

Stanley was almost an hour early, unable to bear any longer the tiny orbit around his bedroom as again and again he flattened his hair and checked over his application form and felt in his bag for the hard laminated edge of his audition number that he would later pin to his chest with a pair of tiny golden safety pins. The foyer was empty. The secretary's office was closed and shuttered and all the arterial corridors were dark. He stood very still and tried to ride out his nervousness, as if it were seasickness or hypochondria or a phantom chill.

He heard the soft thud of the auditorium door and turned to see a boy approaching, red faced and disheveled and carrying an ancient disc gramophone, the fluted brass horn angled over his shoulder. It looked heavy. He was clutching the gramophone against him with both hands underneath its felted base, peering around it to check his way was clear and stepping delicately as he picked his way down the dark corridor.

"Hey," he called, "are you a techie? You don't have a key to the main office, do you?"

"Sorry," Stanley said. "I'm here for the audition."

The boy peered at him. "Oh, you're one of the hopefuls," he said dispassionately. "I forgot it was that weekend already. You nervous?"

Stanley shrugged. "Yeah," he said. He flapped his arms a couple of times and tried to think of something adequately general to say, but nothing came. "Are you an actor?" he asked instead.

"No, I'm Wardrobe," the boy said. "We're just packing out *The Beautiful Machine*. Closing night last night and they need the theater tomorrow."

"What's *The Beautiful Machine*?" Stanley asked. The boy had halted at the foyer's periphery, and it felt a little odd, the two of them calling out across such a large and marble space.

"The first-year devised theater project," the boy said. "It's kind of like proving yourself to the Institute, going off and doing something completely on your own in your first year. The things they come up with would blow your mind. They put it on properly at the end of the year, lights and everything."

"Oh," Stanley said.

"You should have gone," the boy said. "Closing night last night. It was kickass." He nodded toward the gramophone he was carrying. "Lots of musical guys in the batch this year so we went with a sort of a musical thing, really diverse and abstract. If you'd seen it, it would've blown your mind."

Stanley watched the boy inflate, and noted the shift from *they* to *we*. He sensed that *diverse* and *abstract* were key words, buzz words that had the power to set the speaker apart and mark him as one of the chosen. This boy was studied in his carelessness, tossing his head like a pony and turning his hip out so he stood like a model in a menswear magazine.

"This your first time auditioning?" the boy asked. He moved now, walking over to the secretary's office door and bending at the knee to place the gramophone carefully on the floor below the wall of oiled golden pigeonholes. Stanley heard the voice of his high-school drama teacher: Move as you say your line, not after you say it.

"Yeah," he said. "Should I be worried?"

"Nah," the boy said coolly. "Just relax and have fun and don't try too hard. It's way less of a big deal than everyone makes out."

"Did you have to audition for Wardrobe?"

"No."

Stanley waited, but the boy didn't say anything further. He straightened up and tried the door of the secretary's office half-heartedly, but it was locked. He looked again at Stanley.

"The thing that's strange about this place," he said, "is that nobody has anything terrible to say. Even the ones who don't get in—have you talked to the ones who don't get in?"

"No," Stanley said.

"They always say, I know I want it now. I've seen a glimpse of what goes on in there and I might not have got in but I've got a fire in me now and by God I'm going to work and work and try again next year and I'm going to keep auditioning until I get in. They say, What an honor and a privilege to have been able to audition with these amazing people, spend a weekend at the Institute and get a glimpse into where real talent comes from. They say, That place is truly a place of awakening. Do you find that weird?"

Stanley shrugged uncertainly. He had stepped back a half-step while the boy was speaking and he could feel the radiating cool of the porcelain basin against the small of his back.

"Nobody gives the finger as they walk out the door. Nobody says, Thanks a fucking heap. Nobody says, I didn't want to come to your pissant ugly school for dicks anyway. Nobody says, Bullshit I'm not as good as that guy, or that guy, you tell me exactly why I didn't get in. Nobody says anything terrible at all. Do you honestly not find that weird?"

"It's a prestigious school. I guess people just feel really strongly about that," said Stanley.

"Yeah," said the boy, contemptuous all of a sudden, and visibly dismissing Stanley as a person with nothing to offer and nothing to say. "Anyway, good luck. Might see you round here next year."

"Yeah," said Stanley. He felt ashamed of his own dullness but he was too preoccupied with his anxiety about the audition to care. He turned back to the fountain and shoved his hands viciously back into his pockets, listening until he heard the boy's footsteps dwindle away down the corridor and finally the heavy velvet thump of the auditorium door.

THREE

Thursday

The morning paper reads *Teacher Denies Sex With Student*.

"Poor Mr. Saladin," says the saxophone teacher. "Poor Mr. Saladin, with his slender hands and his throbbing lonely heart and his face like—"

"It doesn't show his face," interrupts Patsy, who is feeling cranky. "He's holding his jacket over his head."

The phone rings.

"They imagine it all the same," says the saxophone teacher, "the thirsty mothers with their sad black eyes. They imagine sharp little teeth and a wet gulping swallow. They imagine small bluish pouches underneath his eyes."

Patsy contemplates the article with her head on one side. She dabs her finger absentmindedly at the crumbs on her plate.

"I completely understand, Mrs. Miskus," the saxophone teacher is saying into the phone. "Oh goodness no, I never met

the man, but let me tell you something about him all the same."
(Patsy gets up now, fishes for her coat. The saxophone teacher
follows her with her eyes as she talks.) "Mr. Saladin left a legacy
behind him, a special breed of wide-eyed, fascinated, provocative mistrust which has swept through my students like a virus.
The violated girl is shadowed by whispers and elbows and blind
aching jealousy everywhere she walks. When the lights go out,
the parents cry and ask each other what did he *do* to her, but the
girls are burning with a question of their own: what did *she* do?
What does she know now that makes her so dangerous, like the
slow amber leak of a noxious fume?"

Patsy wiggles into her coat, waves, blows a kiss. She is
leaving.

"They try to imagine her stroking his face and arching her
neck and whispering things, special things that nobody's ever
said before. They try to imagine her up against the wall of the
music room, breathing fast and shallow with her eyes closed and
her hands clenched in fists on the wall above her head. They try
to imagine the ordinary things, like How about lunchtime?, or
I couldn't sleep last night, or I like the shirt with the stripes better. They think maybe now when she clutches her arms across
her chest, when she smoothes her hair down at the side, when
she suddenly falls silent and bites her lip hard, they think maybe
these things mean something now that they didn't mean before.
They try to imagine, Mrs. Miskus. They try to imagine what
these things might mean."

The saxophone teacher is silent now, listening, fingering the
phone cord. The door slams in the stairwell.

"I understand," she says after a while. "Your poor fragile
sensible daughter feels dirty by association and she wants to
put as much distance as she possibly can between herself and
that horrible man. You tell her I have a space on Tuesday at
three."

Friday

A notice goes up to say that rehearsals will resume. A new conductor has been found for jazz band and senior jazz ensemble and orchestra, identified in bold type as **Mrs. Jean Critchley.** The unnecessary naming serves to emphasize the *Mrs.* and the *Jean.*

"Course they got a woman," says first alto darkly. They are standing in the corridor in a bedraggled clump.

"I liked Mr. Saladin," says Bridget in her stringy unfashionable way.

"Is he in prison already?" says first alto.

"Probably under house arrest," says double bass. "So he doesn't reoffend."

"Bullshit," says first trombone. "He'll just be at home in his pajamas watching daytime television."

They run out of things to say and spend a moment regarding the name of Mrs. Jean Critchley, identified in bold type.

"She sounds like a bitch," says first alto, voicing what they are all thinking anyway.

Friday

"I went to see Mr. Partridge about an extension after school yesterday," Isolde says. "He was in his office, and when I came in he sort of exploded out of his desk and said, Let's talk in the hallway, come on, out. They all do that now. They're afraid of enclosed spaces."

The saxophone teacher watches her and thinks, This is the dawn of a new Isolde, a hardened deadened Isolde who has witnessed the dirty and perverted glamour of the world but still

43

nurses a tiny kernel of doubt because she has not yet felt what she has heard and seen.

"Anyway we went out into the hallway," says Isolde. She swings her saxophone around so it is hanging limply off one shoulder like a schoolbag, both hands at her shoulder holding the strap. She shifts her weight to the other leg and sticks her hip out and blinks her big eyes, converting in an instant into a sweet and undeserving victim. The lights change, becoming duller and more diffuse, until Isolde is standing in the creamy lilac light of a late-afternoon school corridor with all the lockers hanging empty and open and the chip packets scudding across the floor like silver leaves.

"So I go, I was just wondering if I could get an extension or whatever, because things have been so hard at home—"

And she seamlessly slides her sax off her shoulder and into her arms, holding it loosely underneath the bell with both hands, and pressing it flat against her pelvis in a casually protective way, as a man might hold a folder against himself, standing in a corridor with a student in a shaft of creamy lilac light after all the others have gone home.

The saxophone teacher reflects how much she enjoys these changes, when Isolde slips out of one person and becomes another. Bridget is good at voices, but with Isolde the performance is always physical and total, like the unexpected shedding of a skin. The saxophone teacher shifts in her chair, and nods to show she's listening.

"And he shakes his head at me," Isolde says, broadening now, rocking back on her heels and sucking in her belly so her chest inflates, "and he goes, Isolde, I am not the kind of teacher who ingratiates myself with my students in order to gain their love. That is not my style. I am the kind of teacher who gains popularity by picking a scapegoat. I do this in each and every class I teach. If I was to grant you an extension I would be a hypocrite and I would undermine my own methods.

"He goes, Isolde, when I set out to gain the love of a student, I do not begin by granting them an extension when they don't really need one. I begin by cultivating a culture of jealousy in my classroom. Jealousy is a key component to any classroom environment, because jealousy means competition and competition means excellence. It is only in a jealous classroom that a true and fervent love can blossom.

"It is only once I am sure my students are well placed to become very jealous of each other that I pick my scapegoat. Picking a scapegoat is not easy, Isolde. It is not as easy as granting an extension to a student when they don't really need one. Picking a scapegoat is a very difficult and delicate task. The trick—" and she brandishes her saxophone now, jabbing it into the air to emphasize what she is saying "—is not to pick the girl that everybody already genuinely dislikes. This will induce the other students to pity the scapegoat, and to become contemptuous of me because I am being cruel. I don't want to be cruel to my students.

"The trick is to pick the least original girl in the room. You want someone unoriginal because you want to be sure that they will behave exactly the same way every time you use them. You want someone unoriginal because you need them to be dull enough to believe that they are being singled out on the strength of their own comic merits. You need them to believe that the laughter you generate is inclusive laughter.

"Isolde, he goes, I am a good teacher who is loved by my pupils. I gain their collective love by choosing a sacrificial victim on behalf of them all, not by currying favor with every individual student. It is a good method and I am a good teacher. I don't want to give you an extension because your sister had sex and everyone found out and I feel sorry for you. I've explained my reasons. I'm sorry."

The lights fade back in. Isolde comes gracefully to an end and reattaches her saxophone to her neckstrap, ready for the lesson.

"So you didn't get an extension," the saxophone teacher says as she rises.

"No," Isolde says. "He goes, What you need to learn, Isolde, is that life just isn't fair."

Friday

It is a new and popular tradition at this secular school to purchase short-snouted plastic Coca-Cola bottles from the tuck shop, and then retrieve with a fingernail the little blue disc with a stiff rim that sits snugly on the underside of the bottle's cap. The girls hold this blue disc up to their lips and with their front teeth they bite a hole in the greasy plastic center to pierce the flesh. They are then able to rip out the middle of the disc so that only the rim remains. Gently they tug at this little translucent hoop of plastic, turning it around and around in their hands, pulling at it tenderly so it stretches wider and wider and the thin hoop becomes a pale band of ribbon through which they can slip their hand. The girls then wear these plastic ribbons on their wrists.

Popularly they are known as "Fuck-me bracelets." It is a mark of a girl's daring to fashion such a bracelet for herself from the aqua seal of a Coca-Cola bottle neck, for whoever breaks the bracelet, however accidentally, thereby enters into a contract with the wearer. Sometimes at parties a boy will lean over to kiss a girl and with his free hand he will scrabble at her wrist to try to break the Coca-Cola seal. Most often the girl will feel him trying to snap the bracelet and she will pretend to struggle, knowing what the breaking of the seal will mean: she will feign resistance and twist her wrist away from him to make the bracelet snap the sooner. Once it has snapped they know that they must go through with it to the very end.

It is a shameful thing to break your own bracelet. The girls snicker at the prospect, and alienate anyone clumsy enough to catch the side of the thin plastic band on a doorframe or on the buckle of her backpack so it snaps.

One of the girls says, "They found a Fuck-me bracelet in Mr. Saladin's tutorial room. Under the piano. It was broken."

This isn't true.

Monday

"Thanks all for coming in, people," says the counselor above the scraping and shuffling, raising his palms like he is a politician or a priest. "I'd really like to build on some of the issues that we raised in our last session. I thought that today we could talk about taking control."

Julia is sitting at the back, low down in her chair, with her arms folded and her ankles crossed and her hair falling across her face. She watches as the other girls trip in from the cold, linking arms with their favorite friends so they advance across the room in a rectangular squadron of favorites. They negotiate seating with whispers and nudges and a desperate narrow-eyed panic, always fearful of one day occupying the terrible seats on the periphery which force you to lean across and be forever asking "What? What's so funny? What did she say?"

Julia watches them slot into place around the current locus of popularity and wit with a feeling of contempt and mild jealousy. Most of the girls are seventh formers, contemporaries of the violated girl and infected only by vague proximity. The rest are the music students, more critically infected and so personally summoned by a solemn pink slip photocopied over and over and signed by the counselor in a delicate whispery hand.

The door opens and Julia sees to her surprise the sister of the violated girl holding her pink summons gingerly in her fist and checking the brass numeral on the plate above the doorknob.

Isolde is only in fifth form, too young for jazz band and orchestra and senior jazz ensemble, and as she enters the room she nods at a few of the girls who must be her sister's friends. The counselor smiles approvingly as she enters, showing them all that he is terribly proud of her, in the way that one might be terribly proud of a mascot or a flag.

Watching Isolde tuck her hair behind one ear and cast around sourly for a seat, Julia feels a flicker of interest in this girl, now thrust forever into her sister's arched and panting shadow, and wonders what she's thinking.

As Isolde sits down, the girl sitting behind her leans forward and gives her shoulders a squeeze, slipping her thumbs into the hollows of Isolde's collarbones and whispering, You okay? in a hot pitying whisper. Isolde squirms away from the girl's hands, nodding, and says something in reply that Julia can't quite hear. The girl shakes her head, gives Isolde a pat and retreats with a motherly sigh. She turns immediately to pluck at the sleeve of the girl on her left, who is already leaning in to listen.

Julia watches the breathy whispers gather and spread up and down the row behind Isolde, and studies the hard impassive look on Isolde's face.

"Would you jump off a bridge just because your friends were jumping off bridges?" the counselor is saying. It's his favorite question and he asks it routinely, his voice ringing and triumphant as if he has just performed a marvelous checkmate.

Julia watches Isolde shift slightly in her chair. She is staring at the counselor dully, frowning but not really listening, her lips slack and slightly pouted. She has the same round cheekbones and innocent round eyes as her sister, but while Victoria's roundness is a fullness, unapologetic and open and challenging, on Isolde it gives her the plump candied expression of a spoiled child. Isolde wears her own face like it is a fashion accessory that she knows looks better on everybody else.

"For some people," the counselor is saying, "seduction is a

means of gaining attention. Seduction is a cry for help, a last and desperate attempt to make a real connection with another human being." He wags his plump finger at them all, ranged around him in a tartan half-circle with their neckties loose and their smooth velvet legs crossed at the knee. "These lonely and damaged people," he says, "may seek out physical and sexual connections that they do not truly want but they cannot live without. These are the people you must beware of." He pauses for effect. "Mr. Saladin was one of these people."

Julia looks over at Isolde but she is still staring at the counselor in the same blank way. Julia wonders if it is an act. She tries to think what it would be like to be Isolde, coming home from school each day like an envoy from a forbidden place, stepping around her sister, watching her across the dinner table as she mashes her potato into a glum paste, walking past the closed door of her bedroom, still with its faded peeling stickers and strip of stolen security tape, passing her toweled and dripping in the hall. Julia imagines a pinched weeping mother and a father picking at his tie as if it's strangling him. She imagines urgent phone calls and people shouting in whispers and a damp shifting silence. She imagines Isolde in the middle of it all, trying to watch television or polish her school shoes or pick through the funny parts of the newspaper, alone and insulated by a patch of dead air like a ship in the eye of a storm.

Julia watches as Isolde examines her fingernails serenely and nibbles at a cuticle.

"This terrible case of child abuse," the counselor is saying, "is a classic case of how seduction can be wielded as a means of gaining control. In preying upon this girl Mr. Saladin destroyed her right to the ownership of her own body. He abused his position of power as a teacher. He wielded his position of power to *gain control.*"

He has moved the lectern aside, and leans casually against a desk edge, one hand in his pocket balled into a fist so it stretches the fabric across his pelvis and tugs gently at the zipper of his fly. With his other hand he plucks at the air as if he is conducting a piece that is very modern and very moving.

"My goal for today," he says smoothly, "is to talk about the ways in which I can help you guys to learn to *take* control. Does anybody want to say anything before we kick off?"

They all shake their heads and smile at him, shifting in their seats like roosting hens. Then Julia says, "I do."

Everyone except Isolde turns to look at her in a rustling swoop. Julia blinks calmly and says, "I don't agree that Mr. Saladin wanted to gain control."

The counselor frowns and reaches up to tug a tuft of hair at the nape of his neck. "You don't," he says.

"No, I don't," Julia says. "Gaining control isn't the exciting part. Sleeping with a minor isn't exciting because you get to boss them around. It's exciting because you're risking so much. And taking a risk is exciting because of the possibility that you might *lose*, not the possibility that you might win."

The girls look her up and down, and marvel with a collective disgusted fascination. Their expression is the expression of any popular girl who takes time to regard an unpopular girl while she is speaking. They watch Julia as if she is a carnival act: intriguing, but it might make you feel a little sick.

"It's like gambling," Julia says, even louder. "If you make a bet that you're almost positively certain you're going to win, it's not going to cost you much adrenaline. It's not that exciting and it's not that much fun. But if you make a bet where all the odds are against you and there's just a tiny, tiny glimmer of a chance that you might make it, then you're going to be pumping. There's a higher possibility that you might lose. It's the possibility you might lose that gets you excited."

The girls start to shift and mutter, but Julia's gaze stays fixed on the counselor, her eyes shiny and narrowed and hard. The counselor is looking at his shoes.

"The fact that Victoria was underage and virginal or whatever wasn't exciting because he could exercise more power over her," Julia says. "It was exciting because he stood to lose so much more if anyone found out." Julia has a way of cocking her head to emphasize the shock value. "He wouldn't just lose her," she says. "He would lose everything."

There is a small pause and then another rustling swoop as all the girls turn back to look at the counselor. He looks up, tugs again at his tuft of hair, and sighs.

"I think we've deviated from the point," he says. "What we're concerned with here is the power imbalance. We're concerned with the fact that, as a teacher, Mr. Saladin abused his position of power by seeking out a relationship with a student."

"We've only deviated from *your* point to *my* point," Julia snaps. "And anyway, isn't every relationship a power imbalance in some way?"

The counselor quickly turns back to the group before Julia can open her mouth to say more. "What do you guys think?" he asks, trying to make eye contact only with the least combative and least articulate girls in the room. "Any thoughts? Agree? Disagree?"

A few girls raise their hands and begin to speak, and Julia loses interest immediately. She scowls at the counselor, and then fishes a biro out of her pocket and begins to doodle on the back of her hand as if she doesn't care. After a while she looks up, and to her sudden thudding surprise Isolde is looking at her. Her expression is no longer childish and candied. Her head is turned slightly so she is looking half over her shoulder like a cold and careless queen with her neck all standing out in ropes.

Julia flushes under her collar and censors herself too late. Her heart is beating very fast. All of a sudden she feels too big for her own body, clumsy and stupid and lumpish, and the feeling washes over her all at once in a horrible thrill.

They hold each other's gaze for a moment, and then Isolde looks away.

Saturday

Isolde and Victoria are watching television. Isolde is curled in the cat-furred hollow of the armchair with her legs hugged to her chest and her head upon the arm. Victoria is lying on the sofa with one leg cocked and the remote control held lightly between her finger and her thumb. Their father has just come through the room and crumpled Isolde's toes in his big hand and said, Goodnight, slugs. Their mother has just called out from the stairway, Bed by eleven please. Their counterpointed footsteps, light and heavy, have just dwindled away up the stairs, and they have just shut their bedroom door with a faint and knuckled click.

Victoria says, "What about that group of boys you used to hang out with? Are they still pissing about with you guys?"

She speaks with the unrequited prerogative of an older sister's demand for the whole truth. As the elder, Victoria's perspective on her little sister's life is always that of a recent veteran, knowing and qualified and unshockable. It is as if, at each new stage, Isolde merely picks up another hand-me-down costume that Victoria has grown out of and cast behind her, and as she struggles with the arm-holes Victoria is entitled to enter the dressing room and watch. When Isolde gets her first period, fits her first bra, plants her first kiss, chooses a dress for her first ball—at all these milestones Victoria is, or will be, present. If not, the elder sister is then always entitled to ask, Why didn't you *tell* me, Issie, why?

By contrast, little Isolde would never dare ask Victoria what really *happened* behind the tiny pasted window of the rehearsal-room door. She would never dare ask for details—the life under his clothes, his breath, the touch of him. She would never ask, Was he nervous, Toria? or Who reached out first? or Did you talk together first, for weeks and weeks—about yourselves, about what you wanted and what you didn't have? All these are questions Isolde is not allowed to ask. She could not ask, Why didn't you *tell* me? when Victoria snared her first lover, began her first affair, broke her first promise, or shed, for the first time, tiny blossom-drops of virgin blood, for all of these slender landmarks are part of a terrain in which the younger sister does not yet belong.

Later, when Isolde is Victoria's age, and Victoria is still two steps ahead, at university maybe, and living elsewhere, smoking her first papered twist of weed, walking home from her first one-night stand with her sandals slung over her wrist, for the first time deciding what, in truth, she is going to *be*—then, perhaps, Victoria might tell her what really happened. Not every detail, because by then Victoria will be airy and deliberately removed, waving her hand and saying, "I just think Mum and Dad were cunts about that whole thing," or "God, that was ages ago." She might say, "We were going to run off together, but in the end he went back to his old girlfriend. I ran into him on the street a few months ago. He's fatter than he was."

But speaking of it now would be impossible. Isolde thinks that it would be like flipping a chapter ahead in a book that she was reading, to press Victoria for a detail, or an answer, or a map. Victoria's life will always be two paces ahead, now and forever, and if Isolde saw the road before she had to walk upon it herself she would simply be a cheat.

"Yeah, but it means you'll never make the same mistakes as me," Victoria says, unwilling to let Isolde feel she has the poorer lot.

"No," Isolde says, "I *will* make the same mistakes, but by the time I do they won't seem interesting because you'll already have done it, and I'll only be a copy."

"Yeah...no," says Victoria. "You've got it better. Mum and Dad are way stricter with me than they are with you. They waste all their energy on me and by the time you come along their standards have dropped and they can't be bothered any more."

"Yeah...no," says Isolde. "I have to pretend to be the baby, and that sucks."

"Yeah, but when I was six I was getting crayons and chalk for Christmas, and when you were six you got a pink tennis racket in a pink glitter sleeve. The older they get, the richer they get. You had way more stuff to play with than I ever did."

"Yeah, but that's just it. I'm always compared to you. You aren't compared to anybody, because you always do things first."

"That's balls," Victoria says. "When's the last time they compared you to me?"

The conversation is a comfort, because underneath it all they know that at least they occupy a place, the older and the younger, a place they each fill as closely and completely as Isolde's body fills the ancient cat-worn dip in the old armchair by the wall. Underneath it all they know that it is more a thing of necessary equilibrium than any sort of failed facsimile. Each sister claims not a mirror copy but a rough-edged ill-formed twisted half of their parents' attention and command.

"What about that group of boys you used to hang out with?" is Victoria's question now, and Isolde says, "Nah, I don't know. All the St. Sylvester boys are dicks, I reckon."

"That's what I thought," Victoria says. "When I was your age."

Wednesday

There is a strange mood in the rehearsal room as the jazz band assemble their instruments and unfold their music stands. It's the first time they've met for practice in three weeks, and privately everyone feels betrayed—not by Mr. Saladin, who was always jovial and tousled and called them Princess or Madam, but by Victoria, who fooled them all by pretending to be one of them.

The girls are silent as they collectively suffer the gross humiliation of being the last to know. They feel a dawning indignation that all along Victoria must have watched them founder and said nothing, that all along she sat among them in silent smug possession of her secret. Now they are compelled to remember with embarrassment their own harmless shy flirtations with Mr. Saladin, every remembered happy-flutter feeling poisoned now by the knowledge that he was already hers and already stolen. They remember their woodwind tutorial when he punched the air and said, *That's* what I'm talking about and grinned his boyish grin, in the quad at lunchtime when he briefly joined their game of hacky-sack and then ran off with the hacky when he started to lose, before jazz practice when he strolled over and started talking about the Shakespeare Festival and the chamber music contest and the changes to the summer uniform—

"He said she looked good in her summer uniform, way back in the first term," says first trombone as she empties her spit valve on to the carpet. "I was standing right there, as well."

It is a mark of the depth of their wounding that they are pretending they suspected it all along. Everything that they have seen and been told about love so far has been an inside perspective, and they are not prepared for the crashing weight of this exclusion. It dawns on them now how much they never saw and how little they were wanted, and with this dawning comes a painful reimagining of the self as peripheral, uninvited, and utterly minor.

"He had this thing he did," the percussionist is saying, "if they were lying in the dark together, if he was talking into the dark and he wasn't sure whether she was smiling. He would make his forefingers into little calipers and he would keep reaching over to check the corners of her mouth. Sometimes he would lie on his side and he would keep his fingers there, just lightly, as they talked on and on into the dark. They used to laugh about it. It was a thing he did."

Bridget is in the corner, lifting her sax out of its gray furred cavity and fitting the mouthpiece together absently. Last week she bought a number of different reeds from different manufacturers to test, numbering each one with a tiny red numeral to remind her which is which. She removes one from its plastic sheath and checks the tiny inked number before screwing it tight. The reed is harder than she has been used to, and probably her tongue will bleed.

"My gypsy girl," says second trumpet. "That's what he called her. My gypsy girl."

The bell rings. There is a vague flurry of chair-scraping and shuffling and they all aim their half-eaten sandwiches at the wastepaper bin and then settle into their concentric half-circle, ready for the conductor to arrive.

"They got her to admit that it had been going on since last year," says tenor sax. "She had to give a statement to the police and everything."

And then they are silent for a while, dwelling separately on the unhappy realization that they, above all others, are the ones who have been deceived.

Wednesday

"If you imagined yourself in French plaits and a pressed school kilt, playing 'Sweet Georgia Brown' on tenor sax at the seventh-form prize-giving and standing coyly in a pool of yellow light, then I'm afraid you made the wrong choice." The saxophone teacher's fingernails are blood-red today, and gently tapping. "The saxophone does not speak that language. The saxophone speaks the language of the underground, the jaded melancholy language of the half-light—grimy and sexy and sweaty and hard. It is the language of orphans and bastards and whores."

Bridget stands with her sax limp in her hands like a wilted flower.

"The saxophone is the cocaine of the woodwind family," the sax teacher continues. "Saxophonists are admired because they are dangerous, because they have explored a darker, more sinister side of themselves. In your performance, Bridget, I see nothing grimy or sexy or sweaty or hard. Everything I see is scrubbed shiny pink and white, sedated and sanitized like a poodle at a fair."

"Okay," Bridget says unhappily.

Tap-tap goes the bloody fingernail on the side of the mug.

"What do you think makes a good teacher, Bridget?"

Bridget draws her lips in between her teeth as she thinks. "I guess talent," she says lamely. "Being good at what you're teaching."

"What else?"

"I guess being patient."

"Shall I tell you what makes a good teacher?"

"Okay."

"A good teacher," the saxophone teacher says, "is somebody who awakes in you something that did not exist before. A good teacher changes you in a way that means you cannot go back even if you might want to. Now you can practice and learn the pattern of the notes and have good control over your instrument and you will be able to play that piece very competently, but until you and I can work together to challenge and awaken and *change* some part of you, competent is all that piece will ever be."

"I was just trying it out how Mrs. Critchley said," Bridget blurts out. "She's Mr. Saladin's replacement. We had jazz band today."

The sax teacher narrows her eyes briefly, but all she says is, "Is that Jean Critchley?"

"She's Mr. Saladin's replacement," Bridget says again.

"I've seen her play live. She plays trumpet." The saxophone teacher is suddenly withdrawn, her voice cold and calm and careful, looking Bridget up and down as if she is seeking visible signs of treachery.

"Why didn't *you* apply?" says Bridget, her eyes widening with the thought.

"I don't like high schools," says the saxophone teacher.

"She doesn't look like a Mrs. Jean Critchley. She has red glasses and she wears baggy tee-shirts with leggings and sneakers. First thing she said," Bridget says, brightening now, "first thing she said was, All right, shut up so I can talk about myself. I'm the teacher who comes after the teacher who had the affair. Let's blow it all out of the water now so we can get on and make some music and have some fun. And you can all relax right away. They made me promise not to have an affair with any of you."

Bridget blinks innocently at the saxophone teacher. She is good at voices.

"Did anyone laugh?" the saxophone teacher says.

"Oh, yeah," says Bridget. "Yeah, everyone likes her a lot."

"So they laughed. They laughed at the sheer ridiculousness of it. The prospect that Mrs. Jean Critchley might seduce one of you, might draw any one of you toward her by subtle and insidious means, might push one of you against the music-cupboard door and press her cold cheek against yours so her lips are almost touching the feathered lobe of your ear. The prospect that one of you might want *her*, even, and pick her out as an object and a prize. That one of you might blush every time she looks at you, might stammer and stumble and take every opportunity to divert through the music block in the hope of brushing past her in the hall."

"Yeah," Bridget says. "She blew it all out of the water, so we could get on and make some music and have some fun."

"So you got on and made some music and had some fun."

"Yeah," Bridget says again.

"And Mrs. Jean Critchley suggested that you play this piece like an ice-cream jingle."

"She didn't say that." Bridget senses she's winning, in some obscure way, and draws herself up a little higher. "She just said, Sometimes it's not about originality. Sometimes it's just about having fun."

The saxophone teacher is frowning. Inside she asks: does she feel jealous? She reminds herself that Bridget is her least favorite student, the student she mocks most often, the student she would least like to be. She reminds herself that Bridget is lank and mousy, with a greasy bony face and a thin hookish nose and pale lashes that cause her to resemble a ferret or a stoat.

She is jealous. She doesn't like the idea of Mrs. Jean Critchley, who is jovial and flat footed and forever appealing to her students to *just have fun*. She doesn't like the idea of Bridget having a basis for comparison, an occasion to see *her*, the saxophone teacher, in a new and different light. She doesn't like it.

"Let's move on," she says. "I think it's time to try something new. Something a little harder, that will make you struggle a little more and re-establish which one of us is truly in control out of you and me. Okay?"

"Okay," Bridget says.

"Let me find a Grade Eight piece," the saxophone teacher says. "One that Mrs. Critchley won't have any cause to comment on."

Friday

Isolde falters after the first six bars.

"I haven't practiced," she says. "I don't have an excuse."

She stands there for a moment, her right hand splayed over the keys and damply clacking. The shifting tendons in her hand make her skin stretch white and purple.

The sax teacher looks at her and decides not to fight her. She moves over to the bookshelf and lifts the plastic hood off the record player. "Let me play you that recording, then," she says. She selects a record from the pile and says, "Tell me what happened at school today."

"They wanted to cancel Sex Ed," Isolde says gloomily. "In light of recent events. They took Miss Clark out into the hallway, and the principal was there and we could hear the whole thing. We're not supposed to call it Sex Ed. We're supposed to call it Health."

The saxophone teacher lowers the needle with a crackle and a low hiss. It's Sonny Rollins playing "You Don't Know What Love Is" on tenor sax. The record trembles like a leaf.

"What is it that you learn in Health?" asks the saxophone teacher as they sit back to listen.

"We learn about boys," says Isolde in the same flat voice. "We put condoms on wooden poles. We learn how to unroll them so they won't break. Miss Clark showed us how much they can stretch by putting a condom over her shoe."

Isolde lapses into silence for a moment, remembering Miss Clark struggling to stretch a condom over the toe of her sensible flat-soled shoe, hopping and red-faced and puffing with the effort. "*There* it goes!" she said triumphantly in the end, and wiggled her foot so they could all see. She said, "Never believe a boy who says it won't fit. You say to him, I saw Miss Clark put a condom over her whole shoe."

The music is still playing. Isolde is only half-listening, looking out over the rooftops and the chimneys and the wires.

"We don't really learn much about girls," she says. "Everything we learn about boys is all hands-on 3-D models and cartoons. When we learn about girls it's always in cross-section, and they use diagrams rather than pictures. The stuff about boys is all ejaculations, mostly. The stuff about girls is just reproduction. Just eggs."

In truth the classes are patched and holey, hours of vague unhelpful glosses and line drawings and careful omissions which serve to cripple rather than assist. Most of the girls now lack a key definition in this new and halting lexicon of forbidden words, some slender dearth of understanding that will later humiliate them, confound them, expose them, because it is expected now that their knowledge is complete. They envisage rigid perpendicular erections and a perfect hairless trinity for the male genitals, groomed and gathered in a careful bouquet. They have not heard of the glossy sap that portends the rush of female drive. They know *ovulate* but not *orgasm*. They know *bisexual* but not *blow*. Their knowledge is like a newspaper article ripped down the middle so only half of it remains.

"Is it useful?" asks the saxophone teacher. "Do you learn things you didn't know before?"

"We learned that you can only feel one thing at one time," says Isolde. "You can feel excitement or you can feel fear but you can never feel both. We learned why beauty is so important: beauty is important because you can't really defile something that is already ugly, and to defile is the ultimate goal of the sexual impulse. We learned that you can always say no."

The two of them sit in that self-conscious half-profile demanded by music-lesson etiquette. Facing each other squarely feels too familiar and standing side by side feels too formal, as if they are amateur actors onstage for the first time, fearful of turning their faces away from the auditorium lest their performance be lost. So they position themselves always at forty-five degrees, the angle of the professional actor who includes both the stage and the audience and holds in delicate balance that which is expressed and that which is concealed.

The Sonny Rollins track has the thin gritty sound of an old recording.

"You can take the record home if you think you'd find it inspiring," the saxophone teacher says kindly. "I really think you'd suit playing tenor."

"We don't have a record player," Isolde says.

FOUR

October

The gymnasium was not a gymnasium but a fluid space, a space that seemed to inhale and exhale and settle around the shapes and figures on the floor. There was a giant accordion made of steel that compressed the plastic bleachers against the wall, and dusty heavy drapes that could divide the space into thirds and quarters and fifths. The stage was formed of many chalky footprinted podiums that could be rearranged or stacked or upended or tiered, depending. Today the drapes were all pushed to the sides and the podiums stacked against the wall in a hasty barricade. The space was clean and full of light.

"Mime is literal embodiment," said the Head of Movement once the doors had closed. "To mime an object is to discover its weight and volume and thus its meaning." He was weighing something in his hand as he spoke, something invisible and heavy. "If we occupy each other, we begin to truly understand each other," he said. "The same is true for all things. Mime is a path to understanding."

He turned over whatever he was holding in his hand.

Everyone was taut and straining and watchful, waiting for an opportunity to say something clever or profound or interesting that would set them apart from the other hopefuls and secure the approval of the tutor. Some of them were nodding slowly with their eyes narrowed to communicate insight and deep reflection. Some were waiting for the tutor to reference something they had a particular knowledge of, so they could snare him afterward and force a conversation. Stanley was sitting on the outer rim, alert and upright but sneaking careful sideways glances at the other hopefuls whenever he could.

"The first and most important point," the Head of Movement said, "is that you must start with a thing itself, not with an idea of a thing. I can *see* what I am holding in my hand. I can see its weight, its shape and its texture. It doesn't matter if you can see it yet or not: the important thing is that I can."

They all strained to see the invisible thing he was holding in his hand. Every pair of eyes followed the Head of Movement as he moved slowly back and forth. He was barefoot, like all the tutors at the Institute, and when he took a step his foot rolled from the heel to the ball in a slow feline movement, lazy and deliberate at once. His feet were milky and lean.

The Head of Movement said, "Many of us fear women. We are afraid of woman as woman, longing for her as virgin or as madonna or as whore. It is not by becoming a woman that we will address this fear. It is by becoming the things she touches, the spaces she moves through, the fractured gestures that are not signs in themselves but are nonetheless hers and thus a part of her. If we discover the weight of these small things, then she will appear not as an idea but as a life and a totality."

He paused at this, and ran his tongue over his bottom lip.

The hopefuls shifted uncertainly, wondering whether they were supposed to argue, and for a moment nobody spoke.

Stanley had gone to an all-boys high school and he felt the presence of the girls in the group acutely. They studded his peripheral vision like scattered diamonds, but when he looked around the room his gaze passed casually over them, in the same way that he might self-consciously pass over a cripple or a drunk and pretend not to notice, pretend not to flinch. He waited uncomfortably for one of the girls to say something, maybe even to object. He looked at the floor.

"*I* don't fear women," one of the boys called out at last, and there was a ripple of relieved laughter.

The Head of Movement nodded. "Stand up," he said. "I am going to tell you a little about yourself." He folded his arms across his chest suddenly, forgetting about the invisible thing that he had been holding in his hand, and the invisible thing disappeared.

The boy got to his feet. He was thin and freckled, his rib cage peaking a little at his sternum and his hip bones thrusting out above the tight gathered waistband of his tracksuit pants. His shoulders and ankles and knees all looked a little too large, like he was a paper figure held together at the joints with brass pivot pins.

"Go for a walk," the Head of Movement said. "Go on. Walk around for a while."

The boy started walking. The Head of Movement watched him in silence for an entire circuit of the gymnasium, following him with his eyes, his arms folded and his face still. When the boy had lapped the gymnasium completely, the Head of Movement fell into step behind him and began to imitate him. He withdrew like a tortoise into himself, shoving his chest out and his shoulder blades together, keeping his upper body rigid while he walked so his arms fell awkwardly from his shoulders, and paddling with each step as if he were walking underwater.

They walked in tandem in this way for a while, the boy looking unhappily over his shoulder and unhappily sideways at the other hopefuls watching from the floor, newly conscious of his big feet and his peaked chest and his stiff paddling arms.

"You may stop now," the Head of Movement said finally. "Thank you." He turned to the group. "Can someone please tell me something about my performance of this young man's walk," he said.

The hopefuls shifted awkwardly but nobody spoke.

"My performance was a parody," the Head of Movement said after a long pause. "It could only ever be a parody because I do not know this young man. I am old and comfortable and I don't really understand his nervousness, or his uncertainty, or his hope. I cannot possibly understand these things just by watching him walk for fifteen seconds. In parodying this young man I disperse all possible complexity. I reduce him and I insult him. *Your* performances will be insulting too if you do not truly understand what you are pretending to be."

The gymnasium was very quiet. The Head of Movement said, "You cannot mime what you don't understand. You cannot penetrate death, or God, or a woman. To attempt any of these things is to aim for sincerity rather than truth. Sincerity is not enough for students of this Institute. Sincerity is a word for hawkers and salesmen and hacks. Sincerity is a device, and we do not deal in devices here.

"Mime," he said. "We will begin very simply. Everybody up."

February

"At the Institute we encourage our students to have sex," the Head of Acting said. "You need to know your body in this profession. You need to know yourself. You need to explore all parts of you. However, graduates of the program will probably tell you it is not a good idea to sleep with each other. This is a small pool, and in any case, two actors together is always a terrible thing."

There was a little rustle of delight as the students looked around at each other to compress their lips and roll their eyes and giggle faintly at the prospect, and just for an instant any coupling, any combination of any pair among them, was possible. In this instant they all became potent, latent, cusping, even the ill-formed and sexless ones who would later be shunned or overlooked. Their hearts beat faster.

"We encourage you to explore the reaches of your body, test its limits and its scope," the Head of Acting went on. "We encourage you to get fit, to fall in love, to get hurt, to masturbate."

He enjoyed the collective flinch, manifested in a kind of sudden unmoving sternness, all of them looking gravely forward in silent straining proof that they were mature enough to hear the word out loud. Boys who, four months ago, would have snickered and reached for the collar of their nearest friend to swipe and then shove his head away, who would have yelled out a name at random, and laughed as the named boy scowled and flushed and hunched down further in his plastic bucket-seat, who would be swiftly and silently adding genitals to every conceivable diagram in the fifth-hand textbook spread open on his lap—these boys were silent and respectful and their eyes were wide.

The girls in the crowd were silent too, holding their jaws rigid and their eyes still. Only boys could be *wankers* and *tossers* and *jerks*: boys were exponents of this solitary function by default, a common fact which softened the shaming, and prevented any indicted boy from being truly alienated or destroyed. For the girls, however, this territory remained inexplicably taboo. Four months ago they would have simply frowned, taken on a pinched and nauseated look perhaps, and shaken their heads very faintly, to forever banish the topic from their lunchtime circle on the dusty grass. Now they were uneasy: they heard the Head of Acting speak the word out loud and were suddenly fearful, lest such a flat and prudish denial of the act was somehow—in the eyes of a man they all sought to impress—*wrong*. Somehow in the short summer between high school and the world beyond, a cosmic dial had turned: self-knowledge was now a quality that lent a girl a kind of husky darkness, a careless self-sufficiency, an appeal that was worldly and yearning and jaded all at once. The girls sat stiff and tense on the gymnasium floor and tried to look as casual and as solemn as they could.

This was the Head of Acting's method: to make sacred everything these students might regard profane, and then challenge any one of them to blanch, or laugh. It worked. The students looked up at him, all of them without the usual proud mechanisms that would make them need to cry, *Everybody masturbates but me.*

"Good," the Head of Acting said softly. "Now everybody get up and form a circle."

In their haste to leap up and obey him they were clumsy and flat-footed and gauche. They scrabbled to unknot themselves and form a ring. The Head of Acting watched them fumble, and he smiled.

October

"What do you think, Martin?" the Head of Acting said, tapping his fountain pen against his cheek. "I thought Number 12 was very teachable."

"Willing," said the Head of Movement. "Eager without being impatient. I'd say definitely a Maybe."

"Too many on Maybe," said the Head of Voice, spinning the whiteboard so the others could see. "We need to start making some definite decisions or we'll be here all night."

"It's because there are more and more Maybes each year," said the Head of Acting irritably. "The kids are losing something. Twenty years ago, kids were soft and supple and compliant. Now they're like planks of wood. Everywhere you look you see fucking Maybes."

He threw himself back into his swivel chair, and the suspension caught him, buoying him back up again so he bobbed crossly for a moment until the momentum died.

At the top of the whiteboard the Head of Improvisation had written Ambition, Teachability, Sociability, Talent in her cramped sideways hand. The words tapered as they advanced across the board, so Ambition was written much larger than the rest, and Talent narrowed to a spearhead against the raised silver lip of the frame. The Head of Acting tilted his head back and regarded the petering list down the length of his nose. Sociability was new. It had been Collegiality for a number of years, and Courage for many years before that. It had been Courage when he had first started teaching. The changes marked a devolution, the Head of Acting thought.

"Teachability," he said aloud. "For the boys, it means their potential to be taught about themselves, about their own bodies. For the girls, it means their potential to forget, to be able to forget everything they've been taught about themselves and about their bodies."

"Oh, come on," the Head of Improvisation said. "You act as if the boys and girls are utterly different species."

"I'm just aware that there are differences."

"I don't think the differences are that huge. How about this boy—Number 12. How are this boy's chances and choices any different from any of the girls'?"

She was cross with the Head of Acting tonight, cross with the pointed sulky air of profound disappointment that was his by rights, as Director of the Institute and possessor of the casting vote. He was sulking majestically, like a spoiled king.

"Well," the Head of Acting said, "he's not concerned about his beauty, for one thing. He's not concerned that every role he takes will flatter him, that every photograph will be backlit and soft focused, forever. He's willing to be ugly for the sake of his art."

"Which is all very convenient," the Head of Improvisation snapped, "because all the unbeautiful roles, all the character roles, are written for men anyway."

From across the table the Head of Movement watched them bicker, and wondered at his own stance. He thought he saw a surly vein of misogyny in the older man, swollen over the years into a bluish pucker at his temple that never quite disappeared, and he thought he saw an exposed nerve in the woman, some hypersensitivity, some indecent raw form of hysteria that made him want to wince and look away. The Head of Movement often felt like this: marooned between two points of view, suspended. He sighed.

"Let's not intellectualize this too much," the Head of Improvisation said at last, repenting. "What's important is that the boy is humble and receptive enough to be able to try different things, to stretch himself and grow, as an actor."

"Humility," the Head of Acting said. "That's what it should say then, up there. If that's what we're looking for."

The others were silent. The Head of Movement rubbed his face with his hands.

"All right. This isn't helping," the Head of Voice said. "We agree Number 12 is teachable. What else?"

They observed the photograph of Number 12, affixed to his application form with a paper clip. He looked slightly wistful, wide eyed with long pale lashes and blond hair.

"My note on Number 12 was Vulnerable," said the Head of Improvisation.

"I saw that too," said the Head of Acting. "I wrote down Virginal."

"Nice," said the Head of Improvisation. "We can work with that."

They were being deliberately polite with each other now. They'll accept him in a moment, the Head of Movement thought. They'll accept the boy and it will be simply for show: as a show of deference on his part, as a show of graciousness on hers.

"I'd be prepared to make him a Yes," said the Head of Acting. "Martin?"

The Head of Movement shrugged. When he was younger this used to excite him, selecting the choicest students from the pool like a gourmand at a spice market, rolling the possibilities around on his tongue, full of hope and ambition for the year ahead. This year as he pawed through the application forms he felt bleak and even a little ashamed of himself, as if he was selling a product he knew to be without use or value. He had been teaching for too long.

He nodded finally. "Yes for me," he said.

"All in favor?" said the Head of Acting, turning to include the others.

They all raised their pens gravely. The Head of Voice nodded a curt satisfied little nod and pulled the whiteboard toward her. She uncapped her pen and wrote Stanley's name in large square letters at the top of Yes.

November

Stanley clutched his Yes letter as he waited in the Green Room to be called upon. The other hopefuls sat around him, perched upon armchairs or stacked wooden forms, or on the swivel chairs that were fixed at intervals in front of the cracked and dusty mirror. Stanley caught sight of himself and realized how frightened he was, stiff in his pressed shirt with a new haircut and long bloodless hands. His gaze slid to the left and he made unexpected eye contact with the boy sitting next to him. They both looked away quickly, ashamed at having been caught observing themselves in such a private way.

Stanley swung his ankles against the crossbar of his stool and looked about him. There was an even split between boys and girls. The final class of twenty always comprised ten of each, so neither the boys nor the girls really regarded the other as a rival: each sex was competing in parallel, vying only against their own. As a result the girls were cautious and deceitful with each other but bright and flirtatious with the boys; the boys, in turn, laughed loudly and publicly when they were addressed but in the meantime they sat apart from each other and watched the girls form their swift bonds of togetherness and false sympathy with something between bewilderment and scorn.

Stanley was watching the girls now. Even as rivals they were pressing together, sowing shallow seeds of friendship and community: "I know it won't happen," they said, "but I hope we *all* get in. I hope we all do. Wouldn't it be amazing, if the tutors came out and said, Let's take them all?" The girls said, "Even if some of us don't get in, we'll stay in touch," and some of them said, "I don't have a chance, really. Not against you guys. I cried in the first audition when you did that piece about the hope chest. You're so much better than me it's not even funny." The girls said, "Underneath it all I just want to be liked by everyone, liked and even loved." One girl was massaging another's shoulders. She ground the heels of her hands into the shoulder blades of her rival, her adversary, a girl whom she had only lately met, and in a low voice she said, "You'll be awesome. You were awesome at the first audition. You'll get in, no problem."

Later Stanley would arrive at the opinion that girls were naturally more duplicitous, more artful, better at falsely sheathing their true selves; boys' personalities simply shone through the clearer. It was that female art of multitasking, he would conclude, that witchy capacity that girls possessed, that allowed them to retain dual and triple threads of attention at once. Girls could distinguish constantly and consciously between themselves and the performance of themselves, between the form and the substance. This double-handed knack, this perpetual duality, meant that any one girl was both an advertisement and a product at any one time. Girls were always acting. Girls could reinvent themselves, he later thought, with a sour twist to his mouth and his free hand flattening the hair on his crown, and boys could not.

Which would be harder for the tutors, he wondered now, choosing between the girls or choosing between the boys? Did they have a different set of criteria for each, a different benchmark that took into consideration this fundamental difference between these unitary blunted boys and these many-headed Hydras, the girls? He realized with a kind of underwater flinch that all the girls in the room were beautiful, all of them glossy and svelte like variations on a theme. The boys, by contrast, were mostly odd and ordinary, not yet grown into their faces and their shoulders and their hands, some of them greasy and brash, some of them thin and spotted and hoarse. Looking around, it seemed to Stanley as if the boys were here to audition for ten different character parts in a play, and the girls were all auditioning for a single role. He got up and moved away.

The room was a mess: costume racks, painted flats, trunks, scaffolds and ladders, swollen cardboard boxes, paint cans, shrouded furniture. On the auditorium wall there were shelves and shelves of faceless polystyrene heads wearing helmets and bonnets and crowns, and in the corner a rusted suit of armor standing with his pelvis forward and his hands upon his hips.

Every five or ten minutes another number was called. The caller was a sharp gray woman who struck each name off her clipboard with relish, and watched them between strikes with pity and mild curiosity, as if they were gladiators dressed up to die.

"Number 5," she called now.

Number 5 jumped to his feet and trotted nervously out of the room. The others watched him go.

"What if this is part of the test?" said Number 14 once the door had shut. "What if they're videoing us now and watching us on live feed just to see how we bond?"

"What if there isn't even an audition at all?" said Number 61. "We just get taken out of the room one by one once they've watched us for long enough, and then they tell us to go home."

"Like rats," said Number 14, as if in summary. They fell silent.

A few of the boys were pacing around the room, trying to stamp out their nervousness and peering at the framed photographs on the wall just for something to do. The photographs showed the class groups that had passed through the Institute, year by year, becoming sharper and more focused as the technology advanced, so the most recent groups shone wetly with a crispness and a brightness that the older classes did not possess. Stanley looked at the faces of all these people who had been opened up, awakened, broken and prevented from forming a crust, and wondered how many of them had now surrendered and become ordinary. In the photographs they looked hard and confident, bright in their theater makeup and their pinned-up costumes, and flushed with the thrill of opening night. He followed the photographs along the length of the wall and saw soldiers, monks, orphans, pirates, housewives, gods, samurai, and a group of silent watchmen in stern feathered masks that for some reason made him shiver.

"Number 33, you're up," came the call.

When they all had first arrived, the Head of Acting swept in, distracted and tilting his face oddly as if he was used to wearing bifocals.

"One of the questions we are going to ask you today," he said briskly, "is why you want to attend this Institute, and why you want to become an actor. I am telling you this in advance so you can think hard about your answer. Let me say that all I am looking for is a truthful answer to this question. I do not want you to tell me that the theater fills you with a noble and holy passion just because you think that is the answer with which you can win. I want you to tell me the truth.

"Let me explain what I mean," said the Head of Acting, still looking at them down the length of his long nose. "I auditioned for a place at this Institute nearly forty years ago. When I arrived for my audition and waited in this Green Room like you are all waiting here now, I was not filled with a noble and holy passion for the theater. I only knew that drama school sounded like more fun than university, and I thought it would probably mean less work. I was wrong about the work," he added, and smiled faintly.

"The real reason I enrolled in any tertiary education at all was that I knew that teenage girls always like university boys better. I had been a scrawny and awkward and unsuccessful teenager and I wanted a second chance. I thought I would enroll in some college, buy a car and try for a girlfriend.

"I am telling you this about myself," the Head of Acting said in his calm distracted way, "because I don't want you to stand in front of the panel and lie. I want you to tell the truth, even if the truth is boring or embarrassing or contemptible. I don't care what you say, as long as it's *you* and as long as it's real." He swept a look over them all, smiled a tiny smile and said, "Good luck."

Stanley moved from the Class of '61 photograph to the Class of '62 photograph and suddenly saw the Head of Acting. He was young and a little thinner but wore the same unfocused expression, as if he was watching something over the photographer's shoulder that none of the others could see. They were all dressed in military uniforms, and the Head of Acting was kneeling at the front with a rifle in his lap, his peaked cap pushed back on his head, showing a darkly oiled curl of hair. Stanley leaned in for a closer look, and wondered if this square-jawed soldier ever found a girl.

February

From the damp-smelling foam-lined pit underneath the trap-door ran a low reinforced passage left and right, and beyond the orchestra pit was another passage that ran underneath the first rows of the stalls in the audience. These passages invisibly framed the orchestra pit, forming a kind of underground moat that offered two quick and unseen paths between the wings on either side of the stage. The outer passage crawled between the ancient foundations of the auditorium, lit along the floor by a dusty string of fairy lights that sometimes winked on and off if the control box was accidentally knocked. The tunnel was narrow and low, the mortar bleeding thickly from between the cement bricks and brushing rough on either shoulder as you passed, the dry itch candyfloss of under-floor insulation wisping out between the joists. The inner passage was lined with gib-board, and narrower still: if two actors met in the middle they had to perform a quick shuffling rotating embrace, like an animate turnstile revolving in the dark.

The secrets of the auditorium were revealed to the first-years in the second week of the school year. They filed silently through the passages, inspected and tested the trap, hoisted themselves up into the flies, and dropped, awkward and untrusting, both hands clutching at the flying harness and craning nervously to check the winch. They walked across the stippled bridge that connected the fly-floors, looking down at the stage far below and reaching out to touch the thick braided cables that ran back and forth. The flies were at least twice the height of the proscenium arch, and the Head of Acting showed them how an entire panel of scenery could be flown up into the space above the stage to hang there, ready and waiting for the cue to drop. He activated the lift in the orchestra pit and they watched the floor of the pit rise up to meet the level of the stage. He showed them the heavy motorized chain underneath the false stage floor that activated the revolve, and then he switched the revolve on and they let themselves be carried around in silent powerful orbit, standing braced like stiff-legged pawns as the red mouth of the auditorium flashed by again and again.

The Head of Lighting came forward and showed them the templates that could turn light into dappled water and wind, the gauzes that gave the illusion of distance, the lights that could make you beautiful or villainous or old, and the followspot with its thick steel handle that could track an actor around the stage. He showed them how to make sunlight and moonlight and counterfeit flames. He showed them how to turn indoors into outdoors and back again.

They stood underneath the steel lighting rig and looked up at the heavy black instruments hanging like a cloud of bats from the pipes, the black barn-doors that shuttered and blinkered the bulbs all folded and unfolded like countless bat-wing membranes settling in sleep. The instruments were each clamped to the rig with a steel yoke which allowed the shuttered beam to be directed anywhere over the stage: the Head of Lighting demonstrated, slipping colored gels expertly in and out of the gel frame holder and pulling the yokes to and fro. He straddled the top of his dented ladder with his ankles hooked around the topmost steps to hold him steady, squinting down at them and plucking at his brown beard with his free hand as he spoke.

The first-years were then shown the lesser secrets: the door-slam, a little wooden box with a heavy sliding bolt that could simulate door-slamming sounds from backstage, and the rain box, a little box filled with dried peas for simulating rain-sounds— "Before everything was digitalized," the Head of Acting said with a nostalgic gravity, as he shook the box and filled the air with the sound of gentle drumming rain. He showed them up close how the false perspective of the painted flats contrived to make the stage area bigger than it actually was. He showed them the grooves and runnels into which the flats could slip, the ancient pulley that hauled at the red curtain, and the curved cyclorama at the back of the stage that gave the space a never-ending vastness, as if it went back and back forever.

"The auditorium is a sacred space," the Head of Acting said at last, looking gravely at them as they stood in the middle of the flooded stage and breathed in the sweet dusty smell of hot lights and generated fog. "We do not hold classes in here. It is only when we come to dress rehearsal that you are allowed to use this space. You may not come in here alone."

The first-years all nodded. Stanley was standing at the back of the group, still craning upward into the vast blackness of the flies and trying to remember everything they had been shown. He was a little in awe of the Head of Acting, but underneath it all he wasn't sure he liked the man very much. There was something cold and pulsing about his manner that reminded Stanley of a lizard or a frog. He had never touched the Head of Acting's ropy liver-spotted hands, but in his mind he imagined them to be cold and moist and snatching.

They all waited for the Head of Acting to say more, but he just drew his heels together and spread his arm to gesture them off the stage, signaling that the tour had come to a close.

The first-years filed quietly past him and he watched them go, down the wheeled aluminum steps into the stalls, up the aisle past the rows and rows, and finally out into the marble light of the foyer. When they were gone he moved to the stage manager's cubicle to kill the lights. He stood with his hand on the cool gray lever, and out of habit cleared his throat and called out a warning up into the flies: "Going dark."

November

Stanley walked out of his final audition feeling light-headed. He paused at the fountain in the foyer to steady himself and gripped the basin with both hands. He breathed quietly for a moment, looking past the porcelain masks into the foggy middle-distance of a recent memory, and after a moment he realized he was being observed. He straightened and gave the spectator a rueful sort of smile. She was an older woman, maybe the secretary, framed like a news-anchor behind the high administration desk in the foyer and watching him with her cheek propped upon her palm.

"You'll be wishing you brought a hip flask," she said. "Just had your audition, I guess."

"Does everybody look like this?" Stanley said, emphasizing his already crippled posture with a little jerk of his spine and holding his hands limp. The woman laughed.

"More or less," she said. "You have to watch the ones who look too happy. In my experience the ones who look too confident afterwards are the ones who don't usually get in."

"Oh," Stanley said, drawing himself up slightly.

"I suppose it's your first time auditioning," the woman said. "Some kids try out three, four, five times. It makes you think what they're doing with their lives in the meantime, just waiting all those years to finally get in."

"Yeah," said Stanley. "Yeah, wow. It is my first time."

"They didn't shake you up too much?" the woman said. "They can be quite mean, in the beginning. To break you in."

She seemed bored, sitting there with her head on her hand in the echoing cavern of the foyer. All the surfaces were bare and clean, and the car park was empty through the high wall of glass.

"Nothing too painful," Stanley said. "Nothing I didn't deserve, probably."

The woman laughed. Stanley watched her laugh. It struck him for the very first time that there were qualities of beauty that were unique to women, qualities that teenage girls could not possess: kindness lines around the eyes and mouth, a certain settling of the body, a weariness of poise and pose that was indefinably sexual, like the old glamour of a dusty taffeta dress or a piece of costume jewelery with a rusted clasp. The thought had not occurred to him before. He had supposed (though never truly consciously) that a woman was only attractive insofar as she resembled a girl; that her attractiveness fell away, by degrees, through her twenties and thirties until it was buried by middle age; that the qualities that women sought were always the qualities they once had, a backward striving that was ultimately doomed to fail. He had supposed that men slept with women their own age only because they could not snare anybody younger, or because they were still married to the sweetheart of their youth; he had not supposed that weary, veined and pear-shaped women were attractive in and for themselves—they were a second-best, he had imagined, a consolation prize. Now, with a weak stirring in the nerve-wracked cavity of his chest, he saw this woman through a different lens.

She was wearing makeup, a thin line of black behind the lashes of her upper eyelid that must have been straight and uniform when she stretched her eyelid out flat to apply the liner, but when she released the skin to blink and appraise herself the line had puckered, giving her a blurred, slightly clownish look that made Stanley think of an old and kindly whore. As she smiled he saw that her incisor was rimmed with the gunmetal gray of an ancient filling. The skin on the back of her hands was loose enough to frame the tendons and the veins, and her knuckles were pouchy whorls of white. A manufactured tan on her collarbone and on the V-shaped glimpse between her breasts gave the skin a fibrous look: the wrinkle-weave traveled both horizontally and vertically so the skin was soft and infinitely lined, like worn suede.

For the first time in his life Stanley saw that a woman was not simply a failed and hopelessly outmoded girl. She was a different creature entirely from the glossed and honeyed girls in the audition room: those girls, Stanley thought, could never play this woman until the day they became her, and from that day onward they could never play a girl.

"You're right about the hip flask," he said. "I reckon I'll walk out of here and straight into the pub."

"Have one for me," the woman said. "And good luck. If luck counts for anything."

Stanley passed through the double doors and out into the drowsy warmth of the late afternoon. As he turned the corner and left the gabled heights of the Institute behind, he thought to himself that he was probably the twentieth student that day to have exited the audition room, passed through the foyer, walked by the administration desk and exchanged words with the secretary before leaving the building. He wondered what she had said to the others, and how she had said it, and what they had thought when they looked her in the eye.

October

"Let's see some chemistry," the Head of Acting said, and nodded for them both to begin.

"I met him last week on the damp satin dance floor at the inter-school ball," she said. The words tumbled out of her too quick, too early, before she had swallowed her nervousness and found her rhythm. "Everyone was balled up in a tight knot near the stage, forming a human noose around the girl and the boy in the middle. It's so the teachers can't see in. From the outside it looks horrible, all tight and pushing and pushing, like they're trying to watch a cock fight or a captured bear. They all take turns in the noose. I was down the other end, just watching, and he walked up to me and asked me very quietly if I wanted a drink."

She was sitting on the edge of the podium, her ankles hooked over each other, kicking out her legs in an idle, gentle way so her heels bounced and bounced. Stanley was standing a little way off with his hands in his pockets, watching her calmly.

"Soon I will walk you home in the bluish dark and ask if your hands are cold just for a reason to touch you," Stanley said.

"He asked me if I wanted a drink," the girl said again. She wasn't looking at him. She had found her rhythm now, and her eyes were flashing. "I thought that meant he had some alcohol so I said, Yes. We're breath-tested now, at the door before we walk in, we have to say our name and our address, and always there's that little spasm of fear that you feel, coming out of nowhere, in case it comes up positive. Some of the boys take cameras in, just so they can fill empty film canisters with rum and drink it once they're inside. Or they strap hip flasks to the inside of their legs. Most of them just bring pills. I thought he meant he had some alcohol so I said, Yes. He disappeared."

"Even as I saw you I was disappointed," Stanley said. "Can anything come of such an ordinary beginning? I asked myself. I looked at you and I thought of all the things you aren't. Even before I spoke to you I was angry at you for not being more than you are."

"He came back," the girl said, "and I almost laughed. He had gone and bought us both a Coke, still all dewy and frosted from the fridge behind the bar, and he opened mine up for me with this quiet little flush of pride, like he was some black-and-white hero lighting my cigarette and fixing my drink just the way I like it. We talked for a while about leaving school and going to university and he told me he wanted to be an actor, and we watched the noose for a while."

"I didn't like you," Stanley said. "I didn't like you for detaining me at this never-ending stage of nervous silence and nothing-talk and worry. I didn't want what you were offering. I stayed because I was angry and I wanted to show you that I thought that you were boring. I wanted to make you *feel* boring."

The Head of Acting was watching them impassively. Stanley could see him out of the corner of his eye, holding his head very still.

"I'd already decided," the girl said. "He wouldn't have known that. As soon as I saw him I decided the way it was going to be. He never had a chance."

November

"Why do you want to be an actor, my boy?" Stanley's father asked. The capillaries were standing out in his cheeks in bold little threads. Stanley could tell he was drunk only by the way he ducked his head slightly every time he blinked.

"They asked me that in my audition," he said. He watched his father refill his wineglass, and suddenly didn't feel like being honest. "I just want to have fun with it, I guess."

"Not in it for fame and fortune?"

"Oh," Stanley said, watching as his father reached across the table and emptied the bottle into his own glass. "No. It's more of a...no. I just want to have fun."

"Good man," said Stanley's father. "I've got a joke you might like."

"Yeah?" Stanley said. This was his least favorite part of the evening. He tried to read his father's wristwatch from across the table. They had already ordered dessert, tiny splashes of cream and color on vast white plates, and soon his father would be hailing a pair of taxis and slipping fifty dollars into his breast pocket and clapping him on the shoulder and walking away. Outside the street was slick and oily with rain.

"What's the most common cause of pedophilia in this country?"

"I don't know."

"Sexy kids."

"That's funny."

"It's good, eh?"

"Yeah."

"I got it off a client. Have I told you about him? The one with the angel voices. You'll love this, Stanley. This guy is honestly something else."

Stanley sometimes tried to imagine what it would be like to live in the same house as his father, to see him every day, to walk past him dozing on the couch or brushing his teeth or squinting into the fridge. Their yearly outing was always at a different restaurant, and Stanley could catalog his relationship with his father in a string of names: The Empire Room, The Setting Sun, Federico's, La Vista. Sometimes his father rang him on the telephone, but the two-second delay of the international line made him sound distant and distracted and Stanley always worried he was talking too little or too much.

"You were an accident," was how his father explained it many restaurants ago. "Our relationship was casual, respectful, and very brief. She found out she was pregnant and decided to keep you, even though my practice was moving to England and it was likely I'd never come back. I said I would keep in touch and help out wherever I could. And I saved your life—she was going to call you Gerald. I stepped in."

"Thanks," Stanley said.

"No problem," said his father, waving a piece of squid. "But believe me, sperm is a serious business."

Stanley looked at him now, drunk and flamboyant and mischievous and laughing at his own story. He was a little afraid of his father. He was afraid of the way the man delivered his opinion, afraid of the crafty watchful antagonism that left Stanley uncertain whether he was meant to argue or agree. His million-dollar insurance policy idea was a typical trap, a raw slice of bloody bait laid out with a flourish and a double-crossing smile. Did his father expect him to second-guess the idea? Was he supposed to follow through with it, or admonish his father for being macabre and coarse? Stanley didn't know. He reached into his pocket and touched the edge of the glossy brochure from the Institute.

"Well, I think that's us," his father said, returning his glass to the table and reaching up to smooth his lapel with his hand. "This time next year, my boy, you will have become a sensitive and feeling soul."

November

"Tell us about yourself, Stanley," said the Head of Acting. He made an abrupt gesture with his hand. "Anything. Doesn't have to be relevant."

Stanley shifted his weight to the other leg. His heart was thumping in his rib cage. The panel was sitting against a wall of high windows so their faces were all in shadow and Stanley had to squint against the glare.

"I don't know whether I'm any good at feeling things," he said. His voice was tiny in the vast space. "Nothing big has happened to me yet. Nobody has died, nothing terrible has happened, I've never really been in love or anything. In a funny way I'm kind of looking forward to something terrible happening, just so I can see what it's like."

"Go on," said the Head of Acting when Stanley faltered.

"I was always a bit jealous of people who had real tragedy in their lives," he said. "It gave them something to feed on. I felt like I had nothing. It's not like I want anyone in my family to die, I just want something to overcome. I want a challenge. I think I'm ready for it."

He was trying to look at them all equally.

"In high school I kind of tried things on," he said, "just to see what it was like. Even when I got mad or upset or had a fight with someone, it was like I was just trying it on, just to see how far I could push it. There's always this little part of me that's not mad, that stays sort of calm and interested and amused."

"Good," said the Head of Acting abruptly. "Tell us why you want to be an actor."

"I want to be seen," said Stanley. "I don't really have a bigger answer than that. I just want to be seen."

"Why?" said the Head of Acting, his fountain pen hovering above the page.

Stanley said, "Because if somebody's watching, you know you're worth something."

FIVE

Monday

"Thanks all for coming in, people," the counselor is saying as Isolde walks in. He raises his palms like he is a politician or a priest. "I'd really like to build on some of the issues that we raised in our last session. I thought that today we could talk about taking control."

The room is almost full. Isolde looks around for a seat, nodding tersely at a few of her sister's friends who look at her with sad round eyes as if they are imagining themselves in her shoes and feeling very sorry for themselves indeed. Isolde scowls. She slips into a chair and tries to scrunch down as low as possible. The counselor smiles at her, a horrible rubbery proud smile that makes Isolde's skin creep, and she quickly looks away, down at her fingernails and the worn tatty cuffs of her school jersey. She suffers being questioned and patted and caressed by the girl sitting behind her, a stout motherly figure who was Victoria's tennis partner in intermediate school and once shared a paper bag of sweets with Isolde under the trees at the end of the lawn.

The girl settles back into her chair like a fat tufted hen, and Isolde can hear her say to the girl sitting next to her, "They're keeping her in the dark I reckon. Makes sense."

"Who can tell me what the issue is here?" the counselor is saying, spreading his arms to include them all. "It starts with B," he adds, silencing the girls who are about to volunteer possible answers that do not start with B. The girls lean back and think of all the B words they have heard the counselor use.

"*Boundaries*," the counselor croons at last, and there is a collective exhalation. "Boundaries, people."

Isolde sits very still and gives nothing away, folding into herself and glassing over as if she is pushing her face into a mask. Vultures, she thinks to herself, using her mother's word. Her mother had said it when she saw the contented headlines in the morning paper. Vultures, she said, and then swooped down and ripped off the front page, but ineffectually so the column headline was vertically halved and the piece that remained read *Teacher Sex*. Vultures, Isolde thinks now, as the whispers eddy around her and the counselor smiles his plump greasy smile.

The counselor is saying, "Maybe you might let this sort of thing happen because you just don't know how else to respond."

Isolde sighs and wishes she were dead.

"Why do I have to go?" she asked her mother last night, slapping the pink form down next to the chopped onions and the flour. "It's seventh formers and music students and then *me*. I'll be the only fifth former there and everyone will know and it's *humiliating*. They all pity me and I hate it."

Isolde's mother chewed at her lip in the way she did when she knew she was out of her depth.

"I suppose you could refuse to go, honey," she said distractedly, "but it might end up seeming like you were taking a stand.

You might draw attention to yourself, and that might not be what you want. It might be better for you to just go along and put your head down. I'm not sure. You decide." She smiled in a vague but encouraging way. "Poor lamb," was the last thing she said before turning back to the onions, her disinterest settling over her daughter like a damp chemical mist over a household fire.

Isolde snatched back the pink form and stalked out of the room. "I have to go to counseling because of you," she snapped as she passed Victoria in the hall.

"Why?" Victoria asked, stopping and looking thoroughly surprised.

"Because they want to quarantine," Isolde shouted. "They want to keep us all in one place so the sickness won't spread and they can figure out a vaccine. They want to put us in a concrete yard and take our clothes off and hose us down and scrub us with sandpaper and turpentine and rags made from old Y-fronts that have turned gray. It's like you've left big inky handprints on all of us, everyone you've ever met, but especially me, I'm the most inky, I'm like dripping ink, it's running down my legs and arms and off my fingertips and pooling wider and wider on the floor."

Victoria stood there in the hall with the last of the sunlight slanting across her face and didn't say anything for a while. Isolde breathed raggedly and glared at her, and stood just inside her bedroom door, her hand on the door edge and ready to slam it on cue. Then Victoria said, "Sorry."

"You bloody aren't," Isolde said. She slammed the door.

"Does anybody want to say anything before we kick off?" the counselor is saying now, and one of the girls in the back row calls out, "I do."

Isolde is still broody and wrapped up in herself and doesn't turn around when the girl begins to speak. She hears her say, "I don't agree that Mr. Saladin wanted to gain control," but it takes a moment before she registers what the girl is actually saying.

The girl says, "Sleeping with a minor isn't exciting because you get to boss them around. It's exciting because you're risking so much. And taking a risk is exciting because of the possibility that you might *lose*, not the possibility that you might win."

Isolde turns around to look at her.

The speaker is a seventh former, a hard-edged ink-spotted girl who smokes lonely cigarettes by the goalposts of the soccer field and sits in after-school detention with a satisfied smirk on her face to show that everything is going precisely as she has planned. She is a loner, too bright for the slutty girls and too savage for the bright girls, haunting the edges and corners of the school like a sullen disillusioned ghost and pursued by frightened vicious rumors that she is possibly probably *gay*.

The fact that the rumors about Julia are unsupported by witness or report means that Julia's sexuality remains an elusive property, threatening but not entirely quantifiable, predatory in an unpredictable, unpreventable way. Julia herself, surly and caustic and isolated by her headphones and her paperbacks and the curtain of hair across her face, never chooses to actively dispel the whispers that shadow her. If she is provoked she might scowl and give the finger, but provocation isn't in fashion right now, so mostly she is simply left alone.

Now, while the girls watch Julia as if she is a carnival act and the counselor tugs nervously at the tuft of hair at the nape of his neck, Isolde becomes aware that the atmosphere in the room is changing. A cold dawning fear is rising from the girls like a scent. The belated threat posed by the now absent Mr. Saladin is plainly diminished in the face of this more insidious and unnameable threat posed by Julia. It is not simply the voicing of the opinion that frightens them. Julia is an infiltrator, a dangerous and volatile mole who might without their knowledge have a *crush* on any one of them, who might at any moment be *imagining* any one of them—there are no counseling sessions to prepare the girls against the advances of one of their own.

"The fact that Victoria was underage and virginal or whatever wasn't exciting because he could exercise more power over her," Julia is saying. "It was exciting because he stood to lose so much more if anyone found out." She cocks her head to emphasize the shock value. "He wouldn't just lose her. He would lose everything."

Isolde looks her up and down in fascination. As she contemplates what Julia is saying, she begins for the first time to feel an interest in Mr. Saladin: Mr. Saladin, who saw in her sister something worth pursuing, who whispered things that nobody had ever said before, who risked and lost everything he had.

Why did Mr. Saladin choose Victoria? Isolde finds herself considering the question properly for the first time. She pictures her sister's round cherry pout and round wide eyes, and the flash of red satin whenever she leans over and exposes the artful low waistband of her school kilt. She pictures Victoria in jazz band, leaning forward to turn the page with her sax slung slantwise across her body, the weight of the instrument pulling the neckstrap downward and tight against her sternum so that the upper end of the instrument lies brightly golden between the blue woollen swell of her breasts. And then Isolde thinks, Why did Victoria choose Mr. Saladin?

In the beginning, watching her parents quarrel over Victoria and clinging to her shoulders like the conscience angels of a morality play, all Isolde could feel was a preemptive stab of injustice as she wondered whether her parents would ever find cause to attend so closely to *her*. She applied herself gravely to her parents' distress and watched Victoria from a careful distance, but she did not think to ponder or picture Mr. Saladin as he paced his camel-cream apartment and handed in his hangdog resignation and in shame telephoned his family to confess.

Even now Isolde has only a dim and tangential perception of Mr. Saladin. She remembers him suited and conducting the orchestra at the end-of-year showcase concert, and once she saw him jogging from the music department to the staff car park with his necktie whipped over his shoulder and a sheaf of papers in his fist. She vaguely remembers him slouching on stage at the first assembly, running a hand through his hair and furtively checking his watch as the third formers were welcomed at length into the school. She recalls that he used to call his students Princess, in a teasing despairing sort of way, as if to say that there was nothing to be done.

Isolde tries to imagine Mr. Saladin in a sexual context, and falters. She casts about and tries to place him among his peers. Mr. Horne with the cellulite smear of acne scarring on both cheeks and the chalky fingerprints around his pocket rim. Mr. Kebble who teaches maths and musty French, his underarm sweat-stains blooming like secret bruises. Mr. MacAuley from the bursar's office who is pert and brisk and shines like an apple from behind the sliding glass. She imagines unbuttoning them and tugging their shirttails from their trousers and pushing them hard against the music-cupboard door. She imagines smiling at them in lessons and making their hearts race. She imagines saying, How about lunchtime? and, I like the shirt with the stripes better. She imagines saying, I don't believe you that it doesn't fit. I saw Miss Clark put one over her whole shoe.

Isolde is lost in this contemplation when Julia looks up and meets her gaze. It takes a moment for Isolde's trance-glazed eyes to focus, and then she suffers a swoop in her gut, panicking for an instant in case the subject of her thoughts was in some way visible. Her heart begins to pound. Again Isolde thinks about the rumors that shadow Julia everywhere she goes, and suddenly she feels a little frightened, as if she has just made herself terribly vulnerable in a way she can't quite understand. She panics and turns away. The counselor is talking again, and all around her the girls are nodding, full of contentment and pity and a deep satisfied peace.

Isolde's heartbeat returns to normal. Julia's words return to her in a late echo, washing over her with sudden volume like the unexpected slapping rush of a spring tide. I don't agree, she said, that Mr. Saladin wanted to gain control. Isolde slithers down her seat in confusion and shame, and when the bell rings she slips out of the room without looking back.

Wednesday

"Bridget," the saxophone teacher says, "I told you that if you didn't play that bar perfectly first time I was going to scream."

"I know," says Bridget unhappily.

"Did you want me to scream? Did you imagine the sharp edge of each wrong note stuck like a little barb into the side of my face? Is that what you wanted?"

"No," says Bridget.

The saxophone teacher draws out the silence between them for three minim rests, the metronome on the piano keeping dogged time. "Are you under pressure at home?" she asks. "Or at school?"

Bridget's eyes fill with tears. "Did my mum call you?" she asks, dreading the inevitable. "She said she wouldn't. She always says she won't and then she does."

The saxophone teacher looks her up and down, and then she asks, "Does your mother lie to you, Bridget?"

Bridget falls into miserable silence as she ponders the question.

Whenever she is bullied or short-changed or mistreated in any way, Bridget's first panicked thought is always that she must make sure her mother doesn't find out. Bridget's mother marches into the school administration block almost fortnightly, complaining or querying or demanding on behalf of Bridget, always on behalf of Bridget, who trails in her mother's righteous wake and once heard the secretary whisper, "That girl has got her mother wrapped around her little finger. Wrapped around."

"Please don't come in to school," Bridget said in dread alarm last week, when her mother discovered she'd paid twice the cost of her sax rental for the month by mistake. "I'll sort it out at jazz band. Please don't come."

"All right," her mother said at last, peering at Bridget in a distrustful, grudging sort of way. "But make sure you get a receipt." Later she doubled back on her way home from the supermarket and went in to the music department after all, before Bridget had a chance.

"I said I'd sort it out at jazz band," Bridget said.

"Gave me a chance to ask what measures have been put in place," Bridget's mother said. She eased a puffy foot from her shoe and massaged it slowly. "After this whole Mr. Saladin ordeal, I said, I just want to know what measures have been put in place." She peered at Bridget, brandishing her shoe in her fist. She said, "*Nothing*, that's what. *Nothing* is what's been done."

"I asked you not to go," said Bridget quietly. "They think you're wrapped around my finger."

"Bridget," said Bridget's mother, "it's my money you're spending on that saxophone. I can manage my money as I please. Plus. It gave me a chance to stir them up a bit. *Nothing* is what's been done."

The saxophone teacher is waiting quietly for Bridget's recollection to end.

"I suppose it is lying," Bridget says at last. "I suppose she does lie to me." The betrayal twists sourly in her stomach.

"It's undermining," the saxophone teacher says.

"I suppose so," Bridget says. The metronome arm is still swinging back and forth, measuring the space between them.

The saxophone teacher lets Bridget's misery weigh heavy for a moment, and then she says, "Your mum *did* come and see me last week, actually. Just to catch up. She'd had a run-in with one of the teachers at your school."

Panic floods Bridget's face. "What did she say?"

The sax teacher likes playing Bridget's mother. She shrinks into herself until she looks pale and stringy and rumpled and slightly alarmed, toying with the end of her scarf in a mincing compulsive fashion, her little eyes darting to the edges of the room as she speaks.

"Bridget hasn't had much luck with teachers," is what Bridget's mother said. "Teachers just don't seem to click with her. It's not that she's a bad kid—she isn't a troublemaker at all—and she's not stupid. But there's something about Bridget that seems to rub teachers up the wrong way. It seems that she's just not a likeable girl. It's not something I understand. How do you make your child likeable? I seem to have missed that opportunity. Somehow it passed me by."

It is an accurate performance. The saxophone teacher returns to herself with a pleased expectant expression on her face, as if she knows that she qualifies for full marks but she wants to hear it confirmed all the same.

"She always says things like that," Bridget says unhappily. "Talking about me like that. Going to see my teachers and telling them I have ideas, or asking them why I don't have enough ideas and what they're going to do about it."

"It's because she wants the best for you," the saxophone teacher says.

"No, it isn't," Bridget says. "It's because there's nothing else happening in her life and she has to stick her nose in or she'd be bored out of her brain."

"Come on, Bridget," says the saxophone teacher in a scolding voice. "All that drama at your school—the sex scandal—it really shook her up. She's worried about you."

This sea change is characteristic of the saxophone teacher's conversations with Bridget. A sudden about-face always provokes a satisfying wounded bewilderment that clouds Bridget's face with shame and with the throbbing irreparable guilt of having said too much. The saxophone teacher watches the effect with satisfaction.

Bridget looks at her music miserably for a moment. Her pigtails are drooping and her ribbons are gray. "She said thank God you're a woman," she says suddenly, as if she is contemplating the words for the first time.

Thursday

The school that these girls so reluctantly attend is called Abbey Grange, colloquially known as either Scabby Grange or Abbey Grunge, depending on your mood or point of view. The boys from the high school opposite hang from their armpits along the iron fence and shout "Scabby Abbey!" through the bars, and when the girls take a shortcut through the St. Sylvester grounds they always shout out "Syphilis!" or "Saint Molester!" sometimes without an audience, but always with a judicious sense of evening the score.

Today Isolde is picking her way across the balding field toward Abbey Grange, threading a path around the wind-blown litter and the scuffed mud-holes crusted beige with last night's ice. Steam rises from the netball courts as the sun warms the wet asphalt, and the patched netting behind the soccer goal is bright with dew. The painted divisions on the courts have faded from white to a dirty thready gray. The school is mostly weatherboard, cream and fawn, but there is a clump of newer buildings among the old, recently painted and brighter than the rest, standing out like shiny patches of skin over a new burn. All the trees are restrained with iron collars and ringed by chiseled seats that spell the name and fate of every student once imprisoned there.

Isolde walks slowly, watching the creeping tidemark of gray

mud and lawn cuttings advance over the lip of her school shoes and into the damp wool of her socks. Most of the girls are pouring into the school through the main entrance, and Isolde is thankfully marooned as she makes her way toward homeroom. Thus far since Mr. Saladin left the school Isolde has enjoyed a special kind of freedom, all the students awkward and stepping around her as if she is very fragile, all the teachers brisk and absent and clearly trying to treat Isolde in the most ordinary, invisible way. The privacy is welcome but Isolde knows that soon the mileage of this reflected notoriety will run out. She has noticed with a kind of indifferent contempt that none of her teachers now draws comparisons between her sister and herself, not even the netball coach who was once so fond of repeating, "I swear, you two— there must be something in the water at your house."

Isolde aims a kick at a flattened Coca-Cola can and it advances a few meters toward the school. She resolves to kick it all the way to homeroom. The first bell rings. Isolde aims another kick at the can, shifting to her other armpit her English project, a hand-drawn poster rolled stiffly into a tube and secured with rubber bands.

For this particular assignment Isolde has drawn a king dead in his bed with a sword through his heart, and the spreading bloodstain on the blanket forms the shape of Scotland. Underneath is the quoted line "Bleed, bleed, poor country." Isolde is good at drawing, portraiture especially, and she is proud of this particular effort, drawn in colored pencil and charcoal, and sprayed with an aerosol lacquer to prevent it from smudging in the tube.

"You know whenever the word 'country' is used in Shakespeare it usually means something to do with 'cunt,'" Victoria said when she saw the poster, leaning her elbows on the back of one of the dining-room chairs and looking down at the drawing with a critical eye. "Everyone was way more smutty back then."

Isolde put down her pencil and pulled the text of the play

toward her. She scoured the quoted passage uncertainly, and then said, "I don't think it means that here. There's nothing in the notes."

"Well, it's a school edition, isn't it?" Victoria said. "They're not allowed to put the filthy stuff in. Trust me, country always means cunt. Country matters—that's *Hamlet*. And same with the word 'cunning.' O cunning love. Means cunt."

They spend a moment looking at the picture. Then Victoria adds, "You learn it in seventh form. After English stops being compulsory they let you in on all the good stuff."

"Do you think I should start again?" Isolde said, pinching a pencil shaving between finger and thumb and looking down at the static image with new eyes.

"No, I reckon it's even cleverer now," Victoria said generously, putting her head to one side to see the picture better. "The bleeding and everything. I bet you get top marks."

Mr. Horne is standing by the entrance to the car park as Isolde trudges quietly past with her poster under her arm. He is shaking his fist intermittently at the scarved and mittened flood of girls pouring into the school, shouting "Get off and walk!" at the cyclists who stand up on their pedals and weave around their classmates and trail their helmets from their handlebars by a single strap.

"Morning, Isolde," Mr. Horne calls across to her, touching his first two fingers to his forehead in a kind of salute. Isolde smiles and waves and mounts the steps to the music block where she has homeroom.

As she enters, one of her classmates swoops down and says, "Hey, Issie. You all right?" She makes a mock-sad face at Isolde, pulling down the corners of her mouth like she is begging, and in her mind's eye picturing herself as motherly and caring and kind.

Isolde scowls. "Today is not a good day," she says, because it's easier to pretend that it isn't.

Saturday

"A man can be powerful and still be loved," Patsy reads aloud, "but it's rare to see a woman loved for her power—women must be powerless. So as women gain power in our society, they also find love more difficult to attain." She closes the book and looks at the saxophone teacher questioningly. "Do you agree?"

This is a scene from a long time ago. The saxophone teacher looks younger. Her skin is tighter underneath her eyes and the droopy muzzle lines around her mouth have not yet started to show. Patsy is surrounded by books and papers and ballpoint pens. Outside it is raining.

The saxophone teacher leans back in her chair and ponders the question doubtfully. "I knew a couple with a baby," she says at last, "a baby boy, maybe fourteen months. The father worked all day, came home every night, and the baby would smile and simper and reach out his little arms and perform for his daddy. But if the mother left for a while, maybe left him with a relation or a neighbor if she popped out on her own, when she came back the baby would be furious. He would scowl at her and turn away from her and refuse to be held by her, and howl if she came too close. In the baby's mind, *she* had no right to go away and leave him. The father's love was conditional and it had to be fought for. The baby had to win his father over, and he did. But he saw his mother's love as rightfully *un*conditional, and when she took it away he felt nothing but injustice and contempt.

"At first," the saxophone teacher says, "I felt sorry for the mother. I thought the baby was being terribly unfair. But then I think I changed my mind."

"You changed your mind?"

"Yes," the saxophone teacher says. "She had a kind of power too. She had a kind of influence. That's what I saw, in the end."

"You haven't really answered the question," Patsy says. "I

asked, do you think that as women gain more power in the world they find love more difficult to attain?'"

"No," the saxophone teacher says. "I object to the wording of the question. I object to the assumption that power and love are necessarily two discrete things."

"You *always* object to the question," says Patsy in mock-irritation. "We never arrive at any answers because you are always objecting to the question."

"It's what you learn at university," the saxophone teacher says. "At high school they expect answers, but at university all you're supposed to do is dispute the wording of the question. It's what they want. Ask anyone."

Patsy sighs and brushes a crumb off the dust jacket with the flat of her hand. "Ridiculous," she says, but she sounds defeated.

"I had a friend in first-year," the saxophone teacher says, "who would begin every essay the same way. Suppose she was set an essay on Images of Violence in Mary Shelley's *Frankenstein*. She would begin the essay, 'The problem of violence in Mary Shelley's *Frankenstein* is twofold.' It was always the same. No matter what she wrote on. 'The problem of nationalism in prewar Britain was twofold.' Always the same."

"What if it wasn't twofold?" Patsy says, scowling afresh at the textbook on the table.

"It always is," the saxophone teacher says. "That's the secret."

Wednesday

"There's this girl at school," Bridget says, "who tells these weird lies. The reason I think they're weird is that I don't think she even knows she's lying when she does it."

"Which girl?" the saxophone teacher says.

"Willa," says Bridget vaguely. "But you wouldn't be able to tell. She's good."

Bridget fiddles with her reed for a second and then looks up.

"Like, I always made this mistake," she says, "whenever I read the word *misled* I didn't realize it was *mislead*, to lead somebody astray. I thought that there was a word *mizle* which meant to diddle somebody, and if you were *mizled* then it meant you'd been diddled. So I always said *mizled*, not *miss-led*."

The saxophone teacher's fingertips are on her saxophone hanging from her neck, and when she moves her hand she leaves gray ovals of damp that pucker and vanish in seconds.

"This girl, Willa," Bridget says, "she was in my remedial English last year and heard me say *mizled* out loud and the teacher told me the right way to say it and we all laughed about it, because it was such a stupid mistake. And then last week we were sitting at lunch, a whole group of us, and Willa starts telling us about how she always thought *mizle* was actually a word, and she says *mizled* instead of *miss-led*. She repeats the whole story back to us as if it's her own.

"I watched her really carefully," Bridget says, "and she was looking at me when she said it, all casual and laughing at herself, and I truly don't think she knew that she was telling my story. She would have looked guilty or avoided me or something. I think she'd just heard me make the mistake and she liked the sound of it and after a while she made herself believe that the story was hers."

"Did you shame her?" the saxophone teacher says. "In front of everybody?"

"No," Bridget says. "Everyone would have thought I was lame."

"So nobody knew she was lying."

"No."

"And the next time you say *mizled* by accident, everyone is going to think you only want to be like Willa."

"Yeah," says Bridget. "If I make the mistake again."

"And you know that Willa definitely does not read *mizled* in her head whenever she sees the word *misled*."

"No," Bridget says stoutly. "It's my thing. And anyway she laughed at me in remedial English."

"Well," the saxophone teacher says. "It's certainly not the most heroic story to poach from another person and call your own. I'm sure I can think of better." She moves her hand again and the gray finger-spots of damp turn to vapor and melt away.

Bridget is flushed, unable to voice coherently the indignation and even rage she feels toward this liar Willa, the plunderer, the unashamed thief. Bridget is never rich in tales about herself, however unheroic, yet she is now a fraction poorer, her life shaved a fraction thinner, her mind a fraction less unique, because of this girl's theft.

"But now she's got this memory," Bridget says, struggling on. "A real memory of it, of every time she's ever read that word. And she laughs at herself and says, What an idiot, like she can't believe how silly she is. And she isn't. Silly. She knew the right way to say it the whole time."

"Maybe she's just a liar," the saxophone teacher says.

"But if she doesn't know that she's lying," Bridget says, almost desperately now, "and nobody else knows that she's lying, and she's got this real memory in her head—"

Bridget breaks off, working her mouth like a caught fish.

"Then it might as well be true," she says at last, and in her distraction flaps her hands against her sides, once, twice, and then she is still.

Monday

"I had Mr. Saladin in fifth form," Julia says offhand in her lesson on Monday afternoon.

"Did you?" the saxophone teacher says.

"For School Cert music," Julia says. "I always thought he was just a bit of a nerd."

"Oh," the saxophone teacher says in surprise, this concept of a nerdy Mr. Saladin being altogether new to her. She rolls the idea around the inside of her mouth for a moment.

"She was in my music class that year," Julia continues, a little dreamily. "Victoria was. That must have been way before they got together—she wasn't taking woodwind tutorials then. I remembered that the other day, and ever since I've been thinking and thinking, trying to recall some incident where I remember the two of them together, some incident that I can extract from the rest of the year and make it mean much more than it actually did."

"And?"

"Once," Julia says, "once Mr. Saladin said, Victoria, if you touch that recorder one more time in the next hour you are going to meet a swift and untimely death, and don't you dare test me to see if I mean it." Julia erects the flat-edged arms on her music stand that hold her music in place. "I should bring it up in counseling," she says. She snorts inelegantly. "And then I should cry."

"What happened in counseling today?" the saxophone teacher says.

"Criticism is constructive, comparison is abuse," Julia says. "Like, 'I find your attitude hurtful'—that's criticism, that's okay. 'I think you are so much like your mother'—that's comparison, that's not okay. We learned that first, and then we did role-plays. Role-play is a useful tool for exploring a situation from a different perspective."

The saxophone teacher says nothing, waiting for Julia to continue, and strokes the rough ceramic edge of her mug with her thumb.

"So I put up my hand," Julia says, "and I go, But what if it's a same-sex relationship? I go, Surely comparison plays a much bigger part in same-sex relationships. Like, I'm fatter than you, or I'm more masculine than you, or I'm the mumsy one, or I'm

the sugar daddy, or whatever. I said to the counselor, If comparison is abuse, does that mean you reckon same-sex couples are
more abusive than ordinary couples?"

Julia rocks back and forth on her shuffling feet, exultant in
the pale afterglow of her faulty teenage logic and remembering
the fearful disgusted silence of the classroom, the counselor rubbing at his forehead and the girls scowling back at her across the
void.

"The counselor just goes, Julia, we are not discussing same-
sex relationships right now. Mr. Saladin was a man and Victoria was a girl. Let's not deviate. And he uses past tense like he
always does, as if they're both dead."

Julia comes to an end now, picks up her saxophone and begins
to play. She has censored the last part of the scene just before the
bell rang, as the girls turned back to face front and the counselor frowned and fished for his notes. One of the beautiful girls
turned around in her seat and hissed, "Why do you always have
to bring up things like that? Every class you say something like
that, just to watch how uncomfortable we all get. It's like you
can't get it out of your head and you say it just for kicks. It's
disgusting."

Thursday

Sometimes, for her own amusement, the saxophone teacher tries
to imagine what it would be like if the casting were to change.
She imagines the girl who is playing Bridget in the coveted role
of Isolde, and in her mind's eye she converts the girl, ironing out
her lanky nothing-hair into a glossy sheet that falls sheer from
a center part, rosying her cheeks and transforming her expression into the careless wounded look that has become Isolde's
signature. She adds a silver watch and a delicate silver link necklace beneath the collar of her school uniform. Isolde's character

twists this necklace vaguely around her fingertip from time to time, or else lifts it into her jaw and chews it while she is thinking, the chain link biting into the smooth skin of both cheeks like a fine silver bridle.

Needless to say, Isolde's part is not coveted because of any qualities inherent in Isolde herself: Isolde's part is coveted because of her proximity to the scandal surrounding her sister. The resounding echo of dishonor and disgrace renders her powerful, in the same way that the beautiful girls who say "I just need to be alone for a while" are rendered powerful, thereafter attended at all times by grave concerned servants who flap about and whisper to each other, "I'm worried she might do something to hurt herself." Even dim-witted Bridget can see that Isolde's proximity counts for a great deal.

It makes the saxophone teacher smile to imagine mousy Bridget in Isolde's role. It makes her think fondly that maybe there is a glimmer of hope after all for this pale stringy rumpled girl who chews at the end of her hair and wears her kilt just a fraction too high and tries so desperately hard.

For the role of Bridget the saxophone teacher imagines casting the girl who is currently playing Julia, mentally redressing her in a school uniform that is musty and overlarge and ever so slightly wrinkled. She imagines the girl's posture changing, becoming withdrawn and apologetic, withering in the way that a rind of raw bacon shrinks away from the heat of the pan. The role of Bridget would be the easiest of the three, because Bridget is a victim, and victims are easy. After playing Julia, the role of Bridget would be a cinch.

Into the role of Julia the saxophone teacher inserts the round-faced girl who is currently playing Isolde. This transformation is the hardest to picture, because it is the most subtle. The saxophone teacher reflects that the girl behind Isolde is possibly too virginal to play Julia: the perfect vanity of Julia's self-loathing is something that this girl is not yet sullied enough to grasp.

The saxophone teacher thinks fondly of her students as she sits at the window with her chin on her fist and looks out over the rooftops and the clouds. Then there is a knock at the door and she puts her mug of black-leaf tea to one side. She smoothes her trouser leg and says, "Come in."

Friday

The ginkgo tree rises out of a small square patch of earth in the middle of the courtyard. The concrete bulges and crumples in peaks around the base of the trunk where the tree has shifted in the ground. The fallen leaves are trodden by now into a yellow-smelling paste, choking the drains and fouling the cobbles with a dirty sallow film.

She is still early, and dimly she can hear the low honk of a tenor sax playing an ascending scale, the sound drifting over the slate tiles and down into the empty courtyard with its naked ginkgo tree. Rising above the courtyard is the old observatory tower, closed to the public now, the white-ribbed dome stained a patchy lichen green, the stippled wrought-iron staircase waxed over with bird droppings and dirt.

The saxophone teacher's studio is in a sprawling cluster of buildings that once housed the museum and a few obscure departments of the university. Now the bricked quadrangles and cloisters and narrow unexpected gardens are privately leased, the old exhibition rooms divided into offices and studio spaces and stores.

The tenor sax moves up a semitone and repeats the exercise. Isolde checks her watch: she is almost fifteen minutes early. She swings her sax case idly and looks around the courtyard for something to do. The concrete is blackened and dulled with the recent rain, glum puddles pooling underneath the drainpipes, the birds shrugging off the drips as they hop between the wires.

Isolde steers herself vaguely away from the tree and the high observatory tower, and wanders into an alley with the dim purpose of finding a bakery and buying a hot bun.

As she passes through the cloisters she begins to hear the low thump of a far-off drumbeat. Sometimes there is free theater or performance art by the hot-bread wagons that park on the far side of the cloisters, and she absentmindedly pursues the sound through a narrow arch and down a wet bricked alley until she comes to an open door.

The door is halved horizontally by a steel bar, and at chest-height there is a shiny patch where the oil from thousands of hands has worn the paint away. At present the door is wedged open with a brick, and from within Isolde can hear shouting and the clear thump of a drum.

She slips in quietly, padding down the corridor and up a small set of white-nosed stairs. She passes several dressing rooms with doors ajar and realizes that she must have entered the old auditorium by the players' door. She hesitates and almost turns back, but the drum-thump is louder now and she can hear voices, and she resolves to go on and at least take a look before slipping back the way she has come. She emerges in the thick velvet blackness of the wings, and inches forward in the dark until she finds a gap in the cloth that will give her a view of the stage.

From the wings the stage looks chaotic, the chalk and pencil lines all visible, the painted flats slantwise and cramped together and unbeautiful, and on the far side the jumbled mess of props and costumes in the wings opposite. Isolde can see a small number of backstage watchers, separated from each other by the quivering upright cloth of the wings, some in costume and standing tense on the balls of their feet as they wait for a cue. She can see past the footlights into the foggy dark underbelly of the two-tiered auditorium, and in the foreground the silhouetted players lit around their edges like the bright thread around the rim of a solar eclipse.

In center stage there is a boy in a scarlet turban, wearing shabby coat-tails, a torn dirty ruff, and white gloves that are loose at the wrist and soiled. Vertical black diamonds are painted over each eye, spearing down his cheeks and cutting a sticky greasy track through the white powder on his face. They give him an odd haunted look, merry and melancholy at once. From where she stands Isolde can barely see his profile, just the curve of his cheek and the swell of his turban above his temple and a flash of black diamond every time he turns his head.

"This is a complete deck of cards," the boy is saying into the dark, shuffling a deck of cards so they cascade neatly from his right hand to his left. "No joker. Aces low. The card you draw from this deck will be yours to keep. You will carry it around with you always like a dirty secret."

With a flourish the boy fans the cards in an arc on the felt table in front of him. Her eyes are focusing now, and Isolde becomes aware of others on the stage, clothed in red and black and foaming around this central boy like lepers. The boy is tall and proud and glittering, harshly lit as if he is a figure in an overexposed photograph, bright and misted and glassy-eyed against the glare.

"If you pick a card of a black suit you will be attracted to men. If you pick a card of a red suit you will be attracted to women. The number value on any spot card indicates your sexual prowess. Ten means you're good; ace means you only think you're good."

The boy is whipping the cards out of the pack as he speaks, holding them up between his fingers and his thumb, then puckering his hand swiftly so the card pops out and flutters into the air above him. He catches the fluttering card with his free hand, his other hand already reaching to pick up the next. The effect is rather like he is juggling, the cards tossed up in an explosive little arc and snatched away before they fall.

"If you pick a court card, your sexual life might get a little more complicated. In general, a queen of any suit forces you to cross-dress, a king will give you a sadistic tendency and a jack will give you a masochistic tendency. But there are exceptions."

The kettle-drum roll is building and building. As the drum roll gets slowly louder, the boy becomes gradually more urgent. His movements get faster and his throat gets tighter and his voice gets more insistent. The black-clothed figures on the stage have begun to writhe.

"The King of Diamonds is the only king to carry an axe instead of a sword. For this reason he is known as the Man with the Axe. If you draw the Man with the Axe, your sexual appetite may well develop into a perversion.

"All the court cards are shown in full face except for three: two of the jacks and one of the kings are always in profile. If you draw one of these one-eyed cards, you will be prone to self-deception and dishonesty.

"But the most important of all the court cards is the Queen of Spades."

Someone collides heavily with Isolde from behind. She staggers painfully and whips around. A boy has fallen back against the wing-cloth, swearing and clutching a handful of fabric to steady himself, his feet slipping on the worn chalky floorboards and his free arm sawing back and forth as he tries to regain his balance. He fumbles to keep hold of the scepter he is holding, but it falls with a clatter and rolls away under a fold of cloth.

He peers at her sharply and frowns. "What are you doing here?" he hisses, already ducking down to retrieve his scepter.

"I was just watching," Isolde says, taking a hasty step back as the boy scrabbles around in the half-dark. "Sorry."

"Stanley!" hisses one of the lepers on stage. "Stanley, that's you!"

There is no time for Isolde to say more. The boy grabs his scepter, jumps to his feet and hurries onstage, righting his crown and flipping his scepter up in the brief half-second before he is illuminated. Isolde's last glimpse of him before he dissolves into the harsh stage light is of a face in transformation, caught between a natural expression and a caricature, changing from the inside in the way the bathwater skin begins to pucker and depress when the plug is pulled from underneath.

Isolde's heart is still thumping from the collision and she suddenly feels ashamed that she is watching without invitation. She turns and slips away, retreating down the white-nosed steps she entered by, padding softly down the narrow corridor and finally bursting out into the ginkgo-smelling bright of the day.

SIX

April

"Masks or faces? That's what I keep asking myself. Masks or faces."

The Head of Movement was leaning against the radiator in the staffroom, his thin hands wrapped around his mug, frowning in a glassy sort of way at a faint stain on the linoleum floor. "The tall girl," he said. "Today. Doing that... that piece from... The piece she did today—oh, start me off?"

The Head of Acting dipped his newspaper and looked at him over the top of his glasses. "Come, you spirits..."

"*Come,* you spirits, that tend on mortal thoughts, unsex me here, and fill me, from the crown to the toe, top-full of direst cruelty. Yes." The Head of Movement stood quivering for a moment. "She will never convincingly play that part. She is trapped inside her little round eyes and inside the smooth perfect symmetry of her face. All I could think while I was watching was that *she* would never think those lines. Not her. Not that face. That face would never dare. If I went and saw her in performance I would walk out and say, Lady Macbeth was all wrong." The Head of Movement tossed his head in frustration. "I look at them all," he said, "and I see so much hope and vigor and determination, all trapped inside faces that will never sell, that will never be remarkable—modern, pampered, silken faces that have never known tragedy or hardship or extremity, or even...God, most of them have spent nearly their whole lives *inside*. That girl—Lady Macbeth, today. It is like she's made of plastic. She is too smooth and round to be real. She will never escape that smoothness and that roundness. She will never escape her face."

"You're in a very bleak mood, Martin," the Head of Acting said, unwrapping an aspirin and dropping it neatly into his coffee. "I didn't think she was that bad. I rather liked her freshness. 'Come to my woman's breasts, and take my milk for gall'—I thought that was marvelously seductive. She wasn't trying to be *evil*."

"She wasn't trying to be evil because she didn't understand a damn word of what she was saying," the Head of Movement snapped.

There was a silence. The Head of Movement bent his head and gulped from his mug in an indelicate snatching way, gasping between each hot mouthful, his throat contracting like a reptile's when he swallowed. The Head of Acting thought, That's a bachelor's habit, bred of always eating alone. He felt sorry for the Head of Movement suddenly, and put his paper down.

His dissatisfaction with the world always has such a terribly personal quality, the Head of Acting thought; he is freshly disappointed each time anything falls short of an ideal, and he wears his disappointment like a child. It showed a curious kind of innocence for a man of his age—a foolish self-sabotaging kind of innocence, for he knew that he was going to be disappointed, and still he believed.

The Head of Movement's instinct inclined toward simplicity

and scruple, and yet he was not a scrupulous man: instead he was anxious and undecided and complaining, suspended between points of view. He was forever in the shadow of a principle, forever in the shadow of some floodlit cathedral swarming with bats in the dark, and while he might admire it and worship it and fear its massive contour, he could never bring himself to truly touch it; he would never knock and enter.

The Head of Acting watched him wince and scowl into his coffee and draw his shoulder blades together and toss his head as if his skin had shrunk. The Head of Acting thought, It is as if, in some deep recess of him, he is still a teenager who has not yet lost that selfish blind capacity to fall in love, and fall badly. He wondered if he was jealous of the man's anxiety, jealous of the agony of his choices, jealous of his tortured sense of failure and the failed justice in the world.

"Is it a bad batch this year?" the Head of Acting said. "Is that what's getting you down?"

The younger man flopped into a chair like a punctured balloon. "No," he said, drawing out the word in a doubtful way.

"You were asking yourself, masks or faces."

"Yes," the Head of Movement said, and sighed. "I used to believe in faces. All my life I believed in faces. I think I might have finally changed my mind."

February

Whenever a door was closed at the Institute another always opened, popping gently forth, invisibly nudged by a draught that could never be contained. The shifty current gave the buildings a muttering, ghostly feel. If Stanley closed a door behind him, he always listened to hear another click open, like a faithful echo, out of the shadows further up the hall. All the doorknobs rattled. Hairline cracks webbed the enamel like dirty lace.

112

The academic year began with a lavish production of *King Lear*, directed by the graduating students and starring all the tutors, proud and flashing in burgundy and gray. The title role was played by the Institute's previous Head of Acting, long since retired, a sinewy man with long teeth and thin white hair scraped neatly forward over his forehead like a monk. About a month after closing night a costume, freshly flattened, was mounted on the peeling corridor wall. The collar was still stained black from the blood that ran down from empty eye-sockets and dripped sticky and scarlet off the Head of Movement's gray unshaven chin.

The year began in earnest. The production of *King Lear* had been in part a challenge, presented to frighten the first-years and to show them an inheritance they would have to fight to earn. For a time it worked. In the beginning the first-years looked up at the tutors and older students with a kind of meek reverence, but as the weeks wore on they slowly began to inflate, growing ever larger with purpose and self-belief.

"I'm an actor," Stanley was surprised to hear himself say, and after an initial pause he found that the definition pleased and even empowered him. "At the Drama Institute," he then added, and waited confidently for his interlocutor to say, "Oh, the *Institute*. That's supposed to be very hard to get into, isn't it? You must be rather good."

The first few weeks of the year seemed to pass in a flurry. Initially the first-year batch appeared tentative and apologetic and bashful with each other, but in fact each student was carefully carving out a place within the context of the group: those who variously wanted to be thought of as comic or tragic or eccentric or profound began to mark out their territory, fashioning little shorthand epithets for themselves and staking claim to a particular personality type so that none of the others would have a chance. One of the girls might drape herself over her classmates as they walked from Movement down the hall to Voice and say, "God, I love you guys! I love you all!," just to secure her place as someone who was indubitably *sweet*. With that place occupied, the others scurried to make known their social or musical or intellectual talents, each defining a little space for themselves that no one else would be able to touch. The other students all said, "Esther is so *funny!*" and "Michael is so *bad*!," and just like that each won the double security of becoming both a person and a type.

Stanley wasn't sure what marked him out as a person. He hung back at the beginning of the year and let the other boys claim the roles of the leader and the player and the clown, watching with a kind of uncertain awe as they worked to recruit admirers and an audience. He guessed he wanted to be thought of as sensitive and thoughtful, but he didn't pursue the branding actively enough and soon those positions were taken. He found himself thoroughly eclipsed by several of the more ambitiously moody boys, boys who were studied in the way they tossed their hair off their forehead, thin boys with paperback copies of Nietzsche nosing out of their satchels, boys wearing self-conscious forlorn looks, permanently anxious and always slightly underfed. Whenever these boys began to speak, the class would peel back respectfully to listen.

Stanley found himself quietly shepherded into the middling drift of the unremarkable students in the class. Like the rest of them he nursed a small hope that one day he would come into his own and surpass them all, but the hope was half-buried, and in his lessons Stanley rarely bloomed.

"We'll make something of you yet," the Head of Improvisation said to Stanley one morning, reaching over and tapping his chest with her finger. "There's something in there," she said, "that one of these days is going to just *ripen*, overnight. You'll see."

She walked away and left Stanley with the hot echo of her touch on his sternum and a feeling of joyful arrival that stayed with him for the days and weeks following. He applied himself more vigorously to his technique, spurred on by this germ of confidence that swelled his chest to bursting. He began to believe in his own ripening, waiting for it with a pious kind of expectation like a cleric awaiting a response to prayer. He became more patient with his own failures, safe and confident in the knowledge that one day soon he would surely succeed.

"It's a strange thing," the Head of Improvisation said later in the staffroom, pausing to count stitches with the pearly edge of her fingernail and tug the woollen square out flat to check her progress. "It's a strange thing, how we caress their egos like we do. I see how much it affects them, lights them up, and I feel so responsible, even guilty, like I am handing a loaded pistol to a child."

"All actors are perverted by their profession," the Head of Acting replied, shaking out his newspaper and folding it crisply along the existing seam. "We inflate their egos to make up for everything about them that gets trampled and broken. You're not damaging them, Glenda. You're just softening the blow."

Most of Stanley's friends from school had now dispersed, swallowed up by the local university and the polytechnic or packed off overseas to pursue better chances somewhere else. Stanley buried himself at the Institute. The first-years were required for long hours each day, and more and more often Stanley found reason to come into the buildings on the weekends, nosing around the script library or taking a book up to the viewing gallery above the dance hall, where he could watch the weekend school groups take classes in ballet and rope work and basic tissue. He found a flat with two other first-year actors, thin solemn figures who, like him, had let all the other bones of their lives fall away. He became consumed by the Institute so totally and wholeheartedly that he sometimes thought about the sour-faced boy from Wardrobe with the ancient gramophone in his arms. He had seen the boy several times on his way to and from the art department, always hauling cans of paint and bags of fabric scraps and half-finished puppets stuck with pins.

At home the boys talked nothing but acting, film and theater, and street performance and revolution, snug in the shell of their own irrelevance but all of them giddy as if they were standing together and alone on the edge of a new uncharted world. They talked long into the night and drafted plays on greasy scraps of newsprint and imagined what marvelous lies they might one day be paid to tell.

"When they write our biographies," his housemates said, "when they write our biographies, all this will be in the opening chapter, the chapter before the big break, before we get famous, before everything starts happening. And this is the chapter that everyone will find really interesting and inspiring, because it will show that we are just people like everyone else, people who started from an ordinary beginning, people who were once poor and struggling and earning an ordinary wage. In that way, this chapter will be the most interesting chapter of the whole book."

Stanley began to look at himself differently, cherishing the parts of himself that he might be able to use, delicately prodding himself for weaknesses, both fearful and hopeful that he might cause himself to bruise or break. His father, who had never before figured very prominently in his daily life, began to surface as a source of tragedy to be mined and exploited and spent. In class he talked about his father more and more. Gradually and unconsciously Stanley began to regard himself as a tragic figure—not a victim of the ordinary lash of adolescence, but a person more profoundly wronged, a kingly figure, an emotional hero. At night he sighed and pounded his pillow and sometimes cried.

"Always the *arriviste*," the Head of Acting said in the staffroom, with a kind of paternal amusement. "We get them too late. That's the problem. We should have a school for sixteen-year-olds. They'd get their degree at nineteen. They'd have to drop out of high school to audition. It'd do them good."

"They're already formed by the time they enroll," said the

Head of Voice. "Psychically formed. Morally formed. Everything happens so early now."

"And they love themselves so dearly," the Head of Improvisation said. She tugged sharply at her wool and sent the ball rolling away under the table. "That's the hardest thing to break."

In the students' cafeteria on the floor below, the first-years were clumped together in a similar debate. Stanley picked thoughtfully at his gray slip of pork as he listened.

"You have to admire people that come here," one of them was saying, "people that choose to put themselves on display, people that choose to play with the very aspects of themselves that make them the most vulnerable. These people are the bravest people in the world."

April

A fine mist of slanting rain was falling, darkening the slate and beading the swollen moss with a thin film like a silver dew. Stanley was sprawled on one of the vinyl couches that lined the corridors of the technical wing, lying on his back with his legs wrapped around the radiator pipe and reading, his thumb spread over the top edge of the spine to hold it open.

"Are you doing your reading for Early Modern?" said one of the first-year girls, coming up beside him and flopping down on to the floor.

"Yeah," Stanley said, shifting his thumb slightly to hold his place on the page. "I've got *The Revenger's Tragedy*. What have you got?"

"*The Alchemist*," the girl said, pulling her bag open and taking out a dog-eared copy of the play. "I haven't started. What's yours about?"

Stanley thought for a second, and then said, "It's about a man who puts on a disguise in order to avenge the death of someone he loves, but after his revenge is complete he finds out that he can't take the disguise off. He's become this person he's pretended to be for so long." He flipped the book around to take another look at the cover, which showed a cloaked man attempting to ravish a skeleton. The skull was brightly painted in peach and scarlet, the cheekbones rouged and the eye sockets ringed in glossy black.

"Cool," the girl said, thoroughly unmoved. She sighed and stretched out her legs, reaching down to grip her toes with both hands. "Dance class yesterday actually *annihilated* me," she said. "I hobbled all the way home. Like actually hobbled."

"Yeah," Stanley said. He stalled a second, trying to think of something to say next. He almost began to say how much the dance class had made him sweat, but stopped himself with the words already in his throat. He almost began to chatter in a self-deprecating way about his fitness, but stalled again and instead cast around for something to say about the dance tutor or the class itself, but he took too long to come up with something and at all once he froze in the compounded panic of realizing he had paused for too long. The girl shifted and began to stretch her other leg. The rough-edged copy of *The Alchemist* fell sideways off her lap and on to the floor.

"All the dance tutors at this place are sadists," she said. "Look at that bruise."

Stanley looked. Slender fingers of gray and purple carved across her hip and melted into a reddish cloud above the bone. She stroked the bruise impressively with one finger, her other hand peeling back the waistband of her tracksuit to expose the skin.

"Wow," Stanley said.

"But I do bruise really easily," the girl said. She tucked the bruise back under her waistband and resumed stretching her leg.

"Hey, this play is actually really good," Stanley said, loosening his tongue and trying for a second time. He flapped his copy of *The Revenger's Tragedy* half-heartedly against his leg. "It's so grisly and sick."

The girl glanced at the cover briefly. "Is that the one where the guy nails the other guy's tongue to the floor with his dagger?"

"Yeah!" Stanley said. "And while he's dying he's forced to watch his wife having sex with his bastard son."

"Yeah, I know that scene," the girl said.

Her indifference seemed to close the conversation completely, slamming it shut with a slap that left no echo. She sighed. Stanley tapped his fingers and wondered briefly if he should reopen his book and keep reading. He compromised by turning the book over and rereading the blurb on the back.

"Did *you* bruise after yesterday?" the girl said after a moment, looking at Stanley with a narrow-eyed interest and flicking her eyes over him, up and down.

"I just sweated a lot," Stanley said, feeling as he said it a wash of resignation, as if he had known he would say it all along. "Dance class makes me sweat."

"Gross," the girl said, and touched her bruise again through the fabric of her waistband, cupping her fingers carefully around her hip.

March

"Let's see some chemistry," said the Head of Acting, and nodded at them both to begin.

This time Stanley was sitting on a park bench with his feet tucked underneath him, drawing his shoulders up to his ears against the cold. The air was crisp and ginkgo-smelling.

"I've seen you here before," Stanley said, "on your way to your music lesson, stepping around the leaves."

The girl halted a little way off. She slung her music case down from her shoulder and placed it on its end in front of her, resting her wrists upon it like a teller at a tollbooth. Stanley spoke again.

"I thought," he said, "that maybe I could make you feel like you were worth something. If you were interested. Maybe this weekend. I'd kiss you only once you were very sure that you could trust me. I'd look out for you. I promise."

"Why?" the girl said.

"I think you're interesting," Stanley said. "I want to know you better."

The wind caught the edge of the girl's skirt and tugged at it gently. She moved her knees closer together against the draught.

"Last year," she said, "I was standing at the bus stop after netball and one of the boys showed up on his bicycle, and I smiled at him and we talked about the people we knew and then he said, Guess what I got my girlfriend for Valentine's Day? Pregnant. So I smiled and said, Congratulations. And then he scowled at me and he said, Jesus, we went to the doctor. She's sixteen."

"I don't understand," Stanley said.

"There's no such thing as innocence any more," the girl said, "there's only ignorance. You think you are holding on to something pure, but you aren't. You're just ignorant. You are handicapped by everything you don't yet know."

"But I see something pure in *you*," Stanley said quietly. "I see something in you that is different from all the others. I see a purity in you."

"The only difference between me and any of the others," the girl said, flatly but with a kind of relish, "is at what price and under what circumstances I am prepared to yield."

April

"Stage fighting," the Head of Movement said, "is also known as combat mime."

Everyone was upright and alert today, hopping up and down on the balls of their feet and shaking out their fingertips. This was the class they had all been looking forward to, underlined on their timetables in red ink and attempted in advance in the secret of their bedrooms at home.

"Stage fighting is not a form of violence," the Head of Movement said. "It is a form of dance, a controlled dance that is rehearsed very slowly until it is perfected, and then brought up to speed. Next year you learn basic fencing, épée and sabre and foil. This year we focus simply on how to slap, punch and kick, drawing on the arts of kickboxing, capoeira and basic acrobatics. By the end of this year you should be able to choreograph and perform a fight that simulates punching, kicking and throwing your opponent, as well as being punched, kicked and thrown yourself."

He smiled at their eagerness and added, "You'll learn that losing a stage fight is just as difficult and demanding a task as winning one. Now. Who can give me the definition of a special effect?" He looked around, but the students were blank and distracted, hopping from foot to foot and aching to begin. "A special effect," the Head of Movement said patiently, "is something that does not happen, it only *seems* to happen. Stage fighting is a special effect. The violence that you simulate *does not happen* on stage. Anybody who doesn't understand this will fail this section of the course. In previous years we have had students removed from this class because they do not understand the definition of a special effect."

He pointed at a chalked rectangle drawn on the gymnasium floor, and said, "All right. Everyone get inside the line, please."

The students moved forward in a crush to get inside the rectangle. The area was small and they had to cluster tightly, shuffling together and clutching at each other to keep their balance and stay inside the line. The girls drew their shoulders together and became ever so slightly concave, carefully bringing their upper arms forward and together from an instinct to protect their breasts. The boys snickered and shoved each other with their shoulders and the backs of their wrists. Stanley found himself in the middle of the crush, uncomfortably pinned between a pair of girls both facing inward. The girl in front breathed into his collarbone and carefully shifted her feet so they were tucked inside his own. The rough edge of her foot touched his, and she quickly shifted her weight to twitch away.

"Before we begin fighting I want to start with a few exercises that will get us comfortable with touching each other," the Head of Movement said. "This exercise is called The Raft of the Medusa. The aim of the exercise is to be the last person standing inside this rectangle. When I say you may begin, you must all start pushing each other. If any part of your body touches the floor outside the rectangle, you must leave the raft immediately. The last person to remain inside wins. Does everybody understand?"

There was a flurry of nodding from inside the cramped rectangle.

"Pushing only," the Head of Movement said. "No punching. No kicking. Not yet."

Everybody tensed their elbows and braced their legs, ready to fight. The students on the outer edge realized too late their disadvantage, and all at once they tried to angle themselves better to worm their way into the center.

"All right," the Head of Movement said. "Go."

The rectangular crowd immediately began to boil. A few of the students were shoved out of the rectangle within seconds; they skipped backward and retreated with a kind of rueful disappointment to watch. Stanley found himself surrounded by girls, and at first he shoved at them gingerly, careful with his hands lest he touch their breasts by accident, using mostly his shoulders and his hips. The girls were less polite. Little palms were shoving at the small of his back all of a sudden, pushing and pushing, and he found his feet slipping on the floor. He grabbed a fistful of somebody's sweater in an effort to resist. The whole crowd lurched suddenly sideways; everybody's bare feet arched and skidding over the floorboards, and half the class tumbled over the western chalked perimeter and off the raft. The disqualified students hopped neatly out of the way and left the rest of the group to fight.

With a large part of the class gone, the winning students could move more freely. The game became more tactical and more deliberately hostile. Stanley had one of the smaller girls in a clumsy underarm headlock and was trying to force her over the line when another student fell sideways on to him and sent all three of them staggering off the raft. The Head of Movement was standing calmly to the side. He checked his watch.

When the raft had been emptied of most of the students, the remainder formed a ring around the final fighters and began to chant and cheer. The winning three were locked in a sweaty embrace in the chalky center of the raft, skidding sideways and occasionally dropping painfully on to a knee or a hip and tugging the others down as they fell. Their legs were braced and bowed as they grappled with each other, two boys and a girl—a wiry muscular girl with the shapely and decided figure of a dancer.

Somebody on the perimeter set up a stamping rhythm, and soon all the students were stamping and stamping, their bare feet sending up tiny clouds of white dust, the steady beat filling the massive space, rising up to the lofty stippled ceiling where the hooded bulbs hung from their bluish rack unlit. The Head of Movement did not join in the stamping, but his long fingers tapped in time against his forearm and his eyes moved carefully from the ring of cheering watchers to the fighting three, and back again. Every time one of the winning fighters was shoved hard or forced closer to the chalk perimeter there was a whoop of appreciation from the crowd and an explosion of clapping and laughter. The beat got faster and faster. The Head of Movement nodded his head and sometimes smiled a tiny smile.

In a sudden fluent movement the dynamic of the struggling three abruptly changed, the boys turning upon the girl and moving to work in tandem for the first time. The tacit flare of cooperation made the Head of Movement inhale gravely and stroke the corners of his mouth with his finger and his thumb. The girl was finally ousted, hauled over the line by the boys shoving at her in a parallel surge. The boys then turned to face each other, skipping quickly away from the perimeter and back into the safety of the middle of the raft. The girl added her voice to the cheering and the stamping, and the boys were once again locked in a skidding headlock, a weary inching dance that finally ended when the two of them fell across the southern line in a tangled heap.

The first-years performed The Raft of the Medusa six times, repeating the exercise again and again until the students were flushed and sore and strained. As the morning wore on, their posture gradually began to change, hardening and drawing upward and becoming more aggressive and finally losing the curving self-conscious protectiveness that in the beginning had handicapped them all so plainly. The chalked line soon bled out into sticky tracks of gray and white, tearing outward like a dying star.

"Thank you," the Head of Movement said after almost an hour, when the red-faced victor had sent his opponent lurching over the line for the sixth and final time. "Now you should all be nicely limbered up and you should have gotten used to touching each other. I want to start with the very basics of stage fighting and build upward." He gestured for them to gather round. He said, "We'll start with learning how to punch."

May

The boy in the mask said, "I need a volunteer."

The mask was cut away around his mouth like a jowl, curving over his upper lip so his chin and his lower teeth were exposed.

The hard plastic curve around his mouth made him look a little like a marionette, shiny and rigid and hinged. The surface of the mask was smooth and flesh colored, with almond-shaped eye-holes, and attached to the boy's face without elastic.

Several of the first-years in the audience raised their hands, grinning in a self-conscious, defensive way, and the masked boy pointed at one of them. "You," he said, and beckoned. This was evidently a sound cue: the gymnasium was suddenly filled with the sound of a classic accordion, jolly and scissoring and gay.

The gymnasium door opened and the secretary darted in, trotting over to the Head of Acting and whispering urgently in his ear. The Head of Acting nodded, rose, and followed her out. The door closed behind them.

In the audience Stanley shivered with unknowing delight. He watched the volunteer make his way through the audience and mount the stairs to the stage. By now other masked figures were drifting coolly on to the stage from the wings, pacing about and looking impassively out at the audience through the fleshy almond holes in their cutaway masks.

"This is an exercise in the Theater of Cruelty," the masked boy called out above the rising sound of the music. "This exercise is a challenge."

He moved behind his volunteer. The boy stood and smiled uncertainly at them all, waiting for his instructions, listening for sounds of the masked boy's movement behind him, and rocking back and forth self-consciously on his heels. Then the masked boy knocked him to the ground. As he fell forward on to his knees, the boy's head was flung painfully backward, his expression hurt and bewildered by the split-second impact but still half-smiling his nervous defensive smile. Swiftly the masked boy darted forward and hit him again, and the boy fell flat on to his stomach, jarring his chin on the floor. In an instant the masked boy was kneeling on his back, pinning him flat on the ground and twisting the boy's wrists around behind his back so he couldn't move.

Somebody ran forward with a water-trough, a wide, flat basin filled with slopping water, and shoved it roughly down onto the floor. The attacker grabbed a fistful of his volunteer's hair, reared up, and plunged him headfirst into the water. He held his own breath as he struggled to keep the volunteer's head submerged, looking at his writhing victim down the length of his stiff veined arms and pinching his lips together in concentration. The victim began to thrash out in desperation and fear, his legs kicking out on the floorboards, panicked and flopping like a bloody gutted fish dying on the edge of a pier.

From where Stanley sat cross-legged in the audience, the pinioned drowning boy looked headless. Stanley could see only his damp collar and the last white knob of his spine over the lip of the water-trough as he tried in vain to struggle free. He watched as the boy slapped the floorboards and writhed and the water slopped and thrashed and the accordion kept playing its jolly provincial tune. After almost twenty seconds the audience began to shift and mutter, and someone shouted, "Let him go!" The masked boy looked up with a jerk, as if jolted out of a reverie. He released his victim immediately, jumping up and stepping backward in a nimble little leap, and the volunteer reared his dripping head, coughing and spitting and taking great savage lungfuls of air. His eyes were streaming and pink-rimmed and his face was white. He sat for a moment in hurt bewilderment, quivering and gasping weakly in the middle of the stage.

The audience watched him regain his breath in silence. They met his gaze with a kind of wary suspicion, all of them thinking that he was probably a plant, a prearranged assistant who any moment now was going to leap up and laugh and cuff them on the shoulder and say, "I got you good." They regarded him doubtfully. They were not yet convinced. A few of the students looked around to measure the approval or affirmation of the tutor, but the Head of Acting had gone and they were alone, a baffled motley patch of black in the middle of the gymnasium floor.

On stage the masked boy was standing impassively, his legs apart, his hands together behind his back. Then in one fluid motion he raised his arm, and two other masked boys ran forward, grabbed the gasping volunteer by his arms, and hauled him to his feet. The first boy ran forward and there was a flurried snipping shoving movement, and then the volunteer boy was shoved to his knees once more and slapped hard across his face. The two boys who were holding him began to tug at his shirt, and Stanley realized that the boy's clothes had been cut off him, sliced from the hem to the collar up the length of his spine. The masked boys tore away the ragged shirt and jumper, and then darted back, leaving him pale and shirtless and shivering in the middle of the floor.

The masked boy looked directly at the audience now, as if in challenge. The first-years looked back in bewilderment.

"That sucks, man," the volunteer boy said suddenly, looking at the torn remains of his jersey and his shirt wadded in a ragged pile in front of him. His voice was thin. "That's my favorite shirt."

The masked boy didn't flinch. He kept looking at the audience, as if waiting for somebody to speak. Nobody did. He leaped forward, and the scissors flashed out again, and in a swift careful movement he grabbed a fistful of the volunteer boy's hair from the top of his head and cut it off with a thick silver *snip*.

There was a collective intake of breath from the students on the floor. The masked boy stood holding the clump of brown fur aloft like it was a trophy scalp. Nobody moved. There was a long and horrible pause, and then all of a sudden the volunteer boy jumped up and bolted. The masked boys tried too late to grab him—they missed. He jumped off the edge of the stage and ran out of the gymnasium without looking back.

The masked boy watched him leave and drew himself up a little higher.

"This is an exercise in the Theater of Cruelty," he said. "We are here to show you what it means to really feel something." He gave an odd little bow and then the curtain fell, whistling swiftly down like a blade. The bottom folds hit the stage floor with a thump and then the first-years were alone in the gymnasium. They could hear the soft apologetic patter of the actors' feet as on the other side of the curtain they dispersed and then finally disappeared.

May

"Come with me," was all the Head of Movement said when Stanley found him, and Stanley followed his sloping barefoot tread all the way from the courtyard to the office upstairs, both of them silent, Stanley falling back as he tried to swallow and mask his tears. He was surprised at the violence of his feelings.

"I've come to complain," was all he'd said, standing with his bony knees together and squeezing the blood from his hands. "I can't find the Head of Acting. I want to complain."

Through his distress Stanley found himself a little relieved that he had found the Head of Acting's office locked and the staffroom empty. The Head of Movement was infinitely more approachable than the older man, who peered through his glasses at the students with a kind of impassive chill and wore short sleeves even in winter, as if he were cold-blooded and felt no difference.

Now, in the still of the office, the Head of Movement placed his palms together in an entreating way. "Stanley," he said. "Stanley, what do you think you would do if you paid to go and see a play which included a rape scene, and during this rape scene the assailant began to really rape his victim?"

"I'd say something," Stanley said. His voice quavered a little and he reached up to rub his cheek with the heel of his hand.

"You would not," said the Head of Movement. He laced his

fingers together. "You would shift in your chair and you would think that this was terribly avant-garde but still it really wasn't your thing and you would marvel at how realistic everything was looking and maybe if you were very uncomfortable you would look around you to see what everyone else was making of it. And then if you really started to feel like something was amiss, maybe if the victim was obviously crying out for help, or if everybody in the audience was clearly feeling uncomfortable, *then* you might stand up and shout something out. But it would take you a very long time. Most likely by the time you got the courage to fight back, the scene would be over."

Stanley was at a loss for what to say.

"I know it's a horrible thing to have to imagine," the Head of Movement said, "but I'm trying to make a point. I'm just trying to point out that if a person is standing onstage in front of an auditorium full of people then 'real' is a useless word. 'Real' describes nothing on stage. The stage only cares whether something *looks* real. If it *looks* real, then whether it is real or not is immaterial. It doesn't matter. That's the heart of it."

"That's not what you told us in Movement class," Stanley said, with rising anger. "You said what was important was truth and not sincerity. All that stuff you said about mime. I *believed* all that."

The Head of Movement sighed and pressed his fingers to his lips. "No," he said, and paused for a moment, shaking his head and gathering his thoughts together. He drew a weary breath. "No. We're talking about two different things now.

"Stanley," he said, "think how you would feel if you acted in a play in which your character had to die, and after the performance everybody came up to you and said I really believed you, I really honestly believed that you had died. I saw you dead onstage and I felt myself thinking, Oh my God, he's actually *dead*. You would be rapt. It would be the best possible compliment anybody could give you: that your pretence, your big game of let's-pretend, looked so real that somebody actually thought it *was* real."

"But *I'm* real," Stanley said, realizing to his displeasure that he was again on the verge of tears. "My performance might be pretend, but I'm not."

"That's exactly it," said the Head of Movement swiftly. "If you are a good actor, you will be using *your* emotions, displaying *your* laughter, *your* tears, *your* sexuality, *your* insecurities. There's always this doubleness at play. You and the character you are playing both have to be transparent. You have to look through the one to see the other. That is why being an actor is such a difficult job. It really is you up there."

"But there *wasn't* any doubleness today," Stanley cried out. His voice was high and tight and choked. "It was just him. It was his shirt they ruined. It was his breath. It was his hair. They were hurting *him*."

"You're angry because they betrayed you," the Head of Movement said simply. "They lured you into feeling something truthful and real, and then they destroyed it in front of you."

"They betrayed *him*!" Stanley shouted.

The Head of Movement sighed and looked down at his hands.

"Why is this not a problem for you?" Stanley said after a moment, still breathing quickly. "How can it be okay by you that something like this is able to happen?"

"I understand your anger," the Head of Movement said. "Please believe that it wasn't meant to happen in the way that it happened. In fact I don't think the boys properly understood what they were doing. The manifesto of the Theater of Cruelty is really a lot more complicated and interesting and life-affirming than its name suggests." He closed his eyes, recalling a loved passage to his mind, and said, "'I have therefore said "cruelty" as I might have said "life" or "necessity" because I want to indicate that there is nothing congealed about it, that I turn it into a true act, hence living, hence magical.'" He opened his eyes and smiled sadly at Stanley. "Artaud," he said, "in his own words."

Stanley sat for a moment, breathing heavily and feeling stalemated. He tried to remember what they had been talking about a few minutes earlier, to renew his argument and try to force the Head of Movement out of this tired apologetic apathy.

"I like that you had the courage to talk to me," the Head of Movement said now. "I'll be speaking to each of those students very seriously so they really understand the emotional impact of what they did." He blinked at Stanley and waited. The minute hand moved forward with a solemn *thock*.

When the Head of Movement was younger he acted for the Free Theater, a mothy ragged band of minstrels and failed gypsies who squatted in derelict houses and camped in parking lots and traveled around the country each year to perform at prisons and rural schools. On the wall above his head were a few snapshots from those days showing greasepaint and street-side juggling and oil-drum fires and scratched guitars. Now he sat bowed with age and a clinging fatigue, reaching up to stroke his thin hair with a dry wrinkled palm, crisp and graying and faded like a piece of parchment left too long in the light.

"Has it ever happened to you?" Stanley said suddenly. "Like the rape thing. Have you ever gone to see a play where something real happens and everyone just watches and thinks it's part of the play?"

"Yes," the Head of Movement said. "A long time ago. I saw a man die of a heart attack. He was old. The curtain came down, that's all. They asked us to leave. Everyone left very quietly."

"Who was he playing when he died?" Stanley asked.

"Oh, it was an obscure little play that didn't do especially well, as I recall," the Head of Movement said, leaning back in his chair and looking at the ceiling to better conjure up the memory. He was relieved not to have to look at Stanley anymore. "Everything was rather beautiful, in a funny kind of way. He died in the last scene of the play and on closing night. We didn't know at the time that he was dead—we thought perhaps a stroke. It didn't look fatal from where I was sitting. But we read about it the next day in the papers."

The Head of Movement was rarely asked to recall scenes from his life in this way, and he savored the feeling.

"The character he was playing was a man who has become rich by impersonating people and forging things and lying. Late in his life he returns home and finds that his family have no memory of him. It was as if he had never existed as a real man. That was roughly the way the story went.

"I suspect that his character was going to die anyway," the Head of Movement said, "in the final few pages. But of course I never saw the ending."

SEVEN

Saturday

The saxophone teacher is waiting for them by the Coke machine. At first Isolde cannot make her out: the Coke machine is the only really memorable landmark in the Town Hall foyer and so it is typically besieged by a throng of waiting strangers who have also arranged to meet friends and family there. Then the crowd thins and Isolde sees her, tall and angular in a brown leather jacket, her hands folded in front of her, studying the people around her with a calm critical up-and-down gaze that Isolde has come to know very well.

"Hi, Isolde," the saxophone teacher says when she sees her, and smiles. "Did your mum drop you off?"

"Yeah," Isolde says, feeling strange. She has never seen the sax teacher outside her attic studio, and (the thought registers oddly) never at night. She accepts a program and bends her head to read it, affecting more interest than she feels.

"There she is!" the sax teacher says, waving across the crowd at somebody. "That makes three of us."

A group of young musicians jostle past, edging between the sax teacher and Isolde so for a brief moment they are separately marooned in the crowd. The musicians sweep by in a cloud of cigarette smoke and perfume, nebulous and bubbling and clutching each other at the elbow with their slender musician fingers.

And then the sax teacher says, "Isolde, do you know my student Julia? Julia has been my student for three years now."

Isolde looks up. She suffers a sick abdominal jolt of recognition as their eyes meet. Julia's eyes widen very slightly and her cheeks flush pink.

"Hi," Isolde says quickly, struggling to mask a dawning bewildered embarrassment, and Julia nods hello, pressing her lips together in a brief and complicated smile.

Out of her school uniform Julia looks older. She is wearing a black cardigan and long black skirt, her hair piled casually at the back of her head and coming loose in wisps around her temples. The dour and surly and willful Julia that Isolde saw in the counseling room is all but gone: somehow now she seems more fragile, as if the care she has taken with her appearance has exposed a sensitivity that she had no cause to exhibit before. Isolde's heart is beating fast.

"Do you two know each other from school?" the saxophone teacher says curiously, looking from one to the other with new eyes, as if the juxtaposition of the two of them together is making her see elements of each girl that she has never seen before.

"Sort of," Julia says quickly. "I've seen you around anyway."

"Yeah," says Isolde. "But I didn't know you played sax." For some reason the thought of Julia as the saxophone teacher's comfortable old-time student is strange to her. She startles herself with the realization that the private confidences and successes and failures that she has shared in her lessons each Friday were, for the saxophone teacher, only one recurring episode in weeks and months and years of shared confidences and successes and failures—that she herself is only one among many. Isolde wonders what Julia tells the saxophone teacher when they are alone.

"Why aren't you in jazz band?" Isolde asks quickly. Her shyness makes the question sound accusatory. She is aware of the saxophone teacher's eyes flicking from her to Julia and back again, as if Isolde is the final piece of a puzzle that will enable her to understand Julia, and Julia is the final piece of a puzzle that will enable her to understand Isolde. It makes Isolde hot and uncomfortable, and inside her shoes she squeezes her toes together in frustration.

"I don't really have school spirit," Julia says. "I'm not that kind of person, I guess. If there was something smaller and more underground I might give it a go. I've thought about starting a band."

"Oh," Isolde says, wondering at this new concept that you might be good at something but not have to prove it by playing for the school.

"I played in a band in my first year of university," the saxophone teacher says. "We had some dreadful name. I can't even remember what we called ourselves now."

"Was it the Sax Kittens?" Julia asks. "Was it Sax, Drums and Rock 'n' Roll?"

"We weren't nearly that clever," the saxophone teacher says. "God, we were awful. We used to do this thing at the end of each gig that was really easy but it always got the crowd going. I'd stand next to the guy who played tenor and at the end of the song he'd flip his sax around so I'd blow into it while he was still fingering the notes, so we were both playing the one instrument. I suppose it must have looked quite difficult—people always screamed like we were doing something amazing."

Julia is grinning now. "You've got a dark jazz past," she says. "You've played *gigs*."

"I've done some things in my time," the saxophone teacher says, pretending to be haughty.

They both turn to Isolde to let her share in their joke, and Isolde smiles quickly.

"Oh, I remember," the saxophone teacher says. "We were called the Travesty Players."

"What does the Travesty Players mean?" says Isolde.

"It's a term from the theater," the sax teacher says. "A travesty role is a part which is meant to be played by a person of the opposite sex. So if you were going to play Hamlet, the program would say, 'Isolde in the travesty role of Hamlet.' "

"Oh," says Isolde.

"Why did you choose it for your band name?" says Julia.

"We were all into gender back then," the saxophone teacher says cheerfully. "Ask your mother."

She is lively tonight, but Isolde finds herself shrinking back, finding the intimacy too forceful and defiant, as if the saxophone teacher is a prisoner released for this night only, drawing the girls close to her in a hard and glittering pincer-grip and demanding they share a part in her slender lonely joy. Julia seems at ease, smiling and pressing the saxophone teacher for more details about her dark jazz past, and Isolde regards her jealously.

Her cardigan is buttoned with gold dome buttons and is unraveling slightly at the hem, giving her a careless scholarly look that makes Isolde feel young and clumsy and naïve. She is wearing a silver turquoise ring on her ink-stained nail-bitten fingers, and tight-knit fishnet stockings underneath her skirt. Isolde drinks it all in and then feels oddly disappointed, looking at this newer, more complete version of Julia who is a whole person and not just an idea of a person. She feels jealous and excluded and even betrayed, as if Julia has no right to exist beyond Isolde's experience of her.

Isolde turns her attention back to the program. The soloist is a foreigner, photographed in black and white with his chin on his fist and his saxophone gleaming against his cheek. He looks moody and implacable and gifted. He is playing in front of the symphony orchestra tonight, and pictured opposite is the conductor, a plump jolly man with his baton loose in his hand like an idle dagger.

"A great soloist," the saxophone teacher is saying, "is never some perfect airtight freeze-dried package who has studied and studied and studied. A great soloist is always born out of a partnership or a group. A great soloist is always someone who has had something to feed on."

Julia is listening politely but frowning all the same. Isolde notices that her nibbled skepticism, which at school seemed an index of aggression and dissatisfaction and gloom, now seems an index of something different, a carefulness or guardedness maybe, something more instinctive and less hostile.

"This is the first concert you've come to this year, isn't it, Isolde?" the saxophone teacher says suddenly, and Isolde nods.

"This guy is awesome," Julia says, flapping the program. "I've got all his recordings. Hey, do classical players have groupies? That's something I definitely need to look into."

She is trying to be kind to Isolde, but Isolde finds that all she can do is blush and smile and mumble that she's looking forward to it. She is squeezing her toes together tight.

The gong sounds a gentle arpeggio to remind them to take their seats. The crowd at the Coke machine begins to disperse, and the sax teacher smiles at them both in turn.

"I really hope you find this inspiring," she says. "This is a special night for me as well—last time I heard this arrangement live I was only a little bit older than you. It woke me up."

Saturday

The orchestra is plush and dazzling against the polished wood of the stage. In the first row of the balcony the sax teacher sits between her two students, calm and matriarchal and silent, the two girls sloping off on either side of her so the three of them seem to form a kind of heraldic crest, a heroic grouping that might be placed above a shield to complete a coat of arms. Julia sits with her hands in her lap, watching the flashing silver and gold with an intent glazed blindness, her eyes unmoving as if she is concentrating on holding something very still in her mind. Isolde is more restless, deliberately leaning away from the saxophone teacher lest their elbows touch, and watching the musicians in a detached, musing way, her gaze drifting from the stage and over the dim unsmiling wraith-faces around her.

As Isolde peers vaguely at the pale faces in the audience she thinks about the different ways you can perform the act of listening. Some in the audience have their eyes shut and their faces tilted slightly upward, enjoying the rain of the music on their skin. Some are nodding in a slow, meaningful sort of way, perhaps every four or five bars, as if something is slowly and majestically taking shape before them. Some, like the sax teacher next to her, are simply sitting still.

Isolde thinks how strange it is, that every person in the auditorium is locked in their own private experience of the music, alone with their thoughts, alone in their enjoyment or distaste, and shivering at the vast feeling of intimacy that this solitude affords, already impatient for the interval when they can compare their experience with their neighbor's and discover with relief that they are the same. *Am I hearing the same thing they are hearing?* Isolde wonders half-heartedly, but she is distracted from pursuing the thought any further, turning her attention instead to watch an elderly woman in the stalls flounder noisily in her handbag for a tissue or a mint.

Julia is listening in a dreamy, sleepy way, the music drawing from her one slow, definite impression rather than a slide-show series of impressions that she can cobble together later and divide to find the arithmetic mean. She is thinking about

Isolde. She can't quite see her past the stern unmoving profile of the saxophone teacher, just a flash of her knee every time Isolde crosses her leg, but even so she finds her left-hand peripheral vision is sharpened with a tense hyperawareness whenever the younger girl shifts in her seat. She thinks about the long look that she and Isolde shared in the counseling class, probing the thought again and again like a bloody tooth and wondering, as she has wondered many times, where the look might have come from, and where it might lead.

Sometimes when Julia's thoughts circulate like this she becomes stricken by the irrational fear that she might open her mouth and say exactly what she is thinking, just to spite herself. She thinks of what she would say, if she did say something, and then she bites her lip and fights back a cold rush of fear at the thought of actually saying it.

The saxophone teacher is thinking about Patsy. She is thinking about Patsy in the smoky afterward bar, still with her concert program tucked in her fist, ordering glasses of wine which they will later refill, in a secret giddy way, from a screw-top bottle in Patsy's handbag. She sees them both folding themselves into a corner, unwrapping scarves and coats and talking about the crowd and the arrangement and the soloist, and then Patsy saying, "What did you imagine?" and already half-laughing in her eagerness.

"I imagined the music was pouring out of the saxophone like water," the saxophone teacher said, "pouring over the lip of the bell and pooling on the floor at his feet, and the water level was getting higher and higher and the tide was churning stronger and stronger and in the end he had to finish the piece just to save his life. And then we clapped and he started a new piece and I imagined that the sax was sucking his breath out of him, instead of him blowing the air in, and that the mouthpiece was pushing and pushing to get further and further in, that the sax was trying desperately to suffocate him, and he had to keep playing to save his life."

Patsy laughed and clapped and they touched glasses and drank, and the saxophone teacher said, "What did *you* imagine?"

"I imagined that noise had the power to seriously hurt you, even kill you," Patsy said, "depending on the quality of the musicianship. The more elegant the playing, the more total the death. The Town Hall would be like the arena where you were sent if you had done something truly terrible. You'd be marched into the auditorium, strapped down and buckled on to the red velvet seats so tight you couldn't move. The soloist would be the executioner, playing faster and faster and watching you over the footlights with wet greedy eyes."

The saxophone teacher laughed and clapped and they touched glasses again and drank, and Patsy said, "That concert changed me forever."

Saturday

On Saturday nights Bridget works at the local video store. She sits glumly on a high vinyl stool and watches the lonely people drift from shelf to shelf, keeping one eye on the black-and-white security television that dimly shows the curtained nook where the adult tapes are shelved. The clock says half-past nine. Bridget watches the inching revolutions of the minute hand and listens for the padded thump of a late tape through the dewy drop-slot.

"Hello, Bridget," somebody says.

Bridget shoves her chewing gum to the side of her mouth and turns her tired head to see Mr. Saladin standing by the door, crisp in beige trousers and a woollen coat. He smiles at her in a boyish way.

"Hi, Mr. Saladin," says Bridget, brightening and slithering forward off her stool. "I've never seen you here before."

"My nephews live in the area," says Mr. Saladin. "Two blocks over."

"Oh," says Bridget with genuine surprise, because she has never thought of Mr. Saladin as the type of man to have nephews. She regards him a little shyly.

"How is it that you're allowed to work here? You're not eighteen," Mr. Saladin says, folding his gloved hands across his chest. "You must not be allowed to watch half the movies here."

"I'm not watching them," says Bridget, "I'm only selling them."

Mr. Saladin chuckles. "And I suppose after I've gone you're going to look up my record for porno," he says.

"Probably," says Bridget, with a rush of gratitude at being granted ownership of the joke. "And I'll find out how old you really are."

"Now you've gone too far," Mr. Saladin says, feigning gravity. "That is privileged information. Don't you dare."

Bridget giggles and then stifles the sound quickly, covering her mouth with her hand. Behind her, the row of mounted television screens flashes its sequence of silent silver car-wrecks and swift untimely deaths.

"Working on a Saturday night," Mr. Saladin says, shaking his head. "What happened to drinking and taking drugs and smoking and playing loud music? I must be out of touch."

Again Bridget's hand flies to her mouth to smother her laughter. Mr. Saladin smiles, his gaze sliding upward for a second as he is distracted by an image darting by.

The clock moves forward.

Until this precise moment in her life Bridget has understood flirting only as a self-promotional conversational tool, wielded with the intention of winning a short-term companion or a grope. Now as she looks at Mr. Saladin, calm and smiling and unruffled in his clean pressed clothes, his scarf knotted neatly around his throat, his elegant triple-veined leather gloves and his windswept hair, Bridget suffers a lusty rush of bewildered wanting that tightens like a fist in her groin. For the first time in sixteen years she feels impelled to flirt for the sole purpose of ruining somebody else, driven to recklessness by the dim and thrilling notion that *here*, at least, is a man who will see her in only sexual terms. She reaches out and pinches the laminate edge of the counter between her thumb and her fingertips, rocking back on her heels in a flirty way, offering herself as bait just so she might have the pleasure of watching him bite in vain.

"What are you doing now? Do you have a new job?" she asks. "We miss you at jazz band."

"For now I'm painting houses," Mr. Saladin says. "I'm in between things. So the new conductor is putting you through the paces?"

"Mrs. Jean Critchley," Bridget says. "She's okay."

"I know the name," Mr. Saladin says. "I've seen her play live. She's good."

"Yeah," Bridget says casually. Mr. Saladin smiles and looks around him, as if he means to amble off, and so Bridget says all in a hurry, "We had to go to counseling after you left, in case we were damaged. It was lame."

Mr. Saladin raises his eyebrows. He doesn't speak for a moment. Then he says calmly, "That doesn't sound like much fun."

"It was lame," Bridget says again, and she almost feels inept, but then she remembers that *here*, at least, is a man who will understand and forgive her naïveté: to this man, her clumsy adolescence is not a handicap but a prize. The fist in her groin stiffens again, clenching like a swiftly tightened screw.

"Victoria still hasn't come back to school," she blurts out before Mr. Saladin can speak again, trying in her gauche and rumpled way to talk casually, like the beautiful girls at school talk casually, tossing their hair over their shoulder and turning out their feet like show ponies. "Has she left for good?"

"No, I don't think so," says Mr. Saladin. "I imagine she'll be back before exams."

"That's good," says Bridget. She smiles in what she hopes is an encouraging way, wanting to show that she is on Mr. Saladin's side.

"Good to see you, Bridget. Keep on with your music," says Mr. Saladin. He smiles at her and strolls off toward the neon wall of new releases. "I'll go and see what you've got on offer."

"It's two for ten," Bridget calls out after him.

She stands there for a moment before retreating back to her stool. Out of habit she checks the security screen and sees a couple furtively entering the adult nook, clutching each other and giggling as they trail their fingers along the spines. She watches as the woman selects a title and they laugh at the various postures pictured in miniature on the back. The man says something quietly, and the woman pretends to be furious and slaps at him with the end of her scarf. They laugh.

After Mr. Saladin leaves, Bridget looks up his rental history and is disappointed to find no porno. She learns that he is thirty-one.

Saturday

After the applause, the three of them sit for a moment in silence. The lights come up over the audience, restoring color to the wraiths, and all around them the crowd begins to shift and laugh and chatter, reaching down for their scarves and their programs and their clutch purses as if released from a spell. The saxophone teacher is lost in a memory and doesn't stir, her hands limp from the applause, her eyes large and vacant and turned toward the stage. Julia sits forward on her seat and turns to Isolde suddenly, and says, "Do you want a lift home? I've got my car here. It'd be no problem."

Isolde hasn't yet learned to drive and Julia's offer makes her feel young and inexperienced and graceless, as if she is being forced to reveal that she can't read or that she is still afraid of the dark. The older girl seems impossibly mature to Isolde, like Victoria's friends always seem impossibly mature, powdered and scented and full of secrets and private laughter, contemptuous of little Issie for all that she does not yet know. "Thanks," is what Isolde says to Julia now, smiling quickly and ducking her head. "That would be great. I was going to have to taxi."

"I won't tell your mother," the saxophone teacher says to Isolde, returning at last from her memory. "I know you're going to keep the taxi fare she's given you."

"How do you know *I* don't charge a taxi fare?" Julia says.

The saxophone teacher laughs. "I've seen your car, for starters," she says. She starts chatting about the music, speaking mostly to Julia. Her big hands are spread open as she talks, turning her impression of the concert over and over like a potter at a wheel.

Isolde nods and smiles. She darts a look at Julia, and wonders if Julia had been preparing the offer for some time, sitting silent in the gray dusk of the stage-glow and all the while preparing how best to phrase the question. Do you want a lift home? I've got my car here. It'd be no problem.

"It's not a popular configuration," the saxophone teacher is saying. Isolde keeps nodding wisely, trying to mask the shrinking sensation in her pelvis, which registers as part exhilaration and part dread. What did the offer mean? Isolde almost imagines the older girl leaning in across the gear shift and the handbrake and reaching out an ink-stained jeweled hand to tuck a wisp of hair behind her ear. She almost imagines it, but in a fleeting shock of panic she snuffs out the thought.

"Pretty inspiring stuff," the saxophone teacher says in conclusion, slapping the armrests in a jolly way and standing up to join the inching exodus. "Pretty inspiring stuff."

Saturday

"Cheers for the concert," Julia says to the saxophone teacher after they have shuffled their way out of the auditorium and through the marble foyer into the cold. "It was incredible. I'll be thinking about it all week."

The saxophone teacher draws the belt of her leather jacket tighter around her waist. "I'll see you Monday, then," she says to Julia. "And I'll see you on Friday," she says to Isolde. She looks lonely all of a sudden, standing stiffly on the gritty Town Hall steps with the crowd pouring out on either side of her. She is backlit by the reddish velvet light of the foyer behind her, and it strikes Isolde that she is rather pretty. She registers with something a little like triumph that the saxophone teacher is now the outsider, looking down at the girls with a halting expression as if she wants to detain them further but she is uncertain how.

"Sounds good," Isolde says, and gives a little wave. Julia smiles, and then the two of them turn away from her and walk out into the night.

Sunday

Mrs. De Gregorio clutches her purse in the crook of her lap while she sips her tea. She sits with her knees together and her thighs elevated a little because she is resting her heels against the crossbar of the chair and only her square toes touch the ground. Her breasts almost reach her lap, and as she sits down she wedges her purse into the gap where her body hinges. The saxophone teacher thinks how very strange it looks, Mrs. De Gregorio curving herself around her purse in this protective way. From where the sax teacher is sitting, she can see only the twin-balled golden clasp peeking out from beneath the soft acrylic bulge of Mrs. De Gregorio's breast.

She smiles. "What can I do for you, Mrs. De Gregorio?"

"I've come about my daughter," Mrs. De Gregorio says, and as always the saxophone teacher marvels privately at this woman's performance, this single unitary woman who plays all the mothers so differently, each performance a tender and unique object like the veined clouding on a subtle pearl. "This might seem like a bit of an odd errand," the woman says, "me marching in here like this to ask you such a personal question, but lately at home we've noticed a few changes, and—" Mrs. De Gregorio looks down into her lap and sighs. "She's just become *impossible*," she says at last.

"Let's start at the beginning, then," the saxophone teacher says briskly, tugging down her shirttails and smoothing flat the wool of her jersey as if she means business. "First of all—why the saxophone? Why did you choose this particular instrument? The saxophone has connotations, as you know. A saxophone is not a piano or a flute. A very particular type of girl gravitates toward the saxophone, and quite frankly it's the type of girl who is not very likely to keep the peace. Why did you choose the sax for your daughter?"

"Oh, it was *her* choice," Mrs. De Gregorio says, but the saxophone teacher shakes her head and swiftly interrupts her—

"Let's not play that game, Mrs. De Gregorio. Your daughter is your project, we both know that. The elements beyond your control are really very few indeed. I can see you're the type of mother who likes to hold the reins. The type of mother who regards her children as free agents is a slapdash mother, a vague uncaring mother who simply doesn't appreciate a job well done. You are not that person."

Mrs. De Gregorio nods, a little defeated.

"So you chose this fate for your daughter," the saxophone teacher continues. "You pushed her toward the instrument of her undoing. You could have had a daughter who played the violin, long-haired and eccentric and quietly confident, but you chose the saxophone. You made that choice."

"I wanted to say," Mrs. De Gregorio says, fumbling for the words, "I wanted to say that we've noticed a definite change, that's all. She won't talk—well. You know what it can be like. And I just wanted to ask what she says to *you* each week. Whether you might have any clues. A boyfriend or something. Something we could work through, and understand."

"Why do you think that your daughter would tell *me* the truth?" the saxophone teacher asks.

"About her studies," says Mrs. De Gregorio weakly. "Or her life at school. Something like a boyfriend, a problem that we could work through, and understand."

The saxophone teacher doesn't speak for a moment, just so Mrs. De Gregorio feels uncomfortable and wishes she hadn't spoken so freely. Then she says, "But how can you ever know?" She is more brooding now and less abrupt. "How can you ever get to the kernel of truth behind it all? You could watch her. But you have to remember that there are two kinds of watching: either she will know she is being watched, or she will not. If she knows she is being watched, her behavior will change under observation until what you are seeing is so utterly transformed it becomes a thing *intended only* for observation, and all realities are lost. And if she doesn't know she is being watched, what you are seeing is something unprimed, something unfit for performance, something crude and unrefined that you will try and refine yourself: you will try to give it a meaning that it does not inherently possess, and in doing this you will press your daughter into some mold that misunderstands her. So, you see, neither picture is what you might call true. They are distortions."

"*Has* she said anything?" Mrs. De Gregorio says. "I know it's an odd question. It's embarrassing to have to ask. But is there anything we should know about?" Her hand disappears under her breasts, checking that her purse is still tucked into the vast crux of her lap. Her fingers find the wadded leather lump and touch it briefly.

"Oh, Mrs. De Gregorio. I'm her music teacher," the sax teacher says. She returns her mug to the table and folds her hands.

"But then what do I do?" Mrs. De Gregorio asks with a kind of rising panic. "What options have I left?"

"You could ask your daughter," the saxophone teacher says. "You could sit down and actually talk to her. But you always run the risk that she might lie."

Monday

"What did you imagine while you were watching?" the saxophone teacher asks when Julia arrives for her lesson on Monday afternoon. "At the concert."

"I liked the second half better than the first half," Julia begins, but the saxophone teacher waves her arm impatiently and says, "No, I meant what did you think about while you were watching? What sorts of things were you thinking about?"

Julia looks at her curiously, as if this might be a test. "Why?" she asks.

"It's a game I used to play with an old friend of mine," the saxophone teacher says. "We had a joke that the better the performance, the more catalytic the effect. A poor performance might only make you think about what you had for dinner or what you were going to wear when you woke up the next day. But a great performance would make you imagine things you would never have been brave enough to imagine before."

She is speaking eagerly, like a child. Julia unclips her saxophone case and says, "I was just thinking about the music."

"Yes, but *around* that. When your mind drifted. What did you imagine?"

Julia slips her reed out of its gated plastic sheath and holds it for a second. "I imagined what was going to happen," she said, "when I dropped Isolde home."

The lights change. The overhead lights and the bright overcast light from the window are doused; a template falls into place in front of a solitary floodlight and the attachment begins to rotate, so that the yellow light is thinly striped and ever changing, playing over the pair of them like passing streetlights striping the dashboard of a moving car. Julia sits down. The streetlights come and go, streaking over her knees and curving away over her shoulder to disappear, and she is dark for a moment before another streak of light rises up to replace the first, and then another, and another, all yellow and forward bending.

"I imagined," Julia says, "that on the way home we would talk about the concert a bit, and what we thought of it, and the teachers that we had in common at school, and we'd keep coming back to *you*, to talk about you, because you are the only real thread of connection between us. We'd talk about you for a while back and forth, only we wouldn't be quite honest, because the most important thing would be to create an attractive impression of ourselves, and what we truly thought didn't really matter. We'd say whatever things would put us in the best light. We'd lie. All the way home we'd lie to each other, back and forth."

The saxophone teacher is unmoving. She looks Julia up and down with her eyes only. Her face is like a mask.

"And then I imagined," Julia says, "that after I killed the engine we would sit there for a moment, not looking at each other, just looking up through the darkness at Isolde's unlit house. My key ring would still be swinging from the ignition, and we would listen to the sound of the wind whipping the leaves. My mouth would be dry."

The rotating template has stilled and Julia's knees are in a square of light which falls through the car window and across her lap. Her face is in shadow. She is sitting stiffly, one leg for-ward-stretched and cocked at an angle, as if on the brake pedal. Her saxophone is lying on the couch beside her, and she is hold-ing it casually with her left hand, lifting the upper end slightly off the couch, so it looks like her hand is curled casually around the handbrake, her knuckles in the plastic shallow beneath the handle and her wrist loosely arched. With her other hand she plucks at her sternum, testing the tension of an invisible seat belt strap, lifting it carelessly and letting it slap back against her chest.

"And I'd go, You know what everybody says about me. At school and everything. It isn't true."

Julia wets her lips with her tongue. She isn't looking at Isolde: she's looking out the window, peering into the dark silver of the wing-mirror, one hand still plucking at her strap.

"Isolde goes, I know. She says it really quickly and then she says it again. I know. She's not looking at me, she's looking for-ward, up at the house, and her finger is at her throat, twisting her necklace around and around, cutting all the blood from her fingertip. The end of it has gone gray." Julia looks back at Isolde again, quickly, and tightens her grip around the handbrake. "And then I go, I was just worried that you might think I was going to come on to you, or jump you when you least expected it or something. I was worried you might think that."

She reverts to gazing into the wing-mirror, turning her face away.

"Isolde goes, I don't think that. And I go, Good. And then we sit for a moment, looking up at Isolde's unlit house and listen for each other's breath, and then I go, That's all. That's all I wanted to say."

The lights come up a little, just enough to include the saxo-phone teacher and bring her into the scene. She shifts and crosses her legs. She looks uncomfortable.

"What is it that everyone says about you at school?" she asks reluctantly. Sometimes Julia makes her feel cornered, and she is feeling cornered now.

"Everyone thinks I like girls," Julia says.

"I see," the saxophone teacher says. The lights dip back down again, receding back to the single streetlamp casting its square pool of light across Julia's lap. The saxophone teacher disappears again into the dark.

"We parked the car," Julia says, "and sat there for a while, and whatever we were talking about sort of trickled away like water until there was nothing left and we just sat and waited for something to happen. My mouth was dry. And then Isolde goes, Do you mind waiting here in the car for a while? My mum thinks Victoria came to the concert with me, and we have to walk in at the same time in case she's still up.

"And even while she was saying it a car pulled up and stopped a few houses in front of where we were, so both of us were lit red for a moment in the glare of the taillights, and then the lights went off but nobody got out. We watched but the car just sat there. And Isolde goes, She doesn't know we're here. She hasn't seen us. Isolde's watching the car with a hard tight sort of expression and I don't want to say anything in case it's the wrong thing, and then she says, We had it all arranged. Mum dropped both of us off at the concert, and I went in to meet you guys and Victoria went off to meet him. It's the only way she can still see him. She's grounded most nights, and none of her friends will cover for her now. I don't mind."

The saxophone teacher leans forward in the dark. She is frowning.

"And then Isolde goes, I'd better go. If we sit here for much longer it'll be weird. I have to go."

Julia smoothes her knees and tugs again at her seat belt, nodding.

"But she doesn't go. She stays in the car for a moment longer, and through the back window of the car in front we see Victoria lean over and put her head on Mr. Saladin's shoulder. It looks awkward, stretched across the gearshift with all this space in between them, and he reaches his arm up and strokes her head. He's saying something but we can only see their silhouettes. It's like a shadow-play, and all of a sudden my heart is hammering and I look at Isolde and she looks at me really quickly, but then again, and she says, Please don't tell anyone, and I say I won't."

Julia's voice has become dry and choked, and her tongue keeps darting out to wet her lips. Spots of crimson have appeared high on either cheek.

"And then she gets out," Julia says, "and the silhouettes turn around and see her, and then Victoria kisses Mr. Saladin good-bye, not on the mouth. He turns his face to the side so she can kiss his cheek, and then they both smile and maybe even laugh, like it's a joke. And then the red taillights come on again and Mr. Saladin's car is gone, and Victoria and Isolde go into the house together. Isolde is the one who unlocks the gate, and while she reaches for the latch Victoria steps into the light and looks at me, really gets a long look at me, and then she says something under her breath to Isolde like she's unhappy. And then they disappear."

Julia comes abruptly to an end and looks at the saxophone teacher for the first time. Her mouth is twisted and her expression is sour, as if the performance has made her remember an unpleasant feeling that she would rather have forgotten.

"Was that really what happened?" the saxophone teacher says, as the lights return to normal and Julia reaches for her sax. "Was it Mr. Saladin in the car, Julia? Could you be sure?"

"I was just telling you what I imagined," Julia says, all of a sudden grouchy and withdrawn and peering suspiciously at the saxophone teacher like she is an enemy. And then she adds, "It was dark." She picks at one of the keys on her sax, just to hear it clack.

"This could be very important," the saxophone teacher says.

"It's what I imagined," Julia says again, retreating further. She turns away and plays an arpeggio to warm up.

"Julia," says the saxophone teacher. Her eyes are gleaming. "Tell me what you saw."

"Nothing," Julia says, and although she is sullen and inward the saxophone teacher senses in her something like triumph, as if Julia has led her somewhere remote and treacherous only to abandon her. "I dropped her home. She said goodbye. She got out. She shut the door. Nothing happened."

Saturday

"Can you remember losing your innocence, Patsy?" the saxophone teacher says.

They are in the afterward bar, Patsy sitting sideways in the booth with her legs up and her brown boots crossed at the ankle. There is a bottle between them, and two glasses, each stained with the pale gray kiss of a woman's lower lip, like a fingerprint just below the rim.

"Do you mean a specific event?" Patsy says. "The actual loss of it, do you mean?"

"Yes."

"Losing my virginity?"

"Not necessarily. Just if there was a moment when you ceased to be innocent. The moment you fell. Can you remember your fall?"

Patsy thinks about this quietly for a second. The saxophone teacher raises her wineglass to her mouth and drinks. Patsy is beautiful tonight. Her hair is swept back into a tumbling handful at the nape of her neck, and her eyes are clear and bright. She wears a heavy brass locket, a gift from Brian, an antique and accidental-seeming piece that suits her perfectly, suits the stout capable breadth of her chest and the soft notched hollow of her collarbone. Patsy always suits her clothes, her costume. The image of her is always complete, the saxophone teacher thinks: it is impossible to halve her, undress her, subtract from her. The sax teacher cannot imagine removing the necklace, even in her mind—she can't imagine Patsy unclothed, Patsy without the trimmings and trappings that she inhabits so completely.

Patsy rolls the stem of her wineglass in her fingers.

"I was never veiled or misted as a kid," she says slowly. "You know, Santa Claused, Easter Bunnied, cabbage-patched, euphemized. I can't remember any illusions. I can't remember ever *not* knowing. Sex was never really a mystery. And there was no God in our house, so no mystery there. Of course I had first experiences like everybody else, made mistakes like everybody else, repaired and reinvented myself like everybody does. But I can't remember ever really *falling*. I can't remember if I *was* ever really innocent. I have no nostalgia for a time before."

She looks up at the saxophone teacher. "Is that terribly sad?" she says, and laughs.

The sax teacher smiles and says nothing, and they both sit quietly for a while, touching their wineglasses with their fingertips, looking away.

"Everything had a precedent," Patsy says after a time. "Everything I have ever done had a template, a formula, a model, something public and visible and *known*. I knew the shape of everything I would ever meet, before I met it. The template always preceded the reality, the experience, the personal truth of a thing. I learned about love from the cinema, and from television, and from the stage. I learned the formula and then I applied it. That's how it happened for me. My whole life."

She gives another little tinkle of a laugh. "Is that terribly sad?" she says a second time. "Is that very sad?"

Up on the little dais next to the piano the double-bassist leans forward and says into his microphone, "One last song, folks. Here's one last song."

EIGHT

May

The day after the Theater of Cruelty lesson Stanley ran into the victim of the exercise on the main staircase. The boy was walking quickly with his head down, taking the stairs two at a time. His hair was cropped close to his skull now, to even up the patch on the crown that the masked boy had snipped. The shorter cut didn't quite suit him. He looked a little frightened, his ears and forehead protruding too obviously from under the shrunken cap of hair. He was wearing a new shirt.

"Hey," Stanley said, reaching out a hand to stall him.

The boy turned guilty eyes up at him and nodded a shy hello.

"I just wanted to say that I went and complained," Stanley said. His voice sounded huge in the stairwell, spiraling up and up to the floors above and ringing clear and hollow in the vertical shaft like the pealing of a bell. "About what happened. I went to the Head of Movement and complained."

155

"Thanks," the boy said quietly. "But it's all right now. It was just a dumb thing." He made as if to continue downstairs, but Stanley stopped him, moving closer and cornering him so he was trapped flat, pinioned against the banister with nowhere to go.

"I'm going to talk to the Head of Acting as well," Stanley said. "I can't believe that nobody else is doing anything about this. It's disgusting. What they did to you was disgusting. And nobody cared."

The boy looked at Stanley inscrutably for a moment. He reached back with both hands for the banister, and stood there with his arms behind him, tugging gently on the handrail. Then he said, "I was a plant."

"What?" Stanley said.

"I was a plant. The main guy—Nick, the guy in the mask—he asked me and arranged it all beforehand. I knew they were going to pick me, and I knew what was going to happen, mostly. I knew about the water, and he said they might slap me around a bit. I thought it would be funny. Just for a laugh."

Stanley was frowning. "But you bolted."

"I didn't know they were going to go that far," the boy said. "My shirt and everything. Cutting my hair. He only told me about the water-trough. I thought it would be okay. I thought I'd help them out or whatever. I said yes."

"Is there always a plant?" Stanley said. "Every year?"

"I guess," the boy said. He jerked his gaze away, past Stanley's shoulder and down the stairs. "They'd never get away with it otherwise."

"They shouldn't get away with it."

"Yeah," the boy said, and shrugged. "It was just an exercise. It was only to make a point."

"But *why*?" Stanley said. He spoke with more aggression than he intended. He felt the same dawning feeling of helplessness that he had felt in the Head of Movement's office. In his confusion he was scowling at the boy, and now the boy scowled back.

"I was just helping them out. They needed someone for their project. It's no big deal."

"What about your shirt?" Stanley said. "Your shirt was a big deal."

The boy gripped the banister tighter. He was flushing. He clenched his jaw, and his shorn golden cap of hair moved angrily backward on his scalp.

"Hey look, I appreciate your concern, all right," he said, "but I'm not like a little bandwagon, you know, or some sort of a just cause that you can fight for. It was my fault, I should have asked them what they were planning on doing. It's no big deal. You didn't have to complain."

"They *hurt* you!" Stanley shouted.

"Yeah, and came and found me afterward," the boy said loudly. "After they'd taken off their masks and it was all over, and we talked and everything, and we sorted everything out. It's not your problem. You weren't there."

Stanley looked at the boy for a second and then stepped aside to let him through. The boy ducked his head and muttered, "Thanks anyway." He slipped past Stanley, bounded down the stairs and disappeared.

Stanley looked up through the high mullioned window that lit the stairwell, and breathed heavily. He found his hands were balled into fists and he vaguely felt like hitting something, but he wasn't sure what he wanted to hit, or even why. He stepped back as a flood of second-year actors thundered down the stairs, and as the crowd dwindled he looked up to see the Head of Acting descending calmly in their wake, holding under his arm a bundled mainsail, patched and rat-tailed and studded around its edge with reef-point eyelets filmed with rust. He looked preoccupied.

"Stanley," he said as he approached. "You're the man who wanted to see me, is that right?"

"It's all right. I sorted it out with the Head of Movement," Stanley said, stepping respectfully aside. "It's all sorted out now."

May

"This is an exercise in control and communication," the Head of Movement said. "I want you all to divide into pairs and face each other. Starting with your palms together and your feet square, you will begin to move in exact tandem, each the mirror image of the other. You can move however and wherever you like, but I want to be able to walk among you and not be able to tell who is leading and who is following."

The class lumbered to its feet and Stanley found himself paired with the girl who had been sitting nearest to him. They smiled at each other quickly as they turned to face each other, and Stanley felt his heart leap. He felt a little stab of self-contempt and frowned to quash the feeling. He turned back to look at the Head of Movement, narrowing his eyes to show the girl that he was listening hard, and that he intended to take the lesson very seriously, and that despite what she may expect or believe he was utterly indifferent to the fact of her sex. In his vague peripheral vision he saw the girl watch him for a moment longer, and then turn back to the Head of Movement herself.

"Between you," the Head of Movement continued, "choose one person who will begin as the leader. You must also choose some sort of physical signal to indicate to each other that the leader will change. You can swap between yourselves as many times as you wish, back and forth. Eye contact is essential. We will conduct this exercise in silence."

The paired students leaned in to confer with each other in whispers. The Head of Movement turned away and pressed a button on the stereo surround system, wiping the dust off the protruding edge with his finger while he waited for the disc to load. The dust was thick and silver-gray, accumulating on his fingertip in a soft feathered wafer. He rolled it into a ball and flicked it away. The disc began to spin, and he twisted the volume knob slowly up and up so the music faded in, swelling larger and larger until it filled the gymnasium completely. He had chosen a cinematic score, instrumental and surging and overblown.

"Please take your places and begin," he called over the opening bars. "The music is your pulse. Take inspiration from it. Detach yourself and divide your mind between watching your partner and listening to the pulse. You should feel alert but at peace. You may begin."

Stanley turned to face his partner and held up his palms for her to touch with her own. They looked clearly at each other, and at first he squirmed and frowned, unsure as to what she might be seeing, looking at him in such a clear, frank way. She was a little shorter than him, and her chin was tilted slightly upward to meet his gaze. She had determined gray eyes and a straight thin-lipped mouth. Stanley was close enough to see the down on her cheeks, glowing soft pink in the slanting light, and the fawny scatter of freckles across the bridge of her nose.

The heavier instruments dwindled to let the strings build their own quiet plucking crescendo. Stanley peeled his right palm away from the girl's and felt her make the same movement, slowly and carefully, lagging perhaps a quarter of a second behind. She was frowning slightly, but even as he registered the expression he realized that she was attempting to mirror his own. He relaxed into a more neutral face and saw her do the same, his movements reflected back at him in a delicate feminine echo, like a cave that threw back a finer, female version of his own call. He balled his hand into a fist and brought it up under his chin, trying to move slowly and carefully so she would see the whole trajectory of his movement and be able to replicate it simultaneously. She watched his eyes, not the movement of his hand. They were both wide eyed with the strain of trying to communicate without words. Around them the other paired couples were moving similarly, waving their hands about in a slow and measured way. As he spread his fingers out and laced them through the thin cold fingers of his echo-girl, Stanley thought to himself that from above the class must look like some sort of windswept crop, swelling up and back like tiny quivering blades thrusting up out of the soil and into a stiff and ever-changing breeze.

From the stage the Head of Movement watched them all in silence, his fingertips still resting on the stereo and filmed gray with dust. His gaze drifted over them and came to rest upon one of the boys, standing on the edge of the group and reaching out his hand to touch his partner's neck with his index finger. The Head of Movement watched the mirrored pair trace an invisible line down each other's windpipe and into the hollow at the center of the collarbone, and thought, The boy is leading. He could always tell.

The boy was standing with his chin high and his legs apart and wearing a solemn burning expression on his face that almost made the Head of Movement smile. It was the first time he'd had class with the boy since the teary outburst in his office following the Theater of Cruelty exercise, and when he had walked into the gymnasium that morning and called for the attention of the class he'd at once spotted Stanley bobbing on the periphery, anxious and desperate to be seen. The Head of Movement had looked away. He did not want the boy to cling to him in such a fearfully filial way, craving attention and recognition and time, unaware that all the trembled first-experiences and thought-dawnings that affected him so wholly were, for the Head of Movement, only the vicarious latest in a long line of the same.

Every year at least one of the students complained about the Theater of Cruelty exercise. The lesson fell into the Head of Acting's domain and mostly it was he who took the distressed student into his office and soothed any lasting damage. Some years, as with this one, he contrived a reason to leave the class at the last minute, scuttling up the back staircase to the lighting booth above the gymnasium to watch the students from behind the darkened glass. The view was always different. One year the victim-student had been able to wrestle free and fight back, and several of the students on stage had been seriously hurt; another year, the watching students stormed the stage in a mass rescue. But lately, year by year, the acting students had been losing something—a readiness to *act*, he thought, without irony. Take this year—a shirt, a bit of hair and the water-trough, and one student crying into his shirtsleeve afterward from the pain of it.

Sometimes the Head of Movement wanted to strike them, to rush down on to the gymnasium floor and slap them and shake them until they stirred and snapped and fought back; sometimes he felt almost driven mad by this cling-film sheet of apathy that smothered them and parceled them and stopped their breath until they were like dolls in shrinkwrap, trademarked and mass produced.

He tossed his head. They were cushioned, that was all. They needed a wakeup.

Down on the floor Stanley had invisibly passed the leadership to his partner, who was now drawing away from him and fanning out, the two of them black-tee-shirted against the wooden floor like a symmetrical inkblot on an aged card. Not quite symmetrical. The male movements could never quite match the female, and vice versa: there was always something missing, some bright edge that gave the deception away. The Head of Movement sighed and looked at them all in panorama for a second, the silken apathetic crowd of sleepwalkers who had watched their classmate get stripped and shorn and nearly drowned, and had done nothing. He thought, How can I possibly wake them up? And then he thought, Who will awaken me?

June

"I am here to tell you about the end-of-year devised theater project," the Head of Acting said briskly, "which is by far the most important event in the first-year calendar."

The Head of Acting always commanded a fearful unmoving silence whenever he spoke. He did not need to raise his voice.

"First of all I must stress that you will be completely on your own. The tutors will not oversee rehearsals, scripts, lighting rigs, costume designs or concept discussions. This is your project. When we arrive in the auditorium at eight in the evening on the first of October, we want to be surprised. And shocked. We want to see why we chose *you* out of the two hundred hopefuls who auditioned. We want to leave feeling proud of our own good taste.

"I might add that this project has an impressive legacy at the Institute: the work that has been dreamed up as part of this project has many times been later reworked into greater productions, some of which have toured internationally. You have big shoes to fill."

The Head of Acting brightened now, as he always brightened when talking about past students. His admiration and approval was only ever retrospectively bestowed, a fact which these first-year students did not yet know. In their ignorance they gazed fiercely up at him and champed at this new and shining chance to prove themselves.

"It is a tradition at the Institute," the Head of Acting continued, "that on closing night the cast will choose one prop from their production to be handed on. The prop they choose will serve as the driving stimulus for the production the following year. Last year's production, titled *The Beautiful Machine*, received from the previous year's students a large iron wheel. In the original production the wheel had been part of a working rickshaw. In *Beautiful Machine* the wheel was redressed as the

Wheel of Fate and became a central visual component of the beautiful machine itself."

One of the boys was nodding vigorously to show he had seen *The Beautiful Machine* in production and remembered the wheel very well. The Head of Acting smiled faintly. He said, "The cast of *Beautiful Machine*, last year's first-year students, have chosen a prop from their production that will become the locus of yours. I have it here in my pocket."

He paused for a long moment, enjoying the tension.

"Does anyone have any questions, before I leave you all to conduct your first meeting?" he asked.

Nobody could think of a question. The Head of Acting reached into his pocket and withdrew a playing card. It was a card from an ordinary deck, thinly striped on the reverse side, pinkish and round edged. He held it up for them all to see and turned it over in his fingers to show the King of Diamonds, bearded and thin lipped and pensive, holding his axe behind his head with a thick hammy hand. The Head of Acting tossed the card on the ground, inclined his head politely, and left the room.

The gymnasium door closed softly in his wake and sent the King of Diamonds scudding sideways. The card was ever so slightly convex, shivering on its slim bowed back like a small unmasted ship lost at sea. For a moment there was only silence. Then one of the girls said, tentatively, "The King of Diamonds is one of the Suicide Kings. In case anybody didn't know." She spoke in an apologetic way, as if meaning to excuse herself for breaking the silence and speaking first.

"The King of Hearts is holding his sword so it looks like it goes into the side of his head—" she demonstrated "—and the King of Diamonds is shown with the blade of his axe facing toward him. It's the same on every pack. The two red kings are always called the Suicide Kings."

Everyone craned to look, and saw that she was right. There was another silence, a different sort of silence this time, a silence ringing with the last words spoken: *the Suicide Kings*. It's always a different sort of silence once the first idea has been cast, Stanley thought.

After a few moments more the collective concentration broke. They looked up and grinned sheepishly, and laughed and stretched and shifted and began to chatter and looked around for a leader who would guide them on from there.

July

"Do we get to a stage, do you think, as teachers," the Head of Movement said, "when the only students who can really affect us are the ones who most remind us of a young version of ourselves?"

The Head of Acting laughed. "And always a very flattering version, too," he said. "Only ever the vigor and the ideals. And the bodies. The supple, fit young bodies that we all imagine we must once have had, before everything else set in."

The Head of Acting was some ten years older than the Head of Movement, and he had not aged well: his pale eyes were rimmed on their undersides by a wet pink rind that always made him look rather ill.

"I think it's sadly true for me," the Head of Movement said. "There's this one acting student this year—a boy. He's very much like how I was, I suppose. How I imagine I must have been. When I'm teaching his class I forget all my doubts about... about everything, really. I watch him so closely and I really delight in his progress—I mean *really*—I keep seeking him out and watching him change, little by little, and I feel excited and generous and all the things that teachers are supposed to feel."

As a teacher the Head of Acting had always maintained a deliberate distance from his students, but his withdrawn and profoundly unmoved manner seemed to cause them, strangely, to worship him the more. It was the Head of Acting who most of the students sought to impress, and it was the Head of Acting who most of them remembered in the years that followed. His coldness and his deadness attracted them somehow, like puppies to a master with a whip. The Head of Movement did not possess this gift of indifference, the Head of Acting thought now: he showed too much of himself, wore his skin too plainly; he was too contemptuous of his students when they let him down.

"The illusion of depth in a character," the Head of Acting had said only this morning to his second-year class, "is created simply by withholding information from an audience. A character will seem complex and intriguing only if we *don't* know the reasons why."

The Head of Movement was stroking his knuckles with his fingertips. He shook his head.

"And I keep reminding myself that in all probability it's just *vanity*," he said, "my seeking out a younger version of myself and watching so greedily, like someone in a fairy tale bewitched. It's a sad thing. I don't think I can connect in the same way with the other students. I just don't—" He spread his arms and shrugged. "I just don't *care* enough," he said. "I don't care enough in what makes them different. They'd never know. I get up in front of them and teach and it's like any stage performance, knowing the role back to front and getting on and doing it. But underneath it all it's just an act."

"Maybe you're being too hard on yourself," the Head of Acting said. "Putting too much of an expectation on yourself that you actually *have* to care. Maybe you don't have to care. Maybe you can not care and still be a great teacher."

"Maybe," the Head of Movement said.

"Who is the student who captures you?" the Head of Acting said. "The younger version of you."

The Head of Movement hesitated, squinting up at the light fitting above the Head of Acting's head.

"I'd rather not say," he said at last, a little shyly, as if the boy was a crush that he held still too close to his heart.

"All right," the Head of Acting said. "But if you let me, I bet I could guess."

April

"My dad has this theory," Stanley said. "He reckons schools should take out insurance policies on the students they think are most likely to die."

There was a pause, then all six of them put down their forks and turned to look at Stanley properly.

"What?" they said.

"Because there's always one kid who dies," Stanley said. "In any high school, right? During your time at high school, any school, you can always remember one kid who died."

His smile was faltering now. He had intended the remark to be flippant and amusing and slightly shocking, but his classmates were looking nauseated and confused. He tried to let a surprised and disappointed look flit across his face, as if to communicate that his audience was not as debonair and outrageous as he had hoped, that the six of them had let him down somehow by this pinched and prudish outlook, by their backward and unfashionable scope that left no room for wit or scandal. He tried to make his eyebrows peak in the center and his smile turn down slightly, a worldly look that was contemptuous and cheerful and uncaring. He tried not to care.

"That's retarded," one of the girls said.

Stanley smiled wider. He could not rightly retreat now. He was committed to voicing, and thus partly owning, a point of view that wasn't his own. He felt trapped, and so tried to redeem himself by becoming jolly and charming, like his father could be, and amplifying his own part, his own sponsorship of the idea, until it seemed as if the idea really was his own.

"You can take out an insurance policy," he said, "for something like two hundred a year. Insurance policies on kids are really, really low. Making money is all about seeing something's going to happen before it happens, right? So if you can get in there and make something good of it—if you can pick the kid who's most likely to die—"

He spread his hands and shrugged, as if the logic were self-evident.

"And you reckon the money should go to whoever takes out the policy," a boy said. "Like, it should go to the school as a reward for being clever enough to spot the kid that was likely to die?"

"What does it mean, 'most likely to die?'" snapped the girl. "That's retarded. How can you tell if a person's likely to die?"

Stanley was feeling hot now. He started to feel resentful, not at his father, whom he was instinctively moving to protect, but at this nauseated audience, who were scowling at him across the mirror-glaze of the linoleum tabletop as if he had mentioned something truly dreadful. He forgot that he himself had met his father's insurance idea with something a little like nausea; he forgot that his father's deliberate provocations often gave him a tight feeling in his chest and a helpless clenching anger that lingered for days and weeks afterward. He glared back at the six of them and said, "Who's to say something good can't come out of a death? Who's to say it's wrong to make something good out of something terrible like a death? To spot it before it happens, and pounce?"

He was imperfectly paraphrasing, and the words were lopsided and unlikely in his mouth.

"Something good of it—like making a million dollars off some kid coming off his skateboard on the way home from school?"

"Maybe," Stanley said. "Maybe, yeah."

"That's the stupidest idea I've ever heard of," one of them said. "Life insurance is all about having a backup in case the person you depend on dies. Like if my dad died, my mum would be screwed because she needs his salary to survive, to pay the mortgage and the bills and all that. So life insurance would pay out if he died, just so she wouldn't be screwed for a few years until she found someone else. Why would they let you take out life insurance on a kid? It doesn't even make sense. They'd know you were up to something."

"I'm just talking about the possibility, though," Stanley said, slipping into first-person ownership after all. "I mean, the idea's possible. Something to think about. If you could pull it off."

All in an instant he remembered a scene from two restaurants ago, La Vista, the two of them silhouetted against a wall of frosted glass and ivy and an artful water fountain that dribbled and never ran dry. His father wiped his mouth on a bunched handful of linen and said, "Want to hear the worst dirty joke I have ever come across in my entire life? I promise you won't have heard it."

The restaurant was quiet. The couple opposite were chewing and looking out the window. Stanley dabbed at his mouth. He said, "Yeah."

"I'm warning you. It's pretty bad. Shall I tell it?"

"Yeah."

"All right. What do you get if you cover a six-year-old kid with peanut butter?"

"I don't know," Stanley said.

"An erection."

There had been a long pause, Stanley's father grinning with his eyebrows up, unmoving, like a clown. The woman opposite had looked across at Stanley casually, meeting his gaze and then lazily drawing her eyes away and returning to the silent dissection of her meal. He wasn't sure if she had heard. He slid his gaze back to his father, his grinning expectant father, and switched on a smile. His own smile felt horribly false, as if the corners of his mouth were clothes-pegged or fish-hooked, and for a second they were both silent, both of them grinning, both of them still. Finally Stanley nodded, and his father said, "It's pretty out there. Right?"

"Yeah."

"That the worst one you've ever heard?" His father's head was tilted at a jaunty angle, and he was rocking merrily in his chair.

"Probably," Stanley said. "Probably the worst."

The memory came unbidden into Stanley's mind and he scowled more deeply now, feeling freshly betrayed. His audience was scowling back at him across the mirrored depth of the table-top which showed them waxy and foreshortened.

"Nobody would ever let you profit from the death of some kid," one of them said. "It just wouldn't happen. Nobody would allow it to happen."

Stanley shrugged his shoulders and looked away, out over the other tables in the cafeteria, as if the conversation had finished and he didn't care. "You're taking it the wrong way," he said, without looking at any of them. He scratched his cheek care-lessly, his eyes roving around the room and his mouth bunched and faintly sneering in the defiant pout of a child. He said, "You're taking it too literally. It was just meant to be a joke."

July

"What is a taboo?" the Head of Acting asked, his voice ringing out in the vast room. The group was sitting cross-legged in a circle, clutching their cold white-dusted toes, their faces grayed and ghostly in the diffused light.

Somebody said, "A taboo is something you want but you can't have."

"A taboo is something that's forbidden because it's disgusting."

"Or because it's sacred."

"A taboo is something we're not allowed to talk about."

"A taboo is something that makes people feel uncomfortable."

"A taboo is something that we're not ready for."

This last interjection was from the girl sitting on the Head of Acting's right-hand side. When she spoke he started in surprise and sought her out with his clear pale eyes, and after a moment he smiled a rare and unexpected smile. "Something that we're not ready for," he repeated. "Good."

They talked about magic and ritual and sacrifice for a few minutes, and then the Head of Acting asked, "Is death a taboo?" He looked searchingly at each of them in turn. "Once upon a time death was a great taboo. Is it still?"

Stanley sat and frowned at the floor. The Head of Acting's pale darting gaze unnerved him. The tutor asked every question with majesty and a pointed reservation, as if emphasizing the profundity of the issues at stake and reminding them that none of them was really capable of a meaningful answer. The cold simplicity with which the Head of Acting spoke made something flutter in Stanley's pelvis, as if the forbiddenness was amplified somehow by the tutor's detachment: it was as if the Head of Acting was being deliberately casual, Stanley thought, like a veteran reprobate offering a cigarette to a child and pretending not to notice the child's blush, and shrug, and stammer.

There was something powerfully strange about the conversation as a whole, as if taboo itself was a forbidden subject. Stanley had the vague sense that they were being tempted, and none of them quite understood how. He squirmed and waited for the flutter in his pelvis to pass. Most of the students, like him, were looking uncomfortable, sitting with their eyes cast down and waiting for the tutor to pounce.

"Stanley," the tutor said, pouncing. "Is death a great taboo?"

Stanley made his hands into fists and pressed his knuckles into the floorboards as he thought.

"No," he said at last. "Not anymore."

"Why?"

"Because people pretend to die all the time," Stanley said. "I watch people pretending to die every time I turn the television on."

"So?" said the Head of Acting, but he looked eager, and his lips were drawn back.

Stanley said, "If death was a great taboo, then pretending to be dead would have consequences."

The Head of Acting gave a brisk satisfied nod and turned back to the group. Stanley drew a breath. He was sweating.

"Let me tell you about my father's death," the tutor said. "He died in his own bed, and after his death my family spent one evening with his body before he was taken away. I had heard about rigor mortis. I found it an interesting concept, but I was also a little suspicious of it, as if it might be an old wives' tale, something archaic that didn't happen anymore.

"I sat by my father's bed and watched over him, and every hour or so I would sneak forward and give him a little poke, just a little poke with my index finger, in the fold of skin underneath his cheekbone where his skin was all pouchy and soft. I kept touching his cheek like this, routinely, waiting for the stiffness to set in. And after a while it did. I leaned forward and poked at his cheek and it was hard as a board.

"It was the delay that I found frightening," he said. "He was soft for so long, and then it was like somebody flipped a switch. The delay frightened me. The delay between two of death's symptoms—rigor mortis and the stopping of the heart. All of a sudden I saw death not as something solitary and final but as an incremental process, a slow accumulation of symptoms, a gradual stepping-down. I had never thought of death in this way before."

They were watching him warily now.

"This is a very personal memory for me," the Head of Acting said, "because I had always imagined that at the death of my father I would feel very great sadness, even hysteria, that I would cry and cry like I'd seen my sisters cry, that afterward I would feel a deep longing for what was irreplaceable about my father, and I would have to work to rebuild my life as normal. I imagined that after it happened I would take time to think about my own mortality, but with a new appreciation and reverence for the brevity of life." The Head of Acting's voice was steady but his voice was very soft, and somehow intensified by the hush, like the savage clear-blue flame of a gas hob turned low.

"But that didn't happen for me," he said. "I didn't cry. I didn't feel a great sadness, and I quickly replaced everything about him that I needed to. My own mortality was just as it had ever been, that was all. I thought I knew how I would react to the death of my father, and I was wrong.

"Like Stanley," the Head of Acting said, quickening and shifting into a new, brisker gear, "any one of you can turn on your television set and watch somebody pretend to die. You all will have seen thousands of deaths which are *not* deaths but merely people pretending. If I said right now, 'You have been shot!' you would all roll around on the floor and clutch your bellies and twitch and moan, and what you would be doing—*all* you would be doing—is copying a copy.

"What I am asking of you for homework," he said, "is not to prepare a performance of death, for most of you have no firsthand knowledge of what it means for somebody to truly die. Instead I would like each of you to prepare a performance of your most intimate experience. You will place yourself at the mercy of this experience by showing this intimate moment to the rest of the group. The aim of this exercise is to see how we can *use* these terribly private experiences as a form of emotional substitute when we come to act a scene or a situation that we don't understand."

There was a grudging silence. Everybody tried not to look at everybody else. They quickly tried to think up all the relatively unpainful moments of their lives that they would be prepared to re-create in front of the class and pretend that it was the most intimate experience of their lives.

The Head of Acting let the silence gather for a moment. Lazily he thought, What would happen if one of them performed a scene from one of my classes? What if the most intimate moment in one of these kids' lives was actually a connection with *me*, some kind of precious moment with *me*, and they had the gall to re-create it in class in front of the rest of them? He pursed his lips as he weighed the possibility in his mind. He thought, It would never happen. None of them would dare.

"I myself have used the memory of my father's death many times in my acting career," the Head of Acting said at last. "I have recalled it, I have re-imagined it, I have replayed it until the memory is sucked of all useful juice and I have *learned* something. I used it as Løvborg. I used it as Kent. I used it as the Chief Tragedian, believe it or not. I used it as Algie."

On the floor, Stanley was thinking of his own father: he pictured him with them now, leaning against the barre with his hands in his pockets and winking solemnly at Stanley as he caught his eye above the sea of nodding heads on the gymnasium floor. He would hate the Head of Acting, Stanley thought, and he imagined what his father would say now: That's right, worship the things that break you down. Worship the deaths and the divorces, and learn to listen to your own sufferings above all other noise. That'll put everything into a nice healthy perspective for you. Just the ticket. Stanley imagined his father shaking his head and laughing in a disgusted, helpless sort of a way, shrugging his shoulders under the gray pilled sports jacket he always wore when he was with a client at work.

But perhaps he wouldn't. Perhaps his father would jerk his thumb at the Head of Acting and say, I have to hand it to him.

It's people like this guy who eventually give employment to people like me. Let him screw you all up, slowly but surely. After you've robbed yourselves of everything that's spontaneous and good about your lives, after all that, I'll have twenty new clients to fix. So go ahead. I'm right behind you, son. I'm right behind all of you. Dig deep.

"If the memory is one of sin," the Head of Acting was saying, his voice ringing out now as if he were quoting from a beloved text, "afterward you will be free of this sin. It is a kind of redemption."

Stanley wondered whether he had done anything in his life that required redemption. He felt ashamed that nothing came to mind. He wished he had a secret, a dark blooming ink-stain of a secret that he could brood over and shrug away.

Finally, with the minute hand on twelve o'clock, the Head of Acting said, "I have one final question before we close. What is the last taboo? The taboo that is graver and more sacred than all others?"

"Sex," somebody said. The answer sounded cheap, and some of the students frowned and shifted and looked at the floor and thought hard. Stanley felt a stirring in his groin again, and he stiffened, wanting very much to leave the room and disappear. Then the girl sitting on the Head of Acting's right-hand side looked up and said, "Incest is the last taboo."

The bell rang. The Head of Acting said, "You may go."

August

It took the best part of a morning for twenty students to reenact the most intimate scene of their lives. Most of them chose a key moment from their parents' divorce. Some attempted a sexual encounter or a scene of public shame. One of the girls brought a pile of pizza boxes on to the stage. She chewed through each slice until it was mush and then spat it out into a white bowl she held under her arm. She wept and wept, and had chewed her way through three cold pizzas before the Head of Acting finally clapped his hands and said, "Good. Thank you. We can work with that."

A bleakness descended on the class as the morning wore on. Stanley was one of the last to perform, and he clutched his little paper bag of props against him as he watched the performers replace each other, one after another, all of them weeping and shouting and caressing invisible lovers with the backs of their trembling hands.

"When I was sixteen," a girl was saying now, "I was going through the drawers in my dad's desk to find a compass for a math project. I came across this photo of my dad in the bath with a little kid. I didn't recognize the kid, or the bath. I flipped it over but there was nothing on the back. I showed my mum."

She yanked down the handle of an old retractable map affixed to the top of a spattered freestanding whiteboard. The map unrolled. The girl had stuck an enormous painted rendering of the photograph to the map-roll. Her father was bearded and laughing, throwing his head back and showing the secret scarlet of his throat. The girl affixed the handle of the map to a hook at the bottom of the whiteboard to hold it open, and stepped back.

"He had two families," she said. "That's how we found out. He'd had this affair with this woman years ago and she got pregnant, and then she got pregnant again, and again, and all of a sudden he had two families, two batches of kids. He divided his time between the two, I guess. When we found out, he didn't try and explain or anything. He just up and left. I haven't seen him since. I wouldn't want to. Mum destroyed the photo so I had to make a copy. So this is him with the third kid of the new batch."

Stanley stared up at the fleshy father in the bath, grossly out of proportion, with his fingers wrapped thick and pink around the small figure of a baby, laughing in the pale soapy lagoon between his legs. The Head of Acting was nodding and writing furiously on his jotter pad. Stanley watched the girl roll up the giant painting and descend quietly from the stage.

A boy began to describe the worst fight his parents had ever had. He was one of the comedians of the group, cheerfully self-deprecating and witty and successful with the girls, and as he spoke the class visibly relaxed and brightened, and sat up with a new generosity and willingness to laugh. The Head of Acting turned to a fresh sheet and looked up at the boy over his glasses, his head tilted and his finger-pads splayed on the desk in front of him.

"And that was the point," the boy was saying, "where Dad goes, You are a neurotic, compulsive woman and one of these days you are going to need to accept that. He really screamed it, and it was a bit frightening just for a moment because my dad's a really quiet, patient sort of a person. After that something just broke. Mum ran off, she really ran away from him, right down the corridor into her study, and slammed the door. We thought the fight must be over, but ten minutes later or so she opened the door again with her head so high and proud, like this—" he demonstrated, holding his arms out like a ballerina "—with her arms full of paper, and she'd typed it out, the whole phrase, in thirty-six point, and she'd got fifty copies printed. She put it up everywhere. She hid copies in his briefcase and in all his pockets. She pinned it to the noticeboard in the kitchen. Everywhere in our house there were these signs that said, You are a neurotic, compulsive woman and one of these days you are going to need to accept that."

Everybody laughed. The boy gave them a quick thumbs-up and then made as if to return to his seat on the floor.

"Stay there a second, Oliver," the Head of Acting said. He wasn't smiling. "Why did you choose this as your most intimate memory?"

The boy shrugged and shoved his hands into his pockets. "I guess because it was the day I learned about revenge," he said, and everyone laughed again.

"Really?" the Head of Acting said. "Or was it because the easiest thing in the world for you is to make everybody laugh? And you chose the easy option, took the easy way out, instead of choosing to actually share yourself in a sincere and honest way?"

The room had gone quiet. Everyone picked at the floorboards with their fingernails and avoided looking at the comedian Oliver, who was still standing with his hands in his pockets and scuffing the soles of his shoes upon the stage. Stanley watched the defensive smile flicker like a flame at the corners of the boy's mouth.

"Everyone else here has really shared something," the Head of Acting said. "They have willingly shown themselves at their most vulnerable. They have relived the most painful and most sacred moments of their lives, and laid them out for us to see. That's a brave thing to do. There's been a lot of trust in this room this morning. I don't see a lot of trust in you, Oliver. Playing to your strengths isn't brave. You knew everyone was going to laugh, big deal."

Oliver was nodding now, chagrined and visibly straining to get down off the stage and melt back into the seated crowd so he could ponder his disgrace in private. He had known this was coming. All the first-years endured a breaking-in of this sort, a forcible public fracture of their ego-mold in the interest of rebuilding a more versatile self. About half the first-years had been targeted so far, and the rest sat glumly and waited for their own turn.

"Do you have a girlfriend, Oliver?" the Head of Acting asked.

"Yes." She was part of the first-year batch and his eyes sought her out briefly in the crowd.

"Is there any aspect of your relationship with your girlfriend which you would not want the rest of the group to see?"

The boy turned back to the Head of Acting. He paused and looked at the tutor suspiciously for a brief moment. "Yes," he said again, but Stanley thought to himself that he could not very well say no. The girl looked faintly stricken, as if anticipating some forced revelation that would cheapen or destroy her, but all the same the boy's admission gave her a rush of pleasure and she almost smiled, looking quickly around at her classmates to see if they were jealous.

"That is what intimacy means," the Head of Acting said. "Intimacy is all the moments that you would be unwilling to share."

The Head of Acting looked at the boy Oliver and tapped his fountain pen against his desktop in a disapproving way.

"You can get down," he said at last. "But I haven't finished with you."

The Head of Acting was sitting behind the students, arranged sideways behind a small writing-desk, with his long legs folded and one palm absentmindedly stroking his calf as he wrote. He watched the shamed Oliver return to his seat next to his girl-friend on the floor, and then capped his pen crisply.

"Stanley," he said. "Up you get."

NINE

Friday

Julia's cue cards are swollen at the edges from the damp of her hands.

"The girls are like wax models in a living tableau: it's always the same scene and they're always in the same configuration," she is saying. "Whoever is the most sexed-up functions as the snare. The snare is always in the middle. She can't be too near the edge or she'd be an easy target."

A crisp spotlight nails Julia flatly to the wall.

"The snare is not necessarily the most beautiful," she says, "but she is always the most provocative. Sometimes the snare will do things that will shame or embarrass the other figures, mostly by adopting a crass or deliberately scandalous manner. That's a normal part of her role.

"The most beautiful girl sits to one side of the snare, and she is known as the prize. The prize is characterized by her untouchability. She is often the only figure in the tableau to be in

179

a stable long-term relationship. The objective of this relationship is always to emphasize her untouchability. Typically the prize is clean and successful and unknowable.

"Standing behind the snare and the prize is the manager. The manager orchestrates all movements within the tableau. The manager is often hard to spot: methods of management naturally differ from group to group. Some common methods of covert management include the use of wit or cruelty, or sometimes the adoption of a motherly persona.

"All other figures in the tableau are the aspiring servants of this central trio. They are used as foils, scapegoats or canned laughter."

Julia has a peculiar flat way of delivering her lines sometimes, as if somebody has forced her to read them and she wants to make clear her private feelings of contempt.

"The depressing fixity of this tableau," she says in conclusion, "makes it clear to us why girls value reincarnation and reinvention above all things."

Monday

There are no counseling sessions about Bridget's death. A flag is retrieved from the sports cupboard, ironed, and hauled to half-mast where it spends a glum week slapping against the rusted flagpole. The girls move around the campus in a vast ghostly drift. They are ashamed that they feel nothing and so respectfully they affect to feel very much. They self-consciously contemplate their own mortality as they watch the raindrops travel down the glass. They sigh and take too long in the toilet cubicle, and say to each other, "I think I need to be alone for a while."

"It's the little things," Julia hears a girl say to her friend while they wait in the line for the tuck shop. "It's the little things that you remember."

In assembly the counselor says, "Bridget was a very special person." He says *special* in the same way he says *important*, cupping his lips around the word as if he is trying to suck an acorn and unwittingly conferring its opposite meaning. In the auditorium, girls who never knew Bridget nod their tremulous assent and pluck at the sleeves of their neighbors for support.

In the staffroom the teachers discuss a memorial for Bridget. Somebody suggests a mural. Somebody suggests a commemorative plaque in the music corridor, to honor her commitment to the jazz band. The weeks go by.

In the meantime Isolde's sister, Victoria, returns to school.

Friday

"You and Julia seem to get on very well," the saxophone teacher says after Isolde has trundled in and unwrapped her scarf and pulled off her mittens.

"Yeah," Isolde says. She flaps her arms about. "God, it's cold!"

"Do you see her much around school?"

"I guess," Isolde says. "The seventh formers have their own commonroom and their own study lounge and stuff. We're not allowed in. Hey, I tracked down some of the recordings of that guy we saw—they've got a whole bunch at the library."

"Good," the saxophone teacher says. "And?"

"Awesome," Isolde says. "Made me want to start playing with other people, like properly."

"You could join Julia's underground band."

"She'd be way better than me," Isolde says. "Hasn't she been learning for ages?"

"She's sitting her letters this year," the saxophone teacher says. "I must say I was so pleased you two got on so well. Is she a friend of your sister's at school?"

"God no," Isolde says with a snort. "Victoria's friends are...
I was going to say brain-dead. No. They're just...much more
girly."

"Julia's not girly?"

"No way."

"What's the opposite of girly?" the saxophone teacher asks,
thinking to herself that only matters of social hierarchy or branding ever produce this sort of conviction in her students.

Isolde reflects for a moment, twirling her necklace around
her finger. "Hard-core," she says at last, pronouncing the word
definitively, as if to deny all other options.

"So Julia is hard-core," the saxophone teacher says.

"Hey, there was something I was going to ask you about one
of the albums I got out," Isolde says, reaching down to rummage
in her bag. "I brought it along."

The saxophone teacher scowls. She wants a performance. She
wants the lights to change, becoming the red tail-glow of Mr.
Saladin's car, and she wants to see Isolde all lit up red for a second before Mr. Saladin kills the engine and the lights go out
and Isolde is sitting in the low half-light of the streetlamp in the
darkened car, and she wants to hear Isolde say—

"It's just the voicing on this particular track," Isolde says now,
unearthing the disc and flipping it over to find the track title.
"Do you mind if I play it?"

"Of course not, go ahead," the saxophone teacher says, sitting down gracefully and watching Isolde stab at the stereo and
insert her disc. She masks her disappointment, reaching over for
her cooling cup of tea and watching Isolde feel for the power
button, sweeping over the dials on the stereo front with light
patting fingertips as if she is blind.

Isolde turns the volume knob and the music begins and, as
it does, the lights change, the overhead bulb fading to black
in time with the upward swell of the saxophone. The two of
them are in perfect darkness for a moment, and then the lights

come slowly up again. They are now reddish and warm, dim and pocketed as if cast by scattered lamps in booths and tables at a backwater bar. The music is lazy and chromatic and low. The saxophone teacher lets out a little sigh of contentment, and settles back to watch.

"When we walked away from you," Isolde said, "this is the tune we heard, coming out of one of those little smoky afterward bars in the alleys by the Town Hall. There was a gig somewhere, not the kind of jostling sweaty gig where everyone's fighting to use their elbows, but just some three-man band jamming away the hours in a quiet bar. Julia turns to me and says, Do you want to get a drink? and I must have nodded because the next thing we're pushing open this foggy door and walking into a warm late-night café—"

Isolde pushes the volume knob up a little bit and the music swells, as if a door has just been opened—

"—and they're playing drums and double bass and keyboards, all of them barefoot and happy, and the drummer is leaning over to talk to the man at the bar while he plays."

The saxophone teacher nods as she pictures the bar in her mind: she knows it very well, the stained diamond pattern of the wallpaper, the dark paneling that ends in an elegant lip at shoulder-height, the reddish brass lamps collared to the wall and bleeding artful fingers of rust in downward rays. It's Patsy's favorite place to sit and drink, and the sax teacher has spent hours in that sticky shadowed corner over the years. She can see the ornate plaster frame of the mirror behind the bar, chipped gold and peeling, and the brass plaques on the lavatory doors, spotted gray with age.

"We walk in," Isolde is saying, "and Julia says sit down. She'll order drinks for the both of us, so I go and fold myself into a corner booth, peeling off my coat and my scarf and checking my reflection in the dark glass of the window by the door. I watch as she leans over the bar and says something to the barman, and she picks up her change and two glasses, and he waves his half-cut lemon at her and says, Get away from me! and they both laugh. She slips into the booth and says, Sorry, I didn't even ask, is red okay? And I don't want to say that mostly what I drink is vodka or rum mixed with fruit syrup to mask the taste, and the only time I've had red wine is when we stole a bottle from Nicola's mum and decanted it into half a bottle of Coke so you wouldn't be able to tell."

Isolde's mouth is dry. She wets her lips.

"I take a sip," she says, "and it's foul, fouler than when we mixed it half with Coke and drank it under the bleachers on the rugby field. I ask Julia if she's turned eighteen yet and she looks a bit annoyed, as if she'd rather talk about something else. She says she has, last week. It was her birthday last week. I say the wine is good. Then we start talking about you, what we think of you, probably because you're the only real thread of connection between us."

The music is crooning and uncomplicated. The saxophone teacher can see it: the cheerful aging three-man band, stepping with their bare feet over the yellow extension leads, the double-bass player nodding and smiling over the glossy wooden shoulder of his one-legged woman-shape, the pianist leaning in and out of the light, the drummer dropping down to a one-handed beat for a couple of bars as he reaches over to take a drink from a sweaty beaded glass of beer, golden under the tasseled fringe of a lamp.

"Afterward," says Isolde, "after we finish our drinks, we're walking down the street toward her car and I'm a bit light-headed. I'm laughing too much. And then Julia says, Most of the girls at school are afraid of me, a bit. It's nice that you're not scared."

Isolde stops. She's in a yellow pool of streetlight now, wide eyed and short of breath, with her fingers clasping convulsively at the cuffs of her jersey. The music slips into a new accelerated phase, becoming more insistent and discordant. Isolde stiffens.

"I looked at her and I said, I am a bit. I am a bit scared. But it wouldn't be worth it if I wasn't."

Isolde gives a little cry, a strangled involuntary half-sob that afterward will be the only thing the saxophone teacher can remember.

"And Julia looks at me," she says, "and then grabs the sleeves of my coat, real fistfuls, grabs the fabric and pulls me toward her really hard. And I think I remember there's one tiny moment before we come together, it's like we stalled for a moment just at the last instant, and I could feel her breath on my upper lip, sweet and hot and quickly panting. I could smell the black spice of the wine in the small pocket of space between us, and then she kissed me."

Isolde isn't looking at the saxophone teacher; she's looking out, out over the mossy rooftops and the clustered antennae and the pigeons wheeling and wheeling against the sky.

"Only it wasn't a kiss how I thought it would be," she says. "She took my bottom lip between hers, and she bit me. She bit my bottom lip, but not so it hurt, more like she was tearing at it very gently, pulling at it with her teeth. And I guess I kind of pulled my head back and gave this gasp and opened my mouth a bit and she still had my bottom lip in her teeth, not so it hurt, really tenderly, like she'd captured it and she couldn't bear to let it go.

"And then we were up against the wall," she says, "and I remember my eyes were closed and my hands were clenched in fists on the wall above my head and Julia presses up against me and her hands are pushing and pushing to find the skin underneath the bottom of my jumper, and then she slides her cold hands up my back and she whispers all salty and hot into my ear, I can't believe this is happening. I can't believe it. I can't tell if this is my fantasy or yours."

The lights ease back up again, just as the track on the disc comes to a chordal close. Isolde moves over to the stereo and ejects the disc before the next track has time to begin. The sax teacher wipes her face, pulling her hand down over her chin so the soft skin of her cheeks is drawn downward for a brief moment, like a sad clown.

Tuesday

"I understand that this is something you couldn't possibly have prepared yourself for," the saxophone teacher says to Bridget's mother. "I'm shocked myself. I feel partly it's because Bridget was so dull. I always imagine that the ones who die are the interesting ones, the wronged ones, the tragic ones, the ones for whom death would come as a terrible, terrible waste. I always imagine it as a tragedy. Bridget's death doesn't quite seem to fit."

Bridget's mother fiddles with the button on the cushion. She looks gray. There is a jeweled stack of gold on the penultimate finger of her puffy left hand, trapped between two swollen knuckles and sunk into her finger like a tattoo or a brand. She pushes the cushion impatiently off her lap and shakes her head in a despairing way.

"If she'd been more original," Bridget's mother says, "it might have been easier. If she'd been more original, you see, then we might have worried that she might commit suicide one day. Then at least we would have thought about her death. We would have prepared ourselves for the possibility just by imagining. But someone as unoriginal as Bridget would never think of suicide. She just wouldn't be clever enough to consider it an option."

"Yes," says the saxophone teacher. "I saw that too. Despair is not something that Bridget would have been clever enough to feel."

They sit quietly for a while. Down in the courtyard the pigeons are fighting.

"And how do you prepare yourself for an accident?" Bridget's mother says limply, mostly to herself. "How do you prepare yourself for a car speeding in the dark?"

After a while the saxophone teacher says, "Do you have other children?"

"Oh, a boy," says Bridget's mother. "Older. He doesn't live at home anymore."

"I suppose you called him on the telephone."

"Yes," says Bridget's mother.

"I suppose he's coming up for the funeral."

"Oh, the funeral," Bridget's mother says. She lapses into silence again and then she says, "I just didn't think this was going to happen. I wasn't ready. I'm still not ready. It's not fair."

Friday

"Do you know," Patsy says in a dreamy voice, swaying at the table with her chin upon her fist, "the moments when I'm the most dishonest with Brian are usually the ones when he believes I'm at my most intimate."

"What do you mean?" says the saxophone teacher. She is sitting stiffly, with her saxophone held upright on her knees. It is a long time ago. She is still holding the instrument with a careful reverence, gingerly even, with both hands, as if it is a new wife and not yet fingerprinted or commonplace.

"I'll be sitting there and thinking how much he is irritating me," Patsy says, "maybe if he's sniffing when he reads, sniffing and sniffing, every half page. And then he'll look up and smile at me and I'll feel compelled to say something, in case what I was thinking was in some way visible to him. So I'll panic and in my guilt I'll say, It's so lovely that we can sit here in silence and read like this. It's so peaceful. I love doing this with you. Which is virtually the opposite of what I really mean. It happens so much. I'll be thinking how he really is getting rather fat, and then I'll feel guilty for thinking such an ungenerous thought, so I'll panic and blurt out, I love you. I'm always motivated by the oddest things."

"But you do love Brian," the saxophone teacher says, mostly because she feels it ought to be said. She has only met Brian once so far, at a recital in the old university chapel. He shook her hand and praised her performance and spoke in a booming voice about the renovations to the tapestry and paneling, twinkling down at her from his great height as if enjoying her lack of interest very much. Patsy flitted in and out and slapped at him and said, again and again, "Come on, Bear, she doesn't want to hear about that."

"Oh, God yes, I *love* him," Patsy says now. "Nearly all the time. A good percentage, anyway. My best percentage yet."

She laughs and shrugs her shoulders lightly, inviting the saxophone teacher to join in and laugh as well at her foolishness, and the foolishness of all duplicitous women who say the reverse of what they mean. The saxophone teacher gives her a tight-lipped smile and watches Patsy's laughter dwindle to a head-shake and a sigh. She wants to kiss her mouth. She wants to feel the other woman pull back minutely in surprise, to almost recoil at how strange and forbidden it feels, but then, all in an instant, to respond—even against her will. Especially against her will.

If there was no Brian—the saxophone teacher's thoughts often begin in this way. If there was no Brian, what then? Is Brian just one man, just one circumstantial, incidental man, or does Brian stand for all men? Is he a symbol for a general preference, a general tendency, and if there was no Brian would there be another, maybe a Mickey or a Hamish or a Bob? She sometimes fears that Brian's solidity and physical presence has transformed Patsy's very shape over the years, bowed her and crooked her until she is simply a negative space that parcels the man up, each defining the other. She fears that Patsy will always exist in this way now, Brian or no Brian, curved to define herself around a man, always a man: a yin that reaches out for its counterpointed yang with one arm always curled and one arm always arched, forever.

Patsy shakes her head again, as if she can't believe her own folly, and reaches the heels of her hands up to her temples to smooth the hair away from her aging face. Her wrists are delicate. The saxophone teacher follows the movement with her eyes.

Wednesday

"I heard she's on Prozac," everyone is saying by the second week, or, "I heard they had to put her on Ritalin after she was found out, she was that out of control." Victoria is now marked, doomed to accept one of the polar fates that diverge before her. "Either she'll end up being totally promiscuous for the rest of her life, and her body will become this weapon she depends on but she's not really sure how to wield," the girls whisper, "or she'll end up this emotional shell, hollowed out and listless and blank. It's one or the other. You'll see. She's screwed up now. It's one or the other." They watch her greedily to see which road she will take, craning forward when she comes into a room, and deflating with disappointment and relief when she leaves again.

Victoria shows no signs of taking either path. She is downcast and polite with all her teachers, and in the schoolyard she tries with limited success to patch up the friendships that have been so damaged by her betrayal. The girls look askance at her, especially the ones who were once Victoria's closest, with whom she should have shared her secret but did not. She asks polite things about the months she has missed, and the girls respond truthfully, but all the while looking at Victoria as if from a long way away, caught between pity and disgust.

"Did your parents ever meet Mr. Saladin?" one of the girls asks one lunchtime. "I mean after you left school. Was there like a meeting or something?"

"Yeah," Victoria says. "All four of us together."

There is a sudden fascinated hush. All the girls pause and look at her.

"He's still way younger than my dad," Victoria says, "so it was still kind of us against them." She doesn't say anything more. She finishes her apple and wanders off across the quad to drop the core in the rubbish bin. When she comes back the bell has rung and the girls are dispersing, looking longingly up at her as they fish for their bags and stow their lunch wrappers away.

"You realize the only way you can make up for this betrayal," the girls want to say, "is by telling us everything, sparing no detail."

"You would be a celebrity among us," the girls want to say, "if you only gave us everything, told us everything, let us in."

The girls want to say, "It's unfair that you should have this advantage over us. You are selfish to keep such valuable and dangerous knowledge for yourself."

The weeks go by.

Monday

"I enjoyed your performance last week," the saxophone teacher says when Julia arrives. "Your performance of the ride home after the concert, both of you in the car together. What you were feeling. What you saw. I enjoyed it."

"Thanks," Julia says.

"Did you practice?" the saxophone teacher says eagerly. "Like I asked?"

"Some," Julia says.

"What have you been focusing on?"

"I guess big-picture," Julia says. "How one girl comes to seduce another."

"Let's start big-picture then," the saxophone teacher says, and gestures with her palm for Julia to begin.

"I've been looking at all the ordinary staples of flirting," Julia says, "like biting your lip and looking away just a second too late, and laughing a lot and finding every excuse to touch, light fingertips on a forearm or a thigh that emphasize and punctuate the laughter. I've been thinking about what a comfort these things are, these textbook methods, precisely because they need no decoding, no translation. Once, a long time ago, you could probably bite your lip and it would mean, I am almost overcome with desiring you. Now you bite your lip and it means, I want you to *see* that I am almost overcome with desiring you, so I am using the plainest and most universally accepted signal I can think of to make you see. Now it means, Both of us know the implications of my biting my lip and what I am trying to say. We are speaking a language, you and I together, a language that we did not invent, a language that is not unique to our uttering. We are speaking someone else's lines. It's a comfort."

Julia's saxophone is lying sideways across the lap of the cream armchair, the mouthpiece resting lightly on the arm, and the curve of the bell tucked in against the seam where the seat-cushion meets the steep upholstered curve of the flank. The posture of the instrument makes the saxophone teacher think of a girl curled up with her knees to her chest and her head upon the arm, watching television alone in the dark.

"I don't know how to seduce her," Julia says. Her eyes are on the saxophone too, traveling up and down its length. "Sometimes I think that it would be like trying to bewitch her with a spell of her own invention if I tried to smile at her and bite my lip and cast my eyes down, if I tried to look vulnerable and coy. Would it even *work*? Even the thought makes me feel disarmed and sweaty and undone. But what's the alternative? Should I behave like a boy, play the part of a boy, do things she might want a boy to do?

"Is that how it works?" Julia says, rhetorical and musing now. She is still looking at the saxophone, lying on its side upon the chair. "Like a big game of let's-pretend? Like a play-act? It feels like there's this duologue about a girl and a boy who fall in love with each other. And maybe the actors are both girls but there's only these two parts in this play, only two, so one of them has to dress up: one of them has to be mustached and breast-strapped and wide-legged and broad to play the boy.

"If you're just looking at the costumes and the script and the curtains and the lights, all the machinery of it, then you'll just see a boy and a girl having a love affair. But if you look at the actors underneath, if you choose not to be deceived by the spectacle of the thing, then you'll see that it's actually two girls. Maybe that's what it has to be like whenever two girls get together: one of the girls always plays the part of the boy, but it's both of them that are pretending."

"Oh, but why can't the two girls just perform a duologue about themselves?" the saxophone teacher says, enjoying herself. "A play written for two girls."

"There aren't any," Julia says. "There aren't any plays about two girls. There aren't any roles like that. That's why you have to pretend."

"Surely you're mistaken, Julia," the saxophone teacher says. "Surely that isn't right."

Julia shrugs and looks away into the sheen of the piano and her own blurry image reflected back. She says, "There is one thing going for me, despite all this. Danger. There's a seduction in that. That's the card I'll have to play, I suppose. I'll have to amplify how forbidden it is, how unscripted and unprecedented, the danger of it.

"The element of danger is what will turn any happy-flutter in her chest into a powerful and thudding fear. That's what I have going for me: the force of her feeling, the massive release of her trepidation, when at last she surrenders and responds. If she surrenders. Whatever she ends up feeling, at least it won't be ambivalent. It will be either the terror-struck forbidden heave of her desire, massive and explosive like the breaking of a dam, or it will be the massive repelling force of her revulsion, her opposition, her denying me. Either way, I've made her feel something. She'll have to feel something. Whatever happens next."

Friday

The girls at Abbey Grange are forever defining each other, tenderly and savagely and sometimes out of spite. It is a skill that will be sharpened to a blade by the finish of their fifth and final year. It is the darkest and deadliest of their arts, that each girl might construct or destroy the image of any of the rest.

They say, Who do you think is most likely to marry first? and Who do you think will get with the most boys? and Who is most likely to cheat? and Who will be best in bed? and then, inevitably, Who is most likely to be a lesbian, out of all the girls in our form?

The last question is always met with shrieks and slaps and a swift intake of merry breath. In their minds they weigh up the girls with the least conquests, the girls currently not in their favor, the girls that are marginally less attractive than the rest. Unpopularity, silence, bookish introversion, any disinclination to follow in the footsteps of the flock—all these are symptoms, the girls agree, as they huddle round to diagnose. They shout out names and laugh and laugh like a coven of giddy witches casting a terrible fate.

If Julia's name is mentioned, however, the girls will frown and flap their hands and say, "Yes, but apart from Julia." Julia is no fun to diagnose. She somehow does not exist in this breathy, shrieking realm of social and sexual investiture where girls are named without their knowledge, convicted, and condemned. The girls cannot alter Julia's fate by saying, I reckon Julia's most likely to be gay. Their power has no meaning for her. She is like a loaded gun cast into their toy-box and half-buried among the plastic rifles, the plastic revolvers, the toy cannons, the caps. They fear the glint of her.

A few of them have kissed each other for the satisfaction of the St. Sylvester boys, perhaps to earn a ride around the block in a low-seated car, or in exchange for a stolen bottle or a crate of beer. A few of them have kissed each other at parties in their mates' front rooms while their friends are outside being sick into flowerpots. Not passionately—that is their defense—but casually, and experimentally, and with no eye for affection or the promise of a sequel or a trend. These are not romances, but selfish tallies that they will later use as a mark of their own liberalism, their own worldly free-spiritedness: the kiss is an insurance, a proof for the later remark, Yeah course, I've kissed a girl.

By not speaking of Julia, the girls have the subtle advantage: they reduce the threat to almost nothing. When they pass her in the hall, they turn their heads and simply walk on by.

Monday

There is a message waiting on the saxophone teacher's answer machine after Julia's lesson. The speaker swiftly and gracefully identifies herself as one of the uninspired mothers, one of the cloying snatching mothers who would rather smother their daughters in the fold of their bosom, clasp their daughters' faces tight to their chests and let them be stifled and choked than lengthen the ribbon of their leash and see them walk away.

The saxophone teacher pauses the machine with the edge of her fingernail, and stands a moment with her finger on the dial.

"The mothers always imagine that my allegiance lies with them," she says aloud, "that our mutual adulthood functions to bind us together against the daughter, the child. They imagine that the daughter is simply the pursuit that draws us together, the activity we both enjoy, the monthly book club, the tennis game. The daughter is simply a medium for our friendship, an opportunity for our togetherness, a shared interest that allows us to explore and reflect upon our adult selves.

"The mothers imagine that I am their ally against the daughter, and that they are mine: they imagine that I have to work as hard as they do in order to forge a connection with the girl, and they roll their eyes at me and shake their heads and laugh like the daughter is impossible, and the both of us know it. They invite me to be tender toward the girl, frustrated with her, even despairing of her, but above all to treat her as an object, as the mere occasion for this reciprocal connection, adult with adult, like with like."

She comes to a halt now and then stabs the machine again, bringing the voice back to life, bringing the woman back into the room.

"So I look forward to hearing from you," the recorded woman continues. "Stella's fourteen, been studying the clarinet for almost three years now, and before that nearly six years piano. She's really very interested in moving on to the sax. There's just something so dowdy and unfashionable about the clarinet, as you know, and I think she's looking to make the move on to something a bit sexier. Something with a bit more bite, that gives her a bit more appeal. It's a welcome move, in actual fact. We were worried for a time that she wasn't interested enough in that sort of thing, just didn't care enough. About boys and nice clothes and all the rest of it. We were worried for a time, I don't mind telling you that. Not that she had trouble making friends—it was almost the opposite, really, that the friendships were just so close. You couldn't prize them apart. Whoever it was, the current favorite. Always one after another, there was always a favorite, right the way through. I'd ferry them around, to and from the cinema and all that, and they'd always sit together in the back seat with an old rug thrown right over their heads so they could talk quietly and I couldn't see. I'd watch in the rear-view, this shrouded tartan thing with their two heads together and both of them whispering away. Looked like they were kissing, even. It unnerved me. I don't mind telling you that.

"If you could call me back on this number," the woman says in closing, and then there is a little pip to show that the message has come to an end.

Saturday

It is thirty-five minutes before Bridget is going to die, and she is sitting on her high upholstered stool in the video store, the till already cashed up and waiting under the counter in its dirty canvas slip. The car park outside is empty and slick, and she can see the line of yellow streetlights peeling away from her into the black.

Bridget is remembering two girls at her primary school who had for a time become obsessed with gathering facts about sex. They always referred to the act as *It*, and sat together for hours in grave dutiful conference as they revised and expanded their combined wisdom on the subject, from time to time closing their eyes in long-suffering horror and saying something like "Two-on-one It. That is *so* gross." They were secretive and guarded and unwilling to share their wisdom, like proud and weary sphinxes guarding the door to a world that the others could not hope to understand.

Bridget recalls one athletics lesson from this period, the two girls standing together with their arms casually linked, and watching the PE teacher with the expression of forbearing solemnity that was appropriate to their studies of It. The PE teacher called out, "Today we're practicing sprints from a crouch start," and the smaller girl immediately whispered, "Crouch start for It." They exchanged a grave nauseated look as if the conjured image had pained them both. Bridget felt a little jealous as she watched these two girls share their mutual feeling of pious disgust. The smaller girl's deliberate revulsion fascinated her. "Crouch start for It," she said. The subject was just too painful to say more. The taller girl looked down in sympathy and shook her head as if to acknowledge how sickening and inescapable the whole business was. It was all around them.

The eight-year-old Bridget had been unable to comprehend the terrible relation that this particular athletics lesson bore to the act of It, and now as she reflects upon the scene she realizes that she still has no idea how to recognize or execute a crouch start for It. Is there even such a thing? she asks herself doubtfully, but then she recalls once more the poise and perfect confidence of this ten-year-old girl, who is eighteen by now and probably thoroughly schooled in arts beyond the reach of Bridget's imagining. Bridget reflects on how little she knows. The raindrops reach the sill and quiver there. She feels ashamed.

Tuesday

The saxophone teacher smoothes the newspaper and looks again at the article. The paper is old now, and there have been others, subsidiary stories that recap this first account, stories about holding inquiries and questioning witnesses and deciding who to blame, but this paper remains, folded into eighths, limp and graying with the hangdog look of old news. The headline reads *Girl's Death "Terrible Waste,"* and the article is short. Bridget is unnamed, which is fitting, the saxophone teacher thinks, given just how forgettable Bridget was. The unnamed girl was cycling home from work, the saxophone teacher reads over and over, and she was hit by a red sedan as she made a right turn out of the video store car park. The car drove on.

The saxophone teacher thinks, She would have been at the concert with the three of us that night, if only I'd liked her enough to invite her. The thought nibbles at her for a moment, just as a possibility, like a new shirt that she may or may not try on. Finally she shrugs and snuffs it out. Outside in the courtyard she can dimly hear a group of students from the drama school, chanting and stamping their feet. She pushes the newspaper away and moves to the window to look.

Near the trunk of the ginkgo tree, six students have formed a human pyramid on a thin square of foam matting, while in front of them a larger group pace back and forth. They are like a seething flock of dark crows in the uniform black of the Institute, their feet bare and bloodless against the paving. From where the saxophone teacher is standing, the pyramid looks a little like a card castle, wobbling slightly but standing firm, growing outward and upward as more and more actors withdraw from the foreground drama and add their bodies to the tier.

The saxophone teacher watches the black flurry in the foreground for a long while. Looking back to the solid pyramid of bodies at the base of the ginkgo tree, she is startled to see that she is being watched. One of the boys in the front row, kneeling on the asphalt with his arms extended stiffly to either side, is looking up at her. His head is flung back, and the open collar of his shirt shows the length of his white throat. The saxophone teacher's first impulse is to step away from the window, but she stays, and she thinks she sees the boy smile up at her. She looks away.

The rehearsal is coming to a close. One of the girls at the front rears up suddenly and calls out, in a rich clear voice that fills the courtyard, "*I* imagine things when I watch people."

And as she says it, as the marvelous peal of her voice breaks off and the stamping and drumming comes to a swift and terrible halt and the courtyard fills with silence like a sudden rush of water, as she says it, the card castle behind her begins to fall. It tumbles down in a stately and choreographed cascade, a slow-motion melt. The figures of the actors tumble off to land on light heels and knees on the foam matting, scuttling off and leaping away until the pyramid has disappeared utterly, thawed out to a nothing-puddle of black stillness, all of the actors unmoving and silent where they have come to rest.

The girl at the front is the only figure standing now. She spreads her arms and says, "I imagine—"

There is the tiniest of pauses, the girl outstretched and full of curtailed breath that swells her ribs to bursting. Then it is as if a spell is broken, as if an invisible curtain has come down and an invisible blackout has blanked the stage, and all the fallen figures begin to move. They jump to their feet and dust themselves down and break into conversation, and the saxophone teacher hears "That fall was heaps better that time, you came in right on the beat" and "We can still get that tighter, guys" and "From the top."

TEN

June

"So we agree that sexuality is an issue that we're all interested in, at least," the boy Felix said loudly, the first time the first-years met to discuss the devised theater project and the King of Diamonds playing card. Felix was bossy and pert and did not understand the humor of what he had just said, scowling at a pair of boys on the far lip of the circle who faintly snickered.

"I liked the idea of using found stories," one of the girls said. "From the media and our communities and all that, taking them and using them and making them theatrical. I liked that idea."

"All right," Felix said graciously, drawing with a fat felt-tipped pen a spiky cloud around the word SEXUALITY. The others watched. At the beginning of the year Felix had labored to snare the role of the group's organizing mind, to the irritation of most of the students, who looked at the tiny protrusion of his tongue as he wrote and felt they could do better.

"Then what about that story that Grace brought in?" Felix

said when he had completed the bubble. "The teacher–student thing at Scabby Abbey."

He used the nickname to show them that although he was organizing the group, they were not allowed to resent him or regard him as a teacher-figure.

"My sister's at Abbey Grange," one of the boys said. "In sixth form. She reckons they don't know the half of it yet. What she heard was that after all the girl's friends found out, the teacher kept them quiet for a few months by paying them out. Mostly buying them booze, on behalf."

"But wasn't the girl a seventh former? So most of her friends would have been eighteen anyway."

"It's what I heard," the boy said, shrugging.

"How did they get caught in the end?" somebody asked.

"I heard it was another teacher," the boy said. "The guy had been dating someone else on staff, and then they broke up and she was the one who found him with the girl. That's what Polly said."

"I thought it was her friends," one of the girls said. "They caught on and went to the principal and dobbed her in."

"I heard that it wasn't just the one girl who was abused," somebody said, "it was a whole bunch of them—he was playing them all at the same time. She was just the one who got caught."

"Do we know whether anything actually happened?" one of the girls put in. "What if nothing actually happened between her and the teacher at all?"

"They had evidence. Like there were some of her clothes at his house. And there was a toothbrush."

"A toothbrush doesn't mean *rape*," the girl said, with a sharp little laugh. "A toothbrush means the opposite of rape. It doesn't even mean a one-night stand. A toothbrush means you've got foresight. It's like if they found *pajamas* at his house, little girly flannel pajamas, pastel pink with a pattern of clouds. It can't be *evidence*. It's an investment. A toothbrush is an investment."

There was a silence as they all digested this new concept.

Then one of the boys said, "Wasn't he like sixty?"

"He wasn't that old. There was a photo in the paper last week. He's got brown hair."

"So we don't really know very much at all," Felix said crossly, swiping his fringe away from his face. He was feeling the helpless boiling irritation of an officious person struggling to control a group too large and original for him. He uncapped his pen and wrote ISSUES at the top of his butcher's sheet.

"We need to make really awesome use of the card itself," one of the girls said. "Playing cards need to be an integral part of the performance, not just some little byproduct scene that's tacked on."

"I think that's a given," Felix said. "Well, let's talk about the card then, and the different ways we could use it." He underlined the word ISSUES, recapped his pen with a careful snap and looked expectantly at them all.

"Just the one card, or the whole pack?"

"I reckon the whole pack," somebody said. "It's a really great aesthetic for costuming and we can use it to shape the play kind of, like if we have four acts, each with a suit name, or thirteen scenes that each have a card name in a particular suit."

"That's a good idea."

"Yeah! We can dress up like the court cards, with their weapons and stuff. Don't they all have weapons?"

"What if we made up a *game*? A card game that we could use as the focus of the play. If you draw a red card you will be attracted to women. If you draw a black card you will be attracted to men."

"Yeah, and every individual card could stand for some sort of particular—I don't know. Some sort of particular habit or trait or something. Something to do with sexuality or whatever."

"If you draw His Nobs, you leave before the morning?" one of the boys said, and everyone laughed.

"What's His Nobs?"

"One of the jacks in cribbage."

"Hang on," said Felix, scribbling. "We're going too fast."

"We're going fine," one of the boys said. "You're just writing too slow."

Felix felt his authority begin to ebb. He scowled and wished he had appointed a scribe.

"What if we make the whole play a kind of fantasy, like set in a fantasy world or whatever, where as soon as you turn a certain age you have to draw a card?"

"You get sent to a fortune-teller or something—"

"Like a tarot reader."

"Yeah! It's like a coming-of-age ritual thing. A rite of passage."

"The card becomes like your identity card. You keep it with you always."

"You can't show it to anybody."

"So queens might mean drag or something, and if you drew a queen you'd have to take up drag."

"Queen—like drag queen!"

"That's what I meant."

"Is that what we really believe, though?" Stanley said. "Do we really believe it's like that—that your identity is dealt out to you, given to you the moment you grow up, and from then on it becomes your—your motif or something? Like a badge?"

"Yeah," the first boy said. "Do you not believe that?"

Stanley opened his mouth but then closed it again. He wasn't sure.

"But doesn't that mean you'd have one card for the rest of your life?" somebody said.

"Yes," the emphatic boy said. "Unless you gamble it away. In a high-stakes game of chance. In a deadly game of chance in an underground bar, where you run the risk of ending up with nothing."

"We could do that really well."

"It would dramatize really well."

"Really steam-punk."

"I reckon."

"Anyway," one of the girls said crossly, "it doesn't matter what we actually believe. It's a great idea. The Head of Acting would go nuts for it. It's just the sort of crossover thing he loves."

"What do you mean, crossover?"

"With the teacher–student thing. Using stories from the media. Did anyone see the production a few years back about the witch hunt, and they had actors in disguise all through the audience pretending to be members of the public?"

"Yeah, I saw that."

"Until you didn't know who was acting and who wasn't, all around you. It was really scary, actually. The season totally sold out. They had to extend by a week."

There was a small hush as they all imagined extending their opening season by a week. Felix had stopped writing and was looking around with his pen limp in his hand.

"I like the Abbey Grange idea," someone said.

"So do I."

"What are we going off, though? Just a few articles in a local paper? That isn't enough."

"We'll have to research it. We'll have to find out more."

"Because at the end of it everything collapses," one of the girls said. "For the girl, the victim, the one who was abused. It all comes down around her like a castle of cards."

July

The blinds were open on the corridor side when Stanley and the girl passed, carrying their costumes down to the art department.

They heard the noise and turned their heads, and then they stopped and moved closer to the glass, to watch.

A boy was howling, squirming and bent almost double with his hands at his groin. The Head of Voice was crouched over him, leaning right over with her feet planted sturdy and apart and her cheek against his, and her plump arms around him, clasping him tight. She was muttering urgently and inaudibly into his ear as he howled. His howl was unpitched and irregular and ever-changing, morphing into a guttural hum, a throaty kind of gurgle, even a bat-shriek that was too high and whispery to be heard. He appeared to be trying to twist away from the Head of Voice but she was clamped tightly to his back and the boy could only writhe and struggle. His eyes were closed.

"What's happening to him?" Stanley whispered.

"Remedial Voice," the girl whispered back. "He's working through a lot of stuff from when he was a kid, I think. Really bad stuff that's all locked inside."

The boy was slack faced and open mouthed and his expression showed no pain, but the noise he was making was raw and brutish and full of hurt. It was frightening, this terrible noise coming out of this boy's calm unworried throat. If it weren't for the leaping of his Adam's apple, Stanley would have thought the noise recorded.

"It's horrible," Stanley said.

The girl shot him a disdainful look, as if he couldn't hope to understand. "Better than releasing it any other way," she said. "Putting kittens in a microwave or whatever."

"Is that what he's doing? Releasing it?"

"Course," the girl said, and tossed her head. "That's her specialty. Head of Voice. People hire her out, outside the Institute—she goes to people's private homes and stuff. It's like a special type of therapy. She's really good."

They watched the boy howl for a while, thrashing stiffly with the dead weight of the Head of Voice clamped around him. His expression changed. He peeled his lips back so all his teeth were exposed and his nose was wrinkled in a snarl, and inside his mouth the hump of his tongue rose up, quivering and taut. He snapped his jaw and barked a little, short gasping barks from the back of his throat like a cough. The Head of Voice had begun crooning in his ear now, a gentle private lullaby that welled up underneath the frenzied barking and caused the boy to wither and gasp. Stanley felt suddenly ashamed.

"Come on. We should go," he said, and tore his gaze away. The girl was already gone.

September

One Saturday afternoon in spring Stanley was huddled in a cubicle in the empty art department and trying without success to untangle the bobbin on his sewing machine. He was near finishing his Queen of Spades costume, sewing in a large waxy piece of cardboard behind the patterned front of the bust to give himself a more angular thrust. He had spent all morning struggling with the wire halo that fitted around his forehead. The headpiece was spangled with wire spokes designed to lift the geometric wimple higher off his head. After nearly five hours squinting at the seams and bruising his fingertips as he molded the rough end of the wire, he was finally satisfied that the effect was rather good. He was wearing the wimple now as he bent over the sewing machine, obscured to the rest of the room by a cluster of colonial furniture that had been carried to the art department for painting and left over the weekend to dry. All around him was the sweet smell of acrylic paint, as always at the Institute laced with detergent so the paint could be easily removed when the production closed.

Stanley bent over his costume. In his research for the production he had come to know his card very well: he knew that in the traditional French deck of cards the Queen of Spades was supposed to represent Joan of Arc, and in the game of Hearts the Queen of Spades was so unlucky she was known as the Black Bitch. He knew that she was the only queen to carry a scepter as well as a daisy flower, and for that reason she was sometimes called the Bedpost Queen. He had pored over the court cards in his deck at home for such a long time that he found the red-and-black images appearing after he closed his eyes at night. He disentangled the bobbin finally from the thready mess below the foot, and snipped the stray threads away. He pinched the end of the bobbin-thread in his fingers to pull it through the notch in the bobbin-holder, and heard the spool spin cleanly.

The door opened and Stanley caught a faint swell of music from the dance hall near the foyer, where a group of schoolchildren were taking their Saturday lessons in jazz.

"In here, then," he heard somebody say, "Nobody should disturb us in here. It's a bugger they're using the staffroom. Sit down there if you like."

The voice belonged to the Head of Movement. Stanley was still intently returning the bobbin to its tiny hinged cavity in the base of the sewing machine, a scrap of thread in his mouth, and he did not reveal himself at once. He wound the wheel at the side of the sewing machine and watched the needle plunge down to retrieve the bobbin-thread, bringing it up in a little scarlet loop that he flicked up with the tip of his scissors and tugged gently outward. He was so intent on the task that when it was done the Head of Movement and his guest were already in mid-conversation, speaking easily and with great relief, as two people who have longed for time alone to talk.

"They all want it," the Head of Movement was saying. "Not just the first-years—everyone, right up until the day they leave."

"Why doesn't the school offer that sort of thing, then? One-on-one tutorials or whatever. If it's what the students want."

As slowly as he could, Stanley leaned sideways around the

edge of his cubicle and saw, through the tiny sliver of view between an upended wing armchair and a sideboard, the central figure from the Theater of Cruelty exercise, the masked boy from second year who had slapped and shorn and nearly drowned his victim on the stage. Stanley watched him for a second, his smooth face unmasked now and taut with eager concentration as he listened to the Head of Movement speak.

"With you," the Head of Movement was saying, "I think that this Institute will fall short in several respects. That's what I wanted to say yesterday—I recommend something postgraduate, even an internship. The mime school. You're going to be unfinished at the end of next year. Unfinished and hungry."

The Head of Movement was speaking earnestly but without the clipped, rehearsed quality that usually characterized his speech. Stanley regarded the pair of them jealously through his sliver. The boy was sitting with his leg hiked up under him and his fingers stroking the frayed upholstery, nodding carefully as the Head of Movement spoke, and suddenly it struck Stanley what was so odd about the situation: *they are friends*, he thought in wonder.

"I value your opinion completely," the unmasked boy said, leaning in close, and in that instant Stanley remembered the golden boy, greased and glittering like an artificial dish sprayed with lacquer to be photographed for a cuisine magazine. The golden boy had gleamed, and this boy was gleaming now.

Stanley swallowed and felt a bitter injustice in his throat. He recalled a vision of himself, in the Head of Movement's office, pushing away tears as he shouted in complaint. Even now he felt a flicker of self-congratulation that he had responded to the Theater of Cruelty exercise in that violent way. Why hadn't the Head of Movement been impressed, then? Why hadn't the tutor relaxed into a rare and sudden intimacy, inspired by Stanley's fragile openness to confess a vulnerability of his own? Why this boy, Stanley thought, this smooth-faced unmasked boy who was no better or worse than the rest of them?

"It's funny," the Head of Movement was saying now, "in many ways you've really...well. Woken me up, I suppose."

"My growth is projected on to him...it is *found in him*," the unmasked boy quoted, and through his secret sliver Stanley saw both of them smile.

"Shared or double birth," the Head of Movement said. "Not the instruction of a pupil but utter opening to another person." He was silent a moment, and then he added, "Well remembered."

They sat there and looked at their shoes, enjoying the shallow silence of the room. Behind the cold discolored flank of the sewing machine, Stanley watched and felt bitter. He waited two long hours, with cramp in both knees and a terrible hunger gnawing at his insides, until the boy and the Head of Movement finally ended their conversation and left the room.

July

"Let's improvise it," one of the first-year boys suggested. "Let's start with what we had last week and see where that goes. I really liked what was happening with the two characters together, both of them saying things that the other doesn't really hear, like neither of them is fully present for the other."

"We'll just start rolling," one of the girls said. "First Mr. Saladin and then the girl, rotating like that. Anyone can get up at any time. Anyone can play either of them, doesn't matter who. We'll just try and keep the scene moving and see what happens."

"We'll get a real dialogue going."

"That's right."

There was a brief pause as everyone digested the formula and swiftly began to prepare what they would later say. Then one of the boys got to his feet. He transformed into a different person as he stood up, a man rising like a phoenix out of the pallid, ashy figure that had been the boy. Once he was standing, hands on hips and his jaw thrust back and his bare feet apart and solid on the floor, nobody doubted who he had become.

The man said, "When the girls spoke of it, they said *all the way*, as if the process was a passage, a voyage, some sort of ritual first crossing of a dimly charted sea. Victoria said those words to me—*all the way*. She asked a question. She asked, Do you want to go all the way with me? as if her departure were already scheduled, her moorings already cast, and I could simply choose to board and join her, to sail away with her and disappear. *All the way*, she said. Every inch of it. Every inch of that windblown ocean-salted bucking rolling passage. Every inch."

He sat down. There was the briefest of pauses again, and then Stanley stood up. He stood with his weight on one leg like a girl, one arm crossed over his chest and holding his hip, the other gesticulating with a crooked elbow and a flat palm.

"He took a long time to answer the question," Stanley said. "At first he gave this little shout of a laugh and gathered me up into him and kissed my crown. Sometimes when he kissed me he'd make this keening sound in the back of his throat, like a puppy almost, some kind of ghostly underwater voicing of some deep-felt feeling, right inside. Once he burrowed his head into the pilled blue wool of my armpit and moaned out loud and he said, I just feel so blessed, Victoria. I feel so incredibly, incredibly blessed. We were sitting there on the cream leather sofa in his living room and I said, Do you want to go all the way with me? and he said, Oh, you precious, precious little girl. Not yet. Not just yet. Let's just enjoy the innocence for a moment, before it dissolves and we can never have it back again. Let's just take this moment to enjoy how much is still to come."

Stanley sat down. All around him the students were stern and glassy. They had only half-listened to his performance, all of them preoccupied already with the inward rehearsal of what they would say when they got up in front of the rest, and how they would contrive to make the words seem spontaneous and unrehearsed and pure.

One of the girls got up. Like any girl who tries to play a grown man, her performance was disproportionate and slightly embarrassing. She let her voice deepen and placed her feet wide apart and assumed a manner that was overly earnest and gruff. She raised her chin and said, "Could it have been one of the others, if this girl had never dared? Could it just as easily have been the girl to her right or left, another saxophonist in the front row of the jazz band, some girl whose breasts were smaller, whose gaze was sharper, whose fingernails were squatter, maybe, and poorer in shape, whose jersey was coming unraveled at the hem? All of them have smiled at me, looked hard at me, laughed with me. When we won our section at the high school jazz festival, some of them even hugged me. Would it have been different, with one of them?"

Another girl got up as this Mr. Saladin was returning to her seat on the floor. The new girl spread her hands and said, "It's funny to think that I never saw him wake up. I never rolled over to see him still sleeping, never saw his eyelids waxed and still in the pale morning light, never burrowed down into the sweet hot breath of the bed and felt him stir and lift his heavy sleepy arms to let me in. We had no mornings-after. We had no nights, no long uninterrupted nights where we could sleep and sleep and sleep. We had no silence. We never breakfasted together. We never swam together, shopped together, walked to the cinema together; I never called him at work to check when he was due to come home; I never pegged his laundry on the line. I never knew his mother or his nephews or his life.

"All these are adult things, and they're all things I never had with him. People say, now, that I was a child wrongfully thrust into an adult's role. People call it an adult relationship, illicit and untimely and premature. In fact it was the opposite. It was Mr. Saladin who had the adolescent relationship, all backseat whispers and doorway fumbles and getting home before mid-night, waiting for the parents to go to sleep or leave the house, sending messages in code and on the sly. I didn't play the adult. Mr. Saladin played the child."

August

Opening night drew nearer and nearer. Without a central script, the devised performance did not seem to be approaching any kind of finished state, but merely began blooming and swelling in odd places, like an ancient wrinkled party balloon that was being forcibly refilled with breath. Tempers in the group ran high, and fractures began to form around the strongest person-alities as the dissatisfied students met in whispering mutinous pairs in doorways around the Institute.

"Andy strutting around in that costume like that makes me *sick*," was how the whispers ran. "Thinks he's God's gift to the stage. Every time he walks past I want to stick out a leg and trip him up."

"Do you know how hard it is to act in a scene with Oliver if Esther's around? Today she was practically humping his leg."

"If Felix clears his throat like that one more time I swear I am going to clock him."

"What is this show, like a two-hour tribute to one guy? Why does Sam get so much stage time? It's not like he's the cream of the crop or anything."

The real risk was that these dissatisfied students, the whis-perers, angry at the comparative insignificance of their parts and sick of the officious prodding from the others in the group, might want so much to disassociate themselves from the per-formance that on opening night they might intentionally act poorly, calling deliberate attention, through their ham acting, to the distance between the actor and the role. This became a tacit threat; it hung in the air around them, and the actors became wary and mistrusting, hugging their costumes tighter to their chests as if they were trying to hold the fractured shell of their ego in one place with the force of their hands.

Leaving the Institute after a rehearsal one day, Stanley bundled his bag of take-home props under his arm and threw his head back for a moment to enjoy the pale afternoon sun. He had left quietly, through the backstage area and out the players' door into the alley, slipping away from his scowling, shadow-eyed classmates who were still arguing as they stacked the chairs away and cleared the rehearsal room for the next morning.

He rounded the corner into the northern quadrangle and to his surprise came face to face with the girl who had appeared so oddly and suddenly in the wings of the auditorium stage, the wide-eyed schoolgirl who had collided with him in the velvet black. He stalled a moment as he recognized her, again recalling the brief and breathy impact in the dark, the girl gasping and stricken and looking down at him in mute apology as he fell.

When his scene was over he had returned to the wings to seek her out, but she had disappeared.

"There was somebody watching," he had said later to the boy Felix, as in their dressing rooms they wiggled out of their costumes and returned their wigs to the faceless polystyrene heads that lined the top of the dresser. "From the wings. She must have come in by the players' door. I guess it was open."

"Did you tell her to get out?" Felix said, not really interested. He was unlacing his bodice aggressively, and Stanley heard the worn and dirty laces rip.

"She disappeared," Stanley said, watching as Felix saw his mistake and swore under his breath. "I guess it's just weird when people watch from the wings and we don't know it. It's like an unfair advantage. If someone had crept in through the foyer and was watching in the stalls I wouldn't have cared."

Isolde was sitting on the slat bench underneath the ginkgo

tree. She was wearing her Abbey Grange school uniform, and was swinging her legs slightly as she flicked the pages of a dog-eared novel, curving her body over the book with her hair falling free about her face. As he approached he saw more clearly now how pretty she was, with full cheeks and a pouting mouth and a slender upturned nose that she was stroking absently with one finger as she read. As Stanley neared her she looked up and gave a puzzled start as she recognized him.

"It's you," Stanley said. "From the wings."

"Oh, yeah," the girl said, and drew her lower lip underneath her front teeth. She looked up at him uncertainly, like a puppy waiting to be admonished.

"You made me miss my cue," Stanley said, and then they both blushed at his rudeness.

"Sorry," Isolde said. "I heard the drum and I just followed the sound. I guess I just wandered in."

There was a little pause.

"It was only a rehearsal," Stanley said at last. She nodded politely and pressed her lips together in a kind of apologetic smile. Stanley pointed at her music case to change the subject. "What do you play?"

"Alto saxophone," Isolde said. "My teacher's studio is up there."

"She must be rich, to afford a studio here," Stanley said. "The rent is insane. I know because the Drama Institute were going to buy out way more of these buildings than they actually did, but it was too expensive." He was growing hot with embarrassment now, the unease spreading like a scarlet ink-stain over his chest and into the stippled hollow of his throat. He knew that it would be visible above the open collar of his shirt, spreading up to his chin like an old-fashioned ruff. He wished he had not sought this girl out, that he had walked past her without speaking, maybe even given her a calm and cryptic nod.

"I don't know if she's rich," Isolde said.

"Are you any good?" Stanley asked.

As soon as he said it he felt ashamed at having asked such an unanswerable question of this round-faced, blinking girl. He hoped she would not ask him the same question back. But Isolde only said, "I'm sitting Grade Eight," and shrugged to show that the question didn't much matter to her anyway.

"I hear you guys sometimes," Stanley said. "Well, probably not you specifically, but the music travels down to where we are."

"Yeah, I hear you guys sometimes too," Isolde said, inexplicably blushing now too. "Mostly drums and shouting."

"And screaming probably," Stanley said, trying to make a joke out of it, but Isolde just smiled and said, "No, I've never heard screaming."

"Okay," said Stanley, flapping his arms. "Well, I guess I'll see you around." He had meant it to sound aloof, but instead it sounded expectant, as if he were anticipating another chance meeting. He looked away from her to show he didn't care, out over the cobbles at the pigeons and the banked rim of litter framing the courtyard with a little crust of silver and white.

"Okay," Isolde said, giving him a curious look. She made no move to take up her novel again, and followed him with her eyes as he stumbled away from her and across the quad, the bag of props slipping from under his arm.

June

"Stanley," the Head of Acting said, "I want you to become your father."

Stanley nodded tentatively. He was standing with his legs slightly apart and his hands behind his back. All the other students were sitting on the floor and looking up at him, hugging their knees tight against their ribs.

"This is a question-and-answer session," the Head of Acting said, smoothing the page in front of him calmly with the flat of his hand. He was sitting at a desk to one side, his legs crossed at the knee, one bare white foot rotating slowly to relax the ankle joint. "We are going to start asking questions of you, addressing you directly as if you really are your father. I want you to stay in character for the next half hour. If you don't know the real answer to any questions asked of you, then make them up. Don't worry if you have to lie, just don't break character."

Stanley nodded again. He looked down for a moment, drew a breath, and then looked up again with his father's wry twitching smile. He spread out his hands and said, "Hit me," and all at once he was guiltless and unapologetic and mischievous.

"How well do you know your son Stanley?" the Head of Acting asked first.

Stanley raised his eyebrows and smiled. "He's a good kid. We swap dirty jokes, that's our thing. We get along fine."

"What kind of dirty jokes?"

"Oh, we try and shock each other, back and forth. It's just a game we play." Stanley smiled again and looked at the Head of Acting coolly, as if he could see right through him, as if all of the Head of Acting's wants and fears and hopes and faults were laid bare to him. The Head of Acting looked impassively back.

"Tell me one of the jokes that you've told your son," he said.

"What's the best thing about sleeping with a minor?"

"I don't know," said the Head of Acting politely.

"Getting paid eight dollars an hour for babysitting."

There is a smothered giggle from one of the students on the floor. Stanley turned to flash him a smile. "Good, eh?" he said, twisting both wrists around to shake out his cuffs the way his father often did. "But it's getting harder and harder to come up with anything original. I have my secretary look them up for me. Best job she's ever had, she reckons."

There was another ripple of laughter from the floor. Stanley grinned and drew himself up a little higher, placing both hands on his stomach and stroking the fabric of his shirt downward again and again. He contrived to make the movement look almost absentminded.

"Tell me one of the jokes that Stanley has told you," the Head of Acting said.

Stanley paused and thought for a moment. "Can't recall, sorry," he said at last.

"Would you say you have a good relationship with Stanley?"

"We don't see each other that often," Stanley said, "but he's a good kid. Good sense of humor. A bit sensitive maybe, but that isn't going to hold him back. We get along fine."

"What's your son good at?"

"Stanley?" Stanley said, buying time the way his father would buy time. "He's pretty well liked everywhere he goes, I think. He did well to get into drama school. Is he a good actor? I don't know. You could probably tell me that."

"So what would you say he was good at?"

"The arts," Stanley said doubtfully, thinking hard. "He's a romantic. He got that from me. He sure as hell didn't get it from Roger."

"Is Roger his stepfather?"

"Yes."

"What's he like?"

"Mild," said Stanley. "Laughs even if he doesn't think it's funny. Runs out of things to say and then looks frightened, tries to escape. Sure he's a nice man though. I wouldn't marry him. But he's a nice man."

"Is he a good father to your son?"

"He's a good stepfather to my son."

"All right," the Head of Acting said, turning to include the rest of the group huddled at Stanley's feet. "Let's open up the floor. Any of you can start asking Stanley's father questions. Anything you like."

"Do you see yourself in Stanley?" called out a girl in the front row.

"He's a little more careful than I was at his age perhaps. He's an innocent kid. I wasn't as innocent as he is."

"Do you think he's still a virgin?" This was from one of the tousled boys in the back. The Head of Acting looked around sharply, but Stanley didn't flinch. He shrugged and smiled.

"There's a certain manner about him," he said. "Something unspoiled. I couldn't say. Wouldn't want to say."

"What's the worst thing about him? His worst fault?"

Stanley looked down at the floor and drew his lips between his teeth to think. "Trusting people too much," he said at last. "Trusting people who aren't worthy of being trusted."

"Have you told him that's what you think?"

"No," Stanley said. He flapped his arm irritably. "What would be the point of that? He needs to make mistakes or he'll never get anywhere. And that's not the sort of father I am." He tossed his head impatiently and twitched out his cuffs again.

"What do you think Stanley thinks of you?"

"I think that underneath it all I disappoint him," Stanley said. "He's disappointed and he's angry because on one level he really wants to rebel against me. He wants to tear down everything I stand for, make me see myself for what I am, but he can't. I'm not that person in his life. He doesn't need to rebel against me, because I'm not the one who makes the rules. I'm just the outsider, the man who turns up every now and again. If he tried to really rebel against me I'd just laugh at him. I think he resents me for that. It's a disappointment to him."

"You can see all that?" asked one of the boys from the floor with a pointed skepticism, as if to imply that Stanley wasn't quite remembering the rules of the exercise. The Head of Acting was sitting back with his arms folded, watching Stanley intently with narrowed eyes.

"Yes," Stanley said simply. He spread his hands again. "I'm a psychologist. It's my job to see things."

August

"We've got information!" the boy Marcus was crying out when Stanley slipped into the rehearsal room and took his seat on the floor. "Polly had a friend of a friend who was the abused girl's best friend, and she knew basically everything. We interviewed her and wrote everything down!" He waved a little notebook in the air, flushed with his own success.

"What's some of the stuff?" somebody called out.

"Like, he was her music teacher," Marcus said, flipping open his notebook in excitement, "and she took private woodwind tutorials with him, for alto sax. And when they drove anywhere she used to lie on the floor in the backseat with a rug over her. And in his spare time he painted in oils, just as a hobby, only he never painted her because it would be evidence and he wasn't that stupid. But he wanted to, he said, God he wanted to, because when she came all the blue-map veins on her sternum and her throat would all come up, rise to the surface of her skin just for an instant, and he always said that if he could capture her at just that moment, it would be the best thing in the world he had ever done. He knew it instinctively. They had a joke that he could do a series of paintings, an exhibition. He said he had never seen anything like it, someone who changed so much in that split-second instant, as they came. It was his favorite thing about her."

Marcus flipped through his notebook, turning over the pages.

"Oh, there's so *much*," he said, bouncing on the balls of his feet. "We can use all of it. It's so good, and there's so much. We should buy this girl a present to say thank you. Polly knows her through orchestra."

"We'll make sure to get her complimentary tickets for opening night," Felix said, already making a note on the side of his jotter. "And a voucher for nibbles."

"Read out the rest," someone called out. "Read out everything."

August

Near the end of the first-year calendar was an underlined event described simply as "the Outing" and carefully timetabled so that the first-, second- and third-year actors were all required to participate together. The actors all assembled in the gymnasium, the second- and third-years smug and aloof in the security of having performed the exercise before.

The sixty-odd students were each assigned by the Head of Acting a part from a play. He had appointed the parts carefully, choosing students who bore a temperamental or physiological likeness to the characters he knew so well, and he smiled as he read each name off the long list he had penned into his notebook. "Henry, I'd like you to play Torvald," he said. "I'm looking forward to seeing your Torvald. I'm guessing it's going to be a very interesting mix"—as if Henry and Torvald were transparent overlays that could be placed upon each other to form an amalgam, a newer, brighter image that would be better and more vibrant than either the boy or the man on his own.

"Claire," he was saying now, and turning to one of the third-years perched on the edge of the crowd. "I've chosen Susan from *A Bed Among the Lentils* for you. You're playing out of your age range a bit, but I think you'll manage beautifully."

The rules of the exercise were relatively simple. The students were asked to leave the grounds of the Institute and disperse into the four city blocks that surrounded the Institute buildings. They had to remain in character for two hours. They were to be let out in small staggered batches, one batch leaving as another returned, over a period of three days. The tutors and the off-duty actors would be patrolling the city blocks, appearing to perform ordinary activities, like shopping and ordering coffee and jogging and meeting each other on the street to talk, but all the while observing the actors as they performed.

Dora. Septimus. Martha. Bo. The list went on. Stanley looked out the window and allowed his mind to wander, and soon found that he couldn't distinguish the names of the characters from the names of the students assigned to become them.

"Stanley," the Head of Acting called, jolting him out of his reverie. He looked up, but the Head of Acting wasn't addressing him. "Stanley from *A Streetcar Named Desire*," he was saying, and a student on the floor was nodding vigorously and scribbling down the name of the role in the margin of his exercise book. Stanley sighed and looked down at his hands.

"I know that some of these roles are easier than others," the Head of Acting said, "and with some of these characters it's hard to imagine them out of the context of the play. But remember that every performance is an interpretation. You can be as imaginative as you like. It's up to you what you want to wear, whether you want to try an accent, whether you want to change your appearance to better suit your role."

Stanley's gaze slid sideways to the Head of Movement, standing like a patient shadow behind the Head of Acting, his ankles together and his heels against the wall. He was smiling faintly and nodding his head, but the movement looked automatic, like a weighted pendulum keeping indulgent time behind a pane of glass. He saw the Head of Movement wink at one of the students on the floor, and turned his head quickly to follow his gaze and seek out the recipient of the wink. He was too late to tell. He looked back at the Head of Movement and saw him smile and look carefully down at the floor.

The Head of Acting had reached the first-year group, and all around him his classmates were being branded one by one. Harry Bagley. George. Moss. Irene.

Stanley was assigned the part of Joe Pitt. "Read the play first," the Head of Acting advised, and smiled a tiny smile before returning to his list. Somebody in the crowd giggled faintly and Stanley blushed, wondering what sort of person Joe Pitt was. He wrote the name on a fresh page of his organizer and then tucked the book into his bag.

August

"How long are you in town for?" Stanley asked after they had ordered. His father was busy scratching something into his electronic notebook and he didn't answer immediately. He stabbed at the screen, folded the notebook away, and shook out his cuffs.

"Sorry, champ," he said. "You said?"

"How long are you down for?"

"Just the weekend. I'm speaking at the conference tomorrow and then we fly out. I've got a joke for you. What's the difference between acne and a Catholic priest?"

"I don't know," said Stanley.

"Acne only comes on your face *after* puberty."

"Dad, that's revolting," Stanley said. He thought, A taboo is something that's forbidden because it's sacred.

His father held up his hands in surrender. "Too far?"

"Yes," Stanley said. Or because it's disgusting. He scowled despite himself and took a drink of water.

"Tell me about you, then," his father said. "Tell me about drama school. Oh! I forgot—I've got something for you. I cut it out of the newspaper this morning." He thumbed through his briefcase until he found a wad of newspaper, folded in eighths. He passed it across the table to Stanley and hummed merrily as he waited for Stanley to read it.

The headline read *Girl's Death "Terrible Waste."* The article was brief.

"You know the girl?" his father said when he'd finished. He was expectant, his eyes the gleeful half-moons of the laughing Comedy mask in the foyer of the Institute.

Stanley looked at the article again, and swallowed. "You're going to tell me that this was the million-dollar girl."

His father laughed. "Stanley," he said, "this was the million-dollar girl. Did you know her?"

"What if I did?" Stanley said. "What if I did, and this was how I found out, and you've just been horribly insensitive to both of us?"

Stanley's father reached across to twitch the page out of Stanley's hands. "It's just a bit of fun," he said, tucking the wad back into his briefcase. "I thought you'd laugh. Don't look at me like that."

He shook his finger playfully at Stanley, and reached for his tumbler. "Anyway, if you *did* know her," he said, "then I'd be congratulating you, because you'd have picked her from the start and you'd have taken out a policy."

"That girl is a real person somewhere," Stanley said.

"That girl is a corpse somewhere," his father corrected. He gave Stanley a stern critical look, as if gravely disappointed and seeing him truly for the first time. He said, "I really thought you'd laugh."

ELEVEN

Monday

The catchment area for Abbey Grange is wide and economically diverse. It is close enough to the city center to touch some of the wealthier areas, but covers several suburbs of middling value and a few streets at its nether edge that properly belong in the backwater suburbs, wide crawling streets with vast gutters and unkempt grass.

The poorer girls who work part-time in fast-food and clothing chain stores are able to effect something of a moral victory over the girls who receive an allowance from their parents and don't have to work for cash. When the less wealthy girls visit the white and shining houses of the rich they always come armed with a strong sense of entitlement, opening the fridge and changing the channel and taking long delicious showers in the morning, always with a guiltless and even pious sense of righting some dreadful inequality in the world. It is almost a noble thing to cajole and thieve half a bag of crisps from a girl whose pantry is lit by angled halogen bulbs anchored to a chrome bar: it is not a burglary but a form of just redistribution, a restoration of a kind of balance. So the poorer girls tell themselves, as they close their salty fists around their next mouthful and remark out loud that they are rostered on to work the late shift at the candy bar tonight.

The richer girls are made to feel ashamed of their parents' wealth by these subtle insidious means, and so they begin to overcompensate in justifying the incremented luxuries of their lives, defending each indulgence in terms of sole necessity. "We have to have fresh stone fruit because of Mum's diet plan," they say, or, "I have to have my own car because Dad's away on business so much," or, "We only had the spa put in because Dad's got a bad back." The repeated validations become their mantra, and soon the richer girls begin to believe the things they are compelled by shame to say. They come to believe that their needs are simply keener, more specialized, more urgent than the needs of the girls who queue outside the chippy and tuck the greasy package down their shirts for the walk home. They do not regard themselves as privileged and fortunate. They regard themselves as people whose needs are aptly and deservedly met, and if you were to call them wealthy they would raise their eyebrows and blink, and say, "Well, it's not like we're starving or anything, but we're definitely not *rich*."

This stubborn dance of entitlement, aggressive and defensive, does mark a real fear in the collective mind of the Abbey Grange girls who have moved through the years of high school in an unchanging, unitary pack. Always they fear that one of them might at any time burst out and eclipse the others, that the group might suddenly and irreparably be plunged into her shadow, that the tacit allegiance to fairness and middling equality held by them all might come to nothing after all. In a group their economic differences even out to an ordinary average, and their combined mediocrity becomes something a little like power, each of them with a specialized function that defines her territory within the whole. But if one of them should burst out and shine, the remaining girls would wither. They are mindful of the threat, clinging to each other's elbows and clustering bluishly in the corridor and reining in any girl who threatens independence—any girl who looks as if she might one day break free and have no need of the rest.

It is just such a group that Victoria rent apart and destroyed when she peeled off to pursue a love affair in such a selfish, secret way. In usual practice, boys are privately met and managed but always remain the collective property of the group: afterward, a girl might talk only to her best friend—or perhaps a close few, according to her own network of allegiances and feuds—but it is at least accepted that she will tell *somebody*, that the boy will remain an object beyond the myriad confidences of the group, a thing to discuss but never confide in, never to trust. Victoria's violation of these rules is crippling and total. To have conducted an entire relationship in secret, to have invented commitments and appointments and, above all, to have trusted in Mr. Saladin over this nuggeted faction of girls who depend so utterly upon togetherness: her betrayal weakens the kaleidoscope stronghold of the group, leeches everything of joy and meaning, punctures every illusion of unity and might. The girls begin to shrink away from each other. Even the St. Sylvester boys seem tame and foolish, like dress-up soldiers waving cardboard swords.

"It isn't fair," is what the girls are thinking, all the left-behind eclipsed girls who squat in the dark of Victoria's shadow and stew. "What she stole from us. It isn't fair."

Monday

Isolde wonders whether what she is feeling is merely a kind of worship, a fascinated admiration of an older girl such as she once bestowed upon Victoria and her scornful train of friends: forever desperate to please them, clinging to their ankles like a foreshortened afternoon shadow, and breathless with the impossible hope that they might one day count *her* among their closest. Is Julia really only a mirror image of the person who Isolde aspires to be—worldly, senior, brooding, debonair? Is this all her attraction is—a narcissistic self-congratulation, a girl captivated by the image of a girl? Does falling in love with Julia require Isolde to fall, to some degree, in love with herself?

All she has is one uncertain evening of stalls and snatches and trailings-off, a lone flare of something bright that sent her heart thudding and the blood rushing to the thin skin over the bones of her chest, and then days and weeks of lonely conjuring, a paralytic limbo of self-doubt which seems to shrink Julia to an impossibility, a freak, a daytime wander that recedes in the rear-vision mirror of her uncertain mind.

She thinks vaguely about how nice it would be to be persecuted. She thinks about the two of them parading in defiance in front of her parents, holding hands maybe. She thinks about watching her father pick at his red throat with his finger while he shakes his head and says, Issie, don't close off your options, honey. You never know, it might just be a phase. She thinks about her mother—her shrug, her careful smile. She thinks about her sister, who would fall quiet and look across at them and watch Julia so cautiously, Julia who is properly her equal, her classmate, the girl she once scorned in the netball trials, the girl about whom she whispered once, Doesn't she know what we all think of her? Surely she knows.

It would be nice, Isolde thinks, to know that you had become the image you created for yourself. It would be nice to have a reason to act broody and maligned.

Every one of Isolde's choices is really only a rephrased and masquerading version of the question, What am I?

It will be this way for years to come.

Tuesday

Sometimes Julia is filled with a kind of rage at the fact of her body, the fertile swell of her hips, her cold freckled breasts, the twice-folded inner pocket of her womb. She doesn't wish herself different, doesn't crave a phallus or a mustache or a pair of big veined hands with calluses and blunted nails—she simply feels frustrated that her anatomical apparatus presents such a misplaced and useless advantage. If the other girl's flushed and halting inclinations tend elsewhere, if Isolde does not seek a mirrored lover but a converse lover, a flipside complement of a lover, then Julia is lost.

Julia thinks, Seducing Isolde isn't just a matter of behaving as attractively and as temptingly as possible, and trusting that Isolde will bite. If, instead, she were faced with the prospect of seducing a boy, then such a simple formula would probably work. The mere fact of Julia's anatomy would be enough. She would herself be the temptation—her body, the whole of her. But seducing Isolde requires forcing the younger girl to come to regard herself in a new way: only after Isolde has come to cherish her own self, the concave yin of her feminine skin, will Julia have a hope. Isolde must come to cherish herself, first and foremost. The seduction must take the form of a persuasion, a gradual winning-over of her mind.

Julia thinks of all the usual gifts of courtship, like flowers in homeroom or stones thrown at her window at midnight or a patient watcher at the school gates, waiting with a bicycle to walk her slowly home. All of them seem grotesque. She imagines sending Isolde flowers in homeroom, and all she can think of is the girl's horrified face as she peers over the lip of the red cluster of tissue, the card already plucked off in embarrassment and crumpled to a nub. She imagines a bouquet too big and too fragile to be shoved into the bottom of Isolde's bag, and the beautiful girls all laughing and shouting, What's his name?

Julia is overcome by a fit of melancholy now, and drives her pen savagely through the margin of her homework sheet, causing the paper to rip. She thinks, What's the likelihood? That the one girl who makes my heart race is the one girl who wants me in return? That the accident of my attraction coincides with the accident of hers? She thinks: can I trust in something chemical, some scent or pheromone that will ride on the current of my walking and come to kiss her as I pass her by?

Julia distrusts this chemical, this invisible riptide that sucks away at all her shores. She thinks: I cannot rely on the chemical. I cannot rely on the accident of her attraction. I must seduce her, actively pursue her and persuade her. I must appeal to the questionable autonomy of a teenage girl whose mind is still not rightfully her own.

Tuesday

"Hey Isolde, want to play?" someone calls out, and Isolde looks up. She is walking back from the tuck shop with a brown paper bag pinched in each hand, the icing slowly leaking through the paper and darkening the pale in greasy spots of gray.

"No, thanks," Isolde says, and holds up the paper bags as an excuse.

The questioning girl smiles and returns to the game. Isolde watches as she walks past: four or five of them are attempting to play hacky-sack in their thick-soled school shoes and drooping gray socks, hiking up their school skirts with both hands to show the winter white of their dimpled knees. She rounds the corner of the school library and continues on.

Isolde weaves her way around the groups of girls sitting in

their impenetrable circles around the quad, and then to her surprise she sees Julia sitting in a rare patch of sun on the grass on the far side of the paving. She is wearing her headphones and squinting in a cross kind of way into a paperback novel. Shyly Isolde makes her way toward her. Her heart begins to hammer.

Julia looks up, sees her approaching and tugs her headphones out of her ears.

"Hey man," she says, and Isolde waves her paper bags and says, "Hey."

"What have you got?" Julia says.

"Just a roll and a doughnut."

"You can sit down if you want."

Isolde crosses her legs at the ankle and descends into a sitting position in the fluent scissor-action of girls long practiced at sitting cross-legged, her free hand tugging at the doubled fold beneath the silver kilt-pin so it covers the bare skin of her knee. Julia shifts her ankles to make room. The horizontal gash along the length of Isolde's filled roll is stained pink from the beetroot. Isolde wipes her finger along the seam to collect the mayonnaise and licks her finger carefully.

"You know what I think is shit?" Julia says suddenly, arching her back and reaching over to yank a tuft of grass from the ground to shred. "That they make you come to those counseling sessions about self-defense or teacher abuse or whatever."

"But I've learned so much," Isolde says, blinking. "Like my body is a temple. And we were all abused as children probably; we only need to work hard to remember it."

Julia laughs and shreds her grass even smaller.

"But you were brilliant," Isolde says. "Standing up to him like that. Like you did."

"He's scared of me now."

"So is everyone, after what you said," Isolde says, meaning it as a joke, but Julia frowns and shakes her head.

"I was paraphrasing, anyway," she says. "It's not like I made it up. Dumb shits. Not you."

"Oh, no," Isolde says quickly. Her nervousness has given way to a kind of giddiness, a reckless charged feeling that is keeping her heartbeat in her throat and her vision sharpened in awareness of Julia's total proximity, the fall of her hair around her face and the every movement of her hands as they pick away at the yellow balding patch of lawn. Julia's hands are thin and reddish, with nibbled patches of dark nail polish in the center of each flat-nibbed nail. She has a few loops of dirty string knotted around her bony wrist, and on the back of her hand a few notes to herself in blue ink, several days old now so the ink has furred out into the web of tiny creases on her skin. Even looking at Julia's hands seems unbearably sensual to Isolde, and she quickly draws her gaze away, out across the quad where a group of girls are clapping a rhythm as they rehearse a set for the school dance challenge.

"We're the ones with the power," Julia is saying. "That's the real lesson from this whole Mr. Saladin thing. The lesson they don't want us to learn."

"Oh," Isolde says, looking again at Julia's hands.

"It's because of where we are in the power chain. We can be damaged, but we can't damage others. Well, I suppose we can damage each other, but we can't damage our teachers or our parents or whatever. *They* can only damage *us*. And that means we get to call the shots."

"What does calling the shots mean?" Isolde says.

Julia tosses her head in a brooding way. "Everyone worships the victim," she says. "That's all I've learned from this place, victim-worship. In fourth form I rowed for the coxed quad in the Nationals, right? We turned up and we were clearly the worst team in the tournament. We just didn't have good enough gear, the quad was really old and heavy, we hadn't been training for long enough. But because we were the underdogs we really believed we were going to win. Because that's what happens. In the last ten seconds, the underdogs pull through and win by a canvas, and good triumphs over evil and money doesn't matter in the end. I remember sitting there in the boat before the race with my oars ready and waiting for the buzzer and thinking, We're really going to show them when we win."

"But you didn't."

"Course not," Julia says. "Some rich school with a flash fiber-glass boat won by about a mile. We were the last team over the finish by at least forty-five seconds. But I'm just pointing out the victim thing. If you're the victim, you really do believe you're going to come out on top. It's what we learn here. Worship the victim. The loser will win."

Isolde looks puzzled. She's a little in awe of the way Julia spits out her opinions, little rehearsed pieces that she delivers with her eyes flashing and her head cocked. Her opinion is more like a challenge than a point of view.

"You know," Julia says. "Back in the day, schools would have special desks for the brainiest kid in the class. But the brainiest kid isn't set apart anymore. Instead we have the remedial block, and the special needs block, and the careers and counseling building. They're the ones who are set apart from the rest."

Isolde says, "You think people worship my sister."

"Yeah, I do," Julia says.

Isolde looks sideways at the older girl, and finds that she has nothing to say. She tugs a pale shard of ham out of her roll with her fingers, and nibbles it carefully.

"So what *was* it like," Julia says, "with Victoria?" She has unwrapped a cereal bar but is eating it slowly, pinching off the sweaty grains between her thumb and forefinger, and rolling them to a greasy ball, one by one. The girls often eat in this mincing way when they are in nervous company.

"What do you mean?" Isolde asks.

"I just meant—she's your sister. Did she talk to you about it afterward and stuff? Did you guess, while it was happening? Is she going to be okay?"

Julia's heart is beating fast. Her instinct is to act tougher than she feels, to make no concessions, to woo Isolde by a kind of reckless baldness, a brash and unapologetic ownership of hard opinion that will make the younger girl look up at her in awe. At the same time Julia is burying a thudding feeling of lonely vulnerability, a simple childlike yearning to be touched, to be gathered up in the other girl's arms and kissed and crooned at. Even as she speaks aggressively, as she delivers her opinions and shrugs and scowls as if she doesn't care, a part of her is trying to show the other girl that she could be tender, underneath; that she could be sweet and delicate and thirsty, that the animal precepts of her feminine nature are not quite lost. It's a strange thing to keep the two in balance: the appearance of hard with the appearance of soft. Julia feels ravaged by the effort, as if she might easily burst into tears at this very moment, sitting here on the grass.

Isolde pinches a half-moon of cucumber with her fingers and licks its dewy edge as she thinks about the question. She is about to reply when a shadow falls across the two of them, and they look up.

It's the beautiful girls, and they are all smiling, thin little curved smiles that press their lips tight together into a cruel reversal of their usual slack-mouthed pout.

"Got yourself a girlfriend at last, Julia?" the most beautiful girl says. "Going to take her home to show your mum?"

Julia looks up at her and says nothing. Isolde is looking from face to face and trying to decide whether she should smile, even a bit.

"She going to brush away some cobwebs?" the beautiful girl says again. "Clean you out a bit? Is that the idea?"

They snicker. Isolde's almost-smile fades a little.

"Did you dial her in? Slip her some cash for the privilege?"

"Oh, for fuck's sake, are you like twelve?" Julia snaps. She reaches for her headphones and her paperback, and begins packing her bag to leave.

"No," says the beautiful girl's sidekick, stepping forward in a moment of rare glory, "but *she* is, isn't she?"

She points at Isolde, and Isolde feels herself turn scarlet. She wonders whether she should point out she's actually fifteen, or whether that would simply give them ammunition for another joke. All the beautiful girls laugh. Julia looks thoroughly irritated at her own mistake, and continues shoving the remains of her lunch into her bag.

"I guess you couldn't find anyone your own age who was keen," says the sidekick.

Julia says, "Just fuck off, Tiffany. Whatever you're trying to do, you're not doing it. Fuck off."

"So if she's the tough one," the beautiful girl says, turning now to Isolde, "what does that make you? The feminine one? Isn't that the way it works—there always has to be a man and a woman anyway? Like a big old game of pretend?"

Isolde, nervous and caught between public denial and public defense of something she doesn't yet understand, simply tries to smile, a nervous tight-lipped smile that the beautiful girls evidently take as a confirmation of the taunt. The leader casts around for something further to say, but ends up just saying "Faggots!" as a way of punctuating the scene, and flounces off with her servants in her wake. The group of them spear across the quad like a tiny blue comet, its head bright and beautiful and its ragged tail getting duller and more ordinary as it trails away.

"Cunts," says Julia under her breath, and she tugs savagely at the zipper of her schoolbag.

"Sorry," says Isolde.

"Sorry," says Julia.

The first bell rings but Julia and Isolde make no move to rise. They sit on the grassy verge side by side and shred grass.

"I heard she had a nose job anyway," Isolde says. "The main girl. Last year."

"Can I have a bit of your doughnut?" Julia says, because underneath it all, the ordinary rules of thieving still apply.

Tuesday

The role of Mrs. Bly requires a fat suit, and special latex pouches that slip into either cheek to fatten the jaw. The fat suit is impeccable. It is made mostly of silicone, sculpted especially for the woman's frame, and it is heavy enough to make her stagger when she walks. She is wearing a tubular denim skirt that buttons up the front, and a gold link necklace with a slender golden charm, and she has rouged her fattened cheeks and sprayed her hair with scented mist. She waddles gracefully into the room and descends upon one of the armchairs, sighing and reaching down to rub her artificially fattened calf. You can't even tell it's a fat suit. The saxophone teacher almost forgets to speak, she's so busy admiring the effect.

"You were recommended to me by one of the Tupperware mothers," Mrs. Bly says. "She said her daughter swapped over to you after that whole scandal at the school, and she's been very pleased."

"I'm glad," the saxophone teacher says. "Yes, I've had a considerable influx of students this year from Abbey Grange."

"Wasn't the whole business just terrible," Mrs. Bly says, and she puckers her lips and squints her eyes and gives a merry chuckle.

"Catalytic," the saxophone teacher says in pretended agreement, guessing that Mrs. Bly won't pause for long enough to think about the word. She doesn't.

"It was just terrible," she says again. "The girl is ruined. She's damaged goods now. And all the girls are keeping their distance of course."

"As they should be," the saxophone teacher says.

"Because it spreads like a virus, that's what I said to my girls," Mrs. Bly says, drawing the vast spread of denim over her knee and puckering her lips to form a little thatched smile that draws all the wrinkles around her lips into a single central nub. "That kind of stain doesn't come out in the wash."

The saxophone teacher suddenly feels weary. She sits down. "Mrs. Bly," she says, "remember that these years of your daughter's life are only the rehearsal for everything that comes after. Remember that it's in her best interests for everything to go wrong. It's in her best interests to slip up *now*, while she's still safe in the Green Room with the shrouded furniture and the rows of faceless polystyrene heads and the cracked and dusty mirrors and the old papers scudding across the floor. Don't wait until she's out in the savage white light of the floods, where everyone can see. Let her practice everything in a safe environment, with a helmet and kneepads and packed lunches, and you at the end of the hall with the door cracked open a dark half-inch in case anyone cries out in the long hours of the night."

The spiderweb lasso of creases around fat Mrs. Bly's mouth loosens slightly.

"The good news," the saxophone teacher says briskly, turning now to her diary, "is that I have an opening on Wednesday afternoon, if that suits your daughter's schedule. One of my students was hit by a car."

"Oh, isn't it dangerous," Mrs. Bly says. "I don't let Rebecca cycle. I flat out refuse to let her cycle anywhere at all. Wednesday afternoon is perfect."

"At four."

"At four." Mrs. Bly chuckles again. "She'll be so pleased," she says. "She's practiced so hard to get her clarinet up to scratch, and she's wanted this so badly. It's as if for the first time in her life something has just begun to blossom."

Friday

"I suppose you didn't know Bridget," the saxophone teacher says to Isolde one afternoon.

"The girl who died? She was the year above, in sixth form."

"She was one of my students."

"Oh," Isolde says. "No, I didn't know her." She stalls a moment, looking clumsy and rocking back and forth on her heels. "Are you okay?" she asks finally, wincing to show a kind of concern.

"Wasn't it a great shock," the saxophone teacher says.

"Yeah," Isolde says.

"Everyone must be terribly upset. At your school and so forth."

"Oh," Isolde says. "Yeah, they had an assembly."

"Just an assembly?"

"And they flew the flag at half-mast."

"I suppose everyone is still terribly upset," the saxophone teacher says, "skipping class, weeping, remembering everything that was irreplaceable about Bridget."

"I suppose so. She was in the year above. I don't know anyone that knew her." Isolde is wearing the half-stricken expression of someone who is required, but ill equipped, to offer condolence or advice about death. She shuffles uncomfortably and looks at the floor.

"Bridget," the saxophone teacher says abruptly, changing tack, "was my least favorite student. Bridget had a way of bucking and rearing her pelvis when she played that I privately found a little distasteful. Bridget would lean back with her knees bent and her eyes closed, tensing up and preparing to catapult her weight forward on to the balls of her feet, the saxophone rearing up like a golden spume about to break and fall. The muscles in her jaw were tight. I bent over Bridget's notebook to avoid looking at her, scribbling curt bullet-points in the margin for her to remember in her practice. Tone, I wrote, and then underneath, Brightness."

Shyly, almost respectfully, Isolde slips out of herself and becomes Bridget—not the real Bridget, just a placeholder, a site for the saxophone teacher to aim at, a figure to address. She stands hangdog in the middle of the room with her sax tucked against her hip and her hair across her face. She doesn't speak.

"This was the last time I saw Bridget," the saxophone teacher says. "She came to the end of 'The Old Castle' and removed the sax from her mouth, shoving her lower jaw forward and back several times as if repositioning a set of dentures. She'd practiced. She always practiced. That was one of the things I didn't like about Bridget so much. I asked her, What did you learn in counseling today? And Bridget said, This week we're talking about guilt. About how guilt can be illuminating. We're doing role-plays based on ideas about guilt.

"Guilt, I said. And Bridget said, rushing on with this rare flash of pleasure that she was owning the spotlight, that the voice she was using was for once her own, and worth hearing, she said, Guilt is really important. It's the first step on the road to something better."

Isolde's toes are ever so slightly pigeoned, her knees inward turning and her hips awkwardly thrust. She rubs the bell of her sax with her finger and looks at the saxophone teacher's shoes.

"So I said," the sax teacher says, "Bridget, I think you are being deceived. Guilt is primarily a distraction. Guilt is a feeling that distracts us from deeper, truer feelings. Let me give you an example. You might feel guilty if you become attracted to someone who is forbidden to you. You feel attraction, and then you remember you are not allowed to be attracted to this person, and then you feel guilt. Which do you think is the more primary of these feelings, attraction or guilt?

"I guess attraction, said Bridget. Because it came first.

"And I said, Good. Guilt is secondary. Guilt is a surface feeling."

Isolde nods a tiny nod, to show she's listening. The saxophone teacher is glazed over now, the memory filling her vision like a glossy cataract over each staring eye.

"I said that," she says, "because Bridget was my least favorite student. I said that because I didn't care for Bridget much at all."

The memory dissolves and her vision sharpens once again.

"What have *you* learned in counseling?" she says, rounding on Isolde with a savage, narrowed look, and the girl blinks and straightens and returns invisibly to herself.

Isolde is not sure what answer she should give. As she hesitates and paws uncomfortably at the sax around her neck she thinks about the girl, the one assembly and one half-masted flag, the never-scheduled counseling sessions about her death, and the paper cutout convenience grief that some of the older girls wielded for a week or so, just to earn a half-hour's freedom and a pass to the nurse.

The saxophone teacher is still looking hard at Isolde, waiting for an answer.

Isolde says, quietly and full of shame, "In counseling we all mourn everything that was irreplaceable about my sister. We grieve for everything about Victoria that is now lost."

Monday

Julia comes straight to her lesson from afternoon detention. She is almost late, and when the saxophone teacher opens the door Julia is still red faced and sweating a little, her cycle helmet trailing from her wrist.

"My teacher is an arsehole," she says in summary, once they are inside. "Mrs. Paul is an arsehole. They have to write a reason on the detention slip, and I said, Why don't you write, 'Saying out loud what everyone was thinking anyway.' So she made it double. I fucking hate high school. I hate everything about it."

"Why did you get detention in the first place?" the saxophone teacher says admiringly, but Julia just shakes her head and scowls. She takes a moment to unwrap and to fish for her music, and the saxophone teacher stirs her tea and tilts her head as she waits.

"When you leave, and all of this is over," the sax teacher says, "you will always have one schoolteacher you will remember for the rest of your life, one teacher who *changed* your life."

"I won't," Julia says. "I've never had a teacher like that."

"You will have," the saxophone teacher says. "Once you've got a few years' distance and you can look back cleanly. There will be some Miss—Miss Hammond, Miss Gillespie—there will be some teacher you remember above all the others, one teacher who rises a head above them all."

Julia is still looking skeptical. The saxophone teacher waves her arm and continues.

"But how many teachers are lucky enough to have had one *student* who changed their lives?" she asks. "One student who really *changed* them. Let me tell you something: it doesn't happen. The inspiration goes one way. It only ever goes one way. We expect our teachers to teach for the love of it, to inspire and awaken and ignite without any expectation of being inspired and awakened in return; we expect that their greatest and only hoped-for joy would be, perhaps, a student returning after ten or twenty years, dropping by one morning to tell them just how much of an influence they were, and then disappearing back to the private success of their own lives. That's all. We expect our teachers every year to start anew, to sever a year's worth of progress and forged connection, to unravel everything they've built and move *back* to begin work on another child. Every year our teachers sow and tend another thankless crop that will never, ever come to harvest."

"I'm not a child," Julia says.

"Young adult," the saxophone teacher says. "Whatever you like."

"I've never been inspired or ignited," Julia says.

"But you see my point," the sax teacher says.

"No I don't," Julia says sourly. "You get paid. It's just like any other job."

The sax teacher leans forward and crosses her legs at the knee.

"Your mother," she says, "wants a progress report. She wants me to describe how I have inspired you, how I have awoken you, how I have coaxed you on to a glorious path toward excellence and industry and worth. Secretly she also wants me to tell her just how much you have inspired *me*—not directly, but in a roundabout, subtle way, as if I'm a little abashed, made a little vulnerable, as if we're talking about something dreadfully taboo. She wants me to lie, a little."

"So lie."

"She wants," the saxophone teacher continues, "what all the mothers want. She wants me to tell her that you and I have a special rapport, that you tell me things you wouldn't tell anybody else. She wants me to tell her that I see something in *you*, Julia, that I haven't seen in years. She wants me to say that our relationship functions for both of us as a shared or double birth—not the mere instruction of a pupil, but the utter opening of one person to another."

"So give her what she wants," Julia says. She is stubborn and difficult today, still wearing the injustice of her double detention like a surly veil around her face. She stands ready with her saxophone fitted around her neck.

"All right, let's get started," the saxophone teacher says, not without irritation. "Play me something loud."

Thursday

"I think two of my students are having a love affair," is what the saxophone teacher would say to Patsy if Patsy were here. It would be brunch, as it always is with Patsy, and it would be a Thursday, and the sun would be shining slantwise through the tall windows and filling the apartment with lazy dusty light.

"With each other, you mean?" Patsy would say, leaning forward and putting both elbows on the table and her chin upon her hands.

"Yes," the saxophone teacher says. "I introduced them at the concert. They're schoolmates—well, one girl is two years older, but they attend the same school."

"Oh, yes," says Patsy, "there always has to be an age difference at the beginning. With same-sex relationships. It's an initiation rite. You need an inequality of experience or you never get anywhere."

"Really?" says the saxophone teacher.

"Definitely," says Patsy. "If you don't have gender roles to fall back on, you need the power to be organized somehow. You need a structure. Teacher and pupil. Predator and prey. Something like that." She throws her head back and laughs suddenly, a clear, delighted laugh that peals out in the tiny flat like a bell.

"I knew you would laugh," the saxophone teacher says. She's petulant today, and cross with how Patsy has been tossing her hair over her shoulder and sucking the smear of butter off her index finger and behaving for the most part like a person who thoroughly enjoys being desired.

"Have they said anything to you?" Patsy says.

"Not directly, but—well, you know."

"Showing all the symptoms."

"Yes, exactly."

Patsy ponders this for a moment in a contented sort of way

and then asks, "Is it the girl who had the sister in the news-paper?"

"Yes—the younger girl, Isolde. Her older sister was abused."

"That makes it even more likely, then," Patsy says.

"Does it?"

"Definitely. For all sorts of reasons."

The two of them sit for a moment in silence. The newspaper is spread over the breakfast things, peaking over the jam jar and the syrup bottle, creased and grease-spotted with marmalade and oil. There is a single strawberry left in the bottom of the thin plastic punnet, flat edged like the snout of a cold chisel and frosted white with unripeness.

"I just want to get to the truth behind it. That's all. The kernel of truth behind everything," the saxophone teacher says suddenly, into nothing.

Friday

"Dad's trying to connect," Isolde says, with the special weariness that she reserves for parental efforts to connect. "It's part of his rebuilding thing. He wants to know more about us. Both of us."

"Is that good?" the saxophone teacher says.

"Last night he comes in while I'm watching TV and goes, Hey, Isolde. Do you have a boyfriend?" Isolde snickers unkindly. "I only laughed because he said Hey. So jolly and casual, like he'd practiced it in the mirror or something. I said, Yes, and he clapped his hands and said, Well great, let's have the man around for dinner."

"You said Yes?" the saxophone teacher says. She has stiffened and is looking at Isolde with her head cocked and one hand hanging limp from the wrist, like a caricature of a startled pet.

"Yeah," Isolde says suspiciously, tucking her hair behind her ear. "It's only been a few weeks, but yeah."

The saxophone teacher makes a little twitching motion with her hand, gesturing Isolde onward. Isolde rolls her tongue out over her bottom lip and regards the saxophone teacher a moment longer before continuing.

"Everything's about eating together now," she says. "Eating together as a family solves everything. We do it like a ritual—nobody's allowed to touch their food until everyone's sat down, and then we all thank Mum and pass the sauce and whatever. Dad says eating together is the answer. If we had eaten together from the beginning, then Victoria would never have bumped accidentally-on-purpose into Mr. Saladin in the hall and let her breasts rub against his chest for the briefest half-second before stepping back and saying, Oh sorry, I'm such a klutz. If we'd eaten together from the beginning then Mr. Saladin would never have bitten his lip and ducked his head whenever Victoria looked at him—that shy-schoolboy flirt effect that he'd been using since the eighties but it still worked a charm. If we'd eaten together, Victoria would never have sucked on his fingertips and pushed her tongue down into the V between his first two fingers and made him gasp. None of it would have happened."

"I didn't know you had a boyfriend," the sax teacher says.

"And none of us ever have anything to talk about at the table," Isolde says. "Not even Dad. He just ends up spieling about his work and everyone switches off and tries to eat as fast as possible."

"How did you meet him?" the sax teacher says.

"By accident," Isolde says. "Just around."

"He should come to the recital next month," the saxophone teacher says, still peering at Isolde with a new hard look on her face. "Come and watch you play."

"Yeah," Isolde says, bending the word like a sucked harmonica note so she manages to sound indifferent and aloof.

"Is he in your year at school?" the sax teacher says.

"Oh no," Isolde says smugly, "he's left school. He's an actor. At the Drama Institute," and she waves an airy hand out the curtained window to the buildings on the far side of the courtyard.

The lights change suddenly and the saxophone teacher can see it, playing out like someone else's home video in front of her, furry and striped with grainy black.

"He's an actor," Isolde's father is saying.

"That's what I said," Isolde says.

"He's at the Drama Institute."

"That's what I said."

"How old is he?"

"Only first-year, Dad," Isolde says, trying to look charming.

"I certainly hope he doesn't expect you to have sex with him."

"Dad."

"Because you're only fifteen," Isolde's father says, speaking loudly and clearly as if Isolde is partly deaf. "If you were to sleep with him, that would be a crime."

"Dad!"

"I'm going to ask you now," Isolde's father says, his eyes wide, "I'm going to ask you now, and I want you to give me a straight answer. Have you slept with him?"

"Dad, stop it, it's gross." Isolde is inspired by a rare shaft of genius, and says, "It's like you want to even everything out, play it fair, do by me as you've done by Victoria. Crime for crime. Stop it."

"Why are you sidestepping my question?"

"Why are you talking to me like that? Can't I talk to Mum?"

"You've slept with him."

"Great. You've decided. Now you'll never believe me whatever I say anyway."

"You're only fifteen."

"Can I talk to Mum?"

"Isolde," says Isolde's father sadly, "I never had sisters. Throw me a bone."

The lights return to normal, restoring a yellowish afternoon light to the studio, and the saxophone teacher blinks as if awakening.

"The Institute," she says. "That's supposed to be very hard to get into, isn't it? He must be rather good."

TWELVE

September

Was he supposed to undress her first, or wait to be undressed? He didn't like the idea of undressing her first—it seemed greedy, and the thought of remaining clothed while stripping her naked unnerved him—he imagined someone walking in, and what they would think. Would it happen piece by piece, like a polite duel—her shirt then his, her bra then his singlet, all the way down? Or were they supposed to undress themselves separately, and then come together after they had both been transformed? Stanley's heart was thumping as he led her to the bed and they sat down on its edge, kicking off their shoes in tandem and shuffling sideways to embrace each other and lie down.

He had imagined this moment many times previously, but Stanley realized now that he had imagined the scene mostly in closeup, arching and rearing and heavy breathing and skin. What was supposed to happen now? He tried to negotiate swinging himself on top of the girl without kneeing her in the groin. He was wooden, like someone obeying a director's instruction or responding to a cue. He floundered, shifting his weight to one side and back again, and he had a sudden, unflattering vision of himself from above, kneeling with one arm thrashing behind his back to find the slipping duvet and pull it back over his shoulders against the draught. He felt a surge of anger at his own ineptitude, and almost viciously he slipped a hand inside her shirt, just to prove he was up to the task. He felt her ribs rise up sharply at his touch.

Stanley was wishing that he was much older than he was. He wished that he was a man, and not a boy, a man who was easy with himself and could strip a girl and laugh and know that what he was doing was right. He wished that he was a man who could place his finger on this girl's lips and say, Now I am going to make you come. He wished that he was a man who could use the word "cunt," who could speak it aloud and easily, in a way that would make a girl admire and worship him. He wished that he was a man at home with his body, a man who could say, You are beautiful, and know that the words would have meaning because he spoke as a man and not a boy.

Stanley slithered his hand down her belly, down past the little scooped slit of the girl's navel, hatted by a fold of skin that shrank to a tight little nib as she raised her arms up above her head. She reached to pull his head down to hers and craned up to kiss his mouth. His hand was scrabbling at the button of her fly. He was ashamed at himself for moving so quickly but impelled all the same by a helpless wish for self-annihilation, a desire for the scene to somehow go on without him so he could withdraw. The denim was stretched tight and flat over the bones of her pelvis, and he had to bend the buttonhole cruelly sideways to wrench the button through. It gave. He drew down the zipper and with his fingers felt the thin cotton of her briefs, buoyed up by the tufted whorl of her pubic hair. He felt surprise. Had he imagined her hairless, like a doll?

The girl was breathing faster. He slipped his hand inside

her briefs and cupped the wiry mound of her pubis with the heel of his hand, arching his wrist to loosen the waistband of her jeans. Carefully he moved to part the seam of her, hot against the cool of his fingers. He wanted to speak. He wanted to whisper something that would break the awful fumbling quick-breathed silence that was filling the room, the mousy rustle of his hand.

Stanley found himself watching the scene from the position of a camera, and he began caring too deeply about what he might look like from above, or from the side—he tried to be sleeker, to thrash less, to push the hair gently off the girl's face and let his fingers trail around her jawbone and touch the soft furry pouch of her earlobe, like he had seen done in the cinema so many times. It didn't seem to be working.

"My arm's dead, sorry," the girl whispered apologetically, and wiggled it free.

"*Shit*," Stanley said.

"What's wrong?" the girl said in surprise, drawing the duvet up around her and tucking it carefully under her arms as she withdrew.

"I don't—"

"You don't know what to do?"

"*No*," Stanley said, a little too savagely. "No, I know what to do."

"It doesn't matter," the girl said, pushing his hair off his face with the rough heel of her hand. The action was coarse and tender at the same time, and Stanley was humbled, feeling her easily achieve the truth of the action when he had found it so difficult. "Just give me a cuddle. Come here."

He crept across the bed and she opened up the duvet to let him in. They lay there for a while, Stanley's heart thumping, the girl's hands moving up and down the curve of his shoulder blade and into the thin hair at the nape of his neck.

"I didn't think it would be like this," Stanley said, without thinking.

The girl raised herself up on an elbow and said, "What?"

Stanley realized he had sounded rude, and said hastily, "I mean me. I didn't think I would be like this."

That sounded even worse, and he seethed for a moment in frustration and self-contempt. What he had meant to say was that all the films and television programs he had ever seen that might have schooled him for this moment had placed him in the position of the outsider, the snug and confident voyeur who is able to *imagine* himself in place of the hero but is never physically required to act. Now he felt utterly unscripted, marooned, desperate for the girl to act first so that he would only have to follow and the burden of decision would not fall to him.

"It's your first time," the girl said, and a note in her voice changed, becoming softer, even maternal. She gathered him up closer to her and he burrowed in. "Silly old duffer," she said, and rubbed the top of his head with her knuckles. "You'll be all right."

They lay there for a while, listening as the ice-cream truck pulled into the street and sounded its theme tune for the children to hear. The truck whined away down the road, and it was quiet again.

"That was it," Stanley said, looking up for the first time, into the lights.

"That was what, Stanley?" the girl said, rolling over and touching him lightly on the lower curve of his back with her fingertips. "That was what?"

"That was the most intimate scene of my life," Stanley said. "Right then. That was it."

August

"Cue Mr. Saladin!" one of the students shouted. "King of Spades! Where the hell are you, Connor?"

There was a commotion in the wings, unseen, and then the

King of Spades appeared, red faced and trotting, ejected so swiftly from the parted cloth it was as if he had been physically launched.

"Sorry," he called out wildly in the direction of the pit. He cast about to find his mark on the floor, two pieces of tape crossed in a pale X like a cartoon Band-Aid.

"Get your bloody game on," someone shouted.

They watched with contempt and satisfaction as the King of Spades found his mark, drew himself up and took a breath. The stiff waxy breastplate of his costume had come untied on one shoulder and so hung at an odd angle across his chest. He had forgotten his gloves and his sword, but it was too late now.

The onstage students sighed and retraced their steps to give the boy his cue again. They said, "But look at it from another point of view. She lost her virginity, and in good time, before it began to cling unfashionably like a visible night-rag. She snared an older man. She achieved celebrity. And now she has a secret which everyone craves to know: a sexual secret, the best kind of secret, a vortex of a secret that tugs and tugs away at her edges so she's never quite *there*. Oh, don't pity Victoria. Pity poor lonely Mr. Saladin, who has tasted the bright ripe fruit of youth and purity, and now nothing else will do."

There was a kettle-drum clash from the orchestra pit, on the beat. Its effect on the King of Spades was dramatic. He crumpled, as if he had been clubbed between the shoulder blades, and all in an instant he became crippled and fragile and old. As he began to speak and the lesser characters reformed like children around his knees, one of the boys in the stalls leaned over to whisper, "He's still playing it for laughs. It won't work if he plays it for laughs."

The King of Spades said, "There was something so very endearing about it, right back in the beginning. The way she played it, out of a textbook, big moon eyes and an open collar, and her skirt hitched up to show her knee. It was so touchingly amateur. It was like a child's painting, imperfect and discordant and poorly executed and crying out to be celebrated, to be pinned to the wall or the fridge, to be complimented and fawned over and adored."

He trailed his foot and looked down at the floor and smiled secretly to himself, as if he was remembering something infinitely private. The band in the orchestra pit had struck up a jazzy pulse, drums and double-bass and the throaty murmur of a tenor saxophone.

He said, "In ten years' time she will be able to look at a man in cold blood and think, We are compatible. She will think, given your generosity of spirit, given your ability to provide me with the emotional shelter I need, given your particular wry and self-deprecating sense of humor, your interest in silent film, given the things you like to cook, and your tendency toward pedantry, and the things you do to pass the time—given all of this, I can conclude that we're compatible. Over the course of her life she will gradually compile this dreary list of requisites. Year by year she will reduce the yawning gulf of her desire to the smallness of a job vacancy: a janitor, or a sentry, or a drone. The ad will say, Wanted. That's all."

The King of Spades shrugged.

"But with me she didn't have a formula," he said. "She didn't know her appetites, didn't recognize the jumping pulse that leaped and leaped in the scarlet recess of her throat. Every time we touched she was finding out something new—not about me, but about herself, her tides and tolls, her responses, the upturned vase of emptiness she carried around inside her always, like something unfinished or unmade."

Behind him there were shadow-figures arched and clawing behind mullioned screens. They were silhouettes, crisply lit and dark against the white cloth, and they were all the shapeliest of the first-year students, chosen for their linear form, their profile. They were hand-picked by the others, who squinted until they saw only the positive outline and could judge the massy contour on its own.

The jazz band eased into the main theme now, the recurring motif of the production, and the seething crowd on stage reformed into another shape, another scene. The lights changed and the music changed, and the King of Spades was swallowed by the crowd.

"You missed out a bit," one of the stage managers said, when the King of Spades at last heard his cue to exit and bowed out, stage right. He was holding a sheaf of papers fixed together with a bulldog clip, and he shook the papers in the King of Spades' shadowed face. He said, "You missed out that whole section where he says, How can I protect these girls and excite them at the same time?"

September

"Has anything ever gone wrong?" Stanley said. "In the devised production? Like, the pistol was loaded and nobody even knew it was real. Or the flying harness was unclipped, or somebody fell from the fly-floors and slammed into the action in the middle of the stage. Some tragic story that happened almost too long ago to remember."

"You're nervous," Oliver said, as he slid into the seat opposite. He pulled an apple out of his backpack and began tossing it back and forth between his hands.

"There's just something scary about being let loose," Stanley said. "Without the tutors watching or anything, just us on our own for months and months. And I just wondered if anything's ever gone terribly wrong. Like in a *Lord of the Flies* kind of a way."

"You're worried you're going to be impaled on the spikes of your wimple," Oliver said, taking a cheerful bite and grinning across at Stanley as he chewed. "Suffocated by that big black dress. Death by habit."

"So nothing's ever gone wrong?"

"Well, if not, maybe this year's the year." Oliver enjoyed Stanley's frowning distress for a moment longer, then reached across and slapped him on the arm. "Hey man, you're awesome in that role. Everyone always says so as soon as you leave the room."

"I didn't mean that," Stanley said. He drummed his hands on the tabletop and sighed.

August

Stanley left the Institute buildings at a brisk trot, hugging a long woollen trench coat around his body. He was wearing a suit and tie, and his shoes were shined brightly black. He took the stairs two by two, broke apart from the rest of the group and set off across the quadrangle with his head inclined and his shoulders slightly bowed, his hands clenched in fists inside the pockets of his coat. He walked swiftly, and soon he had left the rest of the group and was walking down the boulevard alone.

Behind him, a motley clutch of characters from Tennessee Williams, Steven Berkoff, Ionesco and David Hare milled about briefly before settling upon an objective and dispersing likewise. One of the girls had costumed herself in a taffeta dress that was cut above the knee, and she looked uncomfortable and underdressed in the chill of the afternoon. Her bare legs were blood mottled and the fine fur on her arms was standing on end.

Stanley had resolved to circumnavigate the park, detouring to avoid the children's playground, then looping carefully around the lake and returning to the Institute buildings from the opposite side. He withdrew further into the collar of his shirt and lengthened his stride. He supposed he was probably being followed: the Heads of Acting, Movement, Improvisation and Voice had all left the premises earlier that morning to station themselves around the city quarter.

"You mustn't leave the bounded area," the Head of Acting had said again and again, tapping the illuminated area with his forefinger and looking down past the steel arm of the projector at the shifting mass of students straining in their seats. He was dressed in canvas trousers and an open-necked shirt, looking only slightly jauntier than usual but nevertheless infected by the same giddy thrill of disguise as the students, some of whom were almost unrecognizable in their pinned costumes and period hair.

Stanley turned off the boulevard and passed through the blunt-tipped iron gates into the botanical gardens. A suited man passed him on the gravel path and gave him a long look. Stanley almost looked away, but quickly remembered he was Joe Pitt, and looked hard at the man for the longest possible instant, not breaking his gaze until he had passed. He felt an unpleasant flicker of guilt at the deception that did not dissolve when the man rounded the corner of the hothouse and disappeared. Stanley thought he saw out of the corner of his eye the Head of Improvisation sitting on a park bench in a pool of sunlight and holding a newspaper on her lap. He drew his coat tighter around himself and walked on.

Pretending to be somebody else gave Stanley a curious feeling of privacy in himself. The inner thoughts and processings of his character, visible only as he chose to make them visible, across his face and in the lie of his hands and through the curve of his posture, enclosed his own thoughts like an atmosphere, parceling the real Stanley up beneath a double-layered film, the inner and the outer Joe Pitt. He felt snug, as if tightly curled within a nut, safe in the knowledge that nobody could truly see him beneath the double fog of his disguise.

"Hello," said a small voice, and suddenly there was the girl from the wings, the music-lesson girl, coming toward him with her saxophone case slung over her shoulder like a quiver. She grinned, the first properly uncensored grin he had seen on her face, and said, "Are you following me?"

"If I was following you, wouldn't I be walking behind you?" Stanley said.

"I meant stalking." The girl was still grinning, now flicking her gaze up and down Stanley's overcoat, which was a little too large for him, the sleeves hanging over his fingertips as if he was a child dressing up in the clothes of his father.

"Oh. I'm doing an acting exercise for drama school," Stanley said without thinking. As soon as he'd said it, he awaited a sinking feeling in his stomach: he'd failed the exercise; someone would surely have seen and noted it. "If you tell *anyone* that you are doing an exercise, or describe the Institute or your profession in any way," the Head of Acting had said, "it goes without saying that you will automatically fail."

"I have to stay in character all morning," Stanley said, rushing on. "Those are the rules." The sinking feeling didn't come. He felt curiously lighter, standing here in the park with this pretty upturned girl, and he flapped his oversized coat around him and laughed.

"Do you want to get a coffee later?" he asked. "When I'm done being Joe Pitt."

"Okay," Isolde said shyly. "Who's Joe Pitt?"

"Well, he dresses like this," Stanley said. "And beyond that, I couldn't really say."

"You're not doing a very good job of being him then," Isolde said.

"I guess not."

Stanley located the feeling of lightness: he felt *real*, more real than he had felt in months.

"How do I know you're not acting now?" Isolde said, which was almost a cliché but he forgave her because of his feeling of lightness and because of how pretty she looked, with her pink ears and her woollen coat and her mittens clapped together against the cold.

"How do I know that *you're* not?" Stanley said.

Isolde smiled and made a funny gesture, turning out her hands and lifting herself up onto her tiptoes to show that her whole body didn't know. Stanley felt a rush of happiness surge over him like a tide.

"I guess that's a risk we're going to have to take, then," he said.

Out of the corner of his eye he saw the Head of Improvisation approaching.

"I have to go and finish my walk now," he said. "But I'll wait for you under the ginkgo tree."

"I finish at five," Isolde said.

"I know," Stanley said. "I've been watching."

July

"You have to follow through with the action to the very end," the Head of Movement called out crossly. His tired hand was smoothing the hair on his crown, over and over. "Right now it's obvious that you both know the scene is about to end, and you relax before the lights go down. It's only a split-second thing, but it matters. You have to give the illusion that the scene is going to keep going on, behind the curtain. You have to follow through with the action to the very end. Again."

Stanley and the girl again assumed their position, Stanley standing with his palm cupped against the girl's cheek and his index finger slipped inside the tight little bud of her ear. They said their lines again, and tried not to loosen or slacken their bodies as the scene came to its invisible end.

"It is what I want. This is what I want," was Stanley's last line, and he gave her jaw a tight little shake with the clutch of his hand, for emphasis. The girl looked up at him. The scene ended.

Stanley's face was close to hers and her cheek was in his hand. He followed the action through: he leaned down and kissed her like he meant it.

"Oh, for God's sake!" the Head of Movement exploded, and the two of them jumped hastily apart. "When did I say kiss her? I said, Follow through with the action to the very end."

"I thought that was what you meant," Stanley said, with hot embarrassment, looking out past the lights. The girl wiped her mouth and looked at the floor.

"We are not going to have the curtain come down on the two of you pashing like a couple of kids!" the Head of Movement shouted. "Think about the scene, man!"

The Head of Movement did not usually yell. He was generally less vicious than the Head of Acting, less inclined to shame or fracture his students, less given to little bursts of irritation or cold contempt. But today he was scratchy, surly and tight chested as if short of breath, and as he glared up at the pair of them from his seat in the stalls he was smothered by a vast glove of anger and blame.

"What is it?" he said. "Just leaped at the opportunity, I suppose? What?"

The boy had a wounded look. He had been expecting congratulations, probably, praise for his physical commitment to the scene, his willingness to put personal considerations aside in the name of his art; he had been shamed, moreover, and shamed in front of a girl. The Head of Movement might well have destroyed all possibility of a relationship between the pair by this public shaming that caused them to flush and leap apart. The tutor knew it, and didn't care. He was suddenly immensely irritated at them both, the boy with his fair lashes and vulnerable pout, the girl with her practiced look of nervous naïveté, worn thin.

"I just thought that's what you meant," Stanley said again. "Sorry."

The Head of Movement did not speak for a moment. They were looking at him with faint pity now, he thought, as any teenager looks at an adult they believe to be utterly incapable of lust. They were looking at him as if they believed their awkward dry fumble against the fold of the curtain had somehow made him jealous; as if their collision had made him yearn for some lost youthful spontaneity of touch, and his outburst had only marked his dissatisfaction, his recognition of his own immeasurable loss. The Head of Movement felt disgusted. He wanted to turn his head and spit on the floor. He wanted to mount the seven steps to the stage and tear them from their cocoon of self-absorption and conceit. He wanted to shout and make them see that he was not jealous, that he could not be jealous of any pathetic hot-light kiss between two ill-made brats, and if anything what he felt was a profound nausea at what he had been forced to watch.

"Again," said the Head of Movement sourly, and threw himself back into his chair.

September

Stanley was waiting for Isolde under the ginkgo tree when she emerged from her lesson, trotting down the sunken stone steps and across the courtyard to embrace him and kiss him briefly on the mouth.

"Look at you, you little gypsy," Stanley said as he stepped back. "All your bags and everything."

"Fridays are horrible," Isolde said. "Sax and PE and art all in the same afternoon."

"Gypsy girl."

Isolde exhaled and flapped her arms and then grinned at Stanley, a broad, honest grin that lit her up completely. It was the same unashamed openness that had lured Mr. Saladin to

Victoria, only it was transplanted here on to her sister, the same smile on a different face. Stanley leaned forward and kissed her on the nose.

"So when am I going to hear you play?" he said.

"I thought you could hear from down here in the quad."

"But I'm never sure which sax is you and which is your teacher," Stanley said with a grin. "I might be thinking you're much better than you actually are."

"Our saxes actually have really different voices," Isolde said. "If you know to listen for that sort of thing. My mouthpiece is vulcanized rubber and hers is metal. The metal piece makes a really different sound."

"Like how speaking voices are different from each other."

"Yeah," Isolde said. "Right. Like the difference between a woman and a girl."

The stone building behind them was now unlit, all the curtains pulled and the lights doused. Inside, the offices were locked for the night and cooling now in the gathering dusk. On the attic level the saxophone teacher's window was dark, as if she had locked the studio after Isolde's departure and departed herself for the night, but if you looked up through the ginkgo branches you would see an inky figure standing by the curtain and looking down into the courtyard at the pair standing together under the ginkgo tree. Stanley and Isolde did not look up. Stanley crushed Isolde in a one-arm hug and together they walked away, talking quietly with their heads together, until they were swallowed by the cloisters and the branches, and they disappeared.

September

"Do you know why you are here?" the Head of Movement said as Stanley sat down.

"Probably my Outing," Stanley said, hazarding a guess.

The Head of Movement raised his eyebrows and twitched up his chin sharply. "Your Outing?" he said.

"I must have failed the exercise," Stanley said, suddenly realizing that he should be cautious, and trying to look a little more innocent and perplexed.

"I don't think so," the Head of Movement said. "I have your report from the Head of Improvisation and she said she was very much impressed. You were Joe Pitt."

"Yeah," Stanley said.

"I believe her report was very admiring."

"Oh."

Stanley tried to shrug and smile, but all he managed was a shiver and a grimace.

"Were you expecting to fail?" the Head of Movement asked, peering at him closely.

"No," Stanley said quickly. "So I guess I don't know why I'm here."

The Head of Movement sat back and placed the palms of his hands on the desk before him. He was wearing a long-practiced look of grave disappointment, and Stanley's heart began to hammer. The Head of Movement said, "Somebody has complained about you. Somebody has laid a very serious complaint about you. Do you know what that might be?"

Stanley looked bewildered. "No," he said. "Who? What was it?"

The Head of Movement did not speak immediately. He looked at Stanley with something between pity and disgust, and Stanley felt himself shrivel.

"A music teacher who teaches in a studio in the north quad," he said, "laid a complaint with us that you had been harassing her students."

"What?" Against his will Stanley felt himself begin to flush.

"Harassing her students," the Head of Movement went on. "In particular a young girl in the fifth form. Does this mean anything to you?"

Stanley sat for a moment without speaking.

"Nothing?" the Head of Movement said.

He drew the silence out between them carefully, like a measured breath. There was a dreadful sinking feeling in the pit of Stanley's stomach. He sat and stared at the glossy sheen of the table under the Head of Movement's hands, and said nothing.

"Normally," the Head of Movement said, "we wouldn't intervene in a case like this, of course. Normally we'd treat you like an adult and expect you to sort it out of your own accord. But the fact that this music teacher has taken up the issue directly with us—you see that we are compelled to talk with you about it. You see that."

"Yes," Stanley said automatically, and he nodded his head.

"The music teacher was very concerned about her students' safety, given the proximity of her studio to this Institute," the Head of Movement said.

Stanley nodded again.

"What happened, Stanley?" the Head of Movement said. "What's all this about?"

Stanley looked up quickly to meet the Head of Movement's gaze, and then drew his eyes away, turning his head to look at the framed posters and theater programs above the filing cabinet. They were ordered chronologically, lined up like a simple recipe for the Head of Movement's life, the plotted path to where he sat right now at his empty desk with his bare feet together and a frown upon his face.

"I don't know," Stanley said at last. "I don't know anything about a saxophone teacher."

"I said music teacher."

Stanley drew in his breath sharply and again glanced at the Head of Movement, even quicker this time, as if the tutor's haggard face was either very hot or very bright, and his eyes could not stand to rest for long.

"I knew she played sax," he said quietly, and the words were like a horrible admission, a statement of guilt. A little cough in the back of his throat broke the last word in two.

"I assume you are keeping quiet so as not to incriminate yourself," the Head of Movement said coldly, after another wretched pause.

"I just—"

In truth Stanley simply had nothing to say. He shrugged, more to communicate helplessness than insolence, but the Head of Movement's eyes flashed and Stanley saw that the gesture had angered him. The Head of Movement's coldness somehow amplified now, and he pressed his palms flatter upon the tabletop.

"Because the young girl in question is in the fifth form," the Head of Movement said, "you understand that she is not yet sixteen."

Stanley was still nodding.

"Because she is not yet sixteen," the Head of Movement said, "you understand that any form of sexual relations an adult might have, or have had, with this girl would be a crime. I'm speaking in my capacity as your tutor here."

Stanley nodded again. He was vaguely aware that he had gone white and that his mouth had started to fill with saliva in an awful tongue-shrinking preface to vomiting. He felt nauseous and all of a sudden found his sense of smell sharpened acutely: he could smell the damp wool of his tutor's jacket hanging on the back of the door, the paper twist of nuts on the dresser, cold coffee pooling in the bottom of a cold mug. He felt his head reel.

The Head of Movement surveyed him for a moment. He had a wide-eyed straining look about him, as if the worst was still to come. He leaned forward, puckering his lips slightly in a dry kiss as he made a careful choice of words.

"Stanley," he said, "I want you to think about something very carefully. You don't have to answer, I just want you to think about it. If the parents of this young girl ended up being *in the audience* when you produce your first-year production at the end of this week, would it change anything? If they were there?"

It was a strange question and Stanley didn't understand it. He stared at the Head of Movement blankly and said, "I don't know what you mean."

"This girl that you have been—"

"Isolde."

"Yes. She has a sister, am I right?"

"I don't know," Stanley said. "Why?"

The Head of Movement was now looking at him with open disgust. "Oh, come on, Stanley, let's not dance around like this. This is ridiculous."

Stanley swallowed and reached up to wipe a film of sweat from his upper lip. "I'm sorry," he said. "I must be missing something."

"Isolde's sister's name is Victoria," the Head of Movement snapped. "Does that ring any bells?"

Stanley stared at him for only a brief half-second before he realized—and the realization descended upon him like the awful downward shudder of a guillotine. *Victoria*, he was screaming. *Victoria*, the celebrity focus of their production, snipped from a column in the newspaper, snatched up and stolen and grafted on to all the posters, black and red, *The Bedpost Queen*. Would it change anything if *Victoria's* parents were there—that was the Head of Movement's question.

And then the second blade of realization fell, if possible more horrible than the first. They think Isolde is a pawn, Stanley thought, a pawn that I wielded to get information for the play. My pawn.

"Of course, I am not supposed to know anything about the content of the first-year devised theater production," the Head of Movement was saying, "and really I do know very little about what you are rehearsing and working on. But I can't avoid walking past an open door every so often, or hearing a scrap of conversation in the hall. You understand."

Stanley sat shrinking in his clammy seat, trying with difficulty to swallow the nausea that was rising like a hard stone in the back of his throat.

"Does Isolde know?" he said stupidly.

"About what?" the Head of Movement said.

"About the production. What it's about, and what we're doing."

"I have no idea," the Head of Movement said. "I have only spoken to the saxophone teacher. We were discussing the situation, and she explained the family had had a difficult year, given the scandal surrounding the older daughter's rape. I recognized the name and made the connection myself."

Stanley was furiously trying to think back to all the conversations he'd had with Isolde—had he ever mentioned it? Had he ever said Victoria's name?

"Are you going to tell them?" he asked. "Are you going to ring the parents?"

"I think that's for you to think about, Stanley. As I said, you're an adult, and you can deal with this yourself."

"What about the music teacher? What if she's rung them already?" he said. He had never seen Isolde's saxophone teacher, but he imagined her as a vicious oily shadow standing by the curtain and looking down past the branches into the courtyard below.

"I don't know," the Head of Movement said. He was looking at Stanley oddly now. "So you're saying you didn't know," he said. "About the sister."

"No," Stanley said. He felt himself shrivel further. How stupid was he? He had never even asked this girl's last name. He had never asked—about her family, about her life at home, about the house where she woke up and showered and ate breakfast and practiced her saxophone with the scruffy leaves of her sheet music around her on the floor: these were scenes he had never imagined. He had never imagined this girl beyond the time he had spent with her: she had simply been—what? A function of himself, maybe. She had simply presented a role for him to fill.

The Head of Movement said, "But you did have a relationship with this young girl." He enunciated carefully, placing a slight emphasis upon *young*, as if he were pressing his fingerprint upon the word.

"Not…I mean…it wasn't…she consented," Stanley said. "Yes, we had a relationship."

"Until she's sixteen, Stanley, her consent doesn't count for much," the Head of Movement said. He drew away and looked down his nose at Stanley as if he meant to wash his hands of the whole affair.

"They can't come," Stanley said. "The parents. They can't be there. They can't know about it."

"No," the Head of Movement said. "They can't."

"What are we going to do?" Stanley asked. "Do we cancel?"

"The play is not my responsibility," the Head of Movement said. "The ticket sales are not my responsibility. This girl is not my responsibility. My job is only to let you know what you need to know. I don't make people's choices my business. I don't want to know what you did with this girl. But if this is in any way damaging to the Institute—I'm compelled to act."

Stanley nodded dumbly.

"Really, Stanley," the Head of Movement said at last, for the first time expressing real exasperation at this pale and twitching victim seated before him in the small room. "I mean, how could you not know that somebody was watching you? For Christ's sake. You must have been being bloody careless, if somebody was watching the whole time."

September

"Stanley," Isolde said, "do you want to go all the way with me? Some time?"

Stanley ran his finger down her cheek. Deep inside he was irritated at her for even mentioning it, for giving the prospect a shape, a voice. It seemed indecent. He would have preferred to leave the act unmentioned until it was over. He would have preferred not to speak at all, to stop her mouth with his and tug at her cuffs and her waistband and unpeel her swiftly like a ripe fruit. Her question was logistical, organizing, reductive. He would not have asked it. He was a romantic.

"Do you think we're ready?" Stanley said, cunningly answering her question with a question, but looking at her with such a grave and contrite expression that she would be fooled into thinking he was truly engaging with the matter at hand.

"Yeah," Isolde said. She began to smile before she'd finished the word, and then he was smiling back at her and moving in to kiss her and laugh with her, laugh against her, his teeth against hers.

"I do too," Stanley said. "I think we're ready."

"Do you want to?" Isolde said shyly.

"Course I want to," Stanley said. "I was only waiting until you were sure. I didn't want to put any pressure on you. I wanted you to be the one to ask."

This wasn't really true, but he was pleased with the way it sounded.

October

The Head of Movement's office door was open, and Stanley didn't knock. He padded up to the doorframe and lingered there for a moment before he began to speak.

"I should have failed," he said. "That's all I wanted to say. I should have failed the Outing. I told someone outright that I was doing an acting exercise. I even told her I was doing Joe Pitt."

The Head of Movement looked up at him, the light from his desk-lamp drawing down the shadows around his eyes and his mouth. "Why?" he said, making no move to gesture Stanley inside, and so Stanley remained at the doorway with his hands tugging at the straps of his backpack, moving his weight from foot to foot.

"Because otherwise she might have thought that Joe Pitt was really me," Stanley said. "I didn't want her to think that."

The Head of Movement sighed and rubbed his face with his hands.

"Stanley," he said, "why are you telling me this? You don't want a failing grade on your card. It'll be a mark against you. If this was weighing on your conscience, why didn't you just resolve to do better next time? Why would you choose to sabotage yourself?"

"To make you respect me," Stanley said.

"To make me respect you," the Head of Movement said.

Stanley was breathing quickly. "To make you see me," he said. "To make you see me when you look."

The Head of Movement looked at the boy and wondered if he should relent. Stanley's throat was tight and he quavered when he spoke, but underneath his nervousness there was that persistent thread of self-congratulation, even now. The Head of Movement felt a flicker of anger. Even now, he thought. Even now the boy is performing, and adoring his performance, adoring himself.

"Every year there's someone like you, Stanley," he said. "And someone just like you will come along and fill the hole that you leave when you move on. Every word that comes out of your mouth—they're just *lines*. They're lines that you've learned very carefully, so carefully you've convinced yourself they are yours, but that's all they are. They're lines I've heard many times before." The Head of Movement tossed his head suddenly, and snapped, "Why don't you see *me* when you look? I could ask that of all my students. All my selfish cookie-cutter students who troop in and out each year like a dead-water tide."

"What about that boy you were with in the art department? Is he a cookie-cutter student too?" Stanley asked sourly.

There was a pause. The Head of Movement raised his eyebrows.

"The boy I was with in the art department?" he said.

"The masked boy from the Theater of Cruelty," Stanley mumbled. "Nick."

"What do you want to know about Nick?"

"Is he a cookie-cutter student too?" Stanley was thoroughly embarrassed now.

The tutor looked him up and down and almost laughed. "Maybe so," he said. "But he's like me. He's like I once was. I listen to him speak, and watch him move, and it is like a kind of rebirth. I can relive myself, through him. I can be new again just by watching."

Stanley looked at the floor and didn't speak.

"Thank you for coming to me today," the Head of Movement said, after a moment. His voice was cold and his face had closed. "We will amend your records to show a failing grade."

THIRTEEN

Friday

"Are you good friends with your sister, Isolde?" the saxophone teacher asks mildly one afternoon, after Isolde's lesson is over and the girl is repacking her case.

"Not really," Isolde says.

"Do you hang out with her much at school?"

"No. It's weird when the juniors hang out with the seniors. And she's got friends in her own year. They don't like me around."

"Would she be someone you'd talk to, if you needed someone?"

Isolde flushes scarlet immediately. She turns away from the saxophone teacher and ducks to fiddle with the clasp on her satchel. "Probably not," she says.

"Okay," the saxophone teacher says kindly, watching her.

"I don't know who I'd talk to," Isolde mumbles.

"Not your friends?"

"No."

The saxophone teacher waits while Isolde shuffles her music and stuffs it into her backpack.

"Actually it's kind of weird that Victoria's so popular," Isolde says, regaining composure, "because she was ruined. Three years ago, in fourth form. Her friends decided they didn't really like her and they had a conference about it to decide what to do with her. In the end they just gathered around one lunchtime and told her that she wasn't allowed to sit with them or talk to them anymore. And then they all ran away."

"I suppose she moved on and found some new friends," the saxophone teacher says.

"You can't, really," says Isolde. "Once you've been dumped by one group. The other groups get suspicious. There's nothing to do except hang out in the library and always come to class at the last possible moment so it's not like you're sitting alone and waiting.

"Most of the girls keep best friends for security," she adds. "You've always got an ally that way, and you're less likely to be dumped."

"So how did your sister climb her way back up?" the saxophone teacher asks. "If she really was ruined, as you say."

"She fell in with some boys," Isolde says. "She started crossing the road at lunchtime and hanging out with the St. Sylvester boys down by the river. Just her and the boys. That was like her weapon. The girls started coming back to her after that."

"Have you ever been dumped?" the saxophone teacher says. "By a group, I mean."

"Nah," Isolde says. She is wrapped up in her scarf and her coat now, and she shrugs in a general, helpless way to show the conversation has come to a close.

"See you next week," she says, and just for a moment the saxophone teacher feels a stab of something like sadness, wanting very much to ask Isolde to stay. These weekly half-hour snatches of Isolde's life are to the sax teacher only the lighted squares of kitchen windows along a dark street, showing a brief and yellowed glimpse into the throat of a house but nothing more.

Isolde has glazed over with politeness now that the lesson has ended, standing near the door with her music case already in her hand. The precious quickened intimacy of the lesson is now lost, and the saxophone teacher can only smile and wave her out and say, "See you Monday, Isolde. Take care."

Friday

Patsy has brought croissants and ham, and a soft yellow cheese which depresses under the blunt edge of the butter knife. Already they have talked for nearly an hour and the saxophone teacher has watched Patsy with a kind of bursting desperate look, straining and wounded like a stuck deer. She looks as if she might burst into tears. Patsy doesn't seem to be noticing.

"Patsy," the saxophone teacher says finally. "Do you know something? Whenever I am alone and intimate with anybody else, whenever I am at ease, or making someone laugh, or kissing somebody, or making someone feel truly good—whenever I feel like I am being really *successful* as a lover, doing it *right*—at all those times, part of me is wishing that you were watching me."

"That's a weird thing to say," Patsy says, giving the sax teacher a quizzical half-frown. She is already withdrawing, sitting back and bringing the heel of her hand to her cheek to push away a strand of hair and becoming swiftly impenetrable, as if she is determined to misunderstand whatever the sax teacher will say next. All in an instant she is stony and aloof.

"I don't mean that I wish you were there," the saxophone teacher says. "What I mean is that everything I do with other people becomes a kind of proof. As if I were invisibly proving something to you. As if I were saying, all the while, This is what you didn't see in me. This is what you could have had. This is what you missed out on."

"You want me to be jealous," Patsy says.

"No," the saxophone teacher says. "It's not that I want you to be jealous. I just want you to see me at my best. Sometimes I act as if you really were watching, just to prove it to myself. Sometimes I say things when I'm at my most intimate that don't even make sense to the person at hand. They'd only make sense to you. If you were watching."

"Honey," Patsy says, quietly.

There is a silence.

"Of course I'm going to rehearse all of this in the mirror," the saxophone teacher says at last. "Before I say it to you. I'll rehearse it over and over. Until I have the confidence to tell you this, out loud."

Monday

"Tell me about Isolde," the saxophone teacher says outright, when Julia arrives for her lesson on Monday afternoon.

Julia raises her eyebrows as she wiggles out of her anorak and slings it over the back of the armchair. She is still radiating the cold winter air she has brought into the room with her, and the sax teacher catches it in a brief current, breathing it in like an alien scent.

"Tell me about Patsy," Julia says.

"Who?" the saxophone teacher says stupidly, letting her arms fall to her sides, and then in irritation she pulls at her sleeve and says, "I mean, I know who Patsy is. I meant why."

Julia shrugs. "There's a sign up in my homeroom," she says, "and it says, Who's asking the questions in this classroom?"

The saxophone teacher narrows her eyes. "How do you know who Patsy is?"

"All your letters are addressed care of Patsy," Julia says, pointing. "Is she your lover?"

The saxophone teacher flushes scarlet. "This is Patsy's studio," she says in a dignified voice. She twitches her chin up. "Patsy left me the studio."

"Like in a will?"

"No, she's not dead. It still legally belongs to her. That's why the letters are addressed care of her post-box."

"So she's not your lover."

The saxophone teacher taps her fingers on the desk. "Tell me about Isolde," she says.

Julia runs the tip of her tongue over her bottom lip, and then she says, "We meet in the drama cupboard at school. Nobody's ever in there, and we wedge the door shut anyway. We make a nest out of nuns' habits and Nazi uniforms and hoop skirts, and when the bell rings we leave one after the other, with a decent break in between, so nobody notices."

"And?"

"And what?" Julia says.

"That's not enough," the saxophone teacher says. "It's not enough, just to know that you're in there. How did you get there? How did it start?"

"Why do you want to know?" Julia says. "You'll still be on the outside looking in. Even if you know everything, even if you know all the things you shouldn't, even then you'll still be on the outside. Why did she leave you this studio?"

They are tense, like two dogs chained apart.

"As a vote of confidence in my music," the saxophone teacher says. "She taught me saxophone, once upon a time, but she got arthritis early. It started in her thumbs and then spread outward, like a slow and painful inkblot, outward from her thumbs across her hands. She had to stop teaching. She went back to university, and I just took over her studio. I replaced her, I guess. I pay rent to her now."

"She was your teacher?"

"Once, yes." The sax teacher hesitates, her hands clutching at her elbows, but then she draws a breath and says quickly, "What do you do in the drama cupboard?"

"Mostly we talk," Julia says. "There's only gib board between the drama cupboard and the practice rooms so we have to be quiet. That's how Mr. Saladin and Victoria got found out, Isolde said. Somebody was in the drama cupboard and they heard them through the wall. It's always pitch dark in there—we don't dare to turn on the light because it'll shine under the door. My favorite thing she does in the dark is she makes her two forefingers into little calipers and she keeps checking to see if I'm smiling, feeling my face in the dark and lying there with her fingers resting, just lightly, at the corners of my mouth. That's my favorite thing."

"What do you say? When you talk. What do you say to each other?"

"We talk about the preciousness of it all," Julia says. "How fortunate we are. How lucky we are that the accident of my attraction coincided with the accident of hers. We just lie there and marvel, and feel each other's skin, and inside I feel years and years older than I actually am—not like I'm weary or wise or anything, but more like what I'm feeling is so huge it connects me to something still huger, something infinite, some massive arc of beautiful *unknowing* that is bigger than any kind of tiny trap of time, or space, that might otherwise contain me. It feels like that one moment, that one tiny shard of *now*, that brief and perfect moment of touching her skin and tasting her tongue and feeling so utterly captured, so caught in her, that moment is all I'm going to need to nourish me for the rest of my life."

The saxophone teacher has fumbled with her hand to find the edge of the desk, and she sinks back against it weakly.

"But at the same time, the feeling is shot through with a kind of sadness," Julia says, "a bittersweet and throaty sadness that sits heavy in my gullet and I can't swallow it down. It's like I know that I am *losing* something; that something is seeping away, like water into dust. And it's a weird idea, the idea that loss—the massive snatching tearing hunger of loss—is something that doesn't start when a relationship ends, when she melts away and disappears and I know that I can never get her back. It's a feeling that starts at the very beginning, from the moment we collide in the dark and we touch for the very first time. The innocence of it—the sweetness and purity of it, the shy and halting tenderness of it—that is something that I am only ever going to *lose*."

Julia takes a step toward the saxophone teacher. "Is that how you felt?" she says. "With Patsy?"

"Julia," the saxophone teacher says, and then she doesn't say anything for a moment. She draws a hand over her eyes. "Patsy," she says, but then she falters and changes her mind.

"Let me tell you something, Julia," she says at last. "That moment you're talking about. That one perfect kiss. It's all there is. Everything from this point onward is only going to be a facsimile, darling. You will try and re-create that one kiss with all your lovers, try and replay it over and over; it will sit like an old video loop on a television screen in front of you, and you will lean forward to touch the cool bulge of the glass with your forehead and you will feel the ripple-fur of static with your fingers and your cheek and you will be illumined, lit up by the blue-black glow of it, the bursts of light, but in the end you will never really be able to *touch* it, this perfect memory, this one solitary moment of unknowing where you were simply *innocent* of who you were, of what you might become. You will never touch that feeling again, Julia. Not ever again."

"Is that how it is for you?" Julia says. "With Patsy?"

The saxophone teacher expels a breath and says nothing.

"Where's Patsy now?" Julia says.

"Oh, she still lives in the city," the sax teacher says, waving a hand vaguely, north by northwest. "We're just very old friends, Julia. Patsy's married. We're just old friends."

"Married to a man?"

"Yes, to a man."

"But you were lovers once," Julia says.

"No."

"Even once?"

"No."

"You're lying."

"What does it matter anyway, how it was?" the saxophone teacher snaps. "I could only ever tell you how I remember it, never how it was. My wrinkled cheesecloth of a memory, all balled up and mothy with the sunlight glinting through. And you lied about your favorite thing. You stole it from someone else and used it as your own."

Julia scowls and says nothing. After a moment she tosses her head and says, "You probably know it all anyway, from somebody else."

Friday

Stanley is waiting for Isolde after her lesson. From inside he can hear snatches of a tune played by two saxophones together, one confidently leading, the other duller and shyer and more ordinary. He is nervous. He wishes he'd scripted something to say.

At last the saxophones cease and he thinks he hears, through the open window, the faint rumble of Isolde's teacher's voice, and Isolde laughing. He shuffles his feet.

After a few minutes Isolde emerges from the building and trots down the short flight of steps to the courtyard, her saxophone case in her hand. She looks strange: she is smiling too readily and too brightly, and her eyes are sad. Stanley doesn't notice. He keeps pulling at his collar and his hair, and when he looks at her he doesn't hold her gaze for long.

"Hey you," she says. "Did you hear me that time?"

"Yeah," Stanley says. "You're pretty good."

"Want to come to my recital? You don't have to. It might be boring."

"Sure," Stanley says awkwardly. He falls into step beside her, and as they walk out of the courtyard he looks over his shoulder at the saxophone teacher's window. Is there somebody there, standing by the curtain, looking down at them? Is the next student waiting patiently in the hall for the saxophone teacher to finish watching, smarten her hair, open the door and invite her in? He can't tell from this distance and soon the window disappears behind the branches of the ginkgo tree.

"My parents will be there," Isolde says. "They're really stoked to meet you. Especially Dad. My sister had, like, this weird thing this year where she slept with a teacher and Dad's really keen to get back to normal or whatever. He's just stoked you're not in your thirties and balding and my teacher at school."

Stanley exhales sharply and almost pulls away from her. There it is: all the information he needed, the clinching information, tumbling out of her mouth in one careless little burst. Too late.

"Why didn't you tell me earlier?" he says.

"Oh," Isolde says airily. "I don't know. I'm just sick of it, I guess. It's all anyone talks about any more—just Victoria and the rape or whatever and how hard it's been. I just didn't want to talk about it with you."

She reaches for his hand and pulls him closer to her as they walk, showing more affection than she has before.

"It's not a big deal," she says.

"What do you mean, slept with her teacher?" Stanley says.

"Well, apparently the story is now that she didn't even sleep with him," Isolde says. "I don't know. It keeps changing. She gets all cagey."

"You must know," Stanley says. "She's your sister."

Isolde gives him an odd look. "I don't," she says. "I don't know anything."

They walk on in silence for a while.

"Do you talk about me to your sax teacher?" Stanley says. His voice is high and strained.

"I guess," she says. "I mean, I've mentioned you. Music teachers are like therapists, kind of. You meet up once a week and tell them everything you need to tell them and then you disappear again. It's like therapy." Her voice is high too, as if she doesn't believe her own lines.

"What do you say about me?" Stanley says.

"Oh, you know," Isolde says. Now she looks embarrassed.

Stanley makes a swift decision to tell Isolde half the truth. He stops walking and turns toward her.

"She laid a complaint about me," he says. "Your teacher. She must have been watching through the window. She complained that I've been harassing you—because you're so young, I guess, and I'm not. Young. I guess that was why." He breathes heavily and watches her.

Isolde opens her mouth a little but says nothing. She drags her eyes from Stanley's face and looks at a pasted advertisement on the wall over his shoulder.

"So what do you say about me?" Stanley says, impatient now. "In your lesson."

"Nothing," Isolde says quickly.

"You said you mentioned me."

"Only briefly."

"So why would she complain? What does she have against me?"

Isolde shoots him a calculating look. "Are you in trouble?" she says.

"I just want to know what you say about me," Stanley says loudly. In his frustration he is forgetting that he is only telling Isolde half the truth after all. He begins to blame her. He becomes irritated by her open-mouthed stare, the plump curve of her pouting lip, how childlike she seems.

"It's this thing with my sister," Isolde says at last. "I suppose she knows how much it affected me. She knows how vulnerable I am, how impressionable I am, how likely it is that I might act out or do something dumb or end up slutting around, just to make myself heard. It happens, when there's trauma in a family. She's protecting me, I guess."

"From me?"

"Well. Yeah. I mean, probably."

"And you knew." He is thoroughly angry with her now.

"No," Isolde says. "I didn't know. She acted behind my back, like a clinging mother orchestrating the life of her child."

"This is bullshit," Stanley says. "You talking to your teacher about me, the two of you together. It's bullshit."

"What are you talking about?"

"You must have made me sound like a rapist."

"I did not make you sound like a *rapist*!"

"It's my reputation," Stanley says. "My reputation at the school which is at stake. Whatever you said, you made her act like that. You made her complain."

"I did not *make her* complain!"

"You must have," Stanley shouts. "You did. With whatever you said."

Cars are passing. The passengers press their faces to the windows to watch the two of them fight. Stanley has his arms flung wide and Isolde's hands are crossed over her belly. Finally Stanley makes a scissor motion with the flat of his hand that means *enough*. He is the first to turn and walk away.

Monday

"What would you do," Julia says, "if I said that you did things to me here, when we were alone? Indecent things. If I confessed to somebody. If I broke down."

The southerly is gathering above the gables, blackening and bruising and seeming to draw the sky downward. The saxophone teacher crosses the room and turns on the lamp, twitching the curtain against the lowering sky.

"I don't know what I would do," she says, without looking at Julia.

"I'd lie," Julia says, already narrow eyed and pursuing the thought. "I would make up silver lies studded with shards of perfect detail like mosaic splinters, sharp and everlasting, the kind of tiny faultless detail that would make them all sure that what I said was true. I would have alibis. I would bring in other people and teach them a story, and rehearse it so carefully and for so long that soon they'd all start to believe that what they said was actually true."

"It sounds like a lot of work," the saxophone teacher says calmly, but her hands and eyes are still and she is watching Julia with all her attention now. "What's in it for you?"

"It would change what everyone says about me at school."

"What does everyone—"

"That I like girls," Julia says loudly. The collar of her school shirt is open and the hollow V of her neck is turning an angry stippled red.

"How?"

"Because if there was some tragic story behind it all," Julia says, "it would be like a reason or a cause. Like with that girl Victoria."

"Isolde's sister."

"Yeah," Julia says hotly. "Isolde's sister. Whatever she does

281

now, if she goes off the rails or whatever, and ends up sleeping with a billion people and drinking heaps and failing all her exams, people won't think that she's just a loser or a slut. They'll know it's because she's *damaged*, because there's a reason behind everything, which is that she was raped. Whatever she does from now on will just be evidence. So it's kind of like she's free. She can do anything and she won't be responsible. She's got a *reason*."

"That's a very interesting way of looking at it," the saxophone teacher says.

"*I* want a reason," Julia says. "If it turned out that I was damaged, then it wouldn't be my fault anymore. It wouldn't be something gross, it would be something tragic. It would be an *effect*—an effect of something out of my control. I'd just be a victim."

"You all want to be damaged," the saxophone teacher says suddenly. "All of you. That is the one quality all my students have in common. That is your theme and variation: you crave your own victimhood absolutely. You see it as the only viable way to get an edge upon your classmates, and you are right. If I were to interfere with you, Julia, I'd be doing you an incredible favor. I'd be giving you a ticket to authorize the most shameless self-pity and self-adoration and self-loathing, and none of your classmates could even hope to compare."

"Yes, that's exactly what I'm saying," Julia says.

The two of them look at each other in silence for a moment.

"What details would you choose to include?" the saxophone teacher says. "Those sharp mosaic-sliver details that would line your alibi like the tight angled coins on a chain-link vest."

"Nothing physical, at first," Julia says. "That would be too obvious. The lie would shine too brightly, and they'd find me out. Something psychological. Something insidious and dripping. Some slow erosion that in the end would be far worse, far more subtle and damaging, than any quick backstage fumble or teasing slap."

"It's still going to be a lie, Julia," the saxophone teacher says. "At the heart of it. You won't be satisfied. At bottom, all it will be is a lie."

"How do you know?" Julia says. "How do you know how you have influenced me? How do you know I'm not damaged? How do you know I don't nurse some small criticism, some throwaway comment that you made and have now forgotten but I remember every time I stumble or I fail? A tiny something that will dig deeper and deeper, like a glass splinter working its way from my finger to my heart? Some tiny something that will change the shape of me forever—how can you know?"

For once the saxophone teacher has nothing to say. She looks out the window at the birds.

Wednesday

The saxophone section of the Abbey Grange jazz band is gap-toothed now: first Victoria, who has chosen not to return, and then Bridget, who never will. The cavities have been filled with lesser players, and the chairs shuffled a fraction closer to tighten the curve.

"Bridget would have really liked this," says first trombone every now and again, knowing that dead people are always very sentimental and always full of joy and appreciation for the simple things. Some of them still weep, not for Bridget, who was unmemorable, but for themselves, imagining that they themselves had died, and how irreplaceable they would be.

The school's Christian group was tight lipped and private about the sacking of Mr. Saladin and its aftermath; on the subject of Bridget's death it blossoms. A man's powerful and senseless attraction to a girl he had been instructed to protect is a human mystery. More marketable is the divine mystery of this one lampless girl mown to extinction in the dewy dark: it is right up their alley, and the Christian group thrives. Advertisements for prayer groups spring up around the school. Enrollments for youth camps run a record high. A Christian pancake stand appears in the quad at lunchtime, managed by a zealous few who roll the pancakes in lemon and sugar and shine brightly with an inner light. They don't hand out tracts or wise words or a summons to a better life. They hand out pancakes. It's enough. Soon many of the girls are exchanging their plastic Fuck-me bracelets for nylon bands that invite them, in mnemonic, to consider what a grown man might do if he were one of them, if he were faced with the same choices and confounded by the same desires. Bridget herself had been a sometime member, a wearer of a nylon commitment band—this is a comfort, the girls agree, as they mutely beg their own salvation and reach sideways for each other's hands.

The lunchtime youth group shifts from a classroom to the school hall to cater for the swell in numbers, and with the counselor long since returned to his frosted cubby between the bursar and the nurse, the youth leaders rise to take his place. They conclude that, in all likelihood, He would do just as they are doing now, and as they regard their bracelets they feel a throb of satisfaction that they possess the single correct answer to the rhetorical question stitched around the band.

In a sense, Bridget comes to eclipse Victoria after all. Victoria's questionable victimhood, the all-too-visible streak of her own reciprocation cannot, in the end, compete with the indubitable victim of a roadside smash. But the posthumous Bridget is not a singular and universal notoriety, celebrated as Victoria had been celebrated, herself the symbol and the locus of her fame; Bridget is an instrument, subtler and more pliable and vastly more diffused. It's the best she could have hoped for.

"There was a girl at my high school who died," the girls will say, years later. "She was hit on her bike coming home from work. God, it was sad. It really affected us, you know? All of us. I hardly knew her, but even so. It was so sad."

Tuesday

"That's it, then," Patsy said, when the saxophone teacher received her teaching diploma. They looked at it, stamped with a blue watermark, silvered and inked and glossy under its pane of glass. "That's it," Patsy said, "you're damned. A lifetime of the world assuming that you are a spinster, a closed thin-lipped efficient spinster who lies spangled and lock-jawed in her bed at nights and has no love or pleasure to light the room. It's the one truth about music teachers, and everybody knows it: they are alone, always alone, limp and graying in their cold offices and waiting in the dark for their next student like a beggar waiting for a meal. Congratulations!"

They touched glasses lightly and drank.

"But you're not a spinster," the saxophone teacher said. She was still looking at the shining diploma, tracing the words with her eyes.

"But everyone still assumes. Or a lesbian. If they are generous, then they assume I am a lesbian."

"That's why she asked for that ring," Brian said, pointing to the penultimate finger on Patsy's left hand. "She said, Make it the biggest fattest old diamond you can get your hands on. This isn't just a symbol, it's a whole bloody advertising campaign."

"And *this* is what you came up with," Patsy said, waving her hand and making a disgusted face, as if the ring was worth nothing. They laughed.

"Anyway, well done, old thing," Brian said, reaching across and covering the saxophone teacher's hands with his own. "It all starts here."

285

Friday

As Isolde unpacks her case the saxophone teacher talks enthusiastically about the upcoming recital, the venue and the other performers, and the chance for everybody to listen to everybody else. Isolde is not listening. She is going to mention the saxophone teacher's complaint about Stanley. The thought of bringing it up makes her heart thump, and the advance phrasing of the question paralyzes her, consumes her utterly. She senses that the topic is dangerous, that she is somehow backfooted at the outset: she has done something wrong without her knowing, and she will lose.

There is a knock at the door.

"Hang on a minute, Isolde," the saxophone teacher says serenely. "I think that's probably Julia."

"What?" Isolde says.

"I thought we could try the Raschèr duet with both of you together," the saxophone teacher says. "You've each been learning one part and I thought it would be fun to bring them together properly."

Isolde goes red. She looks at the saxophone teacher without speaking for a moment, and then says, "I didn't know I was going to play it in a duet."

"Well," the saxophone teacher says, "I wasn't sure if Julia would be able to make this Friday slot. It was kind of a last-minute idea. It really is worth playing against someone else, you know. There's a whole new enjoyment to be got out of playing with another person." She doesn't advance to get the door: she hovers near Isolde, hands on her hips, and surveys her student.

"I would have practiced," Isolde says. "If I'd known." Her mouth is suddenly dry.

"You remember Julia, don't you?" the saxophone teacher says.

"Yes," says Isolde.

"Wonderful." The saxophone teacher walks swiftly to the door to release the latch. "Welcome," she says to the older girl.

"Hello, darling," Julia says as she sweeps in, and all in an instant Isolde knows that Julia has stepped out of herself and become somebody else entirely: she is performing, and Isolde must too.

"Honey," she says, and they kiss on the cheek like old friends, like thirty-something friends who were once teacher and pupil, once upon a time. The saxophone teacher has melted into the shadows by the wall.

"I know this is meant to be a rehearsal, Patsy, and there's work to be done," Julia says, "but I do need to talk to you. After what happened between us. I'm sorry to spring it on you like this. I've been going through what I want to say in my head, over and over, out there in the hall, and I think I just need to spit it all out before I'm too afraid to speak of it. That's all. Is it weird?"

"It's not weird," Isolde says softly, but she takes several steps backward, away from the other woman. Her saxophone is in her hand. Julia's sax is not yet out of its case, so they appear unevenly matched, Isolde with the bright arm of her instrument held close against her chest and Julia weaponless with her hands upturned to show the white of her palms.

"It just seems so desperately unfair," Julia says. "That I am marked so indelibly, so ineffaceably, tattooed and blue with the ink of your name across my heart, and that your ink is washable, Patsy. It was always washable, and you knew that all along."

"Come on, darling," Isolde says. "You're talking about just one kiss. You're talking about a single red-wine-flavor of a kiss, in the dusky dark of one late evening, riding on the giddy thrill of a concert that sent your pulse to racing."

"Yes," Julia says, vehemently.

"A one-off."

"Yes," Julia says again.

"Come on," Isolde says again, but weakly now. "We're over-reacting, surely. We're behaving like teenagers."

There is a pause and they look at each other.

"I think that this is worse than any other shame," Julia says. "To be rejected not because of circumstantial reasons, or pro-visional reasons, or reasons of prior claim, but simply for the unitary and all-quenching reason that I am, and will always be, *unwanted*. I feel spotlit, pinned against the bright wasteland of a bare stage, with nothing to hide behind, nothing to blame." She gives a cruel hard little laugh, not her own. After a moment she says, "Can't you just tell me why? Can't you just tell me *why* it's Brian, and it isn't me?"

Julia advances several steps. The other girl does not retreat. They are closer now, and Isolde looks her in the eye for a long moment before she speaks.

Isolde says, "I had always imagined that any woman's choice to be with another woman would be a reactionary choice, defined mostly in the negative by the patterns she is seeking to avoid. It would, I always thought, only be after deciding she does not want men that a woman might conclude that she wants other women. It is a public stance, itself a kind of activism. It is a com-plaint. It marks a dissatisfaction. It is the kind of attitude only held by a particular type: emphatic, campaigning, radical, the kind of woman who would boycott certain companies on moral grounds, who would picket outside a factory gate.

"I recognize a shade of this quality in you—the hardness of your opinion, your skepticism, the implicit challenge every time you speak. But there is another quality of yours that dawns strangely on me—a childlike helpless quality of vulnerability, a need. It is this quality that has awakened a new possibility in my understanding of the world: that a woman's choice of another woman might be a free choice in and of itself, not a handi-capped pick of second-bests, not a halved choice of remainders once the men have all been censored and removed. This positive definition—that a woman might love another woman simply in and for herself—is what makes me feel nervous."

"Nervous, why?" Julia says, and takes another step toward her. Instinctively she reaches out with her thin red hand and catches Isolde's fingertips in hers. Isolde doesn't pull away. She looks down, watches their hands for a moment, Julia's bony ink-stained thumb moving in a light caress over her knuckles. Her hands are cold.

"You want me to explain this burgeoning *something* with Brian," Isolde says, looking up again, "which may or may not ripen to a fruit. But I don't think I did actively choose between you, representative of women, and Brian, representative of men. Instead I placed myself in a position where I didn't have to choose. I let myself be his temptation; I behaved as passively as possible and did nothing as he advanced. It was the marshy fog-bound unmapped depths of you that made me nervous, darling. What I wanted was something protected, something proved. I wanted a default feeling, not a nervous uncertain forbidden-place of a feeling where everything was overlaid with fear and even guilt. I don't want to be seduced. I just don't want it. I want to be comfortable."

"How can that be what you want?" Julia says. "How can it be?"

"It is," Isolde says. "In the end. It just is."

Julia steps forward and kisses her on the mouth, and all in an instant they're back in the smoky fug of the bar, and the last number is playing, the last song. They're in the corner and they've just got up to leave, to wrap themselves back into their scarves and their coats and turn their smiling faces to the band as a final show of appreciation, a kind of farewell. Patsy turns to the saxophone teacher to say something but whatever she was going to say dies on her lips. Her eyes flicker down to the saxophone teacher's mouth, and then the saxophone teacher leans over and kisses her, her gloved fingertips against the other woman's cheek.

Patsy doesn't reach out and grab the saxophone teacher's coat, real fistfuls. She doesn't slide her hands around and scrabble with the hem of the saxophone teacher's jumper to slip her hands up and feel the skin of the other woman's back. She doesn't step forward so their breasts are touching, so their hips are touching, so the lengths of their bodies are pressed together hard. She doesn't reach up with her hand and cup the saxophone teacher's face. She just stands there and receives the kiss, her eyes closed. When the saxophone teacher draws back, she opens her eyes, smiles sadly, gives a nod, and walks away.

FOURTEEN

October

"Preliminary thoughts?" the Head of Acting says in the foyer, as the two of them slap their ticket stubs against their wrists and gaze over at the crowd around the drinks counter. "Or apprehensions, even?"

"Only apprehensions," the Head of Movement says. He doesn't smile.

"They're a motley bunch, this year," the Head of Acting says in his darting, distracted way. "I am definitely ready to be surprised."

"What was their prop? The playing card," the Head of Movement says, answering his own question and rubbing the back of his neck with his hand. "It's too easy. The aesthetic is half the battle in devised theater anyway."

"I'm still prepared to be surprised. Let's go in."

The heavy doors of the auditorium have opened finally and the flush bolts are being drawn down by a skinny porter, an underling from Wardrobe who has been dressed as an Ace of Spades. He is stiff in his painted sandwich board and careful face-paint as he bends down to clip open the door. He shoves the bolts into their flush sockets and then straightens and adjusts his headpiece, a tight black bonnet that fits like a swimming cap around his skull. He smiles carefully. The tutors hand him their pink-edged stubs, and one after the other pass under the arch and into the stalls.

Saturday

"Thank you all so much for coming," the saxophone teacher says into the dark. Her voice is higher than its usual pitch, and oddly strained, although she does not look nervous and her hands at her sides are still. "It really is wonderful you've all made the time to come." She looks down to draw a breath, and then continues.

"Like all the thirsty mothers present," she says, "tonight each of you will see exactly what you want to see and nothing more. Even now you will be aching for me to leave the podium so your daughters can file onstage and each of you can have the great comfort, one by one, of seeing your existing attitudes confirmed."

Out in the dark someone coughs, giving confidence to someone else, who clears their throat in a relieved echo of the first.

"I like to encourage all the parents to think of a recital as a public display of affection—you're familiar with the term—in the sense that the performances can never be any more than an indication or a hint," the saxophone teacher says. "But I must impress upon all of you that it would be invasive and wrong to expect to truly see your daughter when you attend this recital. As mothers, you are barred from sharing in the intimacy and privacy of her performance."

The saxophone strap around her neck is caught on the side of her collar, tugging it outward and downward to show the thin milky skin of her chest.

She says, "If you were not the mothers of these girls, you might be able to see them differently, as both a person and a kind of a person. If you were not mothers, and if you were looking very carefully, you might be able to see a role, a character, and also a person struggling to maintain that character, a person who decided in the first place that *that* particular character was who they were going to be.

"There are people who can only see the roles we play, and there are people who can only see the actors pretending. But it's a very rare and strange thing that a person has the power to see both at once: this kind of double vision is a gift. If your daughters are beginning to frighten you, then it is because they are beginning to acquire it. I am speaking mostly to the woman beneath Mrs. Winter, Mrs. Sibley, Mrs. Odets, and the rest," she adds, "the actor I pretend not to see, the woman who plays all women, all the women but never the girls, never the daughters. The role of the daughter is lost to you now, as you know."

She is gesturing with one hand cupped and empty and upturned. The mothers are nodding.

"Let me introduce my first student now," she says, "a student of St. Margaret's College who has been studying with me for almost four years. Please let's put our hands together and welcome to the stage Briony-Rose."

October

"Stanley?" the boy Felix says, pausing at the door of the Green Room and looking in with an air of officious concern. "Are you all right?"

"I'm going to bail," Stanley says into the mirror. His face is white. "I can't do this. The girl's parents are in the audience. I can't do it. I'm going to do a runner. I don't want to be an actor anymore. I can't follow through. It'll bugger up the production, but I can't do it, I'm sorry. I can't."

"You're nuts," Felix says in what he believes to be a soothing voice. "Think of all the money we've spent. If we don't get box office it'll come out of everyone's pocket. Everyone will hate you. You can't pull out now."

"I'll move," Stanley says. "I'll move away for a while until everyone has forgotten." He wants to put his face in his hands, but he has already been through the makeup line and he knows his lipstick and powder will smudge. He howls suddenly and slaps the vanity with both hands. "Why are they here? Why? What kind of sadist parents actually want to see a play about their daughter getting physically abused?"

"What?" Felix says, listening properly for the first time. "You mean the parents of the actual girl? The Victoria girl?"

Stanley moans in reply and kicks the radiator hard. He feels a stab of welcome pain shoot up his calf and linger there.

"Rubbish," Felix says. "How would they even know about it? Nobody knows what it's about. It's opening night. Not even the tutors know. Where did you hear that?"

Stanley turns doleful eyes to Felix and then shakes his head. "I've seen them," he says. "In the foyer. With her little sister."

There is a pause. Then Felix says, "What kind of sadist parents—"

"She's come to see me," Stanley says. "Isolde's come to see me. As a surprise."

"Who?" Felix says, by now thoroughly bewildered.

"Isolde," Stanley says. "Oh, God. And she brought her parents. She doesn't know what it's about, she doesn't know about Victoria or any of it, and they're just about to—oh, God. I can't do it. Not in front of them."

There is a glimmer of panic in Felix's eyes as it dawns upon him that Stanley might really make good his word and run away. He looks quickly over his shoulder down the dressing-room corridor, and then says, "Your parents here tonight?"

Stanley gives another howl. "My dad," he says. "To make matters a whole fucking lot worse. My dad."

"Mine too," Felix says. Then he says, tentatively, "If the girl's parents really are here, Stanley, they've got to be prepared to be shocked. You can't actually buy tickets to a show like this and expect to keep your...your innocence. You can't. They must know what they're in for. And they're not kids."

"But they don't know what it's about yet," Stanley says. "It's opening night. Where in the fucking program does it say that this is a play about their daughter? It doesn't. They're coming to see me, as a surprise." He looks again at himself in the mirror. The makeup artist has done a good job, powdering over his blond eyebrows and drawing in black arches that are higher and more angular than his own. He has a little red pout, and all the natural shadows of his face are thickened with gray: the creases around his mouth, the hollows of his cheeks, under his chin. His eyes are ringed with black.

Felix is still looking thoroughly confused. "On the bright side," he says, trying hard to reclaim the situation, "you're absolutely unrecognizable in your costume and everything. If that's what you're worried about. With the parents."

"Yeah," Stanley says. Underneath his makeup his jaw is set and his eyes are red and his face is pale, but in the mirror the pouting caricature that is Stanley's reflection twitches his head and even seems to smile.

Saturday

Isolde and her parents are already on stage when the lights come up, Isolde on the far end of the settee and leaning still further outward, over the arm, every inch of her body craning away from the other two figures on stage: a stout mustached father and a bony mother who buttons all the way to the top.

"What you need to understand," Isolde's mother says, "is that this little taste of what could be is inside you now. You've swallowed it up, like candy from a brown paper bag."

"What you need to understand," Isolde's father says, "is now that we know about it, it won't happen anymore."

"Remember that the only difference between you and any of the others," Isolde's mother says, "is at what price, and under what circumstances, you are prepared to yield."

Stanley and his father enter, through the frosted French doors in the middle of the false backdrop, preceded by Victoria who has her palm out like she is showing the way.

"He's here," she says unnecessarily, making more of the line than she ought to, because it is her only one and she wants to be seen. The mother makes a flapping motion with her hand and Victoria exits, walking with the pursed self-conscious walk of an actor who has too small a part and so has practiced a single move to excess.

The group stand stationary for a moment, Stanley and Isolde looking at each other with an intense smoldering glare that is lost to everyone in the upper circle and in the restricted-viewing sections of the stalls.

Then Isolde's father says stiffly, "I was just about to say, now that we're here, let's sort this out in a civilized way, like adults. But just as it was on the tip of my tongue I realized that the word *adults* wasn't entirely appropriate, given the circumstances."

There is a silence. Stanley's father is the first to sit down.

Saturday

"The purpose of this recital," the saxophone teacher says, "is really to let the students speak for themselves, as it were. It is really just a vehicle to let them voice their own growth, their own awakening, lay it bare like a virgin at an altar for all of you to see. While you are watching tonight, a good question to ask yourselves might be, What is this performance telling me about the performer? What naked shape emerges out of the rarefying mist of this girl's music? What private things are being offered, and what private things are being betrayed?"

Julia is sitting in the second row with her sax held loosely on her lap, waiting for her cue to rise and take the stage.

"I mention this," the saxophone teacher is saying, "because my next student has had a very difficult year. Many things have happened to complicate this girl's life this year, and if we are very lucky we will see some of these tragic and beautiful things reflected in her performance tonight. Through her misery, every note she plays for you will become a lyric, and she will conjure up much more than a sense of longing and of loss. If we are very lucky, and this is my hope, then we will be able to see the vast extent of the hardship she has endured this year: we will see the unspeakable incest of two women together, played out before us like a rare recording stolen from a vault. You will have to listen carefully."

Julia's palms are cold and sweaty, and she wipes them roughly on the knees of her trousers.

"And just before I welcome Julia to the stage," the saxophone teacher says, "can I just thank all the mothers here tonight for allowing me the strange satisfaction that is got by saying something that nobody hears."

October

"You didn't say he had the main part, Issie," Isolde's father says. He points to the program. "Look, his name's right at the top."

"He hasn't told me anything," Isolde says. "He even said don't bother coming. I guess he was nervous." She is looking up at the stage, tense with vicarious pre-show nerves. The lights are on in the orchestra pit and she can see the musicians emerging from the hidden half-door in the wall to take their places in front of their instruments. As they sit down they disappear from Isolde's view.

"Queen of Spades," Isolde's father reads out loud, and then takes his reading glasses off and says "What about this, eh?" and elbows Isolde in a jovial sort of way.

"Maybe we shouldn't have come on opening night," Isolde's mother says, tucking her knees sideways to let a young couple pass. "If he's nervous."

"I told you, he doesn't know I'm coming tonight anyway," Isolde says. She is craning around to look at the crowd. She watches a throng of senior students from the Institute flood into a wedge of seating in the rear of the stalls and suddenly feels foolish that she has brought her parents with her. The acting students are all clasping each other and hugging and gesticulating madly as they talk amongst themselves. Isolde imagines pushing her way backstage to surprise Stanley at the end of the night, knocking on his dressing-room door and waving shyly as she stands on the threshold with the actors shrieking and shouting up and down the corridor behind her, and all at once she suffers a horrible feeling of dread.

"We don't have to go backstage," she says out loud, to reassure herself. "I can just call him tomorrow."

She hasn't spoken to Stanley since the fight on the side of the road.

"Isn't it posh," Isolde's father says. "Look at that plasterwork on the arch. That's a beautiful job."

The band starts up and the house lights begin to fade.

"I wish I'd got some mints now," Isolde's mum says. "I hope there's a half-time."

October

"It's always—and only—vicarious," the Head of Movement is saying, drumming his fingers impatiently on the glossy cover of the program that is lying on his knee. The cover shows a caricatured girl in pigtails and a school uniform, and the title of the play: *The Bedpost Queen.* The Head of Acting is craning around to look out over the crowd, and isn't really listening, but the Head of Movement is speaking with a strange tight urgency that cannot wait for an audience, and anyway the words are mostly for himself. He says, "You never get around that aspect. Even at your most effective, your most vivacious and inspirational, you're always just…looking on."

September

"Do you know something?" Stanley's father says, leaning down the couch toward Isolde. She turns her head, so they are profiled there against the cream: her delicate upturned pout, his sunken cheek and lantern jaw.

"When I do a group therapy session," Stanley's father says, "for my work—say if I have six or seven or more clients in a room, maybe a whole family if that's what I'm working on—my policy at first is to say absolutely nothing. I ask questions, invite people to speak, bring up issues, but I say nothing about what I think. I don't even hint. I do this for the first session, and the second.

"By the end of the second everyone's itching. They want to know who this guy is, this psychologist who only listens, sits and listens and sometimes asks a question, always a mild question, never provocative, never acute. I cost too much, I'm too well known, just to listen. They become wary of me. They bicker among themselves and then look sideways, daring me to act.

"I leave early, always. I never stick around. I never invite them to know me better. I hold them apart, away from me, and by the *third* session when I walk into the room they're like mice. All their dissension has melted away and their attention is focused entirely on *me*, on me absolutely. And then—" Stanley's father pinches his fingertips together and then releases them like a puff of smoke. "After that, I can say anything," he says. "The third session is golden. They listen to whatever I say. They hear me."

"Does this story have a moral that has something to do with virginity?" Isolde says, a little nervously.

"No moral," Stanley's father says. "I don't do morals. I do dirty jokes, and I do stories to pass the time."

"Good," Isolde says. She turns away, and the shadows on her face disperse as she is swallowed by the glaring fog of the footlights and beyond.

Stanley's father looks at her with compassion and says, "Virginity is a myth, by the way. There is no on–off switch, no point of no return. It's just a first experience like any other. Everything surrounding it, all the lights and curtains and special effects—that's all just part of the myth."

Isolde turns back to look at him and all the shadows return, flooding back to fill the dark side of her face so she is once again halved, like a waning moon.

Stanley's father smiles. He says, "Stop believing."

Saturday

"But still the counseling sessions persisted," Julia is saying, "clinging to the school calendar like a baked stain that nobody was willing to chip away. Still we met to discuss the dubious rape of the girl who unbuttoned her shirt collar right down to the central white rosebud of her bra. We sat together and talked about the girl who sucked on a red lollipop at lunchtime rehearsal and let the boiled candy ball tug her lower lip down ever so slightly, so her mouth opened and you could see the moist rolling of her tongue.

"And Mr. Saladin," she continues, relentlessly. "Mr. Saladin, who need only have waited for the midnight stroke in five months' time, the stroke that would transform Victoria from a child into an adult as surely as a carriage into a pumpkin, or a saddled horse into a dirty common kitchen mouse. It could have even been a birthday present, if he had only waited. At our counseling sessions we learned that Mr. Saladin's crime was, first and foremost, impatience. We learned that the moral is: *They stumble that run fast.*"

The mothers are captivated.

"No, we didn't," Julia says. "We didn't learn that at all."

She speaks like a magician or a ringmaster.

"We learned that everything in the world divides in two: good and evil, male and female, truth and falsehood, child and adult, pleasure and pain. We learned that the counselor possessed a map, a map that would make everything make sense. A key. Like in a theater program where you have the actors' names on one side and the list of characters on the other—some neat division that divides the illusive from the real. We learned that there is a distinction—that there is *always* a distinction—between the performance and the performer, the reality and the lie. We learned that there is no middle ground."

Julia surveys her audience.

"Only those who watch," she says, "and those who suffer being watched."

The mothers don't dare to rustle.

"But the counselor lied," Julia says. "You lied. You lied about the pain of it, the unsimple mess of it, immeasurably more thorny and wretched and raw than you could ever remember, with the gauze veil of every year that passes settling over your eyes, thicker and thicker until even your own childhood dissolves into the mist."

The saxophone teacher is watching Julia from the side of the stage. She has a lump in her throat and a tight aching feeling in her chest. It might be pride.

"Just think," Julia is saying, "Victoria is probably with Mr. Saladin tonight, right now, laid out in an adolescent flush of pleasure somewhere, while her sister and her parents sit in the bruising dark of an auditorium on the other side of town. She is probably naked and crooning and stretched over him with her body limp and butter-slick. He is probably whispering into her hair the dwindling number of days until she becomes her own self, the day when her body becomes her own, the day when her body becomes his own. He is probably stroking her with the callused heel of his weathered adult hand."

She looks at the mothers.

"And you wish you were there," Julia says softly. "You wish you were there."

Saturday

Isolde and Julia are alone against the black cloth of the stage. There is no set or scenery. They are both wearing their school uniform, but differently: Isolde's is clean and pressed, and Julia's is limp and darned and grubby and artful. They look across at each other.

Isolde says, "Is it because I didn't learn to love myself that I chose to bury myself instead in the reassuring strangeness of a body that was without that essential similarity which would force me to *compare*? With you I would have been doubled, intensified, mirrored back. With him our differences canceled out to nothing."

"Yes," Julia says. "But that's only part of it."

Isolde says, "Is it because I was scared, then? Is it because there wasn't a template for it, and the unexpected hugeness of my innocence, the sheer and terrible abyss of my unknowing, was simply too alien, too frightening? It was just too big for me—too big for me to hold inside myself, like something perfect or tragic or sublime."

"Yes," Julia says.

"I've never felt like that before, Julia," Isolde says. "Scared like that."

"Don't worry," Julia says. "You never will again."

The lights change.

"I remember being in your car outside my house," Isolde says, "both of us sitting there in the pale gray of the streetlight with our seat belts holding us apart, our seat belts crossed over our chests, strapping us against the crocodile vinyl, holding us flat. And you turned to look at me and gave a little bit of a laugh, like you were really nervous, and you bit your lip and let some of your hair fall across your face and you didn't tuck it back. And then you said, Can I just...? and you let the question die and you reached up your hand to cup underneath my chin, reaching right over, straining against your seat belt that was pulling you back, reining you in, holding you there. I was so scared. I remember licking my lip. I remember my mouth was dry. I remember you kissed me."

"A one-off," Julia says.

"My fall."

And Julia says, "My fall."

Isolde says, "What will happen to you now?"

Julia pulls her gaze away from the other girl and looks out over the wraith-faces of the audience. She doesn't speak for a moment. Then she says, "All I can expect, I guess. Slow fade to black."

October

"It's too easy," Stanley's father says as he steps from the taxi. "Oh, Stanley, it's too easy, and I'm going to say it anyway."

He steps over the gutter and spreads his arms for a hug, wrapping Stanley up tightly. Stanley can smell the familiar blush of cologne on his father's shirt.

"What's too easy?" Stanley says when they have separated, and the taxi has turned the corner and disappeared.

"You've improved on my own methods," Stanley's father says. "You've taken my ideas and run with them, turned them into something I couldn't have dreamed up myself. I'm flattered and impressed and a little ashamed that you don't have more sense."

"Are you talking about the insurance thing?" Stanley says.

"Absolutely I am."

"Because I rang up the insurance companies," Stanley says. "I rang up a few. I asked them about your idea to make a million, and it won't work."

"Of course it won't work. I was just having a tease, and shame on you for following through, by the way," Stanley's father says. "But *this*—"

He laughs and spreads out his arms. Above the double doors of the foyer an enormous glossy banner, *Opening Night!*, snaps in the wind and strains fatly convex against the roped eyelets fixed along the balcony rail. Posters showing a girl in a school uniform coyly sliding a playing card into the pocket of her dress are taped to both doors of the foyer.

"This is brilliant," Stanley's father says. "And it's hilarious. But I'll be surprised if you last a week in performance. They'll shut you down tomorrow night probably."

"That might not be such a bad thing," Stanley says.

"Are you in trouble?"

"Yes."

"Need some help?" his father says, for once not using his therapy manner, but instead peering at Stanley with a curious half-smile, as if he is very proud.

"Yes," Stanley says, more quietly. "I've been accused of something."

"Excellent," his father says. "You can tell me over dinner. Let's get Chinese."

October

"In your organizer," Isolde says, "your black organizer with the gold stripe, I found an article snipped out of the front page of the newspaper. The headline read *Teacher Denies Sex With Student*. Only it wasn't just the article, it was a photocopy of the article, a photocopy of a photocopy, with key phrases highlighted in yellow, maybe by you."

Stanley is sitting a little way off, his head in his hands.

"Half of the article was familiar to me," Isolde says, "the half that had clung to the folded spine of the newspaper when my mum swooped down and tried to rip off the front page, when she said Vultures, Vultures, and she crushed the torn piece into a ball. After she left the room I read the left-behind slice with the headline Teacher Sex and all the words disjointed and coming apart from each other, and piece by piece I tried to put it back together, the sharp-edged fragments of my sister's love."

Stanley is unmoving, clutching his temples in his hands and squatting like a boxer resigned to lose the fight.

"So I read the article," Isolde is saying, "photocopied and whole, with the key phrases highlighted, phrases like Received Special Tuition, and Temporarily Removed From School. I wondered why it was in your organizer, slipped inside with your bus pass and your library receipts and your favorite sonnets written by hand. I decided it was probably an exercise you were doing at school, just an exercise, something about scandal in the news."

In a sudden fluid motion Isolde draws herself up and pulls her elbows in to her sides.

"But *now*," she says, "now I know what really happened. I know now that you saw an opportunity in me. I know now that I am a pawn, a shining pawn advancing all the way to the furry cardboard nether-edge of the playing board to be transformed into a queen—a queen for you, a queen for your performance and your production and your career. I know now that something in me betrayed her after all, some small streak of sameness or familiarity that made you see *her* when I turned my head and bit my lip and tucked my hair back, and all at once you saw all the things in me that you could use. I know that you thought to yourself, Her proximity to her sister counts for a great deal."

Isolde draws herself up tighter, as if she is gathering in all the threads of herself, all the fraying pieces, wadding herself up in order to be able to continue. When she speaks her voice is half-stifled with a kind of muted hurt that makes Stanley throb and look away.

"I am serving a double purpose for you," Isolde says. "That kind of unknowing doubleness that halves me down the middle and carves me into two: a benefit and a use. You want to harness my proximity, squeeze me dry, hoard up all the little stained-glass splintered facts about Victoria that make up everything I know. You want the complete story, for yourself. You want my sister, but you don't want her whole: you want her shadow, her reflection, her image that bleeds out into the newsprint on the front page. You want the air around her and the spaces she moves through and the things that brush her as she passes by. And that's why you want me."

"Isolde," Stanley says in a low voice that is muffled by his hands. "You aren't being used. Nothing about you has been used, or used up."

"But I have used you," Isolde says, trumping him, her voice ringing out clear and bright. "Just as you have used me, I have used you. That's what I came here to say. You're a kind of protection for me, that's all. You're a kind of proof."

Saturday

"Before we close I'd like to say one final thing," the saxophone teacher says, after the last girl has tripped offstage and returned to her seat on the floor. The sax teacher looks small against the wasteland of the stage. Behind her the Steinway grand is sheathed like a vast canvas-covered tombstone fallen backward and left to lie.

"I'd like to pay a tribute to one of my students," the saxophone teacher says, "a lank and wilted student who died this year, hit by a car on her bicycle as she was coming home from the late shift at work."

The room is deathly quiet at once.

"For a long time I have tried without success to see Bridget's death as a tragedy," the saxophone teacher says. "Finally I believe I can see it in that way."

She looks down at the floor to gather her thoughts.

"When Bridget arrived at jazz band on Wednesday," she says, "the Wednesday next that never was, the Wednesday she never saw, she would have been a celebrity. Pale and stringy Bridget, always the girl of small information and small ideas, always the girl shadowing her righteous flat-soled stalking mother, always the girl a few seconds behind the joke, would have found herself armed with something to offer and something to say. She would have been surrounded and petted and prodded as she relived her brief six minutes of conversation with Mr. Saladin at the video store for everyone to hear. Everyone would have listened. The room would have been utterly still. And she would have been

307

warmed by the first narrow shaft of lighted pleasure she had ever really known. She would have been popular, for an instant, because she would have had real information for the first time in her short unhappy life. Bridget was robbed of this small pleasure. It is for this reason that we can see her death as tragic."

The mothers are nodding.

"Poor Bridget," the saxophone teacher says softly. "It is a cruel thing."

November

Julia and Victoria are among a drowsy handful of seventh formers sitting in the common room, all of them unfurled and limp in the lapping heat of almost-summer. The lease of their high school years has all but expired, and it is with a fond kind of nostalgia that they look around them at the world that they will so soon leave behind. Through the window comes the sound of laughter and shouting from the girls on the playing field.

Gradually the common room empties, one by one, until the door clatters shut behind the last of them and only Julia and Victoria remain. Julia is bent over her end-of-year clearance form, and Victoria watches her for a moment from across the room.

"Did you have a thing with my sister?" Victoria says suddenly. Her voice is thin. "Earlier this year. Did you two like hook up or something?"

Julia looks up and studies the other girl with an impassive look. "Is that what everyone reckons?"

"Well," Victoria says, sounding abashed. "Yeah." She looks smaller than usual. Her lip is thrust forward in a way that makes her look, for the briefest half-second, a little like her sister. It is as if the image of the younger girl flashes across her face for a moment, like a ray through a cloud.

Julia watches the image of Isolde flash by and disappear, and then she says, "Why don't you just ask her? If you really want to know. Why don't you just ask Isolde?"

It sounds too intimate, Isolde's name in Julia's mouth. They both notice it, and blush.

"I was waiting for her to come to me, I guess," Victoria says. "I was waiting for her to tell me. Before I had to ask."

"And she never did."

"No."

Julia turns away. "So what's everyone saying?" she says, with her face turned toward the window and the wall.

"Only that you kissed her, one time."

"Is that all?"

"And someone found a Fuck-me bracelet in the drama closet, and it was broken."

"Is that all?"

"Yeah. That's all. So what happened?"

Julia says nothing. Victoria sits and waits. She has an eager coaxing look on her face, and she is leaning forward slightly so it looks as if her whole body is hoping for an answer. Her eyebrows are up.

Julia is still looking out the window. Outside the girls on the hockey field are cheering and cheering.

Finally Victoria sighs and says, "Julia, I'd be happy if you told me just enough of the facts so I could imagine it. So I could recreate it for myself. So I could imagine that I was really there."

ACKNOWLEDGMENTS

My profound thanks to Denis and Verna Adam.

To Damien Wilkins, Jane Parkin, and Fergus Barrowman, thank you for your advice, encouragement, and wisdom.

To Stephen Pike, thank you for your mischief, and for your zany idea about life insurance. Thanks also to Lolo Pike and Emily Nyberg for your love and hospitality.

To Charlotte Bradley, Tane Upjohn-Beatson, James Christmas, Jane Groufsky, Jemimah Walker, Claire Bramley, Nathan McLoughlin, and Gemma McCabe, thank you for sharing ideas and listening. Thanks also to everyone at Tennyson St. Studio—Chloe Lane, Lawrence Patchett, Joan Fleming, Sarah Barnett, Amy Brown, Pip Adam, and Asha Scott-Morris. Your enthusiasm means a lot.

Love and thanks to Felicity, Jonathan, and Sebastian: thank you for sharing your home and easing the fever.

To Caroline Dawnay, Olivia Hunt, Jessica Craig, Lettie Ransley, and Zoe Ross, a heartfelt thank you for everything beyond New Zealand.

Your acumen, your patience, and your many kindnesses continue to amaze me.

To Reagan Arthur, and everyone at Little, Brown and Company, thank you for taking a chance on me. Thanks also to Marlena Bittner, Peggy Freudenthal, and Andrea Walker for all your energy and support.

I also owe thanks to everyone at Granta Books (UK), in particular Philip Gwyn Jones, Sara Holloway, Pru Rowlandson, and Amber Dowell.

Love and thanks to Mum, Dad, and Will.

My biggest debt is to Johnny Fraser-Allen: thank you for believing.